Shadow Angels

Shadow Angels

Peter Morris

To: JP.

So Glad this
was gifted to you,
I hope you enjoy it!

Publisher: BlankPete Artworks
Editor: Rob Bignell, Inventing Reality Editing
Cover Art: Creative Canuck Designs

Issued in print and electronic formats.

ISBN: 9798377785996

For Andrea, Hannah and Erin.

Thank you to my brothers and sisters in the tactical community, especially all the snipers and marksmen /women. If we have ever rubbed shoulder patches or talked tactics, know you had an influence on me and this book.

Ex Umbrus Venimus
– From the Shadows we came.

Chapter One

The feeling struck him suddenly as the driver pumped the brakes in the heavy armoured vehicle on the way to their staging point. Everything in his world seemed to be moving in slow motion; streetlights floated passed the small window across from him in a blur as the big heavy truck lurched away from the stop sign. The lights tried to hold on to the edge of the frame but couldn't, slowly blinking off only to reappear in the next window. His own hands moved slowly, as he fidgeted with the grip on the weapon resting across his right thigh. Even the sound of the fan in the heater sounded slow, so slow he could count each pass of the blades. This happened to him right before every large operation he had ever been involved in, adrenaline was flowing through his body playing havoc with his senses. This was the case now. He could hear each breath of the men sitting around him, muffled as they were by their grey Arc'teryx balaclavas. The smell of their sweat clung to the humid air in the cramped truck, and he could hear the click-clicking as someone chewed on a piece of gum. No one was saying a word, just slowly breathing. It was rhythmic, inhaling for five seconds then slowly out for five seconds. The soft glow from the red lights inside their armoured vehicle created strange shadows on the obscured faces of the men, and the light had a heaviness to it which added to the slow-motion effect he was feeling.

Parker wondered if the rest of the guys on the team were doing the same thing he was – taking in the moment. They had trained for these types of scenarios maybe hundreds of times, but no one ever really expected anything like this to happen here.

Certainly not twice.

Parker's mind shifted back and forth between what they were waiting to do and memories of things they'd done in the past.

"Team Four draws another short straw." he whispered into his headset over their secure channel. He could see shoulders start moving with the giggles of agreement.

"I got a bad feelin' 'bout this boys!" someone replied, laughing at the inside joke. Maybe they shouldn't joke about this one, Parker thought. It didn't really matter though, did it?

He thought quietly to himself, *They shoulda known this wasn't going to go away.* Parker's mind played back over the two other famous counter-terrorism takedowns he had been assigned to. The so called "Toronto 18" and the more recent foiled plot to blow up a railway bridge where a commuter train from New York City ran a daily route. In the cramped confines of the truck and through the dim red lighting Glen Parker looked at each one of the guys around him. Men fidgeted with the shoulder straps of their plate carriers that had been digging into their shoulders during this long day. Others snugged on their gloves and adjusted the Velcro at the wrists. Others tightened their suppressors and blinked the green beams from their MAWLS lasers. These were the guys he would trust his life to in the next thirty minutes. He knew each one of them as well as he knew himself.

They were all very good at what they did.

"Best in the Unit."

They had been told that on more than one occasion. What that meant was that they currently were drawing the bulk of the most serious assignments, going up against the worst of the worst. Dealing with the people who needed to be dealt with was their specialty, and they had a knack for it, too, he remembered. Man, he wished he had a hundred dollars for every time some detective had told them that this suspect was "the worst they'd ever seen" or that "this guy's gonna shoot it out with you guys for sure." No doubt the D's believed it too. But every time the Hogs – Parker laughed every time he thought of the night that nickname came to be – brought them out. Sometimes a little battered, but mostly not; they were consummate professionals, and a bad guy only got what he asked for. A few criminals got their piece of flesh, too, but none of the team had ever been hurt too seriously. Nothing more than a few twisted ankles and black eyes to go with a bucket full of scrapes and bruises.

Once again there they were waiting to be given the green light, to go and do dangerous things under the cover of darkness, all to ensure that Joe and Jane Citizen could wakeup the next day and go to the Eaton Center or the Tower without worrying that some fanatical ideologist might try to detonate a truckload of fertilizer and diesel fuel next to their mini-van. "All this for base pay." the guys in The Group used to joke.

Parker had to shake his head to get himself back on track. It'd been a long day already, cell phones started signalling the callout at about 1100 hrs local time, and it was pushing 0400 hrs. Parker's radio crackled to life, the activity on the command channel rushed his senses back to the present and on full speed.

At about the same time, in a rather unremarkable non-descript building in another corner of the Greater Toronto Area, other people's nerves were twitching as well. Luckily for everyone involved, none of these people were going to be holding the triggers. Nonetheless, their anxieties were not misplaced. Not that they didn't trust the men they had just put in harm's way, nor were they afraid the information used to put those men there was bad. No, they all knew this had to happen. There just was no stopping it now. That understanding is where the anxiety and anxiousness met, and it had created a stew of sweat in the bleak concrete room. One commander in the room knew that he would not be calling anyone off this operation, not today.

"ATTENTION! ATTENTION! Time is 0400 hrs, thirty minutes to green light." the intercom barked piercing the virtual silence in the Major Incident Command Center.

Some strange instinctive act forced everyone to look up at the ceiling toward the voice. They were all paying close attention to the radio chatter between the various units as they confirmed their status.

"Mobile 15 package still stationary at home – site still green."

"Mobile 16 target just entered the house – site is yellow."

"Mobile 17, yep we're set boss – site is green."

"Intel 5's ready, no change – reporting green."

"Intel 9, no change here either. All set. Green"

Things had been falling into place like that over the past several hours. Targets returned home and mobile surveillance turned to stationary. Surveillance teams settled into their seats, and tactical operators checked their gear for the umpteenth time. The proverbial calm before the storm, as it were.

Each of the sub-units involved in this operation were on a common radio channel as they neared the H Hour. The bottom of each hour had been designated as the COMMS check time and each team leader or road boss took their turn calling in a status report. They still used separate encrypted channels to talk to the other members of their team directly for routine matters, but the important stuff was all going over the operational channel. The chatter had started to slow as men were settled in their positions and the targets had mostly been put to bed. The talk consisted mainly of routine check-ins to team leaders.

"62's okay."

"84 looking for a bio."

"19's gotcha, go on bro' but hurry back."

Mostly the surveillance people talked; the tactical guys had better radio discipline and in most cases were sitting within eyeshot of their teammates anyway. Hiding. Waiting. But the most alone of the tactical operators were ghosts in physical presence and in all the radio chatter too. Strangely absent from all the briefings were about fifteen members of the Tactical Intervention Group, TIG for short, or simply The Group. These fifteen members, due to all the excitement around the operation, had gone mostly unnoticed by the other cops present. In fact, they hadn't even been heard on the common channel all day. That was just fine to them and those who knew they were out there.

All everyone had to do was wait for the word. It would come sooner than they thought.

***

Vincent Wismer was the kind of Unit Commander men listened too and respected, but not because of the usual been-there-done-that respect garnered in a specialty unit. He earned that respect because he listened to and respected the men on the teams. And he really did. It was a rarity amongst unit commanders who too often felt like they were above their rank and file. Not Wismer. He was a tall man with a modest build who had spent the bulk of his policing career as an investigator. His last command position prior to coming to TIG had been at the Intelligence Unit, which gave him a very high-level security clearance that he brought with him to The Group. As well, his positions had allowed him to fill a smartphone full of contacts in places like the NYPD, FBI, CSIS, the RCMP and even Black units like the Army's elite JTF II, all of whom he had called upon for advice during the preparations for this operation. This was a strange turn in the tables this time for American counterterrorism units to be calling him to pass along wishes of "Good-luck," "Stay-safe," and "Give 'em hell boys!" to his men. As he sat scrolling through the incoming emails on his phone, he thought of the men under his command. He knew their faces, all 84 of them. He knew names and histories, and he knew about most of their home lives too. He had met their wives, kids and girlfriends, and in some cases parents, and it was as they approached H Hour that the gravity started to hit him. He fidgeted with the band of his watch. Alone in a dark corner of the large briefing room, awaiting his turn to take the lead in the operation, Vince Wismer stole 30 seconds to pray. He was not a religious man, but as he stared down at his folded hands between his knees, he prayed anyway. Wismer didn't know the proper words to use, so instead he had a simple request for God, "Look after my men." He knew it was unrealistic to believe that none of his men would be hurt; he just prayed that hurt would be the worst of their worries. Wismer was a realist, and he had seen the intelligence on what these suspects were capable of. He was asking his God to guide his guys to a win today.

"ATTENTION! ATTENTION! Time is 0415 hrs, 15 minutes to green light. Staff Inspector Wismer you have control, with compromise authority. Lightning Order is also in effect for target one. Please confirm with your units."

The broadcast was barked over the command center's intercom in that loud sterile way like a CODE BLUE at a hospital. There was no emotion attached to the announcer's voice, the words were enough. The wheels were well in motion and the announcement seemed to loiter in the air somewhere near the ceiling, hanging over everyone's heads pressing the building tension down on top of them. Tactical intervention was at hand and the outcomes would be borne on the shoulders of the decision makers in this very room.

Wismer rose confidently. He took a second to adjust his shirt, re-tucking the back and picking up his command folder. Then he casually slipped his pen into the pocket of his well starched shirt, he had abandoned his tie hours ago. As he rose, he slipped on his jacket and paused. This was a deliberate habit of his, never to rush to a briefing or command podium. Wismer believed his calmness would be a visual representation to every one of his Unit's professionalism. As a final subconscious symbolic act, he adjusted the unit pin on his lapel, as if touching it was somehow good luck. This pin was given to all members working within the Unit; it was a small color reproduction of the patches worn on the left sleeve of every operator on the team. Only a team member could wear the patch, as they had earned it, but everyone else in the unit was allowed the pin. The pin was shaped like a shield with a deep red background. Across the top of the shield, the gold letters TIG stood out and flashed in the light. Below that, the two original sections of Unit were respectfully represented: an iron fist clutching an olive branch and a lightning bolt, and an image of Guy Fawkes – assaulters and explosives techs working together. As Wismer strode to the command table, he rubbed his pin. Coaxing the good luck out of it.

The words Lightning Order were hanging over the hum of the computers in the stale air of the bleak concrete command center. Some understood the meaning instantly, doing the math on the members assigned to the operation and those that were unaccounted for as yet. Others wondered, unsure, but they too would soon understand.

***

There was a palpable tension inside the Green Tree Halal Meat store as well. The group had just finished recording its final demand video, which would be sent via taxi to a local news station for broadcast. As before, they would be very careful to cover their tracks. The flash drive would be left in a washroom taped under a sink several kilometres from this place. Next, another taxi would be called to pick up the package.

The terrorists knew the taxi would be compelled to come and get it for religious, political and cultural reasons. No money needed to be paid for this service. Fear had set in across the city; in fact, it gripped the whole country. They were confident that the cab company would deliver the recording to the specified location lest bloodshed should be on their hands. If they refused, the worst that would happen is that the taxi company would call the police notifying them of the package and the police would come to get it. The right people would still receive the message, even if it meant losing the national television audience they had built for their cause; that was no longer the focus of their mission. However random the use of the taxi service may appear, there was some method to their madness. The majority of the drivers for the two largest taxi companies in Toronto were also new Canadians and shared a common struggle as the men from this group. Hoping to cash in on sympathy for their cause, they chose to target these two companies to fulfill this part of the plan. This had worked the first-time days ago, and so Ameer Mahmood had every confidence it would work again. Besides, this was jihad and the hand of Allah Himself would aid them in accomplishing this mission.

"Al-hamdu lillahi rabbil 'alamin!" (All the Praise be to Allah, the God of all men) shouted Mustafa Mahmood in his native Arabic. "Now we can be done with this dog and bring the true glory of Allah to these people."

This made Raahil flash a little smirk. He had actually been to the training camps and fought against the infidels in the mountains of Afghanistan, unlike his loud-mouthed colleague. He recognized the nervous overconfidence men got when stress was built up, could hear it in his colleague's voice. "Allahu Akbar, effendi. We are close to completing what Allah has asked of us," Raahil said, "But let us not become overconfident like our brothers who went before us, yes?" His speech was always soft and calm, and it gave everyone near him a sense of ease. Even his enemies. His reference to their brothers was a reminder for the group of the foiled plot by the infamous Toronto 18 to blow up various symbolic locations throughout the city. *It should have been I chosen to lead this jihad,* he mused to himself. Raahil chastised himself internally for doubting their leader and reminded himself how far they had come in such a relatively short time. He closed his eyes.

A recent convert to Islam, O'Neil Facey had quickly developed into a proud soldier for Allah. Unfortunately, he lacked the ability to see why he had really been recruited into the Western Brothers of Islam. He was smart enough to know it couldn't have been for his ability to memorize and understand the Koran. O'Neil lived in the same low income buildings that the founders of this group did, and he was the de facto leader of the local Crip street gang who ran those neighbourhoods. Ameer Mahmood, the terror cell's leader, had known from the start that he would need local funding to support his movement, as well as access to weapons and soldiers – disposable soldiers – and that was the real reason that O'Neil had been romanced and massaged into the group. O'Neil bought it, too, the whole story and all its promises. It really was much easier to convince the converts than Mahmood had thought it would be.

But being duped is one thing, being stupid is another entirely, and O'Neil Facey was not a stupid young man. At twenty, he was much wiser than the Islamic cleric gave him credit. Sure, he had barely managed to get a grade ten education, but he had a PhD from the streets. His degree taught him to watch everything. O'Neil didn't yet know enough of the language to understand a conversation, but he could read a person's body language from the other side of a crowded after-hours club. That gift had saved his life on at least one occasion during a late night in Scarborough he would like to forget.

O'Neil walked over to the table where Raahil was sealing the flash drive into an envelope and placed the camera down.

"So that's it huh 'cuz? You nervous?" O'Neil surveyed his Muslim brother while rubbing the old bullet scar on his neck.

"Young brother Facey, there is still much work to be done. That is all that worries me. I have faith that Allah will guide us on our righteous path. Fear not, O'Neil, all will be fine as it is a good plan. The infidels will have no choice but to listen to us when it is done."

O'Neil thought that this must be what it was like speaking to a politician. He had grown up listening to lies and murky explanations from the government on all sorts of issues. The lip service about all the great things the latest mayor planned on doing for the poor people of neighbourhoods like his. This gave him a feel for Raahil's tone. Something was being left unsaid, a hidden meaning behind the words. *Maaaan,* he thought to himself, *these dudes get nervous easy!*

There was a fifth person present in the meat shop, without a voice, however, in any of these matters. And he *did* understand the language being spoken by the two Arabs. The feeling of that conversation was worrisome to him – as if the black scarf tied around his mouth and the cord biting into his wrists weren't enough to make him worry. He had endured a whole day of beatings, and yet at his age he had held up. Pain was temporary,

7

he kept telling himself. He wanted to stay alive, so he endured the pain and their angry taunts at him. *They really believe that I am the one who betrayed them?* He repeated this to himself throughout the entire taping of the video. He hadn't even noticed the AK-47 and the sword being pointed at him, he just kept repeating that statement, *They really believe that I am the betrayer?*

Bashir Abdullah was a modest and humble man who kept to himself and ran a small family business that did little more than cover the rent. But he was a proud man who believed that every day in Canada and away from the oppressive regimes of his homeland was a blessing. Because of that belief that he cared little about worldly things. He had been happy to have his crowded little apartment with his devoted wife and daughter in what he thought was the best city in the world, next to Umm-Qasr, the port town in Iraq where he had grown up. A proud fishing town, it sat in a tenuous border position with Kuwait. Due to the strategic importance in times of conflict the town had been fought over time and again. So shattered by years of conflict, the little town was no longer recognizable to the people who originally called it home. Various religious factions had come recruiting in the small town, but as a minority Christian, he knew it would be a matter of time until he and his little family faced more violent persecution. So, he had packed them up twelve years ago and moved them to Canada, a country of tolerance and diversity.

Bashir remembered his town as a sunny, happy place, the market always busy with people and commerce. Where the trees on the hillside overlooking the port always had shade for a weary fisherman. He had professed his love to his wife under those trees, and they had watched many sunsets in their warm shade while holding each other. He wasn't even sure if the trees were still there. He wondered what war, violence and religion had gotten anyone. Bashir longed for the shade of one of those trees where he could rest his head in his wife's lap, eating the dates she fed him while they watched the ships coming into the port.

Where he sat now, however, was far from that oasis, and this humble and proud man was slowly beginning to unravel. He knew all too well the rantings of fanatical extremists. They had taken more than one of his friends to their camps, after they had wilted under the pressure. Bashir didn't know if any of them were still alive.

Bashir prayed the Our Father in his mind and scanned the poorly lit room with his one good eye, the other having long since swollen shut. He saw the four men with him – he thought he had known them. They had come in together for the taping of that second video. His daughter had been with them then, as she was employed these men, doing what he didn't know. The older of the men seemed to be in charge. One of them he had only met a few days ago, the boss. The second one, the chubby old one, had come in that day as well. The third man was the calmest of the group, and he seemed to have the most strategic mind of all of them. He was the one holding them together. This one had come in over a year ago and built up a friendship with Bashir. It had led to a job for his daughter and a simple request to periodically rent a storage space in the basement of the shop.

Suddenly, they had come and insisted on using the basement to film a video. Bashir didn't protest as they had paid handsomely. But he became worried that these men were planning some sort of extremist action when he overheard the taping.

Bashir had noticed that the fourth man, the younger black man, was being treated as an outsider. He would do well to remember that, he thought as it could be the crack he needed to get out of this predicament. What do they want with me, Bashir wondered to himself again, what betrayal do they think I've committed?" He scoured his memory, looking for answers that would never come, because there was no connection for him. He had no idea what they were talking about and what they wrongly believed of him. *Maybe if I can get them to talk to me I can figure this out?* Bashir continued his mental search for answers, but his train of thought was broken when he noticed the taller of the two brown men kneeling in front of him. He had approached from the right, Bashir's blind side.

The man leaned over and ripped the gag from Bashir's mouth and threw a glass of water in the older man's face. Mustafa could see that Bashir recognized his anger and rage, and he was pleased that the old man was obviously intimidated. "Good," Mustafa thought, as he stroked his beard and scowled, "cower like the Christian dog you are!" he yelled. "Betrayer!" he screamed at the cowering old man, spit flying across his face. "You will die for what you have done!" he screamed again, punctuating his statement with a hooking punch to the right side of Bashir's face. This opened the wound above Bashir's eye, causing all the pooled blood to run down his face like some grotesque waterfall.

To his amazement the man refused to flinch or wipe the blood from his eye. This prisoner of the new Western Holy War just sat there staring back at him. "Christian coward." Mustafa smiled and muttered to himself again as his thoughts raced. "He has lost the will to fight." He finished off his little tantrum by spitting on the man that he believed less than human. For his part, Bashir took it all in. He had felt the punch in the face, but it was not his focus. He was more concerned with the looks on the faces of the other people in the room. The Black one he saw smirked at the episode, but there was an underlying message in the young man's face that showed a distaste for the actions of the angry Arab standing over him.

The other face, Bashir observed, cringed in disgust at these outbursts. He watched as the fitter of the Arabs closed his eyes and turned away. O'Neil also recognized that look on Raahil's face. It was the second time he'd seen it today.

Again the coward strikes out at the defenseless old man, the former soldier Raahil realized. Why must there be a coward on every side of a conflict? These beatings undermine our objective. But how could he go against the wishes of their leader, who after all was this coward's brother! Weak leadership had cost them in the mountains of Afghanistan, and he feared it would be their undoing here. Raahil prayed to Allah to keep him honest and safe, but increasingly he wasn't sure if those prayers or even Allah himself would be enough.

***

"Attention! Attention! Time is 0420 hrs, 10 minutes to green light."

Wismer barely even noticed the announcement from the intercom. He stared quietly at his phone and spoke out of the corner of his mouth as he typed. "Ten minutes, Ray?" asked Wismer.

"Yeah boss. Are they ready?" his senior staff sergeant asked, who, for this operation, was the most senior operator involved although no longer at the business end.

"Ready and waiting, no change." reported Wismer.

Staff Sergeant Raymond Farmer had worked in the unit for close to 20 years, where he had risen to his present rank. He had seen tactics change a lot in those years, and he knew that what he expected of his men that day was far beyond anything he had ever dealt with. The fact that he was so far removed from what the guys did these days and what was required of them to do it made him a little envious – a lot proud – and a touch nervous.

But he had faith. Farmer had been to the training days in preparation for this operation. He had seen the guys going through their entry drills progressing from empty weapons to simmunition rounds to live fire drills. He had watched as all six of the teams elevate their skills under the watchful eyes of the Special Forces advisors. The teams had brought themselves as close to the level of their SF advisors as they could get. They had earned the respect of those advisers, and with that came a dramatic rise in confidence.

As they neared the takedown date, Farmer had hated not being able to tell the guys what they were about to walk into. But he knew he couldn't, even if he was pretty sure they'd all figured it out. It was just too risky in terms of the OpSec on this one to give them the details too early. Farmer had gotten over that anxiety two days ago when all the teams had been called to the station for a mass briefing, and he watched the serious looks on their faces, looks of readiness that said, "I knew it!" The men were smiling and nodding to each other, and fist bumps were passed around the room. The atmosphere of confidence and professionalism had impressed him in a way he had not expected. They really were the best in the country.

Sitting at the large oak table in the middle of the command center in front of all the other section commanders and support staff, Ray Farmer nervously looked down at his maps again. He was in charge of the deployments and the taskings for each and every tactical member involved in Operation Sleeper. The process had been a long arduous task planning the minute details right down to what radio number each operator would be given. With all that work behind him, today's task was to keep track of everyone at all times.

As the green-light time approached, Ray watched the plotted movements of his men on a screen populated with the information from their GPS units through their ATAK program and GPS units. That information was then displayed on several large plasma screens at the front of the room for all to see. He quietly began typing on the computer in front of him, entering a series of grid coordinates. Farmer hit enter and looked on with the others as seven new black triangles were plotted at various points around the map. It made him think of a term he had heard Paul Speed use, *Pink Mist*, and he smiled. "They'll be fine," Farmer thought to himself, "there are angels in the shadows tonight."

The other people in the room who were not from the tactical side of the house wondered at the black triangles too. These triangles bore no unit designation, whereas the teams were displayed by a blue circle with their team origin underneath – TIG teams one through six respectively, RCMP-MSERT, OPP Central TRU, PEEL teams one and two, along with Durham teams one and two.

"Attention! Attention! Time 0425 hrs. Five minutes to green light." The cold announcement echoed from the speakers followed promptly by Staff Inspector Wismer speaking for the first time on the common radio channel, which was also echoed through the command center's P.A. system. "All teams proceed to your designated jump-off locations. Hold and acknowledge."

Within two minutes the teams started checking in.

"Team One in position and holding."

"Team Two in position."

"Team Three ditto."

"Four's in position and ready."

"Five in position and holding."

"Team Six in position."

This was followed by similar responses from the other involved tactical teams. The last of which was Peel Region whose response was, "Peel One and Two in position, location secure." Unfortunately Peel had drawn the least exciting of the details this time, which was to secure a facility in which to process any accused persons that may be brought in. Members of the RCMP, CSIS and the American Department of Homeland Security were already on scene there and waiting to interrogate those accused parties.

Next came radio transmissions that the many of the people in the command center weren't expecting. The meaning of the black triangles was about to be revealed. The Group had kept them secret. Upon hearing the whispered voices attached to those call-signs quietly coming over the radio, people immediately began to understand just what, or more properly who, those black triangles represented.

"Sierra Four to CP, ready to designate." came Paul Speed's whispered voice. It filled the command center and instantly grabbed everyone's attention. People stopped and listened to the sniper's conversation with the Staff Sergeant.

"Affirmative Sierra Four, designate." replied Staff Sergeant Frank Goodhall, who was in charge of the communications.

"Sierra Four, we have the Whiskey side at Target One, five o'clock at 130 yards. Badgers have been visible inside, along with the dove. No solution currently. We also confirm Lightning Order at this time."

"Acknowledged. Sierra Four is on the Whiskey, five by 130, no solution and Lightning Order is in effect. At your location only at this time." confirmed Goodhall. Then he waited as the rest of the black triangles checked in. The sniper teams were in place, and many were reporting visuals on their suspects. Good. They had all made it through the last several hours without being detected. "Nicely done fellas," thought Goodhall to himself, "nicely done."

At 0429 hours with all the units properly plotted and identified on the maps, there was but a minute to spare. Tension was high in the command center and in several ordinary looking vans there was a palpable odour of adrenaline ready to ignite around the city.

12

Then it did.

"Sierra Four...Badger at level one door one holding a gun to the dove's head. Looking around nervously. We have a solution."

There was no panic in the man's voice that anyone could tell across the common radio channel and yet lying on the roof of small business kitty-corner to Green Tree Halal Meat Store, or Target One, exactly 130 yards away were two men whose hearts just jumped.

"Sierra Three...solution on Badger Two at the door on the black side. He's with Badger Three. Sierra Three Alpha do you have a solution for Badger Three?"

Men pressed their headsets tightly against their heads as they listened to the current exchange while three snipers were sliding their index fingers onto their triggers and pushing their weapons off safe.

"Sierra Three Alpha...No. Negative at this time."

"Sierra Three, we've lost Badger Three. We still have solution on Two. Options Sierra Four?"

Sierra Four's direction was clear and without hesitation, "Simultaneous. Then scan for number three for a rapid follow-up. Ready? Alpha Team – standby. On my count, five, four, three, two..."

Chapter Two

{*One Year Prior*}

Paul Speed signalled his turn into the Tactical Intervention Group's driveway and slowly eased up to the card reader outside the black gate. It was a warm fall afternoon, and the windows were down in the little four-door Honda, a stark contrast to the rows of pickup trucks and Jeeps in the The Group parking lot. The one thing he had insisted on when he and his wife had bought it was a really good stereo and speakers. Speed was an eclectic music lover, but 1980's and 1990's rap music was at the top of his playlist. Currently the heavy baseline from one of his favourite artists Nas thumped from the speakers.

As he reached his card out the window and taped it against the card reader, the gate started to open and then promptly stopped. A gruff voice grumbled through the speaker box, "No way Speed, not today. You cannot pass through until that crap gets turned off."

Speed laughed, as he pushed his dark sunglasses up onto his forehead, and staring at the camera, replied to the voice on the other end, "Sorry pal, I left my Hall and Oates CD at your mom's last night." Both men laughed sarcastically, and the gate was opened. Speed turned the volume down and pulled the car into the lot. He waved at his team leader Glen Parker, who was headed to the entrance with a group of the Team Four guys. Speed found a parking spot and killed the engine. He grabbed his go-bag from the passenger seat and his lunch box from the back and half trotted to the door.

Man I love this place.

After swiping his access card at the entrance, Speed shook hands with the guys from Team Three that were finishing for the day and made his way to the team room down the back hall. He waved a hello and a smile to the front desk man who was on the phone still trying not to laugh at the call box exchange that had just occurred.

The Tactical Intervention Group had been stood up in 1965 in Toronto and had long since engraved its reputation in the annals of history. Gunfights, hostage takings and large project takedowns, the T.I.G. had seen it all. Speed couldn't help but steal a glance at the black and white pictures adorning the walls of the hallway that captured that history, as he walked to the back hallway to the team room. He passed the pictures of the original members of the unit and watched as the pictures painted a story of the history of this place. A lot had changed over those years.

The last ten years however had seen the most marked advances in tactics, tools and training. After 9-11 cities all over the world braced for the new reality of domestic terrorism and Toronto was one of the first to jump on that bus. The sad reality was that many of the people in power didn't really believe it would ever happen here. But they sure weren't going to let their voters hear them say that. Nope they would pump the terrorism cow hard in order to get funding for a whole myriad of social programs, and oh yeah, a few toys for the cops too. The year 2006 would change that view in more than one plush corner office.

Team Four already had a long distinguish history at the unit and was currently the most senior team in The Group. They were beginning to gel nicely and were operating at a very proficient level. Those facts hadn't gone unnoticed by management either, the team regularly drew the most difficult assignments and was actively sought out by detective units to execute their warrants. It was a good time to be a Hog!

Like most things however, that too was cyclical, and every team had its turn at both the top and bottom. Each of the special weapons teams also had its own unique identity, and those identities were as varied as the ones in any family.

One trait that wasn't unique to this unit was, like SWAT units around the world, there was a genuine brotherhood amongst the members, even if there was a competitive nature with each other. On every team people came and went, but the identity of the team itself stayed mostly the same. Each team also had its own way of welcoming rookies; some rituals were costly and some arduous. Team Four rookies were subjected to a series of initiations and rites of passage which all lead to a feeling of belonging. To really belong though you had to be on the team leader's good side, and on this team getting on the TL's good side was always the hardest hurdle to clear.

Glen Parker had the reputation as the most gifted operator in the unit. He'd been with The Group, as they were often called, for most of his nineteen years as a member of the Police Service. He'd seen just about every possible situation, whether in training or operationally, that you could throw at him. Parker was currently on the phone arguing with his ex-wife about missing a soccer game because he had stayed late at the unit to finalize some training plans for next week.

Before coming on the job, Parker had been a kid looking for direction and he'd found it on a whim in the Army. That career had led him to policing and eventually to The Group, and he had stayed ever since.

He made a point of letting his people know when they were good and when they were not so good. Glen Parker had a way of being up front with you. He figured better to find out what you were made of before rather than after you had been on the team for a year.

This was the start of another week on the afternoon shift for the Hogs, and they had just been told a rookie would be joining them. One of the other Hogs had recently been promoted and the vacancy needed to be filled. As it was, Bryan Robinson walked through the doors that evening full of piss and vinegar, but cautious – even tentative, much like a kid on the first day at a new school. He trotted in and found the team collected at the main counter by the front lobby.

"Hey how are ya' I'm Bryan." he said, making his way around the table in the center of the team room where guys had assembled now. Robinson shook hands with his new mates and he noted to himself that every one of them sized him up as they shook. Not in a condescending way, just in a general first impression sort of way.

He came finally to where Paul Speed sat. Speed had his nose buried in some manual, and his right hand was gently lifting a coffee mug to his face. He looked up as Bryan's hand came out and smiled sincerely. "Hey buddy, nice to see you again. Welcome to the Hogs." Speed caught the look of confusion on Robinson's face and quickly made the fix for him as they shook. "That's us pal, Team Four – the Hogs. Don't ask."

Bryan shrugged and smiled back. "Glad to be here." He didn't immediately notice anything remarkable about Speed other than he seemed to be another young guy. But he'd heard the stories about him. Speed's thick veins were wrapping around his forearms as his rolled-up sleeves choked his arms. His pyramid shaped neck looked like it could hold the whole station up. Robinson thought, "He's the first guy to actually welcome me to the team."

Doubled over a computer at the main desk sat a gray-haired man with an ear cranked over to the radio speaker and Robinson reached down over the high counter shoving his hand right under the guy's nose to get his attention. "Bryan'" he said politely.

The reply was a raised eyebrow and a short, "Nate. Welcome aboard."

The last guy sitting at the end of the counter was another senior looking fella. Michael "Mike" Carter was the next most junior member having been on the team just over a year.

"How are ya' Bryan, I'm Mike." he had said as the two shook hands.

"Is the Sarge around?" Robinson asked the team and then he heard a call from the adjoining sergeant's office.

"That you Robinson?" the voice asked.

16

Walking in the direction of the voice and pointing as he went Robinson asked, "This way?" a series of nods was the only acknowledgement.

In the small office next to the front desk area, Bryan found Team Four's Sergeant Matt Sommers sitting behind a desk. In front of him was a very large mulatto man who didn't even turn to acknowledge him. "Have a seat kid." was the direction from Sommers as he motioned to a seat next to the man across the desk.

Robinson took the empty seat and extended his hand across the desk to the Sergeant, "I'm really glad to be here, Sarge."

"Don't get too comfy yet sweetheart." responded the large man next to him.

Sommers smiled and waved at him. "Easy big fella! Let the kid finish his first coffee here before you break into him. Bryan, meet your team leader, Glen Parker."

Robinson smiled somewhat sheepishly and turned toward Parker extending his hand. "We met on my basic course Sarge. Nice to see you again Glen."

Parker rose and without shaking a hand or cracking a smile he turned to leave but caught himself at the threshold of the door. He turned back and looked at Bryan, who for his part returned a goofy grin. Parker smirked. "When the Sarge is done with you, come find me." The TL turned and left closing the office door behind him.

Bryan turned back to face the Sergeant and shrugged. "Off on the wrong foot?" he asked unsure of himself.

"Nah. He's like that with all the new guys. Every one of those guys out there has gone through the same thing with him. Just follow his direction, and you'll be fine."

The rest of the conversation revolved around some of the S.O.P.'s for the unit and more importantly the team. After about a half hour get-to-know-you session Robinson was dismissed with the advice, "You'd better not keep the TL waiting any longer. I'll give you a heads up. Have your rifle, eye and ear protection and your vest. I think you'll be getting a little range time." And with that the rookie rose and made his way to the team room down the hall, where he found Speed going through his own gear.

The door to their room had a picture of a razorback hog, the team's logo, painted on it.

"I guess this is our space?" he asked.

Speed smiled, "Yeah buddy. Your gear is over in that stall." He pointed across the room. "You'll find your personal C8 and an MP7 in the little gun locker there, and all our team issued shotguns over here. We got your stuff in last week. It should all be there."

17

Robinson went to his new stall and opened the weapons locker finding a brand-new Colt C8 .223 calibre rifle and an HK MP7 submachine gun both with his name labeled on the stock. He saw that his vests were hanging under an equipment shelf and his name was stencilled there as well. "Very organized." he remarked to Speed.

"Hey man, a well-oiled machine runs pretty smooth, but it runs smoother when it can find all of its parts. If you follow?" was the candid response from Speed, who was busy pulling stuff out of a black backpack he'd retrieved off his own shelf labeled SPEED/S4.

"Better not keep Parker waiting." Speed had felt Robinson watching him and had prompted him on.

After retrieving his eyes and ears from his stall, the newest Hog made his way to the lobby with his rifle slung across his chest. As he came through the locked door leading from the team room hallway to the lobby Bryan found Parker who was already wearing his vest and eye protection.

"Got everything?" poised the TL. Robinson almost sputtered out a yes sir but bit his lip instead and nodded. "Come with me." The TL ordered.

The basement of the station housed a 50-meter range and a close quarter battle, or CQB, room There was an ever-present smell of gunpowder that clung to the walls like paint. Robinson had seen both of these rooms before when he had passed selection and spent five long weeks on a basic tactical officers course, he had developed some skills over that time. But when he was ushered into the long range and saw the target at one end and a box of ammo at the other, he began to worry. It had been about a month and a half since his course and he had not been shooting during that time. Robinson knew he would remember how, but the added pressure might cause him to send one off target.

Parker walked to the far end of the range, the rookie following close on his heels, rehearsing in his mind the basic principles of shooting as best he could remember them, "Grip, sight picture, breathing, trigger squeeze, follow through…Hopefully he doesn't go stand next to the target or anything crazy like that."

At the end of the range, Parker's demeanour changed like some sort of a switch had been flicked, "Okay, your course wasn't that long ago, so just relax. I want you to load a mag and put ten rounds as tightly as you can in the middle of that target's chest. You remember how to work that holographic sight and laser?" Parker asked, as calmly as a doctor in the operating room. Parker's delivery immediately put the rookie at ease, time to take care of business.

18

Bryan went through the ten rounds and then the subsequent ten as ordered, and when finished he was glad to find that there were no holes outside the scoring rectangle in the chest. Sure, he hadn't put all twenty rounds into a loonie-sized grouping or anything, but it wasn't half bad.

Parker looked him in the eye and Bryan could see that the switch had been flicked back the other way again.

"Well at least you hit the target. Once you've got this cleaned up you can help check your truck and then hit the gym."

Bryan thought this would be a good time for an icebreaker and offered, "So you're keeping me then?"

Parker threw back over his shoulder, "Don't hold your breath sunshine." as he exited the range smiling to himself and leaving Bryan to pick up the brass. For his part Bryan was smiling too; he was excited to finally be there.

***

There were never many smiles where O'Neil lived and fewer still where he stood now. The night had turned cold, but he had come down anyway. Not because he really cared about the well-being of his man posted there, it was all about money. That was the driving force behind his apparent show of compassion. His money to be exact and he wasn't about to let anyone think they could walk away with it. This was his turf and everyone knew it but that didn't keep him from making the rounds. People had to see the face they both feared and revered. Most of all he made it a point to keep his people on their toes. O'Neil's trick was to be consistent in his inconsistency; that way they never knew when to expect you.

The other trick was to be ruthless when someone disobeyed orders and this further reinforced the fear. It was the way of running an organization that the streets had taught him and had he been to the Harvard Business School, he would have known it was no different in the corporate world. Only the strong survive and currently he was the strongest.

O'Neil hadn't always been such a hard kid. There was a time in his life when he did smile at the sun, run and play tag. A time when everyday had been a dream. Then the neighbourhood started changing. It had always been a low-income part of town, but the residents had at one time looked after the housing project. Now it was run down, dirty and a damn scary place if you didn't belong there.

The Orton Park Projects were a haven for criminal activity, of which the most lucrative was the drug trade. O'Neil had watched the older kids move from stealing to dealing years ago and it had taught him that the only way to survive was to hustle and make as much money as you could. Somehow that never seemed to translate into a retirement plan with a nice car and a house though. There were three ways people left here ambulance, police car or coroner's wagon. That was it. Those were the prospects for a kid from this part of town.

So he grew up hard, and he grew up fast. He learned how to work the system and make others work for him. He knew how to flip up a kilo of cocaine into several hundred grams of heroin and quadruple his money. As for gang life, well it had just followed right along with the rise of the drug trade. Even though this was Canada, Toronto was so closely connected with its American cousins that the spread of "gangsterism" was inevitable. Toronto had all varieties of gangs to choose from. O'Neil Facey's "hood" had gone the way of the Crips in the late 1980s as a means of protecting themselves from the rival "hoods" nearby that were going to the bloods. As such, being a Crip was all O'Neil ever really knew.

Family was a foreign concept to him. Having immigrated to Canada from the islands of the Bahamas, Eluthra to be exact, when he was just three with his mother, they had hoped to start over. They were in search of a better life.

O'Neil's mother worked a lot of menial jobs on shifts which left O'Neil in the care of neighbours initially. As he got older it meant he was forced to fend for himself more times than not. Eventually his mother became another statistic in the dark underworld of a big city. Soon she was carrying her drug dealer – pimp boyfriend's baby. She was in and out of jail and the last time the cops hauled his mother off to jail it was for good. O'Neil was taken in by a neighbour that he knew as Aunty Jean.

O'Neil would see his mother from time to time over the years when she was between programs. It got to the point where coming to see him was too much of a temptation for her to go back to old habits. Her son had become the exact person that had sent her into this lifestyle. She hated herself for leaving him there to become that way.

He fancied himself a sort of father figure to the younger generation coming up under him. In his mind he was doing right by his community. He had paid in cash for the new basketball courts in the courtyard, and he'd also managed to commandeer a number of TV's and game consoles for the community room. Of course, no one asked any questions about where they'd come from.

20

As he sat in the cold stairwell of the building sharing a joint with one of his captains, he smiled on life and on how far he thought he'd come. The dope made his mind kick into a new speed, and that familiar feeling was comforting. He always had felt that he made his best plans when he was high. O'Neil and his soldier bounced some ideas around while the deep melodic bass lines of the latest gangster rap classic from the six filtered from the headphones that were hugging his neck.

A door squeaked opened from a floor somewhere above, and hard soled footsteps descended towards them. Both of the gangsters immediately felt at their waistbands for the guns they were holding. But O'Neil didn't panic because he knew it was only going to be another resident of the building heading out into the evening air. If it were anyone else, his phone would have been ringing off the hook by to warn him. He knew his enemies would never actually try to get in the building and the cops were just too easy for his people to spot. Besides, no one he knew wore hard soled shoes unless it was to the clubs downtown on a Friday night and today was Tuesday. When the sound of the feet reached the landing above them both O'Neil and his associate turned to face the unknown resident and were surprised to find two Arab men standing there.

O'Neil and Strong got up turning to face at the Arabs and the four men stood staring at each other for a few seconds, waiting to see what the other's intentions were. For the Arab's part, they wanted to confirm that they were looking at *who* they wanted to talk to. The two Crips had no idea what these Arabs could possibly want with them.

O'Neil's captain, James Strong, spoke first saying, "Whatchu punks want here?" as he lifted his shirt revealing the semi-auto TEC-9 in his waistband.

One of the Arabs spoke in perfect English without any regard for the weapon. "You will come with us. There is someone who wishes to speak with you on a matter of mutual benefit."

O'Neil stood stone faced for several more seconds, as he carefully chose his response. "Why don't you fuck off with your friend there before you both end up getting shot? Who you think you talking to like that? All 'I will come with you' and shit! Get lost motherfucker."

What he lacked in tact he made up for in confidence. But O'Neil had, in his current altered state, failed to notice how professional these men had been. It became all too clear when, in a flash of hands and elbows, his man Strong was grabbed into a rear naked chokehold after he had made a weak attempt to pull the TEC-9 out of his waistband. In fact, the weapon hadn't even cleared his belt line before the silent Arab had stuffed the hand reaching for the gun and spun Strong around so that there was a serious case of *oh shit!* spreading across his face. The Arab's hand was settling on the gun's grip as he stared calmly at O'Neil.

O'Neil was snapped back into sobriety and immediately realized how deftly and quietly the Arab had moved. It was indicative of some high-level training, military maybe? In fact, the only sound O'Neil had heard was the deep grunt his toughest captain, and bodyguard had made when he had been snatched into the Arab's grip. O'Neil was looking at the one who had spoken to him initially, "What's up then?"

"You'll come with us to visit the Mullah, and you will have a conversation with him. You are permitted to bring your associate, but we will be keeping you weapons temporarily. Trust Allah that if you or your associate should try anything as foolish as that again you will quickly find yourselves face to face with the Almighty."

How could he argue with that? Besides, his right-hand man was already in very precarious position. O'Neil also realized that these men were very serious indeed and if they were willing to go to this extreme to get a meeting with him then maybe there was some benefit in it for him.

"Okay man, we'll go, but I won't forget what you pulled here, trust me." He'd said, in an attempt to salvage his reputation, only to have it dashed again when the Arab responded saying, "I truly hope you never forget my young friend, trust *me.*"

With that, O'Neil and his captain followed the two Arabs to the elevator and up to the 21st floor. O'Neil had been watching the slow but steady influx of Arab families into the Orton Park buildings. But they mostly kept to themselves, he had no customers on these upper floors since they'd moved in, so he was never up here. And as such he had paid little attention to them, he reflected internally that maybe that had been a mistake? Upon exiting the elevator, they noticed several more rough looking Arabs in the hallway on what could have easily been a Secret Service Security detail. He didn't know if they were armed or not, but O'Neil suddenly did not feel so much at home.

The two young black men were ushered into an apartment at the end of the hall nearest the stairwell. As they entered, several Muslim women were ordered in Arabic to leave, and the two Crips were directed to a couch in the living room. O'Neil stared as the burka clad women rose immediately and silently shuffled out of the room. The only sound came from their silk garments wisping as they passed the couch. As they went by O'Neil stared into the bright green eyes on one of the women and was puzzled that he could discern no expression in them.

There was a strong odour of hookah in the air and a slight haze hovered at the top of the room. A tray of coffee and baklava was placed on the coffee table and expensive looking ceramic cups were filled for three. The two gangsters sat looking around the room, Strong most sheepishly as he was still shaking off the humility of the ambush, but O'Neil was taking stock of his surroundings. Blinds closed, lots of tough looking security types, people ordered out, and the whole invitation to the meeting ordeal. All of this had the feeling of being something very high level.

After a time that seemed to last forever, an older Arab man entered the living room and stood at the threshold consulting with the men who had brought O'Neil here. The Arab was in his fifties of average height and slender build. He had dark worn looking skin, and what hair could be seen under his black headdress was a smoky grey. O'Neil noticed that the man was, however, very well dressed compared to the other men in the apartment. It appeared that this man was of some importance, but just how important was still to be seen.

Then it began. Ameer Mahmood walked into the living room and stood opposite his two guests with another man off to his right and introduced himself in perfect English, "Welcome. I am Ameer and this is my associate Raahil, and I believe you have already met Amr and Fattah. I hope that interaction wasn't too concerning for you? After all, you would expect your men to act as swiftly for you, correct? Anyway, that is enough. Welcome." Ameer Mahmood extended his hand across the coffee table and shook hands with the confused O'Neil. The Mullah then sat in a very comfortable looking mahogany and red velvet chair and crossed his legs. He took a sip of his coffee and beckoned for his guests to do the same. O'Neil obliged. "Good. Let us share a drink and talk like civilized men about how we can begin to work together."

O'Neil liked the man's straight forward approach and sipped at his coffee which was much too bitter for his taste; it wasn't his usual double-double. After getting past the first bitter mouthful O'Neil opened the door to the conversation, "So whatchu need homie?"

Ameer smiled. "It's not what I need, my young friend, rather what we need." What followed was a framework, a sales pitch for a partnership that was to be mutually beneficial to both parties. Ameer orated on a series of promises about money, freedom, and long-term prosperity that had O'Neil rubbing his palms. Like any good street deal, both O'Neil and Ameer were already planning to break those promises. Unfortunately, O'Neil couldn't see past the dollar signs.

The meeting lasted for several hours, and there was much discussion about Islam and religion in general. This also ended favourably for the Arabs when O'Neil hinted at his contemplation of converting to Islam.

The last piece of baklava was snatched up by Strong and O'Neil took a final mouthful of the ginger-ale he had been able to get the Arabs to give him. Then the men rose. Ameer stood to meet them and the three exchanged handshakes. Before allowing the young gangsters to leave Ameer taught them their first lesson in Islam, "Gentlemen, it is custom in Islam when we greet or part from each other to say As-salamu alaykum, which means peace be with you, to which the other person responds, Wa alaykum As- salamu and with you peace. As- salamu alaykum, my new friends."

The two gangsters tried in their best possible diction to respond but butchered the phrase. "Close enough for today." replied Ameer with a chuckle and a smile. The groundwork for the plan was in motion and although the process would take some time to foster, in the grand scheme of things it was very close at hand now.

Chapter Three

Anew batch of candidates were in their final week of training on the Basic Tactical Orientation Course, the five-week job interview held by the TIG to weed out undesirable candidates. As Speed stood in front of his locker listening to the nervous chatter of the latest batch of prospects, he thought back on how much the course had changed since he had gone through it. He remembered a time when everyone got a certificate, and the only difference to failing was the wording on the document that read either *Successfully Completed* or *Completed*. That little difference had led to many a grievance from candidates who thought they should have been asked up to the unit, but in reality they had never passed. Selection was now much more rigorous, every minute of every day was not only a chance for learning but for candidates to be evaluated. Speed smiled to himself, as he closed his locker and made his way through the huddle of prospects and down to the gym.

Throughout the course, each of the six operational teams were encouraged to send representatives whenever they were available to act as observers. This facilitated two goals. Firstly, it added tremendous pressure to the candidates having to be evaluated by the guys they hoped to work with, and secondly, it gave the teams a first-hand look at potential teammates. Most often the teams sent their team leaders or next most senior member.

Even though Speed was only fourth in seniority, the team had decided to test his insight as such he was part of the Hog's observer rotation for this class. This week was his turn to follow the candidates. The Hogs were working afternoon shift, and as such Speed was in on his own time at 0700 hrs to shadow the basic course. It was just part of the new way of doing business at the TIG. It benefited the whole unit and therefore some personal time was worth sacrifice.

Especially if selecting the right people meant it kept your ass safe at some point in the future. Candidates for selection came from all over the Service—forensics, patrol, detective squads and the like. The only posted requirements for application were to have completed a minimum of five years on the job; an added benefit would to have gone through a divisional level investigative training program. Other than that, The Group kept its application standards wide open so that they didn't discourage potential candidates; those eliminations would often take care of themselves in the first week of the course.

25

Recently revised, the program was modeled after many Special Forces selection programs, albeit on a much less strenuous level. Week one was really nothing more than a series of tests of the candidate's abilities to follow orders and think while under stress. The training section's job was to slowly and steadily increase the pressure. Like a carpenter closing a vice too tightly on a piece of fresh wood who risks damaging the grain or even splitting the board. Too little pressure and the board won't be stable enough when you try to shape it. The process of selecting suitable members for the Group was a delicate balance but the standards were real, and they were intentionally difficult. They had to be.

There were the usual tests of marksmanship and fitness, but in today's operational environment they would also test the new guy's ability to adapt to changing timelines and requests, as well as their ability to slip in and out of locations without being detected.

The Group needed their new candidates to learn early in their training the mindset of being organized and prepared for anything at all times, readiness was a pillar of the unit.

That first week was all about building a solid foundation. Weeks two through five were about increasing the difficulty. At the end there would be qualifications to pass and exams to write and everything would culminate in difficult skills confirmation scenarios. All of this before any of them earned that coveted patch.

On day twenty-three for this particular course, there were two days to graduation and possible selection to The Group. This batch of candidates was actually doing quite well. Only one candidate had to be removed in week one and one other in week three. They were down to eight potential candidates and the word to the teams from the Training Cadre was that there wasn't one of them that would not be suitable for the unit. Unfortunately for the hopeful candidates, there were only two immediate openings: one on Team Four and another on Team Five. Both teams had recently sent members to a joint task force team headed by the RCMP and thus had openings. There would be other openings in the coming months due to both an on-going promotional process within the Service and the natural attrition of the unit. But the remaining eight candidates all craved those two immediate openings. Being selected straight from the course meant you were thought to be the best of your class. The other candidates would be returned to their original postings and wait for a call.

Paul Speed was in the gym early that morning to work out and observe while the candidates were being put through their paces by one of the trainers. Speed had made it a point to meet all the candidates over the last four and a half weeks and knew them by name without having to look at the back of the blue shirts the candidates had to wear.

Speed had memorized their schedule for the day, *Long day.* Speed thought to himself. Well at least he would be operational at 1430hrs and getting paid to be there watching as the candidates muddled through their interior combat drills.

Finishing his run on the treadmill with a sprint, Speed slowed the machine and his breathing at the same time. He liked to practice this at the end of every run to ensure that if he had to hustle into a firing position, he could quickly slow his breathing and heart rate enough to shoot accurately. A few seconds later, he was breathing normally, and Speed strolled off the end of the machine, wiped it down with the anti-bacterial cleaner and made his way to the water fountain.

At the fountain, Speed was joined by candidate Damon Fernandes, the class's quiet team leader. Damon was on his 30-second rest period during the class's circuit training session and was quite out of breath. But he stopped short of the fountain when he saw Speed coming and stood off to one side, waiting. Speed breezed past him and took a long drink from the fountain then stood and smiled, as he waved Fernandes to the cooling water. There existed a recent unwritten rule for the candidates that stated that they were to clear a path and stand aside for any full-time member of the unit at any time and for anything. That meant the candidates went last for the coffee truck, last for showers, last for parading on and off duty and last for the water fountain. It was another way to test the candidates and it was also to show respect to the men and women who were already serving members.

Speed watched as Candidate Fernandes crawled back to the next station in the circuit's rotation and readied himself for another 30-seconds of chin-ups. A grin of sarcastic joy spread over his face as he grabbed the bar and smiled at Speed. Fernandes was the candidate the Hogs had targeted as their pick, but he hadn't been anyone's pick in week one. He had come across as too timid and too quiet, so much so that the Training Cadre had picked him to be the class leader because they thought he might crumble under the pressure.

He hadn't and in fact he had risen to the challenge.

Under Fernandes' leadership, the class had not been less than fifteen minutes early for a single timing. He was still a bit too quiet, but the Hogs liked what they saw in his personality. He could use some more time in the gym and some work on his conditioning, but this candidate seemed to be the sort of guy the Hogs would love to shape into their style of operator. So far his tactics and marksmanship were holding up with the rest of the class as well in spite of a lack of any weapons handling experience.

Besides, Speed hadn't had any of that either when he came to the team, and he was now their lead sniper. Where Fernandes was lacking the team felt confident that they could polish him up. Speed grabbed his phone and headed back upstairs to the change room for a quick shower and to get suited up for the long day ahead. He thought to himself as he climbed the stairs, *That kid has a lot of potential.*

As he was finishing in the shower, a page came over the intercom: "Speeder, call the front desk. Constable Speed, call the front desk please."

"Shit!" he muttered out loud to himself. Hastily towelling off on his way to the phone just outside the showers. Speed punched in the number for the front desk and spoke to the operator on the other end. "Gus. Speed. What's up, buddy?"

"Hey Speeder. Yeah, the Staff has a briefing for you when you're ready."

"Okay, tell him I'll be down in five would ya'?"

A briefing huh? Well, that could only mean work, and work sure beat the hell out of standing around watching a bunch of candidates tripping on each other during their entry drills. Speed threw on a clean uniform and grabbed his memo book and headed for the Staff Sergeant's office. On the way out, he had to pass the rookie's lockers and there he bumped into Fernandes again, "Survived another PT circuit huh buddy?"

"Yes sir." was Fernandes's only response complete with a look of pain and rolled eyes. "Keep it up, candidate." It was all Speed could do to keep from telling the guy that they intended to pick him right from the course, but he bit his tongue and trotted down the stairs.

Chapter Four

At the Staff Sergeant's door, Speed tapped on the frosted glass and was beckoned inside. As he entered the corner office, he noticed Josh Bender, the lead sniper from Team Three, sitting opposite the Staff. Speed immediately knew this was big but just how big would take some time for him to fully understand. Each of the snipers was handed a briefing package in a crisp new blue folder. At this early stage, it was rather thin but it did list a number of suspects and outlined the case being built around them. Sniper 4 and Sniper 3 exchanged a look of satisfaction. The kind you shared when you were selected for a special task, a task doing something you loved but you knew it was going to involve a lot of work. And in this case potential danger.

The Staff Sergeant spoke first. "Okay guys, I know there isn't much to work with there and there is no timeline for completion, but as you've just read this is a very serious investigation. Once again it comes with national security issues. Because of the unit's performance during the last investigation of this type and the recent work of you guys in the sniper program, we are being given the leeway to begin our own recce's of the targets. You each have several targets in your packages, and what I need from you is to start the planning for assaults on those targets should it become necessary between and the takedown date for this project. We need to be proactive on this one fellas. You plan 'em, you run 'em, but you must not compromise this investigation. Understood?"

Nods from both snipers acknowledged the Staff. As they turned back to their packages one question was asked in unison, "When do we start?"

"Now. Call in your partners and get to it. I expect a preliminary report from each of your teams by the end of next week." Staff Sergeant Frank Goodhall ordered. He looked across his desk at the two snipers as they studied their packages intently, "Okay then, get at it."

The snipers rose and headed back out to the front desk area. Josh Bender (Sniper 3) looked over at the man on the desk who was currently on the phone and when he had his attention whispered, "When you get a sec, could you call in our number two's? Thanks Gus." The snipers smiled in thanks and headed for the planning office down the back hallway on the main floor of the station. As they passed the training cadre's office Speed stopped telling Bender he'd catch up in a minute. Speed poked his head into the office and was greeted by a chorus of "Speeder!" Laughter rang through the room, and he smiled, as he looked around the room for Jake Fischer. Fischer was in charge of the candidates today, and Paul just wanted him to know he would be late due to his new assignment. Fischer was not in the office so Speed left his message with one of the other cadre members and headed on down the hall to the planning office as the laughing and ribbing followed him.

The planning office was a smallish room at the end of the hall and unofficially it was known as the team leader's/sniper's office. Reason being, they were the only ones in general who needed the use of this room. The room was equipped with a series of standalone Internet-ready computers, a map table complete with topographical maps of the city and the surrounding area, as well as a set of internal computers. The walls were also covered in white boards for the guys to rough out any ideas. Currently no one else was using the planning room and that was a relief as the snipers set to work pulling maps and searching the web for information related to their targets.

First things first though. Before they got too far into their work each of them had to assign their details a codename. The snipers had two choices on that. They could search the internal database for a randomly generated one or make their own and submit it for approval. Neither of them had ever used a random codename before so why start now? There was a special sense of ownership when you named your own assignment. Even if the codenames were rejected by the database they would keep trying until they found one that they liked. Speed went first and after several attempts settled on Archangel. Bender was luckier and got his on the first try. With that done two labels were printed out one for each binder. Projects Archangel and City Snake were born and for the next six to seven months would occupy the majority of the sniper's time. Snipers three and four would be spending the better part of this week getting the preliminary work done on their respective files and comparing notes. Their number twos would be starting the rough work on the maps plotting possible spots for them to build their hides. Collectively they would huddle around French presses filled with dark coffee. The aromas swirling around their bent heads coaxing the best possible plans out of them. The two sniper teams would begin the long discussions over the terrain, ingress and egress routes ad nauseam, eventually ending at a well-thought-out set of operational plans.

***

Basic Course Graduation Day – Day 25

The candidates had just finished their course and Speed was there in the crowded classroom for the diploma ceremony along with his team leader and close friend Glen Parker. "You wanna tell him?" Parker poised rhetorically to Speed.

"No thanks big fella', I'm pretty sure that's your job."

"Yeah. Thanks for nothing pal." Parker finished with a smile. He really did hate talking to people even the ones he was supposed to like. Speed watched, as the imposing team leader made his way across the room stopping momentarily to speak with Team Five's T/L. Speed knew that Parker would be giving the man the gears about trying to steal their pick, but it was all in fun because the "Demon Dogs" had their eye on someone else anyway. As Parker made it over to where Fernandes was standing, he stood silently to one side while the rookie received his congratulatory hugs from his girlfriend and family. When the moment presented itself Parker broke in with an introduction to the group. "Very polite! Well done Parker." Speed snickered to himself.

"Hello. I'm Glen Parker. I'm the team leader for special weapons Team Four. May I steal a minute of this man's time from you?"

Smiles around the huddle acknowledged the request and seemed to signify that they knew what was coming next. After all, it is what Fernandes had wanted, that coveted spot on Team Four.

"Damon, I'm not real good at this kind of thing so here it is…we'd like to select you from the course to join us on special weapons Team Four. Do you accept this assignment?"

There was no hesitation and no overreaction from the reserved rookie, "Absolutely sir. Start date for me?"

Parker smiled at him. He held out his hand and revealed a Team Four Hog patch in the shape of a razorback. "Here you go kid, try not to lose this. And look, you've had a long five weeks. Take the weekend off as per Sergeant Sommers and hook up with us on Monday for the back half of afternoon shift. 1430 start Monday. Sound good?"

And with excitement about to kill him, the new S.W.A.T. rookie smiled as big a smile as he could and replied, "You bet! I'll see you Monday then." Parker took his leave from the new Hog and walked back across the room to where Speed was standing, "I couldn't do it, Speeder. Couldn't tell him he'd failed the course."

"You're kidding me Glen, so we're stuck with him now?"

"Yep, I guess so! You saw the look on his face, those sad puppy dog eyes. How could I …" and the two men burst into laughter as they left the room, "Aw shit Speed, he'll be all right. I mean, damn, we kept you didn't we?"

"Yeah! And look how long you've been here ya' dinosaur!"

More laughter and as it subsided and their sides stopped aching, the intercom bellowed, "Team Four, suit up – Team Four, suit up!"

Fernandes watched longingly, clutching his coveted team patch, as his new teammates started running for the stairs. Both men headed to the main floor where they split up. Speed ran to the garage to begin dressing and Parker to the front desk to get the details of the call they'd be going to. Once he had the printout he ran back to his truck and threw on his equipment as the rest of the team was getting into their vehicles. Once his headset was in place, and the radio turned on he waited for a break in the comms checks. "Radio check for Parker."

"Good check brother, what do we got Big Man?" came the response from one of the operators.

"Person with a gun, barricaded and suicidal." Parker gave the Cole's Notes version. "House or apartment?" asked his lead sniper, already planning his next move, as the trucks rolled out of the garage and onto the street.

***

Ameer Mahmood had his own plan mapped out in his head. But some details had to be written in a journal in rough form. Ameer carefully removed the false bottom from the middle drawer of the large mahogany desk. Inside the hidden space he removed a worn leather-bound notebook who's worn edges bore the scars of rough travel. He reviewed his handwritten timeline and after making a few coded notes he closed the cover and retied the leather binds. The book was hidden neatly away in its space and the lid returned. Ameer was careful to keep a close eye on that journal knowing that if it was discovered it could derail not only his plan, but several others. The majority of the work would be done by his own men, and in fact he preferred it that way, but some things had just become too hard for an Arab to accomplish even in this country. He couldn't just send his brother and a gaggle of Arabs into a farming supply company and ask for massive amounts of fertilizer, could he? No. However, he had accounted for that, and his new batch of willing soldiers would be able to do all sorts of important jobs for him. Ameer's gold inlaid pen put the finishing strokes on his signature completing the forms required to register a new business. He ran a damp sponge along the glue strip and sealed them in

32

the official city envelope. Leaning back, Ameer crossed his legs and began reviewing the intricate business plan he had put together, "It must be clear to him Raahil, what to say if questioned. We cannot have Allah's plan undermined by something as simple as a slip of the tongue." he said to the man standing on the desk's other side.

"I agree. I will make sure that our new friends get the appropriate message." Replied Raahil. Leaving a task as important as this to men who had no real connection to their cause was risky, but Raahil trusted the wisdom of the Mullah and set off to find O'Neil. He dialed the appropriate cell phone number and immediately got O'Neil on the other end,

"What's up?"

Raahil hated the vernacular of the people in these neighbourhoods. *Why can't they just speak English? It is demeaning to their own character to bastardize the language this way,* he thought to himself angrily. His advanced schooling would not let him accept such "slang" as part of how civilized people were supposed to talk to each other. Worse yet, how someone being called and treated as a leader should speak. Raahil silently vowed to educate O'Neil just on the off chance he survived all of this, maybe O'Neil really could speak like a leader. *Save that for later,* he thought to himself again as he responded to O'Neil's question, "I need to speak with you and review the next step in the plan. Can we meet somewhere public, but away from here?"

O'Neil thought on it for a minute and then made a suggestion that gave Raahil some pause, "Okay dude, on Spadina just south of Dundas there is a Chinese restaurant called the Goldstone Noodle. It's on the west side of the road at Williamson Square. Let's meet there in say an hour or so."

Could this simple street thug have some real smarts about how to deceive the authorities should they be watching? It was a perfect spot to meet. Neither one fit-in there, but neither one would be out of place either. In this cultural melting pot of a town people from all races and backgrounds mingled in each other's neighbourhoods like tourists and where never given a second glance. The only thing that could spoil this perfect meeting would be if O'Neil had picked a place that would be too busy, or if he came dressed like a regular gangster, for then they would look out of place together. Raahil decided to use this meeting as a sort of test for his new associate. If it looked like it was going to be a bad idea to meet there in that way, then Raahil would simply invite O'Neil for a walk to some random place nearby and talk in a dark corner. In any event, he didn't really think that the Canadian authorities could possibly be wise to them yet.

"Okay, I'll see you there at 8:30 then." Raahil agreed, hanging up the phone and immediately walking to the elevator for the ride to the garage. He figured that he would take the time to scout the location first. "Worst thing that happens is I get a good meal out of it and maybe a laugh at this juvenile kingpin." Raahil chuckled, as he entered the elevator. He tried to stifle the laugh when he noticed the look he was getting from the East Indian woman standing in the corner.

Once in the basement garage, he made his way to his parking space and keyed the remote for the alarm. He climbed aboard the nicely appointed SUV and brought the engine to life. Pulling out of the parking space, Raahil headed for the highway to get downtown in order to complete his reconnaissance of the restaurant and the area. Although he had lived in the city for more than a decade, he'd not spent much time in China Town, and he wanted to have a plan 'B' should something go wrong. Raahil thought he would have made a great spy for his country or any country for that matter. As it was, planning just seemed prudent to him to have a reaction plan and an escape route, rather than flying by the seat of his pants through parts of town he didn't know. As he cruised down the highway toward his destination, classical music floated quietly from the truck's speakers and the former soldier went over the script for the meeting. Raahil was so engrossed in thought and lulled by the music that he nearly missed the exit for Spadina Road. Descending the off-ramp to the inner city, he switched off the stereo and changed gears in his mind. He went from strategist to tactical planner, ready to analyze his surroundings.

***

While Raahil cruised north on Spadina, O'Neil was still at home pulling a black sweater over his head. He sat on the edge of the bed and looked back at Shawna lying there naked staring up at him. His number one girlfriend had no idea what he was about to embark on tonight; she figured it was just another drug deal. But something felt different to her about this one. O'Neil rarely got dressed like he was going to a club for a deal. He had on a white collared dress shirt under a black knit sweater with the cuffs rolled up at the wrist exposing his diamond studded watch that sparkled at the cuff. His black dress pants had just the right amount of sag in them to sit perfectly on top of his favorite black suede Balenciaga's to complete the look. O'Neil stood and went to the mirror on the dresser. He splashed on a healthy dose of that Tom Ford cologne and fit the diamond studs in his earlobes.

As he loaded his pistol and put into the back of his waistband the young lady lying in the bed asked him, "Big score tonight, baby?"

"Shit Shawna, you know I don't like to talk business wit' you. Let's just say that when I'm done this project we'll be able to move out the hood forever." The words were there but the gangster in O'Neil didn't really mean "we". He bent down and kissed her breasts then stood smiling and said, "I'll be back in a couple hours, you be here when I get back 'cause I ain't done wit' you yet. A'ight girl?" With a smile she curled up under the covers and closed her eyes and O'Neil vanished. He also took the elevator down to the basement garage and was met at the door by his bodyguard James Strong. They made their way to the Lexus parked nearby with one of O'Neil's soldiers behind the wheel and climbed in. O'Neil outlined his plan if any trouble came their way, either with the police or their new partner in crime. When he was finished, he nodded to the driver to head out. As soon as they cleared the underground, Strong dialed an associate in the Vanaulley Walk complex near to the restaurant and made the appropriate arrangements for shelter and security in case it was necessary. Hanging up he turned up the stereo and the deep baselines began warming up the car's interior. Strong pulled a joint out of his pocket and lit it taking a long hard hit off the marijuana. He turned to pass it into the back seat to O'Neil who waved him off which left a look of disbelief on Strong's face. He shrugged and turned back into the front seat handing the joint to the driver. O'Neil starred out the window watching the streetlights fly by as he wondered at his own future.

***

Raahil made a second pass through the area. He was quite impressed with O'Neil's selection both in location and the timing. The restaurant was virtually empty, and there were plenty of seats for them to choose that allowed good escape routes if they should need them. As for the area, it was busy with regular vehicle and pedestrian traffic and the restaurant had easy exits out to the Vanaulley Walk neighbourhood, which was a maze of low-income townhouses and laneways. An 8:30 p.m. meeting couldn't have been better. That time of night put them in the restaurant after any dinner rush and before any club or theater crowd might be out looking for exotic tastes. "Maybe the kid is smarter than I gave him credit." Raahil wondered aloud inside his SUV as he took in the location; he knew better than to underestimate anyone. He steered the SUV onto a quiet tree-lined side street a few blocks from the restaurant and pulled it into a space as another car left. The time 8:15 p.m. and Raahil exited the truck making his way down the street through the brisk mid-March night to the restaurant. At this time of year in Toronto the nights were still crisp leaving your breath hanging in the air.

Inside, Raahil selected a large booth near the kitchen and sat with his back to the wall so he could watch the front door. He ordered a tea and waited for his associate's arrival. He was a full thirty minutes early, and he sat comfortably sipping on his tea. Not quite as good as home, but not terrible either. Raahil let his mind wander back to happy memories of home, walking the lush valleys that blended into the edges of his village. He was nine then, and he smiled at his grandfather who held his hand and walked him down the path to school. His mind skipped ahead several years to his time in boarding school in Europe, then to his military Service. He felt himself getting angry as he thought about the invasion and the bombings. He saw the image of his grandfather lying twisted into the rubble of their modest farmhouse. He knew then that he would fight against every last one of the invaders that had killed this humble man.

Promptly at 8:30 p.m. in walked O'Neil flanked by his bodyguard, shaking Raahil from his memory. A tear hovering at the edge of his eye, that he quickly brushed away. O'Neil made his way to the table and nodded for Strong to take a seat near the front of the restaurant. Raahil was impressed by the professionalism with which O'Neil presented himself tonight looking every bit the young entrepreneur they needed him to be. They exchanged a smile and the customary Wa Asalam's to which Raahil was again amazed this time by O'Neil's diction.

"You've been practicing I see." remarked Raahil with a smile.

O'Neil returned the smile, pleased with himself for his hard work. After ordering plates of General Tao's chicken and Singapore noodles, the two associates began their discussions.

Raahil outlined the next phase of the plan and reiterated how important it was that this be a legitimate venture. O'Neil was confused. "So, you want me to give up my drug enterprise to run a landscaping business for you? How is cuttin' fuckin' grass supposed to compensate for the tens of thousands of dollars a week I'll be losing, Dog?" Raahil knew that O'Neil just couldn't see the whole picture yet and it was much too early to reveal it to him.

"You must trust me, O'Neil. You will be well compensated for your efforts. But it is imperative that you let on that you have turned a new leaf and gone legitimate. I would even suggest that you let yourself be seen working for your new business by that local police officer who enjoys arresting you so much. How better to solidify your new reputation? Remember, we will make requests of you to purchase specific items at precisely the right times, which will aid us in what we are trying to accomplish but will not look out of place coming through your new business. Come on, what do you think you will call this new business?"

Raahil worked O'Neil hard trying to massage him into agreement. He told the young thug that the Arabs simply wanted to cut corners on licensing and taxes to establish their businesses. O'Neil would play a part in that by allowing certain transactions to be hidden through his company. The obvious win for O'Neil was a legitimate means of income and compensation on top of that from the Arabs. More enticingly, it would cost him nothing in initial investment. How could he possibly say no? This had been his dream since he was a child, to get out of those buildings and live a regular life.

O'Neil didn't even hesitate, "New Leaf Landscaping." he proclaimed.

Raahil sat back and smiled at the announcement. This kid was smart and had a nice sense of humor as well. After some more preliminary discussions the pair of unlikely partners finished their meal and parted ways. O'Neil still had reservations about this new development and needed to put the pieces together. As he stepped outside Strong asked, "Where to boss?" O'Neil rubbed the old scar on his neck and looked around. "Let's head over to Club 44 and get a drink. I need to think." The pair climbed into the luxury sedan and pointed the driver in the direction of Toronto's club district. Outside the club the driver stopped the car in the valet line and let O'Neil and Strong out to make their way through the VIP entrance. Once in their booth Strong brought over a bottle of very expensive vodka and poured two glasses. He so badly wanted to pry O'Neil for information, but he knew it was too soon, better to let him think awhile.

After a few minutes, O'Neil opened the conversation, "Whatchu think them Arabs want with some fertilizer, dog?" Strong looked stunned as usual but then replied with such clarity that O'Neil was furious with himself for not having seen it earlier.

"Bombs man. They planning to blow some shit up, dude. I saw a documentary about that Oklahoma City bombing from way back. That's what they used."

The light went on for O'Neil, as he slouched deeper into his seat trying to find a way to turn this to his advantage.

A fine young female came over and sat next to him, "What's up, Face? You look tired. Wanna get out of here?"

O'Neil didn't even turn to look at her he just stood and ordered Strong to follow him. Their driver saw them coming and hurried to get the car, he checked his watch. They hadn't even been in the place an hour.

As the car pulled up, O'Neil climbed in without a word and as Strong got into the front seat he ordered the driver to head home. O'Neil just stared out the window the entire ride. Was this the retribution he'd been seeking? Or was this too much even for him to handle, worse yet – was he being set-up to take the fall? He couldn't be sure. He wondered how to play this. He could choose to go against the Muslims, but he knew he could never go head-to-head with their organization. He had seen enough already to know that they were in a different league.

But did he even want to? Did he even care?

This city had done nothing for him or his family, so why should he care? O'Neil's train of thought was broken by the sound of sirens and flashing lights as they pulled into their hood. "That can only be one person." he said out loud, angrily.

As the driver's window went down, he could see the uniform and laughed. "If it ain't Officer Do-little." O'Neil announced.

The officer leaned in the window and looked into the back seat, his hand on his weapon the whole time. "Well, well, well. What do we have here but three bad mice. How are you fellas? Welcome home. Did you boys have a nice night on the town?"

"What do you want officer? You ain't got nothing better to do?" asked Strong, returning the sarcasm. No one was panicking yet, but they knew if Officer Tim Immes found his way into the car and then into searching them that they'd all be going to jail. The three handguns and a quarter pound of weed in the console on top of all of their previous convictions would be the end of their new partnership with the Muslims.

As Officer Immes was examining the driver's identification and paperwork, a black SUV sped past them and swerved, nearly hitting the officer. Officer Immes collected himself tossing the paperwork into the vehicle and racing back to his scout car to pursue the truck. As he sped past them, sirens roaring, the trio sat staring at each other, quietly wondering just how lucky they'd been. After a short pause, they pulled off and made their way to the apartment complex. Ahead of them near the driveway they could see that Officer Immes had cornered his prey and was berating the man in the driver's seat who didn't seem bothered by it at all. As their car eased by, both Strong and O'Neil realized who it was, Raahil.

Raahil was enduring the officer's tirade and politely apologizing, as he watched O'Neil's car creeping by. He had stopped when he saw the officer pulling their car over. Staying back a half a block or so Raahil had watched the interaction and immediately knew that this was the officer who had been a thorn in O'Neil's side for many years. Raahil knew that O'Neil was armed, he had caught a glimpse of the pistol when they stood to leave the restaurant. He had also correctly rationalized that with all the gangster bravado, O'Neil's men would also be armed. Those guns were just waiting to be uncovered by this persistent cop. This would spell the end of their mission and he could not let that happen. So he had put his truck in drive and sped at the officer fully intending to hit him. What was the life of one western cop in the war on the infidels? To Raahil it was nothing. At the last second the cop had heard, or maybe sensed the car coming and jumped nearly onto the hood of the sedan but the diversion had still done its job. The officer had given chase and let O'Neil go free. Raahil was confusing him further with a calm demeanor and plausible story of having dropped his cell phone, he doubled down with a heavy Arabic accent.

"It really was an accident officer. I am very sorry. I hope you are all right, are you?" Raahil put the man at ease and politely accepted the ticket the officer wrote him.

Maybe that little assistance will solidify our trust? Raahil thought as O'Neil's car moved past.

"That guy put himself out for us," O'Neil was saying to his bodyguard in the garage, "that goes a long way in my books." His mind was made up. In the morning he'd go and register the new company.

***

Paul Speed was sitting on the floor smiling as his daughter painted his toenails a bright pink. Giggles filled the living room and overshadowed the sounds of some random cartoon on the television. The dining room table in the sat covered in maps and paperwork, patiently waiting for Speed. He had been using his own time to work on project Arch Angel. Once the nail polish had dried, Speed and little Camryn moved to the couch to watch some more non-educational television and eat popcorn. It was late in the evening and she would have to go to bed soon, but not until her mommy got home. The door opened, and Paul's wife Angie dragged herself across the threshold exhausted from a long day at the office. She was immediately brought back to life when Camryn ran to greet her.

"Mommy, Mommy! We're eating popcorn, and Sponge Bob is on." Camryn exclaimed.

"Wow! You must pretty lucky." remarked a sarcastic mother complete with rolled eyes directed at a completely remorseless father.

Kisses were exchanged, and Angie took Camryn for her bath, "Night daddy, love you."

"Love you too Cammo. I'll come tuck you in in a little while."

As his girls went upstairs, Speed got up and poured himself a scotch and slid into his chair at the dining room table. Again, he reviewed the mission he had just put the final touches on. Almost psychically his cell phone started buzzing with a text message. Speed unlocked the phone and read,

Scotch?

The message was from his teammate and number 2 Mike Carter. Ironically the pair of snipers lived less than fifteen minutes from each other, and more than one drink and a cigar had been shared on each other's porches. Speed typed back:

Must have read my mind? Just poured one, there'll be one cooling for you when you get here...15?

The response came back as if Carter had it cued to send, which he probably did.

OTW.

On the way. Speed thought. He had better mention this to his wife.

He slipped quietly up the stairs and into his daughter's room where Angie was just finishing reading her a story. He smiled at them both and knelt next to the bed. Camryn immediately put her arms around his neck.

"Mike's coming over; he'll be here in a few, okay?"

"Oh, hi honey! Nice to see you too honey." Angie had remarked with a hint of frustration in her voice. "Haven't you guys seen enough of each other? Between work and all the time you've been spending with each other on your days off you should rent a place together and call me when it's over. Whatever *IT* is."

Speed smiled, "Love you babe. Knew you'd understand." He kissed them both and left the room, as Angie let out a huff. As perceptive as any child and sharing her parent's genes, Camryn smiled, hugged her mother and said, "It's okay mommy, daddy will be okay. He just has work to do, right?"

Angie smiled back and pulled her daughter's head into her chest so she wouldn't see the tears welling in her mother's eyes. "You're right honey. In so many ways, you're right."

40

Speed went back to the dining room and folded up all the maps and papers. Then he poured a second drink for his partner and made his way to the door just as he heard Carter's footsteps on the front stairs. Speed opened the door handing his partner the drink and whispered "Shed" lest his daughter hear her uncle Mike was here and want to get out of bed. The pair made their way through the house to the backdoor where Speed handed Carter the pile of papers and pulled on a black fleece before opening the sliding doors again as quietly as possible. The Speed's lived in a modest two-story home with a fair-sized yard. The yard itself had a nicely cared for garden and a wooden playset for Camryn, a cedar deck for entertaining and "The Shed" as it was called. Speed was not at all a handy man but with the help of his friends they had built a cabana-come-man's room in the back corner of the yard. The Shed even had electricity and a space heater making it hospitable year-round. Over many a drink some elaborate additions had been planned the only plausible one being the addition of a sauna. Tonight's conversations would not cover the topic of sweaty drunken men in a confined space however. Speed flicked on the light and heater as they entered. Carter got out the ashtray and wooden matches from the cabinet above the desk and pulled two Cuban cigars from his pocket. H. Upmann was their brand of choice, Pyramide No. 2's the size. The two snipers settled into their usual seats, Speed in the old leather chair and Carter in the corner of the worn love seat. Papers were spread on the table and the two cigars were lit in sort of a ceremony that marked the beginning of the mission. Speed pulled an old, converted ammo can out from under the table and opened the lid so that Carter could place two more identical cigars inside. These cigars would not be enjoyed until the completion of this mission in a similar ceremony. What the old friends didn't know was how different that ceremony would be from one's in the past.

As the aroma of the fresh cigars filled the shed the pair set to work memorizing the mission and all its intricacies and possibilities. They sipped their scotch and for the thousandth time debated making any changes. They found no problems and settled on what they had decided. Angie stood in the darkened dining room staring out the big window that overlooked the quiet yard. Through the window of the shed she could see the smoke of the cigars above the heads of her husband and his partner as they huddled over the old table. Quietly she worried. He had been at this one for weeks now. Every spare minute of every day spent staring at maps and tables of which none meant anything to her. She knew what he did, but she never knew the details before he did it. Secrecy was part of the job, but it made being married to him very difficult. She had thought about

41

leaving more than once but she knew she couldn't do that to Camryn. Afterall, she was a daddy's girl and Paul was a good father. The worst part for Angie really was knowing how dangerous these missions of his could be and how close he could come to getting hurt or killed.

The last mission of his had him hiding in the middle of some housing project in the city on a rooftop watching a drug-den apartment. That night Paul and Mike had been ambushed by three local gangsters who had come to the roof to smoke some dope and shoot off some fireworks. Luckily for Paul, Mike is very good at his job too. Mike had been taking his turn keeping security and the partners were able to secure all three without firing a shot after a brief struggle. Paul had come out of it with only some minor scrapes and sprained wrist and Mike ended up with a fat lip. It had scared Angie to death when Paul told her the whole story the next day. Fighting on a roof some 24 stories high is not what she wanted to hear. As she watched them in the shed, she paid special attention to the expressions on their faces, and she knew this was a mission on a whole other level.

Speed was pointing at the map and out of the corner of his eye caught a glint off something in the dining room window. He knew it would be Angie's glasses. He sat back looking toward the house. The sniper knowing he was being watched. He half smiled as if to say, *I know. But I'll be okay*. Angie saw him looking at her and backed deeper into the shadows. She read the expression on his face and instantly tears leapt onto her cheeks. This *was* different.

Chapter Five

This mid-May morning was dank, wet and a miserable wake up for Toronto. The forecast wasn't calling for much better for the rest of the week either. O'Neil stood on his balcony with a fresh cup of coffee staring out over the lucrative territory he'd been slowly letting go of. Not entirely, however, as he had placed key people in charge, which would ensure that distribution royalties were still indirectly coming back to him. But on the surface the drug trade in this area was no longer under his control. That process had begun several months ago during a meeting he'd had with Raahil followed by the man extending himself without question to O'Neil. That one selfless act had solidified the agreement and as a result O'Neil was the proud owner/operator of New Leaf Landscaping.

Given his local influence, he'd had little trouble securing the landscaping contract for the housing project where he lived, and with his new cleaner image he'd also landed several private properties in the area as well. The front business was in full operation, and it was time to start servicing the customers. New Leaf's crews had already begun an initial fertilization cycle that meant O'Neil had to buy several truckloads of fertilizer which was being stored in a small warehouse rented for him by the Arabs. He felt exposed the first time they had gone to the supply company and asked to buy such a large quantity, after all New Leaf was very small operation. O'Neil figured for sure he would have trouble making the purchase. But Ameer had thought of this as well and in fact had registered several other landscaping businesses in legitimate names. O'Neil was buying in bulk for the conglomerate. The salesman never even batted an eye at the orders.

O'Neil and Strong met in the garage and the pair climbed into the black king cab pickup with the company's magnet on the side. The poor Lexus sat in its parking spot, a sad layer of dust had changed the car's colour from flat black to gray. The landscapers headed out of the garage passing the luxury car without a second look and drove to the new Mazda dealership in north Scarborough where they met the work crew. The guys had recently laid sod around the grounds, and as of 8 a.m. sharp they had been hard at work forming the gardens and planting the shrubbery. As the bosses pulled up, the crew laid down their tools and took their first break of the day. Strong opened the tailgate, and the coffee and donuts were set out for the men. O'Neil could see the impact he was having on these men. Most of them had come from his old gang and previously had next to no prospects in life. O'Neil's new company, although a front, was giving these men something to be proud of. They worked hard for their legit money too, regardless of the fact that O'Neil and his righthand man ran the company like a platoon of Army Rangers. O'Neil often thought he would have done well in the military and likely wouldn't have gotten in so much trouble if he had actually volunteered. Unfortunately, he'd never been introduced to that way of life, and it was too far past it now.

While the men were laughing and relaxing in the cool morning air a light rain started and another pick-up truck rolled into the lot. An older gentleman slid out of the driver's seat. He wore a pair of dirty work jeans that looked a size too big, a black hooded sweater – also too big – with a large New Leaf logo on the back. His favourite ball cap with the torn brim and faded Blue Jay's logo sat snuggly over his forehead. As he walked toward the crew, he flicked a cigarette across the lot and smiled. O'Neil strode across the parking lot and met the man halfway. The pair shook hands, and the crew turned its attention back to the warm coffee and fresh donuts.

"Well. How's she lookin' kid?" asked the gray-haired man in the dirty jeans.

"Pretty good I think," responded O'Neil, "the guys sure work hard, and it actually looks pretty sharp. Whatchu' think, Gary?"

"Yeah, it really does look nice." the old landscaper replied sincerely. "I like what you've done by the front door there with the flagstone. A very nice touch, I'm not sure I would have had the parts to try it." O'Neil had wanted this business to be as legit as possible and hired Gary Stewart to be his horticulture and landscape foreman. A former heroin user and customer of O'Neil's *other* organization, Gary had stopped using two years ago and had been clean ever since. He was working part time at one of O'Neil's landscaping equipment suppliers where they bumped into each other two months ago. It was an instant winning situation for both men, and O'Neil had hired the avid gardener and amateur landscaper on the spot. The odd couple hit it off right away like a pair of lost souls finding each other. It was good for the new company, as they were learning from one another and doing good work. This also pleased the Mullah. He was able to watch as the business took off with the look of a truly legitimate enterprise. It meant there would be no reason for this company to attract unwanted attention and ruin their mission. Everything was running very smoothly. O'Neil and Garry smiled at their work, and across town the Mullah smiled, as he looked out the rain blotted window of the top floor suite.

44

The morning weather was not looking any better at the Tactical Intervention Group's newly christened training facility either. The sprawling training compound was located on a large piece of property in the north end of the city. Formerly this place was an airfield and a Department of National Defence facility. The City of Toronto had bought the entire complex three years ago and set right to work on repurposing it. It wasn't really fair to call it *their* compound, as in reality it was a training center for the entire Police Service. But the units that got the most use out of it and who it was really designed for were the men and women of the Special Operations Command. This command included the TIG, K9 Unit, Mounted (horse) Patrol, Marine Squad and the Public Order Unit. Some of the special units from the Investigative side of the house also spent a good deal of time at the center, their unit crests also lined the hallways of the training areas – Fugitive Task Force, Weapons Enforcement Unit and the Gang Task Force to name a few. All of which had many past members from the teams at The Group. The training center itself was named after famed Chief of Police William McCormack and boasted several outdoor ranges to accommodate all the weapons in the Service's arsenal, including an outdoor 1000-yard range for the snipers. There were two outdoor and two indoor live-fire shoot houses, four simmunition training rooms, several classrooms, and a large briefing/planning room. All the training areas were state of the art and came complete with digital recording capabilities. That was just the firearms training side of the center. The other half of the complex housed various training rooms, classrooms, a large gym and a locker room. The McCormack Center was the official college of the city's police officers and all the in-house training was conducted there. A student at the center could regularly see a truck from the TIG backed into one of the reserved parking spaces near the ranges. Members of the unit could use the indoor ranges at any hour they wished, and the outdoor ranges could be used up until late evening. The city had gone one step further and approved the use of the outdoor ranges well after dark only with special permission from the commanding officer of the training center. That permission was not given out regularly as the center was located on a track of land that was relatively close to several residential neighbourhoods. That restriction had been a small concession to the local residents who fought hard against the idea of late-night outdoor shooting at all.

Speed and the men of Team Four were back on the dayshift rotation and as usual on the first day they were detailed to weapons training at the center. The main body of the team would conduct live fire Hostage Rescue Training while Speed and Carter would be on the long range. The snipers liked to take advantage of sloppy weather like this to build the *dope* for their logbooks. Anybody can shoot on a perfect day with sunny skies and warm temperatures, but it takes a little more fortitude to lay out in the wind and rain for several hours just in the name of training. Today was not going all that well however. The pair of snipers had been laying at the 500-yard line shooting moving targets and doing quite well when Speed started to have problems with his rifle.

"What the fuck?" Speed whispered to himself. The bolt was sticking this time. He had already wiped it down and re-oiled it three times in the last hour. Mike was watching out of the corner of his eye between courses of fire as Speed fought with the weapon. His concern was growing. Speed's gun had never given him any trouble.

"Stubborn today is she?" Mike asked comically.

Speed sat up slowly and removed the bolt from the rifle studying it.

"I can't figure this out Mike. This rain and these temps shouldn't be enough to cause this." replied a frustrated Speed.

They had been at it for two and a half hours already. Having already shot through some 200-rounds. Maybe it was a combination of the weather and the stress on the gun? Maybe it was Speed? Or maybe it was just one of those random bad days that happened after staying up late with a wife and child, too much red wine and not enough sleep. Speed was mad at himself. He shouldn't have days like this. Even though everybody did, and he knew that too.

"Mike, I gotta pack up and take 'er inside. Maybe even go see the guys in the shop. Sorry bud."

Carter knew what it was like since he had recently been issued a new rifle himself. He had gone through a similar situation when it was time to retire his old gun. This was just bad timing given that their current project was progressing along an unknown timeline. The two snipers packed their gear and headed for the control office at the back of all the ranges. Inside the RSO had been sitting in the observation control tower watching the snipers. An old veteran of the Service the snipers were his favourite to watch in training. It was their professionalism and attention to detail he admired. He did not know all of their names but the guys he liked he made a point to know. As Paul and Mike came into the office, "Fossil," as he was affectionately known, came down from the tower and met them at the desk.

"Reapers four and four alpha. How are you Paul, Mike?" He asked nodding to each of them.

The guys laughed at the mythical call signs. Fossil seemed to invent new ones every time they saw him.

"Fightin' with it today huh Paul?" Fossil asked.

"Yeah, she's getting a little like an old pair of jeans that are all tore up, but you can't see your way to getting rid of 'em, know what I mean?" Speed said.

"Hey Fossil, are the boys in the cage in yet? I'd like them to take a look at her for me."

"Sure Paul, head on down. Take care fellas. And you guys be sure to let me know if you need any special arrangements for range time to get yourselves squared away 'eh?"

"Will do Fossil, thanks." The guys returned. The pair of snipers headed through the corridor that led past the shoot houses and back up to the main part of the center where they would head to the basement to see the armourers. As they passed a red access door marked SH #4, one of the indoor shoot houses, the door opened and out popped one of the guys on Team #5.

"Hey Speeder. Hey Carter. Whatchu guys doin'?" asked Steven Pinkner, nicknamed Pinky for obvious reasons.

"Just headed down to the cage to get my rifle looked at. You guys working up your rookies?" asked Speed trying to deflect.

"Yeah. They're coming along. Hope your rifle's okay, Speeder; take care boys." Pinky ran off to the water fountain down the hall. Speed and Carter smiled and flashed him a "high four" with their hands and carried on to the cage.

Once in the basement, the pair buzzed in and were granted access to the new state of the art weapons maintenance area also known as "the cage," although strangely there was no cage anywhere in sight. Speed spoke with the lead armourer and explained the problem while Carter called into the Sergeant's phone attached to Matt Sommers's hip in SH #1.

"Sommers." answered the Sergeant.

"Sarge it's Mike. Just a heads up, we're in the cage. Paul's gun is acting up."

"Okay Mike thanks. You guys will be on a cell, right?"

"Yeah Sarge, or the general intercom will get us in here as well. How're the boys doing?"

"Good, good. Fernandes is picking it up pretty well, and Bryan has a good handle on it now. Hey, nobody's been shot yet so that's good right?"

"You bet Sarge. Be in touch."

Carter hung up the phone and returned to the desk in time to hear the armourer telling Paul that he would need about an hour to look the rifle over. The gun smith was looking Speed in the eye like a doctor about to deliver bad news. The man started slowly as he wiped the cleaning solvent from his hands onto an old rag. "I think she just might be shot out, Paul. It might be time for a new stick, but we'll see what we can do. The good news is I do have a ready to go, brand new Remington. If we have to, it's yours. It's brand new from the optics to the bipod. I'll let you know." The man reported.

The frustration and concern washed over Speed's face; he couldn't hide it.

"Okay Dave, see what you can do. I'll be back in an hour."

Speed turned to his partner like a kid who was about to lose his puppy and pointed to the ceiling. It was a sign that meant he wanted to go to the cafeteria and have a coffee. Hopefully the caffeine would help him work this through.

The large cafeteria was at least the size of the largest college or high school cafeteria you could think of, and for good reason. On any given day there could be upwards of several hundred people at the training complex. Between recruit classes, in service training, and range use, the center was more times than not a very busy place.

As the snipers reached the café, they were pleased to see the coffee line nearly empty except for a few suits. One of the detective courses must have been on a break. As they stood in line, Speed was still daydreaming about the status of his weapon and didn't notice an old friend sneaking up on him. Big Brad Nelson grabbed Speed by the left arm, which generally was a bad thing to do to any operator from the Group, let alone one having a bad morning without coffee. Speed immediately and instinctively grabbed the big wrist and started to twist but stopped when he realized he was in a police facility, and it had to be a friendly grab.

"Getting slow Speed." was the laughing response from Nelson.

"Sorry big man, didn't see you there. I'm a little preoccupied this morning. Head is somewhere else, ya' know?"

"Sure buddy. I think you're just getting too old to play the SWAT game anymore. Maybe you should write your promotional exam and come over to the dark side?" replied Speed's oldest friend on the job – comically. Nelson never really expected Speed to give up tactical work. Not until they dragged him out kicking and screaming.

"So what gives buddy, what's eatin' you?" wondered Nelson honestly.

"Might be losing my rifle today…I'll get a new one of course." Speed had seen the look of surprise on his friend's face. "My current one is shot out man. It just means a lot

48

of work. And I don't need to tell you that the timing couldn't be worse." Which was a direct reference to the pending terrorism investigations that Speed knew he could not talk about, and neither could his old friend who was also "in the loop." Nelson joined the snipers at a small coffee sitting area in a corner near some windows and the three talked shop as cops were prone to doing when in the company of other cops. They had been arguing about the status of the current contract negotiations when Nelson looked at his watch and took his leave.

"Well that was fun, girls. Gotta get back to school. You fellas stay safe all right?" Just as he reached the main door a general alarm and a page over the intercom sounded "ATTENTION! ATTENTION! All ranges stand down, all ranges stand down. Medics to Shoot House Number Four Code One. Medics to Shoot House Number Four Code One!"

Nelson looked back at the two operators and watched them rushing down the hallway toward the ranges.

The sort of page that had just come over the intercom could only mean one thing –

someone had been seriously injured in the shoot house. Given that it was a shoot house and Team Five was in there using live ammo, the chances were that someone had been shot. This was bad. As the snipers ran toward the shoot house, other members from their unit also swarmed into the main hallway leading to the ranges. There was a standing Group policy that if you were at the complex and that page went out you were to immediately respond to the area in question, since it was most likely a brother or sister member of your unit in trouble. Today there were some twenty-five members of The Group training at the center. The two gun teams and five other members on various other training assignments. *Holy Shit!* was all Speed could think. He and Carter were two of the first on scene aside from the other members of Team Four who had been training just a few rooms down the hall. The members gathered there could not believe what they saw. Pinky lay there writhing in a pool of blood in the middle of the shoot house floor. He had been shot twice, once in the right hip and once in the lower right back portion of his vest. Luckily the vest had stopped the second bullet but the one on his hip was going to be a problem. Pinky was in a lot of pain. There were no medics assigned to the training center today, so an ambulance had been dispatched and was in route. The members of Team Five tried frantically to administer some first aid and get Pinky him some relief. Others stood frozen in amazement. The team leader, Speed had noticed, was standing with his arm around one scared shitless rookie. Had the rookie shot Pinky by accident? It wasn't a question Speed wanted to wonder about out loud.

Across the increasingly crowded room, Parker saw Speed and immediately remembered he had driven a marked TIG vehicle to training today. Speed had said something about staying late with his rifle. Parker pushed his way through the crowd and caught Speed's eye. Still fifteen feet or so away, Parker motioned to Speed and Carter with his right arm extended indicating *you*. He then motioned with his hands, as if he were holding a steering wheel followed by a raised index finger. The meaning was clear to the snipers – it meant "Move your ass to your vehicle and be prepared to drive lead on an emergency run to the hospital." Before Speed and Carter could even react, Parker took charge of the chaotic scene, as calm as the eye of a storm. He gave a similar set of signals to two members from Team Five who also raced to the parking lot. Outside, Speed and Carter jumped into their truck and pulled near to where they knew the ambulance would arrive and turned on their roof lights so that the ambulance could easily find them. Speed dialed on a handheld radio as he stepped out of the truck to wait near the driveway for the ambulance whose siren he could hear racing their way.

Christine Jones, the only female operator at the unit, came on the radio looking for Speed. "Speeder, it's Chris. You read?"

"Go ahead for Speed."

"Paul, we're set as number two. Holy shit, Paul, this is bad, real–"

Speed cut her off. "Yep it is Christine. But it'll only get worse if were don't keep our heads on. Get us a fast route okay Chris?"

"We're on it." The radio went quite just in time for the ambulance to wheel into the driveway next to the emergency exit. As the medics raced inside the two TIG trucks blocked the driveway and prepared for an emergency run to the nearest hospital. Jones' partner had gone with the medics to get the hospital information. Given the amount of blood loss and the trauma from the injury the medics had been directed to Sunnybrook Hospital, which was the largest Trauma center in the city, and the best equipped to handle this sort of emergency.

"Speed. Route info when you're ready." came Christine's still frazzled voice over the radio.

"Go." Speed wrote as he listened. Sunnybrook Hospital, southbound Dufferin Street onto the eastbound 401 Highway, eastbound 401 highway to Bayview Avenue, exit southbound and continue southbound to the emergency entrance.

50

"He's stable Paul but they want to rush it there, okay?"

"Will do Chris." Speed paused holding the mic open.

"Hey, he'll be fine. We just have to get him there." He continued and noticed for the first time that there was a crowd of policemen and women gathering in the nearby driveways and vestibules. As he looked around at the faces, he could see their concern. Just then he heard the doors crash open and a rush TIG operators burst out into the light rain escorting the medics and Pinky to the waiting ambulance. As they got Pinky loaded, Speed signaled to the team leader who was climbing in last. Speed taped his earpiece with his fingers. The TL still had his plate carrier on and he instantly reached back to dial the radio to the appropriate channel. A second later, he came over the radio with a muffled "Radio check." Speed acknowledged with a 10-4 followed by the route info. Within minutes, they were racing down the first leg of their journey. As they drove, they passed the stationary patrol cars from the local divisions who had no doubt been detailed to block traffic to facilitate this emergency run. The truck was silent the whole way. Carter was pushing the big Suburban as fast as he safely could. Speed sat staring out the window thinking about the big picture. The tides were turning.

The street posts flew by as they raced to the hospital, going as quickly as Speed's mind raced. He watched the beads of rain streaking across his window and he couldn't shake the feeling that this was a bad omen. Speed wondered to himself at how bad would the outcomes would be if the terrorists were to strike now. What if they were counter-surveilling the T.I.G, just looking for an opportune time to strike? This could be it. Speed often felt like he had a sixth sense for feeling the tides shifting. Maybe it was from years of playing hockey and feeling the ebbs and flows of a game. Speed closed his eyes and envisioned himself holding the side of a massive wooden pedestal table. He gripped the sides, but the thing pulled him slowly around. He opened his eyes again, as the big Suburban pounded over the curbs into the emergency drive at the hospital. Speed shook himself back into the moment. All the franticness of the incident flooded back into his ears. The siren was still blaring, and the radio chirped at him.

"Speed, I need you guys to sweep the inside then secure the lot. Copy?" It was Team Five T/L.

"Copy." was all Speed needed to say.

Carter threw the truck into a police parking space near the ambulance bay, and the snipers jumped out heading for the door. Christine Jones was there holding it open as the medics wheeled "pinky" into the Emergency Department. She was white as a ghost.

"What happened Jonesy?" asked Carter.

"I'm not sure, Mike. It happened so fast! We were going through our entry drill progressions, and Pinky was fourth in the stack. There was a newbie sandwiched on either side of him, kind of so he could watch them. They hit the third door with no problems, the newbie first, and Pinky on his ass. Pinky called for support. We had just reset all the targets, and there was an extra hostage that needed securing in the room. When the next newbie came in, he was confused as to whether or not Pinky had downed the hostage takers, I think, and so he starts to let off rounds. The kid hits Pinky twice! Holy shit guys…Holy shit this is a mess!"

"Hey Chris, do you have Steve's home number?" Speed was looking for a way to distract Pinky's upset teammate. "Why don't you go to the triage desk and sort out getting him checked in and give a call to his missus?"

"Okay Paul. Good idea. Where are you guys going to be?"

"We'll secure you vehicle and look after seeing the bosses in. Toss me your keys."

A warm wave of composure settled over Christine Jones now that she had a task to accomplish. After a quick security sweep of the ER, Speed and Carter headed for the parking lot. On the way out they were met by the TIG's Staff Sergeants and the Inspector near the emergency apron.

"What's the status, Paul?" asked Vince Wismer with obvious concern in his voice. The two Staff Sergeants for their part also had signs of concern written in their furrowed brows.

Speed answered honestly, "We haven't heard yet. They wheeled him straight into surgery in a lot of pain. One round into his right hip. Christine Jones is trying to get a hold of his wife."

"You know they're separated as of two months ago? She may be at a different number?" Staff Sergeant Goodhall said.

"No, I had no idea about that Staff. Either way, Christine is trying it. She'd have better knowledge of Pinky's personal business than I would anyway." Speed paused deliberately. "She needed something to occupy her mind, boss. I think that they are obviously all a little shook up."

With that, Wismer patted Speed on the shoulder and smiled at Carter. The bosses turned and headed into the emergency area. As Speed and Carter were backing Jones's truck into a parking space, two black training vans squealed into the lot. The guys from

Team Five piled out and made their way quickly into the hospital. The one rookie still had a worried look on his face.

"Poor kid." thought Speed. Carter and Speed let the Team Five guys get settled before they headed back inside. Just as they were climbing into their own truck Paul's phone rang. He looked at the display and saw that it was Parker calling. Speed answered, "What's going on big man?"

"Not much. How's Pinky?" asked the team leader.

"No word yet. Looks like one of their kids screwed up pretty good huh?"

"That's not totally clear yet, pal. Might have been a couple of problems there. Anyway, more bad news for you. Your gun is decommissioned. A shiny new one is ready to go whenever you can get here. Ol' Fossil said he'd stay late to turn it over to you if need be. Sorry pal."

Carter watched as Speed's face dropped. He knew what it meant. He did not have to hear the words. The gun was gone. He too felt the momentum swinging away from them.

"Okay. Thanks Glen. Can you let Fossil know I'll be by in a couple of hours at the latest? We just want five to get settled here first."

"Will do, bud. See you tomorrow." Parker knew his friend too well. He knew that Speed would go back to the range and start building data on that new rifle tonight and that he would stay as late as Fossil would let him. Carter knew it, too, but it didn't bother him at all. It was another chance to put some rounds down range and help his partner out.

"What are you thinking Pauly?" Mike asked, as the snipers sat staring out the window of the truck. "It's pretty bad huh? What about your gun, what do you want to do?"

"I don't know Mike. I really don't know." Speed gripped the cell phone so tight that Carter thought it might crack. The gravity and the enormity of the situation were both weighing heavy on him now. He hated being in a position where he might not be able to do his job if something happened. Speed turned and looked his partner in the eyes, *time to go to work*. "Mike, you mind going to the range for a couple of hours? Got a new stick to break in."

"Absolutely bud. They're fine. Let's get out of here. I'll let the bosses know we're leaving." And with that Mike Carter climbed out of the truck and made his way over the where the Staff Sergeants were standing outside the emergency. There were several high-ranking officers arriving looking for the latest update. Speed watched as his partner quietly pulled his old friend Staff Sergeant Ray Farmer out of the scrum and spoke to him off to the side. Carter nodded in Speed's direction and Paul saw the look on Farmer's face, he felt it too.

Could this get any worse? Speed wondered to himself. But it could, and he knew it. They could all be going to a funeral next week for a dead member of the unit. Killed in a training accident. Damn it.

Speed's mind spiraled; he needed out of there. It was like subconsciously he knew he was playing catch up with an unavoidable fate. The driver's door opened, and startled him back to reality. He hadn't even seen Carter coming back to the truck.

"You all right bud?" Carter asked, as he closed the door and settled into his seat. "The Staff says thanks and no problem. To go and get your rifle squared away." Carter was looking at Speed who was still staring out the window. "Speeder, he said something else kinda funny. It didn't make sense to me but—"

Speed turned to look at his partner and cut him off. "What'd he say Mike?"

"He said not to waste any time getting that gun up and running. It's not like him to be that concerned about one rifle being down."

Speed shook his head and turned to the window as Mike put the truck in drive and headed back to the training center. Pulling out his phone Speed typed a quick apology to the Team Five T/L then dropped the phone onto the console.

Staff Sergeant Farmer had edged back into the ring of senior officers and watched out of the corner of his eye, as the sniper's truck pulled away. He was nervous, the old veteran knew things about the status of the pending mission that he could not tell the men yet. It gave him a more realistic appreciation for just how bad this timing was. He hoped that the Team Four snipers could quickly get themselves back in the game. The Service would not be able to afford being down a sniper team when it came time to deal with these terrorists.

Up on the fifth floor, Team Five gathered in the waiting area. Some leaned on the walls and doorframes while others paced circles in the floor. One member was sitting in a corner seat with his head in his hands. The team leader had a hand on the rookie's back trying to reassure him that Pinky would be all right. They were all still dressed in their assault kit and several of them had Pinky's blood spilled over their equipment and hands. Mostly they shared the same blank stares of shock and disbelief. The bosses came and went from the waiting area trying not to overstep the boundaries of the Team's privacy, balancing that against the command staff's need for information. There was a sudden explosion of activity on the floor. Nurses bustled in and out of the room Pinky would occupy. The nurses dragged in a number of large machines and monitors apparently getting it ready for the new patient. The elevator doors opened, and the team stood to see if it was Pinky. As hospital staff pulled the bed out of the elevator, a monitor began to sound a frantic high-pitched emergency tone. A nurse called out "CODE BLUE." The charge nurse picked up the intercom handset and broadcast the code blue throughout the hospital's sterile halls. Nurses and doctors from all over the floor swarmed to the area. Pinky's bed was wheeled at breakneck speed into the room they had just been prepping. The team instinctively spilled into the hall, but were pushed back into the waiting room by one of the young doctors. She explained sharply that the team needed to give the medical professionals room to do their jobs. All but one of the team crowded around the door. A very distraught rookie slumped in the corner sobbing into his hands. Within a couple of tense moments, the excitement settled down and an relieved doctor exited the room. A heart rate monitor could be heard faintly chirping in the background keeping time with Pinky's heart.

"That was a little scary." announced the doctor to the crowd of anxious police officers. "I'm sorry for that. He's stable but he needs time to recover. You are welcome to wait here if you like, however it will be some time before we allow him to have visitors."

***

Speed and Carter walked into the control room of the training center and found Fossil engrossed in a well-loved copy of Tom Clancy's *Without Remorse*. Clearly not the first time he had read it, as evidenced by the worn page corners. A hot cup of coffee sat on the desk next to him under the lamp. Fossil looked up over the top of his book upon hearing the door open and a look of compassion came over his face.

"Dead-eye One and Two." the old man said in his usual way. Fossil caught the strained smile in the corner of Speed's mouth and instantly felt his pain. "Range is prepped. Ammo is on the shelf by the door, your lot number Speed. Rifle is right here." Fossil turned to a counter behind his desk then swung the brand-new Remington 40XB around, presenting it to Paul Speed like a doctor does a new baby to a proud new father. Speed stood for a second staring at the rifle in his arms, gently running his fingers down the length of the barrel. He caressed the stock and opened the bolt. He smiled at the smooth feel of the action. The sniper worked the action a few more times and smiled a little wider. Speed was old school this way, he liked the tried-and-true Remington. He trusted the weight and craftsmanship, and more than anything he knew this rifle. Speed shined his smile around the room looking over at Mike and then up at the old range officer.

"Fossil, you mind if I deal with the paperwork later? I'd like to go get friendly with this thing if that's okay?" He knew Fossil wouldn't mind and as he strode proudly toward the long-range cradling the rifle, Mike in tow. Fossil had grinned at the question and held that look as the snipers walked out.

The sniper team spent the next several hours on the Sniper Range where they began the long process of building a data card for Speed's new gun. This would take months if not the better part of the year to get a complete log. During that time they would shoot in as many different temperatures and conditions as possible. But the data he built tonight would take him out to 800 yards, and that would at least put him back in the game. The situation was far from perfect but at least it was a start. The clock above Fossil's counter read 8 p.m., and Speed actually had a look of content, if not happiness, on his face as the sniper team stepped back into the control tower. Fossil turned from the television he had been watching in time to catch Mike's wink. Speed looked to Fossil and asked if he would mind the pair cleaning their guns in the Range office with him instead of going to the basement cleaning room as per the Center's rules.

"Not a problem fellas. Use the counter." Fossil gestured toward the main check-in counter. The old timer put on another pot of coffee and broke out two more mugs, handing one to each of the snipers. The pair set out their guns and removed their bolts, instinctively slipping them into the cargo pocket of their pants. Cleaning kits were laid out what followed was a strict routine. Each sniper's routine was slightly different than the other, but each performed the same way every time.

As Fossil poured the coffee into the first cup he had to ask. "So, how'd she do?" He nodded his gray hair toward the new rifle.

Speed smiled. "Pretty good, old fella, pretty damn good. Hey, thanks for staying for us by the way. We…I…owe you."

Fossil waved the sniper off and turned to Carter's cup. "You don't owe me anything, kid. Just be ready to do whatever it is you're getting ready to do." Fossil took the opportunity to turn the conversation away from rifles. "Damn Leafs are a bust again this year."

A heated debate erupted on the race for the current NHL playoffs. Again, the Leafs were in jeopardy of missing the post season. Speed's favourite team, the Boston Bruins, however, was making a charge for the conference championship.

56

But they all believed it was most likely going to be the Tampa Bay Lightning and the Colorado Avalanche in the Cup final. The debate finally settled around who was a better player, MacKinnon or Stamkos.

The conversation served its purpose as a distraction for the two snipers, a difficult task in the midst of all that had gone on that day.

Chapter Six

The months were sliding off the calendar and plans were slowly and deliberately falling into place. Just as Ameer had been meticulously planning all these months. He had been working on this plan with no direct supervision or input from his associates in the Middle East and so far, there had been no real glitches. Yes, the arrest of the initial eighteen members of his organization had been a hiccup a few years before. But that was a planned initial probing maneuver that only he was aware of, and it had been deemed an acceptable risk. Not even his brother and closet captain had been told of the strategy. Their group was patient and calculating. What Ameer worried about the most was his brother's uncontrollable personality. It could jeopardize the mission and he had therefore decided to keep information from him. Raahil Abdullah on the other hand was a much better asset than his own brother. The Mullah knew this as a fact but remained cautious as Raahil was not his blood. To Ameer, blood would always be thicker than water. Now into June, and the plan was settling into the next phase. Ameer felt the time was right to have another face-to-face meeting with all of his upper echelon, a chance to restate their goal and go over their mission. For a reason even he could not explain, Ameer felt compelled to include O'Neil in the meeting for the first time, a move his brother regularly warned against.

"Bringing that dog here once was a mistake, but twice could prove to be your undoing brother. And to this meeting?" Protested Mustafa.

"Enough brother! It is decided. Arrange the meeting with appropriate security precautions."

Mustafa pounded his way out of the living room to a table in the foyer where he grabbed one of the burner phones and made several coded calls. The last was to O'Neil.

The young Muslim answered, "New Leaf, how can I help you?"

"Come to my brother's home and pray with us tonight." Mustafa responded gruffly.

O'Neil could feel the tension in the thickly accented voice on the phone but was unsure of the reason. "I'll need a ride man, 5:30 out front here. Okay?"

Mustafa stifled his anger and decided it would be better used at a later time. "Fine my friend, I will personally be there to get you."

With that, the phone was abruptly hung up, and O'Neil was left staring puzzled at the receiver. He placed the phone back on the table and looked across the desk at his most trusted friend and advisor.

"Strong. Something's up man. Jus' doesn't feel right the way that Mustafa dude talks to me man."

"What'd that punk want? We haven't heard from his ass in months?" asked Strong.

"They want me to come to a meeting. Gonna pick me up at 5:30 tonight." Strong matched O'Neil's curious look and wondered the same thing—what was about to or had already changed?

***

An unimpressive building, on the exterior anyway, sits on the perimeter of a commercial park in the northern part of the city. This bland building is owned and operated by the Police Service. The sign on the inside wall beyond the frosted security doors read *Combined Forces Operations* (CFO), and it housed several covert law enforcement units. One often overlooked player in this game of law-and-order chess happened to fall into that category. It is not always the sharp end of the spear that makes the first and deepest cuts in a battle, every so often a little spot way down the blade nicks a vital artery and starts a slow bloodletting.

Such a nick may have just occurred at a small desk in a secure office deep within the heart of the building. At a workspace just like any other in a typical office sat twenty-nine-year-old analyst Naila Rashid. Scattered across her desktop lay pages of printed sheets with red liner notes. There was a half full bottle of water, several pens, pencils, highlighters, and a laptop computer. What was different about this scene was that she worked inside a glass soundproof cube in a long row of identical cubes. Each cube was well lit, and along with the laptop there was a desktop computer. The computer was wired to a larger server in the main portion of the office. Looking out from each cube, the "monitors," as they were called, could see their supervisors sitting at their desks on the opposite side of the room. Those desks were also in soundproof cubes. In effect, this created an airtight information gathering and dissemination center. All of it under the watchful eye of the CFO supervisors from various partner agencies.

Naila was born and raised in Canada, but her family history started in the Middle East, specifically in the tiny country of Qatar. She holds a degree in languages from the University of Ottawa with a major in Political Science – Middle Eastern Studies. Currently she is working on her PhD in the same field. So, it was no surprise that she has been able to quickly move up the security clearance ladder within the CFO to become one of the lead Arab intelligence and wiretap monitors. Although only a civilian member, Naila is held in very high regard within her area of expertise.

Recently the RCMP and the Canadian Security Intelligence Service (CSIS) had been investigating a local ring of taxi drivers and storeowners for some time trying to uncover any links to terror organizations. This sort of fishing expedition had become common after the 9-11 attacks and would be seen by many in society as an unethical breach of Canadian civil rights. Essentially, this was an exercise in sifting through the grains of sand for actionable intelligence, all under the umbrella of the war on terror. Most of the *intel* would be useless in a courtroom, but in the context of National Security it was completely necessary.

During one such investigation, a list of several cell phone numbers was discovered almost by accident. But thanks to the attention to detail of the investigator that list had been scanned into an Intelligence file. The numbers were found in the possession of a low-level courier associated to an offshoot group loosely associated with a known terror organization named Al-Jihad. No plausible explanation for the list ever was uncovered. Nor were interrogators able to glean from the courier whom the numbers belonged to and what they were for. So, as was routine, the numbers were sent to the wire room to be added to an ever-growing list of numbers to be randomly checked and cross-checked for any possible nexus. This type of seemingly pointless scratching of the surface was exactly what had begun to bore most of the monitors.

Daily monitoring of random pointless conversations between average Canadian, American, and multinational Arabs got old quickly. The young highly educated but underpaid minds in the monitor rooms quit frequently. Much information was likely missed or overlooked due in large part to the overwhelming size of the pile of sand they had to sift. As skilled as she was, Naila was no exception to the law of complacency. She too was finding it difficult to stay on task while balancing her work with her education. There had been a lot of doodling and lunchroom loitering. Summer was fast approaching, after all, and many of the young minds in the analysis section were wandering. The girls had a summer getaway planned for the Turks next month. Until then, Naila and her 27 colleagues continued digging through and collecting data relating to more than 3000 phone numbers.

So Naila began her daily routine and began researching the day's assigned numbers, forty-three to be exact, through various open media sources. She used the results of her online searches to prioritize her list and then she began to scan and listen to those numbers. The analyst would diligently record the "take" from those calls and transcribe anything she found to be important. But as was the flavor of the month, she wasn't feeling overly optimistic this morning.

In the initial weeks and months after 9-11 when the CFO had been first set-up, the monitors had been extremely busy. Links were made almost daily. Now the intelligence had slowed to a trickle. Maybe once a month a lead was generated that when investigated generally led nowhere. There were some successes to be remembered, however. This was the office that pulled the pieces together in the Mahar Arar investigation at one point. Most of what had been uncovered in that investigation had been classified and sealed in an attempt to protect other active American investigations, in the end costing Canadian taxpayers a total of $11.5 million. The dollar value of that investigation was irrelevant to the monitors and analysts on both sides of the border. These stories of success kept Naila focused. Kept her listening, recording, writing, and sipping on her dark roast coffee.

As the bright green digital clock in the middle of the office crept closer to noon, Naila pondered her lunch options while she listened to yet another cell phone conversation between Arabs. In general, they discussed everyday Canadian issues and family matters or innocuous business dealings between here and back home, no different from millions of phone calls taking place right on other Canadian citizens' phones. The trick for Naila and the other monitors was to pick out the right nuance of language in the right conversation. It was a little like being in the right place at the right time.

The current conversation she had in her ears was between an Arab male and a Canadian sounding woman. The male was trying his best to convince the female to meet him at his condo by the lakeshore. It was not looking good for him however, and this made Naila laugh. The tenacity of this man kept Naila's attention, and she let herself linger on this call longer than she should have. She leaned back in her chair and blew on her coffee, and propped her feet up on an overturned recycling bin under the desk. Her mind had drifted away to the Turks, and she missed the point in the phone call when the man asked the female to conference him to another number. Naila's head snapped up when she heard a new male voice on the phone. This voice was distinctly urban and distinctly Canadian. The totality of this conference call is what caught the analyst's attention. The conversation was short and to the point. The presence of the second male was being requested at prayers that night. He was going to be picked up at 5:30 in front of what Naila assumed was an apartment building. No address was given, and no names were used. The forwarding of the call and it's tone is what made her take notice. Nalia's instincts told her that there was something behind the words.

This was the new struggle for the analyst, this conversation could be nothing, or it could be a drug deal. Drug deals were something well below the concern of the CFO. They were uncovering more and more of them every day, and the worst part was the information was useless in court since the wiretapping was not authorized for those investigations. The CFO would periodically share their "take" with the drug units, but only if it seemed big enough. That was a rare case, however, as it could compromise the intelligence gathering capabilities of the CFO.

But this call did not have the feel like a drug deal to Naila. She decided that she was going to play a hunch. She had been right before and hoped her supervisor would take a chance again. Naila transcribed what she had heard and filed the appropriate forms with her assessment. Her CFO 1312 (Intelligence Alert) described the conversation as worthy of further investigation. She detailed her "hunch" and grounded it in reality and experience. Her education had given Nalia exceptional writing skills, and she knew that if the report was carefully crafted it would get the appropriate stamp of approval. That required approval would push this bit of *intel* further up the blade toward the pointy end. Naila knew some of the guys up there on the tactical side and always wondered if any of her intel had gotten them "jobs" as they say?

She saved the report electronically and then set about the rest of her day, which was quickly filled with otherwise boring conversations about the latest teachings at one Mosque or another. Whose son or daughter would be attending which university next year? What was for dinner? How was the weather?

"Do you know a good mechanic?"

"Can I get that Kunafa recipe from you?" The same old routine continued. These were average Arab-Canadians discussing normal Arab-Canadian issues, nothing of interest to report. Just that one fragment of a conversation. Naila glanced at the clock for the hundredth time and was surprised to see that it was pushing four o'clock. She had missed lunch again. She finished transcribing her last monitored conversation, saved the file on the central server, and was hurriedly closing up her desk for the day when one of her girlfriends stuck her head through the door to Naila's cube.

"Hey Naila. What's up for tonight? Are we still doing dinner at that Indian Place you're always raving about?"

Naila yawned and shrugged, then slouching in her chair pulled her hair into a ponytail. Pulling off her glasses and twirling them as she spoke, carefully weighing her options. "Tell you what. Call me in a couple hours, and I'll see how badly I need a break from my thesis. Okay?"

"Sounds good hon'. Call you later. But you *are* coming to dinner girl. You are burning out."

"Sounds good." But even as she said it, Naila new all she wanted to do was curl up on the couch and zone out. Naila went back to sending the last of her emails as the girl left, when she remembered the 1312 had not been sent yet. Kicking herself for her lack of focus – she really needed that trip to the Turks to recharge her batteries – she addressed the email to her direct supervisor and hit send. She shut down her computer and removed the secure token. Gulping down the last bit of her third coffee of the day Naila scooped up her sunglasses and purse and headed to the door. She jingled her keys on the way to the door, as she weighed her take-out options for tonight.

***

5:25 p.m. – O'Neil stood out front of the New Leaf office trying not to feel too uncomfortable in his new unflattering white prayer outfit. Choosing to wear the garb of his new allies was his idea. To say the least, it was not popular among his employees and former gang associates. Many a laugh was being had at his expense, an act that in the past would have been met with severe physical repercussions. But O'Neil had a method to his madness. Even if he was the only one that knew he was not truly mad.

Promptly at 5:30, the black sedan pulled up, and the tinted passenger window slowly lowered revealing the car's driver. Mustafa had a look of surprise on his face that he used to try and hide the fact that he was impressed at O'Neil's attempt to fit in. Smiling, he motioned for the former gangster to climb in. The thirty-minute ride to the Mullah's apartment was quiet. Mustafa drove conservatively along the surface streets as he inhaled deeply on unfiltered cigarettes, O'Neil sitting in the passenger seat texting his office manager about some unfinished business, both of them oblivious to the building tension inside the car. O'Neil looked up from his phone, as they drove into the underground of the building, and Mustafa parked the car in its usual spot.

As they climbed out, Mustafa looked across the roof to O'Neil and offered the proverbial olive branch. "It is great, the things you are doing to follow the path of Allah. Not to mention the great respect you have shown to my brother and our family. Thank you, brother O'Neil." Without waiting for a response, he turned and headed for the elevator leaving O'Neil to trail behind. They both smiled privately to themselves.

As the elevator doors opened on the Mullah's floor, O'Neil was surprised to see what looked like some sort of celebration being set up in the hall. All the women were bringing out food and teapots. There were Hookah pipes full of hash-oil being placed in one apartment, and a number of girls in various modes of Hijab roamed from apartment to apartment. The Mullah greeted O'Neil at the door when arrived just in time for the start of prayers. The Mullah and O'Neil had purposely not seen each other in some months. They each smiled genuinely as they took the other's hand and kissed each other on the cheeks as is custom.

The Mullah took O'Neil by the shoulder as he welcomed him warmly, "Murhaba. As-Saalam Alaykum."

Seeing Ameer in his full Islamic leadership role was somewhat inspiring to O'Neil, just as Ameer had hoped it would be. O'Neil was ushered into the prayer space and returned the greeting, "Wa-Alaykum As-Saalam." O'Neil slipped off his shoes as he stopped at a silver bowl to cleanse himself. With the sun fading, the group of men knelt at the edges of their carpets and began their prayers.

When they were done, and all the hugs exchanged, the men headed out to the hallway where the celebration was starting. Ameer kept introducing O'Neil to people he had never seen before like a new son-in-law. O'Neil thought the whole thing was strange, but the atmosphere was too festive to resist. He soon found himself on a couch with slim figured green-eyed beauty. Her abaya was decorated with a very transparent green lace that matched her eye colour and sitting this close to her he could see right through it. O'Neil tried in vain not to look at her beautiful figure being highlighted by the translucent lace. They sat sharing a Hookah filled with hash oil and tobacco for some time, which allowed O'Neil to take in his surroundings. He noticed the same level of security was present, and every so often one of the serious looking guards would pop his head into the room where O'Neil and the green-eyed girl were getting to know each other.

The conversation slowed, and O'Neil took an opportunity to go get some food in the hallway. While filling a plate with samosas, an apartment door near him opened and a security man exited. O'Neil was able to get a glimpse of at least four very young, maybe teenaged, Arab men dressed in white robes. The boys appeared to be in a state of extreme shock. There was dance music drifting out of the room and a half-naked Arab woman crossed the door carrying a clear bottle of alcohol. *What the hell is going on in there*, he wondered to himself?

The security man caught O'Neil's stare and smiled. He then quickly pulled the door closed. Almost as if in rhythm, the green-eyed girl he had been flirting with saddled up next to him, whispering in his ear, as she gently turned him toward the quiet end of the hall. O'Neil looked at her smiling face and soft features that seemed to be glowing from under the edges of her hijab. He was trying to resist being pulled into this dream. Maybe it was the hash, but as he fell deeper, he thought to himself that something else might be going on, like maybe this party was a way of dragging him farther into whatever these guys were up to? But as he focused on the shapely woman walking ahead of him, he quickly forgot about the boys he'd seen through the open door.

O'Neil did not even realize that they were standing at the end of the hall now. The green-eyed girl reached for the doorknob to the last apartment and pulled him into the quite foyer. The dream continued as she led him by the hand down the darkened interior to an unoccupied bedroom. Drifting past closed doors, he heard the moans of passion. There air was ripe with the smell of sweat mixed with that strong tobacco-hash oil recipe. By the time the door opened to the final bedroom, all O'Neil could focus on was her light brown skin, she dropped her Hijab and her abaya hit the floor. His high was fully set in, and he lost all his ability to resist.

Several hours later they emerged from the room, O'Neil's prayer shirt hanging loosely around his shoulders. His green-eyed companion stopped in the living room and sat with another woman on the couch. The two women glistening with sweat covered their heads and began to gossip in Arabic. The green-eyed girl smiled over her shoulder at him, as she watched him feel his breast pocket and find the paper she had written her number on. O'Neil turned for the door and smiled back.

***

Pulling the door open, Detective Gaines called across the state-of-the-art office to his leading Arabic analyst, "Naila."

She stopped in her tracks just as her access card hit the scanner to exit the secure room. "Detective?" she replied quietly.

The seasoned detective leaned out of his cube holding up a couple sheets of paper. "Are you sure about this assessment?" The look on his face seemed to show interest, or at least Naila thought it did.

"Yes boss. The whole thing didn't add up for me." was her tired response. Maybe if she had been more convincing in her reply, the results of this conversation might have been different. Maybe if Detective Jim Gaines had been having a better month his support for her would have been better still. But timing was everything. Too bad, because it was starting to look like today's timing was not going to be very good.

"Sorry Naila. But I can't see anything here worth running up the chain. We've got to do better than this if we want to keep our jobs here. I'm going to save us both the time and shred this one right here. I'll see you tomorrow and we'll go at it again. Okay?" Detective Gaines told her.

Naila wasn't even mad so much that he had turned her assessment down. What bothered Naila was that he had done it so casually. Normally there would have been a mini conference between analyst and supervisor. No matter how brief, before an intel assessment was binned. This process allowed the supervisor to dig deeper into the analysis right from the source. Not in this case, and that was the puzzling part. Naila was too mentally drained to argue or care. She pursed her lips and closed her eyes tightly in frustration as she turned away from him slapping her card against the sensor again. The little light turned green and was followed by the metallic Click of the magnetic lock opening. Naila answered curtly over her shoulder, "You're the boss. I'm just the analyst." As she pushed the door open, the words were barely out of her mouth, but she could already hear the secure shredder grinding her CFO-1312 into tiny confetti. The potential significance registered only a hiccup in her subconscious, as she breezed through the main lobby, her soft-soled flats barely whispering as they carried her out the main door to her parking spot. She flopped tiredly into the driver's seat and started the car.

Chinese. I'll have Chinese tonight. she said to herself.

Chapter Seven

Now into the third week of June, and the citizens of Toronto were settling into their summer routines. People were hitting the local beach on the weekend for volleyball, a run on the boardwalk or to just lay in the sun. Others were having dinner and drinks on a patio then dancing the night away at a downtown nightclub. The good early summer weather was making it increasingly difficult for anyone who worked indoors to look outside at the sunshine and remain productive in the office. People's thoughts quickly wandered to a cottage, or wherever it was that they went to relax. Their minds inhaling the familiar smells of suntan lotion and bon fires, and their fingers feeling the chill of a cold summer drink.

For five friends, the longing was over. The ladies from the CFO were checking into their 5-star all-inclusive resort in the Turks and Caicos. They had been waiting for a long time for this well-deserved vacation. As they huddled around the concierge counter getting their room keys, they could not help but take in the breathtaking view of the beach out through the open lobby. The expansive space was adorned in white marble and dark stained teak wood finishes adding to the exoticness of the resort. A friendly local girl working the counter was just finishing checking in the last of the group and handing over the room keys. The guest turned and found the rest of her friends standing at the edge of the lobby with their bags looking over the pool deck. Hormones and pheromones were running high, and the ladies were already flirting with a group of young men.

Naila was the last member to join the group and as she adjusted her Hijab she smiled awkwardly at her friends and their shameless flirting. The girls quickly made plans to meet by the pool in an hour for their orientation meeting and scattered off to their rooms. Naila couldn't help herself, when she got into her room she leapt into the air landing on her back on the plush bed, sending the folded towel swan flying to the floor. She let out a deep sigh of relief and reached up to the pillows searching for the complementary chocolate. She unwrapped it and popped it into her mouth, savoring the sweet milk chocolate. Naila let herself lay there for fifteen minutes then sat up and began unpacking her suitcase. She set aside a modest one-piece bathing suit and a pair of flip-flops. Naila had time to spare before meeting her friends in the lobby, and since their flight had been at 5:30 a.m., she wanted to freshen up. Naila opened the double doors to the well-appointed bathroom attached to her suite, for this trip she had treated herself to an upgraded room with an ocean view and ran the shower. The weary traveler dropped her clothes in a pile and stepped under the shower head. She stood under the large rainfall fixture, head hanging, and let the warm water begin to wash away the stresses of her life.

A half hour later, the girls found themselves sitting at the pool bar listening to the entertainment director explain how to book the A-La-Carte restaurants and where to get towels. Some of the girls had grabbed a drink before the orientation began and Naila sat quietly fiddling with the straw in her virgin pina colada. She sat in the back of the group and was only half listening. When the half hour presentation was over, the girls quickly headed to the pool deck. The main pool was already quite crowded this late in the day, however they were surprised to find an available sunshade on the beach with five empty chairs. The group wasted no time settling into their R and R, a few rounds of drinks had helped. But something kept nagging at Naila and preventing her from completely relaxing. She could not shake a feeling that she had left something unfinished at home. She lay there, reclined, staring off across the turquoise horizon through her dark sunglasses completely oblivious to the group of young men that had just come over to mingle. A set of powder blue eyes brought her back to the island paradise.

"Hey there." the handsome well-built man started.

"Oh hey. I'm sorry. Daydreaming." She started the process of getting to know the young man sitting at the end of her lounge chair and easily forgot about whatever it was she couldn't remember anyhow.

***

Bryan Robinson eased the black Suburban up to the curb on Queen Street West in front of a coffee shop that the teams often frequented while on duty. The place wasn't one of the popular chains of boxed coffee shops that were cropping up in all the trendy neighbourhoods across the city. The place had pictures of coffee beans and old-fashioned grinders adorning the walls, the beans were roasted in house unlike the Canadian staple Tim Horton's. This cafe was a simple and warm little corner shop that had been forgotten about until recently when it came under new management. One of the guys had found it almost by accident a few years ago when they were finishing a long operation at an apartment building around the corner. They had been dealing with a young woman suffering from paranoid delusions who had threatened her neighbours with a large kitchen knife. The operation lasted through the night and into the early morning hours. As the sun came up that morning, and the neighbourhood started to come alive the guys were waved into the little shop by a vanilla looking white haired man. This was the owner, and he offered hot coffee to the tired team. Stanley Boothe spent twenty-five years as a civilian employee of the Police Service working in the Forensics Bureau. After retirement, he had moved back to his west-end childhood neighbourhood. Being unmarried and collecting a pension meant he had some money to spare. He had always been a lover of coffee, and when he saw his favourite coffee shop going under he had an epiphany of sorts and bought it. Since then, he has built up quite a clientele, mostly due to his pleasant demeanor, but it also helped that he could brew a great cup of coffee. Word of this spot steadily spread around The Group. So, as was becoming customary, the guys stopped in again for their favorite cuppa joe and a quiet place to sit and chat.

As Paul and Bryan Robinson walked through the door, Stanley looked up from the espresso machine, expertly putting the finishing touches on another perfect cappuccino. He smiled his usual toothy friendly smile and gave a nod toward the patio door. The familiar signal that told the guys he would bring them their usual out on the patio. He went back to finish pouring the frothed milk on the cappuccino. Speed looked at the time on his Garmin, it was a little after nine in the morning, and the June sun beat down on the quite patio space. The pair of tactical operators chose a corner table in the shade of an awning and leaned back into the comfortable chairs. Speed pulled off his sunglasses and laid them on the table tiredly rubbing his eyes. Bryan was in full on recline mode with his head thrown all the way back, his mouth gapping wide open. The dark tinted glasses which rarely left his face sliding back onto his forehead due to the painful looking angle at which his neck was bent. A soft *tink* of the spoon against the side of the coffee cup snapped Bryan's head back up into position, the sunglasses nearly shooting across the patio. Speed was leaning forward with his face over the mug taking in the aroma of the freshly brewed coffee and Bryan had to laugh, "How long was I gone?"

"I dunno bud. At least a minute or two." Speed laughed.

Stanley slid Bryan's black dark roast across the table and pulled over a chair. "How's tings then boys?" he asked in his thick East Coast accent. He didn't care about work really. He wanted to hear them talk about home. Stanley had figured out a long time ago that cops don't always want or need to talk about work. Sometimes the best thing for them was to talk about anything other than work. Stanley sat with the boys, as they shared stories of home renos and trips to each other's cottages on their days off with their families. The most recent pictures were pulled up on cell phones and swiped through with pride. They all shared a couple good laughs. But it never ends for the guys on the teams.

Bryan was fidgeting with the antenna on his portable radio, which as always was placed on the table between them. The incessant twisting of the antenna seemed like he was willing it to life. As they sipped at their coffee, the radio spat at them, "Base to team. A monitor for you when you're ready to copy." Stanley quietly excused himself and made his way around the café. One of their teammates prompted the base to continue. The basic details of the call were outlined for the guys. Speed and Robinson cast each other a look. Without saying a word, they finished their coffees, Speed redonning his sunglasses as they headed for the door. Passing back through the shop, Speed dropped five dollars on the counter and waved good-bye to Stanley, who sat visiting with an elderly couple at another table.

The teammates climbed back into their truck in time to hear the request from Sergeant Sommers for them to respond to the call. Speed flicked on the emergency lights and siren and reached for the mic, as Bryan pulled a U-turn and headed for the next intersection that would take them down to the Gardiner Expressway. This would be the fastest route out to the east end of the city. Speed held the mic and acknowledged the Sarge that they were in route. So started another routine day in the City of Toronto. Across the city, the other members of Team Four were leaving the range, letting a stopped motorist off with a warning or u-turning their way out to the call as well.

When the operation was over, no shots had been fired. All ten of the Team Four operators were unharmed, and one door had been disintegrated. Three blunt impact rounds had been discharged, and two conducted energy weapons deployed. In the end, one very agitated young man was in the custody of divisional officers who would take him to a hospital for psychiatric assessment and evaluation. Back at their trucks the team geared down, re-storing their heavy assault gear and weapons. Sweaty and hot, most guzzled down bottles of water brought around by the medics. Speed reattached his shingle to the front of his soft body armour and slid his sunglasses back over his eyes, to look up the row of vehicles for Glen Parker. He found him looking back his way. Parker raised his left hand above his head with his index finger extended and made a circular motion. This told the team to mount up and return to base. That signal was passed down the line of vehicles and all the operators currently pulling security climbed into their seats. The motorcade of blacked out trucks rolled back to the highway for the return trip to the base.

Speed sat quietly staring out the window on the ride back watching the city bleed by, lost in thought, but not really thinking about any one thing in particular. He noticed that

Robinson had not taken the direct route up to the 401 highway. Instead, he was heading along the surface streets in what seemed like the longest route possible.

"Where the hell are you going Bryan?" Speed asked in a heat-induced, lazy tone. He didn't even lift his head from the window or turn to face the young driver.

"I need another coffee, man. Last night was a little rough. There's a Timmie's a few blocks away over at Markham and Ellesmere. You know you need it too. Look at ya'!" Bryan slapped him across the arm.

As they drove along the city streets, Speed found himself mesmerized by two identical white buildings approaching in the distance. He recognized them as the Orton Park Projects. Just after mid-day now, and the sun was crossing over to the western part of the sky. Bright but not blinding due to some thin cloud cover. Through the polarized lenses of his sunglasses Speed kept staring at those buildings. Something on the top floor was grabbing his attention. As they got closer, he could make out a man leaning on a balcony railing smoking a cigarette. He felt like this man was watching him too. Almost unaware that one had noticed the other. As they got closer to the building the man on the balcony seemed to have been called away. Or maybe he had suddenly remembered something, because he quickly stood up and flicked something off the balcony.

The man took a step toward the interior door and stopped. He stood staring out at Speed's truck. His gaze did not leave the black Suburban, as it cruised past the building.

Speed kept his eyes locked on the man for some reason; he was not sure why. When the man had stood, the truck was directly in front of the building. Speed noticed the man wore what looked like a traditional Muslim prayer shirt and white head covering. This didn't really mean much as there were several people outside the building dressed similarly. For some reason though, it triggered a forgotten reminder on Speed's internal to-do list. He slid his cellphone from a pouch on his vest and sent a text to Mike Carter:

Hey Mikey. After the debrief let's hit the sniper room and review the intel on that Archangel thing again. Ok?

Speed stared at the screen. He watched the message go from "delivered" to "read" and then a text bubble and three rolling dots appeared. The reply read simply:

You bet.

He turned to Robinson, who was hunched over the wheel looking up at a red light willing it to turn green and said, "I need to hit the sniper room with Mike after the debrief. Cool with you? You got something you can do at the barn for a bit?"

"Sure thing Speeder." Bryan replied without looking away from the light. As it switched to green, he roared off on their continued quest for coffee.

***

Ameer Muhamed straightened as the Black Suburban crept closer and closer along the street toward his building. He had seen it coming for several blocks given that his balcony afforded him quite an impressive view of the city. Not that these particular neighbourhoods would be gracing the covers of any home and garden magazines. These buildings had been selected out of necessity, and since he had to be there, why not get the best view toward the rising sun? For some reason, he couldn't pull his eyes away from that truck. As the truck got closer, he noticed the push bar on the grill and the low-profile antenna on the roof next to the GPS bubble. And as it passed below him, he could see the man in the passenger seat, leaning against the window looking up in his direction from behind black sunglasses. Ameer noticed the gray uniform and the circular crest on the shoulder. The sight shot him straight up. This was clearly one of the trucks from the tactical unit. He continued to follow the vehicle with his eyes, and he felt a sting as the man inside stared back at him. Ameer was very confident in the operational security of their plan to date. However, this simple chance passing made him immediately question their timetable. He had suddenly remembered that they were due for another integrity test, a test designed to gauge the reliability of their associates from the floors below. As the Suburban got a green light and drove off, he flicked his cigarette off the balcony and headed back into his office. Inside he called for his right-hand man. "Raahil!" he yelled through the penthouse.

A moment later Raahil appeared at the door, expressionless. "Yes." he stated flatly.

"Raahil. It is time for the final test for our friends."

Raahil knew exactly what that meant, and he turned without speaking. He walked down the corridor to the living room to the hall table with the brass bowl on top. Raahil picked a burner off the top of the pile and powered it on. As he sat on the couch in the living room, he dialed a number he had memorized many months ago. A polite female voice answered on the other end. "I have some information to share with you. Yes, tonight is fine. Eight p.m. at the usual place...okay." He hung up and handed the phone to a partially nude young Persian girl, the one with the bright green eyes. She took the phone into the kitchen and placed in the microwave, hit ten seconds on the timer, and pressed START. The completely fried phone was dropped into a garbage bag, which was then tied up and placed next to the door for disposal. As she returned through the living room, the green-eyed girl smiled teasingly at Raahil. She ran her thin fingers up his arm and over his shoulder, passing him and gliding down the hall and through the bedroom door. Looking back over her shoulder, she giggled, as Raahil rose to follow.

***

The door swung open twenty minutes after it had closed and the Hogs spilled out into the hallway next to the Unit Commander's office. Vince Wismer sat perched at his desk and had just placed his phone back in its cradle. He called out for Glen Parker to come in. Parker peeled off from the team, and Speed watched as the boss motioned for him to close the door. Paul's thoughts drifted back to his earlier daydream and a feeling that was gnawing away at his insides. He stopped by the front desk area and topped up his coffee while trading the customary insults with the newest front desk operator and perennial funnyman Brad Turner as he passed.

"Brad, the gym's just 40 paces though this door," Speed sniped, tilting his mug in the direction of the unit gym, "that's 10 calories burned just getting their pal."

Without missing a beat, the man behind the desk returned fire, "When you actually do some police work, Speed, I'll go in there. I don't think there's a threat of you solving any crime or me getting any skinnier."

The pair laughed. Speed continued down the hall to the sniper room just as the phone started ringing at the front desk.

"I think that's for you Brad?" Speed hollered over his shoulder, as he held his ID card to the scanner and entered the planning room. He found Carter already leaning back in a corner chair. Carter sat staring at the two white boards they had commandeered with the Team Three snipers. The computers whirring to life, and Speed slouched into a chair throwing his feet up on the map table. "So. What do we know Mike?"

***

Seven thirty in the evening on College Street in the summer was typically busy. Patios were packed in the trendy party of the city known as Little Italy. Couples huddled over a well-cooked meal and soaked in the atmosphere. Raahil took his time getting downtown and purposely parked several blocks away. He slowly walked through the back streets and alleys, which avoided most of the CCTV cameras along the busy tourist street. Again, he arrived early in order to surveil the location. *Always a good practice before sitting down with the undercover officer*, he reminded himself. Raahil and his team had noticed some new cameras on the patio and in the laneway during the recce for this meet and they planned a route to avoid them. The place he always met his handler was a little Italian café called the

Diplimatico. It had the perfect exterior patio with a quick escape route to a dark laneway devoid of any cameras. Raahil's security team was quietly and expertly defeating the cameras along the sidewalk to that lane as he settled into the patio. It was just a precaution in the event they had to make a speedy exit. A member of his team had managed to slip through an open service entrance into the basement office area of the cafe.

The man was removing the security system's hard drive just as the slender blonde undercover officer was ushered out to the patio. She was in the company of a well-built light skinned partner who Raahil had never met. He shifted nervously in the cold metal chair and inhaling deeply on his unfiltered cigarette, irritated at the presence of this man. *Why the change in the pattern?* Raahil sized them both up. The female officer was not in great shape but not exactly out of shape either. Her streaky blonde hair was pulled back in a tight ponytail which allowed you to count all the piercings in her ears. Nine in total, he remembered as he counted again…no. Wait. Ten. She had added one in the months since their last meeting. Her conservative makeup and lightly tanned skin made him wonder what it would be like to be with her. In his daydream, they were lying naked in bed together in a room that overlooked a beach somewhere. The white linen drapes were gently blowing into the room. His phone buzzed on the nightstand startling them both. The screen glowed with a coded message. He leans over and kisses her shoulder and asks her to turn on the TV saying something is happening back in Canada. He kisses her breast and smiles as she starts to sob watching the footage of the destruction in her city.

His perfect dream was stopped abruptly by the scraping of two chairs on the patio stones. Raahil rose to greet the pair of cops and was introduced to the man standing across from him. The light skinned man offered a firm grip and an intelligent gaze. He was very cocksure and appeared to Raahil to be situationally aware. More so than his pretty partner. Raahil also noted the weapon protruding from under the man's light blue linen shirt and made a mental note that the officer is right-handed due to the gun's placement. Raahil also noted the way the female officer uncharacteristically clutched her purse. He chose not to make things anymore tense than they already seem to be. Instead, Raahil broke the obvious tension by ordering a round of espresso and asked, "So. What do you want to know?"

***

A warm ocean breeze blew gently through the open-air dining room at the resort tonight. Naila and her friends enjoyed some appetizers with the group of men they met earlier on the beach. Naila sat across from the young blue-eyed hunk she had spent the afternoon chatting with. She liked that he didn't seem bothered by her being modest and covered up. They had spent the day talking about everything from politics to music to studies. Naila learned that he was a law student from Boston College in the United States. So intellectual conversation had been easy between them. But they never once talked about religion. She had assumed he was Christian only because he was a white American. Not exactly fair, she knew. But it intrigued her all the same that he may be genuinely attracted to her even though she was clearly Muslim.

As dinner continued, the larger group conversations slowly turned into more intimate huddles and eventually a few pairs. The men and women were starting to make their preferences known. Naila and her new friend sat staring at each other during an awkward moment of silence. Her mind drifted back to the office and that last 1320 she had submitted. Her male companion raised his wine glass and took a healthy mouthful of the red merlot. The movement caught her eye, and she smiled and nervously sipped her iced tea.

The young man smiled back. He leaned forward and in his thick south Boston accent asked, "So Naila. What would I have to do to convert to Islam?"

She nearly spat her drink across the table at him. Not because she was offended, not at all. No, in fact if she had to, she would say that she was extremely aroused by the question. Two things struck her instantly. First was the irony that this man was Jewish. She was much more attracted to him more than she wanted let on. Secondly, and more importantly she suddenly knew what was troubling her about her last report.

Chapter Eight

Naila stared into the bright blue eyes of her new "friend" Stephen, whose face lit up the background on her laptop. She was back at work for the first time since the vacation, and she still had not been able to switch off the vacay-mode. The young analyst reclined in her chair with her feet propped up on that overturned recycling bin again. She nibbled on the end of a red pen with a smile while watching the spinning icon and waiting for more conversations to download to her workstation. Naila had been talking with Stephen nightly since getting home. Those conversations and this relationship, as it was, had given her renewed passion for both her studies and her work. On the topic of the latter, she had produced some very in-depth analysis, which were being noticed by her bosses. Her work was being coupled with a new Data and Social Media Mining Team in the office. This new approach had uncovered some interesting leads in several evolving cases. There was a pattern emerging around the activities of a particular local Taxi company. But as yet no one could decide exactly "what" it is or if it is even criminal in nature.

The young intellect continued staring into the eyes on her screen preparing to try and place a piece into this puzzle. Naila noticed a file icon next to Stephen's nose and hovered her mouse over it. The little window told her it was dated the day she left. Immediately she sat up and clicked the file open. She pushed her glasses back and pulled her hair into a bun, as it opened. It was the 1320 that was rejected the day she was leaving for her vacation; attached was a copy of the recorded conversation as well. Naila remembered the words Stephen had said over dinner that first night, "What do I have to do to convert to Islam?" and immediately she remembered what made this phone call stand out.

Naila quickly opened a new 1320 and began typing furiously. Her thoughts were coming together faster than she could type them. She paused periodically and clicked over to the web browser to scan the latest counterterrorism sites for articles that would support her working thesis. During the next two hours, she kept her soundproof cube door locked. Her internal messenger icon was set to BUSY, and her phone stayed in airplane mode resting in the cubby outside her door. She didn't even notice the six IM's she had missed, the little indicator continuing to flash the number "6" at the bottom right corner of her screen. Three were from co-workers, and three were from her boss who sat watching from across the room.

***

The nameplate read *Detective Gaines* on the wall outside his door. But Jim Gaines had not done much detecting in the years since 9-11. Mostly he had been an overpaid clerk. His job was to evaluate the strength of the work produced by analysts like Naila, not to actually analyze anything himself. Gaines had twenty analysts working for him in this section. The work had become increasingly mundane and routine, and Jim had long since lost that loving feeling for the job. When he first transferred to the CFO from Homicide, he was full of excitement. Gaines had taken the job the second it was offered to him. The offer had come in the hallways of the Superior Court of Justice on University Avenue just two years after 9-11. Gaines had just successfully built a case against and helped convict a young Lebanese man who had killed a 17-year-old drug dealer in an underground parking garage at the Orton Park Housing Complex in the city's troubled east end. The accused was a recent visitor to Canada and had no ties to the community. He had no family, no passport, no criminal record, and no known address. The guilty man had been picked up after a resident, whom he had not seen nearby, called 911. As he exited the underground through a stairwell leading into the courtyard, the man wiped the blade of the knife on a black and white keffiyeh wrapped around his neck then tossed the knife into a garbage bin near the building's loading dock. As he kept walking out onto Orton Park Road, a responding officer in plainclothes in an unmarked car saw him. Tim Immes was the leading expert on policing in that neighbourhood and when the emergency call had gone over the radio he immediately thought of O'Neil Facey and his Crip gang. They had been building a small empire in these buildings, and that meant enemies were always lurking around to cause trouble for Orton Park Crips. Immes had been sure he would see some young black gangster running from the complex with a red hat or a bandana covering his face. The nearby blood gang from Kingston Road was the logical suspect pool. But the witness description of the black and white scarf didn't sit right. So much so that when Immes saw the suspect walking quickly north away from the projects he almost drove right past him. If it hadn't been for the dark staining down one of his pant legs and on the cuffs of the gray sweater he was wearing. Without a doubt it was a career arrest.

Gaines was assigned as the lead homicide investigator and had skillfully pulled all the evidence together from the scene. That is to say, he had directed the crime scene tech's where to look and what to look for. He did spend hours trying to get the suspect to give him a statement or a motive but got nothing. Gaines had the entire neighbourhood

77

canvassed for any link between the suspect and the deceased. Again, zero. Not one of the thousand residents, registered or not, could add a thing. The detective had even sat with O'Neil Facey and Tim Immes in a shitty little coffee shop drinking black mud for three hours, trying – off the record – to find out who could be dumb enough to muscle the Crips in the area?

In the end, Gaines tied his investigation into a neat enough little package. It was all based on the testimony of the one silent witness and the evidence. For a motive, the Crown Attorney and Gaines went with the old story of a drug deal gone wrong. All the evidence lined up pointing in that direction and to this suspect. The suspect was literally caught red-handed leaving the scene. Everyone believed that Gaines had slam-dunked this caper. A case like this was an investigator's dream. The reality was that the suspect made one small mistake, being witnessed during the murder. He then had a second bout of unfortunate luck and was caught by a keen-eyed local cop. The suspect surrendered without incident and pled guilty at the first trial date. Assisted only by a free legal aid lawyer the judge easily served justice by sentencing to the man to the maximum penalty of life without parole. The investigative commander at the time knew Gaines had not done anything spectacular like it may have appeared to other people. He simply was just very efficient at organizing the information for presentation in court. That was exactly what had brought her down to the courthouse that cold afternoon with a job offer. She needed someone to run a new section at the Intelligence Division. She needed an organizer. Gaines would be her guy, besides that, his clearance rate at Homicide wasn't all that stellar anyway.

Fast forward to the present. Gaines had put on twenty sloppy pounds. His eyes were deep and baggy and his hair had gone grey. He rarely, if ever, did his tie all the way up and most days didn't bother to shave. His office reeked of burritos, stale coffee, and the stench of sweaty feet, as he has a habit of kicking his shoes off and propping his socked feet up on his desk. And that is how he was perched again today. His pinstriped gray suit coat was hanging on the back of his open door, and the worn-out brown wingtips were set at the side of his desk. A baby blue tie hung loosely around the collar of his stark white French cuffed shirt. He completed the outfit of course with his custom Homicide Squad cufflinks that he wore almost every day, just in case anyone might forget where he had come from. Gaines sipped away at his lukewarm coffee and picked at the top of the banana nut muffin on his desk. He watched Naila with deep interest. The detective had sent her three IMs in the last half-hour, which she had not responded to. She was focused on something. He could tell by the way she sat ramrod straight, eyes locked on her screen. She was typing madly on her keyboard and her level of energy was exciting to Gaines. It had gone missing in this office since the early days after 9-11. He waited patiently, almost as patiently as he waited for his pizza pocket rotating in the microwave.

***

Naila's paced slowed as she proofread her work. After a second read-through, she was satisfied with the argument and its supporting points. She sat back smiling to herself. Gaines noticed the change in her activity and quickly pulled his size 10's off the desk stuffing them back into his shoes. He tied the laces sloppily and sat up as he heard the *ping* from the computer indicating he had new material. This *ping* was followed by a second notifier, a radar *blip*, indicating a new IM request. Gaines didn't even look to see who the 1320 was from, he knew it would be Naila's. Instead, he immediately clicked on the messenger.

Naila: I need you to review that 1320 today. Can we have a meeting as soon as you're done? This is big!

Jim: Just got it. Give me 30 to review it and then we will sit down.

Naila: K. thx.

Gaines didn't return the reply, as he was already through the opening paragraph and trying to grasp the totality of the initial thesis.

***

Speed and Carter had been going in circles over the intelligence reports that they had pasted to their white boards. It was shift change, and the snipers from Team Three had joined them. What was troubling all of them was a wide disconnect between what INTEL knew and what they let the operators know. So many of the reports were redacted to one degree or another. Even still, the trail of intelligence had been cold for some months.

Josh Bender, nicknamed Freddie, a la Freddie Kruger, was the lead sniper for Team Three. He was locked on the scribbles on the white board and wondered out loud, "What if this connection to the Taxi company is just a convenience?"

"Whaddya mean?" Carter asked.

"Well. INTEL says they're all from the same Middle East region, right?"

"Okay?" the other three snipers prompted him to continue.

"So. Let's say you have some really big thing you're doing, and you don't want too many questions. You just want something, or someone moved around, but don't want to have to tell the whole story. Who would you trust?"

Speed and the other snipers were leaning forward, as Bender pulled them into his theory.

"So Freddie – your theory is that the taxis really are taxis. They just don't know who or what they're dragging around?" Speed was starting to think bigger now. "What if this is just the first kiss? What if our suspects are just building the relationship right now so that when the prom rolls around, they have a sure thing?"

"Right!" Bender replied with some extra excitement.

"If INTEL follows the cabs, they should be able to make a link to someone at the bottom of the food chain." This came from the other Team Three sniper, whose nickname was Handsome Jack, though not at all for the traditional reasons. Jack had a large red scar that ran from the corner of his left eye down under his chin. The scar was a by-product of an unfortunate incident with his brother when they were much younger. As soon as his stitches healed enough Jack had completed his police application.

Handsome Jack's reputation at the unit unfortunately was on a steady decline over the last few years. He had become sort of reserved and a bit of a loner. His weapon qualification scores were consistently at the bottom of the shooters, even having to re-shoot his sniper qualification at least once. This worried Speed, who wondered would he be up to the task if this operation ever came together. Leaning forward on his knees with a coffee mug to his face, Speed watched Jack rubbing his eyes. Was that the issue? Or was he just tired from another late night of drinking? Speed would have to make a point of asking Freddie about it later. For now he needed to start with the answers to some questions from INTEL.

Speed wheeled his chair back in front of one of the room's computers and logged in to the secure side with his token and password. Opening his email he waited while the emails were loaded to his inbox. "Freddie – you guys' mind if I send that theory to Gaines over at INTEL? I have a couple other questions to ask him?" he asked the Team Three snipers. Who each replied simply with a thumb in the air. They were busily pouring over images for an operation they had coming up tonight. Speed dropped his head and opened a new mail and addressed it to Gaines.

Carter stood and stretched which caught Speed's attention, then nodded toward Handsome Jack and smirked as if to say, "Are we sure he's okay?" Speed returned the same look and raised his shoulders, which in no way reassured his friend.

"Paul I gotta run. You need anything else today?" Carter asked, as he headed for the door.

"I'm good pal. Chat with you later. Hello to…is it Lindsay this week?" Speed quipped.

Carter turned for the door and tiredly responded, "Asshole. You know its Lindsay. Been Lindsay for six months now." As he passed the Team Three snipers, Carter said goodbye by kicking each of their chairs, to which the appropriate reply was, "Later ol' man." Most of the guys were in their late twenties or early thirties. Mike had joined the job late in life and come to The Group even later. At 50 he was a bit of an asterisk on the nominal role. But he never missed a pull-up, a timed run, or a qualification. The guys loved him. Carter threw up a sarcastic middle finger, as he opened the secure door and left the room.

Chapter Nine

The late afternoon sun kept beating against the widow of Gaines's office as finished his review of Naila's latest 1320. The document was extremely detailed and organized as always. He had reviewed it twice, and as he finished the second read-through, he leaned back in his chair rubbing his substantial forehead and exhaled deeply. The detective looked out across the office for Naila, but she was not in her cube. Gaines reached for the desk phone and hesitated, his hand on the receiver. Was this really as good as it looked? He decided that he couldn't chance it. This information required more than a rudimentary "Hot Wash." Gaines needed to loop his boss in on this immediately. He dialed the extension and waited. The unit commander's executive assistant answered in her ever-pleasant way, "Inspector Nance's office. How may I help you?"

"Bearnice. Hi. Jim Gaines. Is he in?"

"Afternoon Jim. He is, I'll put you through."

"Barry Nance." came the youngish voice through the receiver. At only 40 with twenty years experience, Nance had quickly risen up the ranks and was overseeing all Intelligence operations within the city. His unit contained not only the Analysis and Assessment Section where Gaines worked but also the Strategic Activities Groups or SAG. Units like Source Management handled all the informants and agents for the Department. This section managed informant evaluation and information dissemination. As well, they paid the informants, coordinating their identity renewal and relocation if required. There were also the Organized Crime Unit, the VIP Protection and Threat Assessment Section, the Undercover Operations Unit, and the Major Projects Sections. Nance had come up through the investigative side of the house and cut his teeth by assisting on homicide investigations and major gang takedowns. His reputation for attention to detail during large-scale investigations was respected internationally. The inspector had given lectures on the subject twice at the FBI academy in Quantico. Nance also had assisted police agencies in England and Germany with the management of their own wide-spanning investigations. his management style was relaxed and informal which made him a very approachable boss.

"Barry. Gainesy. I need a level 3 evaluation with you in the room."

"Sure thing Gainsey. Nine a.m. tomorrow good for you?" the boss asked.

Gaines tried not to sound overly excited and replied, "It's got to be today, boss. Has to be."

The use of the term "*boss*" told Nance all he needed to know.

"For you Jim, 30 minutes. Conference room 2 is open. I'll have Bearnice book it. Who is the analyst?"

"Naila."

Nance did not overreact either. After all, very little actionable intelligence had come out of the Analysis Section lately, so much so that the Deputy Chief had been breathing fire down Nance's neck about laying off some of the monitors and analysts. But Nance knew Naila's reputation and her work.

"Done. See you in thirty." Nance hung up and quickly punched the speed dial for his assistant.

"Sir."

"Bearnice, can you clear conference room 2 for me please? I need it in the next half hour. I'll also need the tech team to conduct a level 3 sweep and scan. Thanks."

The line clicked off, and Bearnice punched the end key. Her left eyebrow sat raised on her forehead, as she keyed the little used speed dial button to the Tech Crimes section head.

"Tech." an older man's voice answered.

"The Boss requires a Level 3 Jimmy. He'll be using conference room 2. Please and thank you."

"Ok Bearnice. We're on it." The man hung up and gathered his team and their equipment.

***

Two men each carrying large black cases headed for conference room 2. They found the room occupied by a small group of investigators using the room to spread out a new case file, they were politely asked to leave. No one questioned the case-toting men in their khaki cargo pants and black golf shirts emblazoned with the Tech Crimes Section logo on the chest.

When the group was gone, the tech team slid the occupied sign across the glass and closed the soundproof door. They placed their cases on the expansive oak table and set to work. Two other members of the section headed for the secure garage and climbed into a relatively ordinary looking black Sprinter van. Ordinary, except for an array of short fat antennae and two black bubbles on the roof. The inside of the van looked like the control room for a space launch. There were many scanners and electronic countermeasures that could be deployed from this vehicle, today they would only need two. One of the men climbed in the driver's seat and started the truck while the other opened a side door and positioned himself behind the electronic controls. As the computers came to life, the van pulled out into the afternoon sun and began a slow drive around the neighbourhood. The operator in the control seat set both the short and long wave scanners. He was looking for anyone operating a listening device in the area. Seeing as how this was mainly a commercial part of town, they shouldn't find any. The scanners buzzed away for the next twenty-five minutes until the van pulled up to the secure gate. The driver swiped his access card to gain entry, as his partner powered down the scanners and the van was returned to it's place in the secure garage. The last step was a one-word text front the scanner tech to his boss:

GREEN

The two Tech officers went back into the building returning to their previous assignments.

The secure phone on the hip of the senior technician buzzed. The officer closed his case having finished his sweep of the east side of the building and conference room 2. His partner returned just then and loaded his case while the first typed on his phone:

COPY

Then a new message was sent, this one went directly to Nance:

ALL GREEN

The Inspector stood and grabbed his jacket from the back of the chair. Pulling it on, he headed for the door. He stopped at Bearnice's desk, "I don't know how long this'll take, Bearnie. You feel free to take off anytime, okay?"

"Okay sir. I'll see you in the morning." She smiled, slowly shutting down her workstation and gathering her things.

Nance strode out of the office and headed to the back of the building where the conference rooms were situated. He thumbed at the screen on his secure phone changing the settings to "In A Meeting." When he reached the conference rooms he stopped at the coffee table outside the door and poured himself a large mug of dark roast. Nance handed his phone to the Tech Section Officer stationed at the door, who placed it in a metal locker on the opposite wall. The key was then handed the boss. Nance swiped his way into the room and being early took a seat at the head of the table. He sat twirling a pen, waiting in anticipation of the pending presentation.

Fifteen minutes after sending the boss the request, Gaines saw Naila return. He waved her over hurriedly. She leaned on the open door to his cube, unsure as to what his response would be. Naila had spent her whole lunch hour on the patio at the local coffee shop wondering if he would take her seriously. Gaines had been so…absent lately. She really had little faith in his response. But Naila had made up her mind. This time she would take it over his head if he tried to shut her down. Naila noticed that Gaines had uncharacteristically done his tie up. He had his jacket and shoes on and had even shaved. She figured this had to be a good sign and her cheeks flushed with excitement.

"Naila. This is great work!" he started. "We have a hot wash with the boss in less than fifteen minutes. Can you pull it off?"

The statement and question caught Naila off guard. She had never given a hot wash directly to the boss. That was something normally done by Gaines. He liked her analysis that much? She was excited and nervous at the same time.

"Let me just pull myself together and quickly throw a proper presentation together." she said.

"Naila. I don't need all that. You can access your working files from the room. It'll be better this way. Trust me, more organic. But in your eloquently organized way."

Naila smiled and skipped across to her cube where she dropped her purse. She adjusted her hijab and took a deep breath. She met Gaines at the outer door to their section of the building and the pair headed off toward the conference rooms.

At the door to the conference room, they both switched their phones to "Do Not Disturb" and set their automatic messages to "In A Meeting." They then handed them off to the Tech Officer, who placed each in a secure locker. As the officer closed the door on the locker holding Gaines' phone, the little screen lit up turning the inside of the metal box a bright blue. It went unnoticed as the door was closed, and the key turned, withdrawn then handed off to Gaines. He was already pouring a coffee and pawing up a pastry from the table by the door. Naila took a bottle of water and waited for her boss to access the room for them. When the door opened, they were both surprised that the boss had beaten them. Gaines shook hands with Nance and introduced him to Naila.

"Boss. This is Naila Rashid. She's my top analyst and the reason I had to have you here now."

"Barry." Nance said extending his large hand to greet Naila. She was immediately put at ease by his gentle but commanding grip, his soft voice and those baby blue eyes. "I've heard a lot about you."

"Well, all good things I hope sir?" Naila whispered sheepishly.

Nance sensed the unease in the room and tried to put it to rest. He pulled his jacket off and set it on the empty chair next to him. As he sat half slouched in his own chair, he told the young analyst to relax. "Just tell me a story, Naila. Call me Barry and pretend I'm another co-worker from you section. You're just telling me a story."

Naila smiled nervously and plugged her secure token into the computer at the opposite end of the large table. The computer came to life, and the large screen on the main wall automatically powered on. The trio watched the computer go through is authentication process. When the access screen faded away, Naila was mortified to see Stephen's smiling face staring at the three of them. All seventy widescreen high-definition inches of his smiling freckled face grinned from ear to ear at them. Gaines' eyebrows raised in an uneasy reaction. He was a little embarrassed for her. He had never seen her nervous like this.

Nance didn't miss a beat to break the ice again. "Your brother?" he asked jokingly.

Naila smiled as she hurriedly opened the folder she had created earlier.

"Islamic extremism relies on extremist actors." She started shakily, her voice pitching in all the wrong places. Naila fidgeted with the edges of her hijab, as if she could hide herself in there. Her eyes were down staring at her perfectly manicured fingernails resting on the edge of the table. She smiled internally at the one nail on her left hand had been painted on the beach by a local girl. It was a palm tree and a sunset. Naila thought of Stephen, *Allah give me strength*. Immediately she began to settle down.

Nance broke in, "Naila. I haven't seen Gaines this excited about police work in a very long time. So, I believe that whatever story you are about to tell me is worth it. Take a breath – relax – and just tell me what your theory is." He smiled gently to urge her on and took a long sip of his coffee while the analyst collected herself.

She started again, this time more confidently. "Islamic extremism relies on extremist actors." Her growing confidence riding the wave of each of her words. Naila's eyes were up and locked onto the boss. For the next hour and a half, she went through her theory. She answered every question with conviction and pushed away every other offered scenario with supported articulation and fact. The only thing holding this theory back was that it was one small snippet off a phone call that was completely untraceable. But Nance was interested and that is all they needed.

Chapter Ten

Raahil sat back and waited for the verbal judo match to start. He had asked them what they wanted to know and waited to see what they might fish for. As he leaned back and crossed his legs beside the table, he sipped at his espresso. The pair of detectives from the Source Management Unit were shoulder to shoulder at the tiny table, just as he had intended. His own posture dominating the small corner they were using. Raahil had purposely pulled the sugar dish and milk cup closer to his side of the table. Again, the staging was a deliberate act designed to make the detectives uncomfortable. It meant they would have to ask him for the things they needed.

The female officer whom he had dealt with on two other occasions fell first. She fidgeted in the hard metal chair. After trying unsuccessfully to reach the milk, she had whimpered at him like a poor child, "Ravi, could you please pass the milk?"

"Why of course. I'm so sorry. Let me pour it for you my dear." He purposely laid a velvety coat over his words and smiled to himself at this small victory. But the male officer would not fall for the tactic.

The light skinned man smiled casually, as he made a big show of reaching all the way across the table. He didn't have to lean forward to grab the sugar and didn't have to ask. The man plopped a healthy spoonful into his espresso then sat back holding the cup above the table, as he stretched his long legs out right under Raahil's. The detective nodded and tipped his glass toward Raahil as if to say *Your move, sir*. In reality, the big detective was saying to himself, *Nice try asshole*.

The female detective spoke again and moved her first pawn. "Ravi, you know how this works. You called us here. We didn't ask for this meeting, you did. So, you tell us whatever it is you have to tell us." She spoke with conviction and the confidence of a little barking bitch that has a large owner attached to its leash.

Let her feel like she's winning, that's part of the game, Raahil had to remind himself. When he spoke, it was calmly. Putting on his fresh-off-the-boat Pakistani accent, Raahil passed on his information like a good concerned new Canadian. He told them of a drug ring operating in the Orton Park Projects. He said they were all young black males and that a man they called "Strong" was the leader. Raahil said he knew all of this because he worked late as a cab driver and would frequently cross their paths. They were always in the stairwells where they did their dealing. He even had an apartment number for "Strong."

Ravi had gotten a gun pointed at him two nights ago when he had accidently stumbled across a conversation in the basement where "Strong" and an associate where discussing what sounded like the timing for a drug shipment.

"Why do you think it's a drug shipment, Ravi? It could have been anything." the dumb female detective asked.

This was the delicate part, Raahil knew. Give away too much knowledge, and it will look too good to be true…too little, though, and they will just dismiss it.

Raahil continued, "Well for one I don't know who gets a shipment to an apartment building at three o'clock in the morning? All I know is I heard them saying it would come in at three in the morning Saturday. Then I heard six packages – crystal – eight thousand." Raahil watched both detectives carefully to see if the bait had been taken.

The big detective looked at his little partner. He spoke next. "Okay Ravi. You know the drill. Standard payment for this sort of information is five hundred. But since this is supposed to be so big, we will make it a thousand. Sound fair? And as always, payment after we verify." He shoved his big hand across the table and waited for Raahil to take it.

Raahil chuckled inside and sheepishly shook the officer's hand like he figured a "Ravi" might. He didn't even acknowledge the little female, as they stood to leave. Raahil simply smiled and bowed his head slightly when she said, "We'll be in touch." Just like that it was done. The pieces were in place for a checkmate. The detectives left, and Raahil knew they would immediately set to work on figuring out who "Strong" was. But that wouldn't take long. He was well-known criminal gang member from the Orton Park Projects, allegedly a reformed drug dealer. The bait was too easy. The last part of the plan would be to lure Strong to the building early Saturday morning, getting him to take possession of six ounces of crystal meth. This would put the Mullah's group in position to start the execution phase of their mission.

Raahil waited another thirty minutes before rising to leave. He sent a text to his security detail that he would be moving and rose. Raahil dropped $20 on the table and slipped off the back of the patio into the lane. There was an abnormal spring in his step as he rounded the first corner. He headed north in the darkened lane. Raahil's depth of experience and training should not have let him be so excited. But it had been so long since he had been in the field that he felt a real rush at manipulating the two cops.

The earpiece whispered quietly in his ear – "He's fifty yards from you now." The man wearing all black sank deeper into the shadows. He was in a yard next to the laneway. Like a statue, he stood perfectly still and listened. The officer heard the scuffing of Raahil's expensive dress shoes first. An instant later he caught him out of the corner of his eye. He watched, as Raahil continued up the laneway oblivious to the team of surveillance specialists watching him. The surveillance man quietly keyed his mic three times, indicating to the rest of his team that their subject was still on his route and they were still uncompromised. A few seconds later, another member of the team reported in. She told the team that the subject's security detail was waiting near his car a few blocks away. Three more silent clicks from another member of the team. Next, an operative reported that the suspect was stopping in the school playground down the road from the vehicle. His security men were still idling in their black sedan at the end of the road. They were watching their boss intently. The subject took out a pack of cigarettes and casually lit one.

***

Taking a long draw on the unfiltered cigarette, he sat on a bench where he scanned the area and the surrounding streets. Raahil counted a total of three homeless people throughout the schoolyard. No doubt there were more hidden in the shadows. He took another long drag and looked down at the phone in his lap. One of the bums stirred under a nearby tree lifting a beer can to his lips. Raahil looked back at the phone and typed: Ok?

***

The bum closest to Raahil had watched him enter the playground from the south end. Raahil moved slowly and scanned the area. The bum lifted the empty king can to his lips and spoke softly into it, "Bravo one. Eyes on. He's scanning. This guy is good." He put the can down just before Raahil looked his way. The bum was playing the part perfectly. He never felt completely comfortable when he was undercover like this. It was a feeling sort of like being half-naked in front of your neighbors. He felt like everyone could see right through his disguise. The undercover operator had long since grown an impressive chest-length gray beard, which was perfect for this operation. He hadn't showered in the last couple of days, and he even went to the extraordinary length of spending time helping out around his father's hobby farm today to get good and dirty. The officer wore an outfit he had pulled together from the Salvation Army, complete with a pair of old running shoes that were entirely beat up and two sizes too big. He wore some baggy old torn jeans, and an old dirty fleece sweater with a teddy bear ironed on the front. Over that he wore a long dirty trench coat. The piece de la resistance was the mangy old winter hat he pulled down low on his forehead and over his ears, his long dirty blonde hair hanging out from under the edges. The undercover officer lowered the can and shook it a little. He was being careful not to stare at their subject. Having been trained to watch mostly out of the corner of his peripheral vision he kept his head turned away from his target for the most part.

***

The phone vibrated silently in Raahil's hand, and he glanced down at the glowing screen to read the message:

ALL OK

Raahil rose to his feet slowly like nothing had changed. The car was to his left less than a hundred meters away. Instead of walking directly at the car Raahil headed away from it. He strode straight off the bench directly toward the bum slumped under the tree drinking from the can of beer. This was all a part of Raahil's countersurveillance plan. It was designed to make a team scramble to cover him, and in the process, they would show themselves. He stepped onto a paved footpath that would take him right past the bum under the tree. Fifty meters ahead, just off the path on his right, the bum guzzled from his can again.

***

The undercover operator remained as calm as he could. He was taken by surprise when the subject stood and walked right toward him. Had he been made? Was the subject going to come and verify his bum's credentials? He slowly brought the can to his mouth and whispered, "Moving my way. No compromise yet." As he brought the can back down, he slouched down a few more inches. He was in a semi-flat position on his back. Only his head and upper shoulders were slightly raised against the tree. Both his knees were up and bent, his feet bracing into the ground. The subject framed perfectly between his knees on the path coming towards him. The experienced operator, a former Group sniper, was in a perfect ground fighting or firing position. He would let the subject decide what it would be. The bum then placed the can on the ground to his right and slowly slid his right hand under the front of his sweater. His left hand rested at his belt buckle. The bum's right hand expertly wrapped around the grip of his Glock G38 with his trigger finger resting lightly against the frame. He had chosen this model for the stopping power

90

of the .45calibre rounds. The old operator spent hours on the range with the little gun and was as proficient with it has he had been with his full sized 9mm version when he was at the T.I.G.. If this came to shooting, he would be winning hands down.

***

The bum continued to sit there slumped against the tree, likely passed out. As Raahil passed him, he had barely even moved. The bum lifted his can again and Raahil heard him mumble to himself. Probably pissed off that he was staring into the bottom of an empty can now.

Raahil continued through the fence to the schoolyard and out to the street then looped his way north of his car and back south through the residential streets. When he returned to his car, the security team pulled out from the curb driving away slowly. Raahil slid into the plush front seat of his nicely appointed luxury sports coupe. He sat there for a minute soaking in the sports car's opulence then eased himself back deeper into the plush red leather seat and caressed the steering wheel. Raahil had never known such luxury and wealth on his own, but since working with the Mullah he had managed to acquire a few nice things. A week ago, he had picked up this latest extravagance against his own better judgment. He knew better than to attract attention to the mission. This risk he figured was well covered by the group's legitimate business holdings.

As Raahil sat in the dead quiet interior, he reviewed tonight's operation. He was looking for errors on his part. He could think of none. It was a flawlessly executed deception that would lead to the ultimate and final test of their associates. Raahil smiled contentedly and reached forward where he pressed the start button. The sports car roared to life, and he couldn't help but rev the engine once or twice before taking off. He inhaled that new car smell and shifted into first gear.

***

"Car is fired up and moving away to go northbound out of the area. Bravo one breaking down." the undercover operator said into his can with a little less concern for compromising himself. He waited ten minutes in position after the sports car drove away and then slowly gathered his cart to shuffle off to his pre-arranged rendezvous location. He was looking for the beat up Econoline van that would be waiting for him. Hidden inside would be three highly skilled shooters from The Group. When the undercover operator reached the laneway, he could see the van backed into the spot exactly where it should be. As he ditched the cart, his shuffle turned to a stroll, and he ambled over to the sliding door of the van. The old veteran stood for a second next to the door opening his fly to take a piss. Manny Horowitz leaned out laughing. John Burke was in the seat behind Manny, and a rookie the old sniper didn't know was perched behind the wheel. All three were in a dressed down uniform, so-to-speak, khaki tactical pants. Manny and the rookie wore black fleece jackets covering their chest rigs, but John had a long-sleeve checked shirt under his rig with the sleeves rolled up exposing his substantial forearms. The rookie was bald as a whistle except for a little soul patch under his bottom lip, and both Manny and John were sporting a few day's growth on their faces. Manny's hair was perfect as always, and John had an old Toronto Maple Leafs ballcap pulled down snug on his head.

"You old salt! I can't believe you're still doing this shit!" Manny exclaimed, and he reached out to pull his old friend into the van.

"Nice to see you fellas too! Always a pleasure, Manny, you prick. Gentleman John, haven't seen you in forever. Everything cool with you brother?"

"All good here my friend. Glad to see you are keeping well. How are Rita and the kids?"

"You see that, Manny? That's a gentleman. Remembers the wife's name and everything. You could learn something from him." The former operator slapped Horowitz across the shoulder with his right hand. The bearded old former sniper kept wiping his hand all down the sleeve of Horowitz's black fleece as Manny just watched.

"You just wiped your dick dribble all down my jacket didn't you?" Manny asked in shock.

The old sniper ignored him and turned his attention with a smile to the rookie in the driver's seat. He extended the same hand up between the seats. "Hey kid, what's your name? How long you been on the team?"

"Damon Fernandes. I just got pulled up a few months back." was the rookie's response. Instead of a handshake, he offered a fist bump to the undercover operator.

John Burke spoke up for him, "He's a good kid Salty. Glen pulled him right from the course, if that tells you anything about him."

The old sniper climbed in and leaned back in his seat pulling a protein bar from his pocket. As he opened the wrapper he smiled. "It does indeed. It does indeed."

With that, Manny reached up and slapped the rookie on the shoulder twice. Immediately the van was started. The lights were turned on, and the little team pulled out into the street for the ride back to the INTEL building. Manny keyed the press to talk on his chest and stated for the rest of the team that was listening:

"Four Two. Package secure. We're on the move."

The van pulled away to the south merging with the nighttime traffic on College Street and meandered its way home as the four men inside relaxed – finally. The warm night air danced into the unairconditioned interior and mixed with the sour smell of sweat. This forced Fernandes to drive with his face half out the open window.

The old sniper was leaned back with his eyes closed and asked quietly, "Hey rookie, any chance this old van has a working radio?"

Fernandes flicked on the old AM/FM radio. It was already tuned to a local rock channel. The announcer was just finishing up delivering the weather for tomorrow and went directly into a City and Colour classic. The opening chords of the City and Colour hit relaxed the three senior members in the van even more and Damon hummed along as he drove through the city, carefully to watching his mirrors for any sign of a tail. The quartet sang the chorus together as they headed home.

***

The subject's car continued to make its way north. As it did, a caravan of some eight surveillance vehicles casually wrapped a rotating blanket around it. At the very rear of this caravan, two city blocks back, sat two very satisfied Detectives. These Detectives were from the Source Management Unit. The small female in the driver's, and the larger, light-skinned Detective sat stretched out in the passenger seat. He nervously cracked his knuckles. The radio hidden in the glove box periodically hissed with updates on the subject's movements as they followed along at a safe distance.

The big man in the passenger seat seethed for the fifth time already, "Janine, I don't know how you put up with that guy. How can you stand to play that dumb little girl role for him?"

Janine just smiled glancing over at him. "I hate it too. But it got us what we wanted right? Trust me Pepper, I'll be laughing at this guy in a few weeks when we slap handcuffs on him! Did he seriously think he could roll in here in that $80,000 car, dish on some low-level drug dealer, and not think we'd be wise to him?"

Her partner just laughed as he paused to key the mic: "Copy. Give him a little space guys. We already know this part of his route, and it'd be hard to lose that car anyway. Air One, you have the eye for now."

Air One's "copy" was lost in the conversation. The detectives were busily going over all the little nuances of the meeting, making sure they had read the subject's play correctly. He clearly wanted to feel in charge. After all, he had gone to great lengths to make himself feel that way. They had watched his team, as good as they were, disabling cameras and prepping the site for their arrival. The detectives were right to use extra caution for this meeting, especially after seeing the level of tradecraft employed by this subject and his associates. The subject's wholesale dismissal of Janine during the meet was clearly intentional. She had been his only contact up until today, so he should have no reason for that move. The partners were happy with their own tradecraft and planning as well. They had gotten the subject to play into their hands while letting him think he was in charge the whole time. Their surveillance plan had been perfectly executed so far and they had no reason to think otherwise at this point.

The large detective took a big mouthful of his dark roast coffee and removed a tin of cigarillos from the pocket of his shirt. Opening the tin, he drew one for himself. Janine looked over at him from the driver's seat and rolled her eyes. "Fine." she said, taking one for herself. "You're a bad fucking influence on me. You know that right?"

Her partner just smiled with the cigarillo between his teeth, as he leaned over with a match and lit hers. Lighting his own, he drew deeply on the tobacco and exhaled a cloud of smoke saying, "But ya know ya love me!" It sent the partners into a deep spat of laughter, the kind you get when everything seems to be going your way.

***

Raahil continued his drive without paying much attention to his surroundings. He was fully mesmerized by the car. The engine purred along in perfect harmony with the soft Arabic pop hits coming from the sound system, this lulled Raahil into a false sense of security. He continued cruising along into the city's Greek Town on the Danforth. At a redlight, the car went quiet, as the soundtrack paused between songs. Raahil looked around at the drivers and vehicles near him. Nothing seemed out of place. There was a little Asian woman sitting entirely too close to the steering wheel of her compact car in the lane to his left. Behind her, a balding heavyset man wearing a white tank top was behind the wheel of an old beat-up Buick. Directly behind his own car Raahil could see a middle-aged white woman, blonde, frazzled looking and texting on her phone inside a mini-van. The last car at the light was directly in front of Raahil. A sporty two-door coupe, loud rap music pumping from the open windows and vibrating the license plate cover on the trunk. A small thin white male and a muscular black male were in the front seats. Both had their hats on sideways – he hated that – and were slouched low in the seats. Subconsciously, Raahil processed the scene as All Normal.

The light changed, and the little Honda speed off noisily. Raahil eased onto the gas and pulled ahead of the little Asian lady who was getting a slow start. She stared straight ahead like she was fixed on her destination. The other cars eased away from the intersection, and all continued on their journeys. As the next song started Raahil thumbed the volume control on the steering wheel. The sweet voice of Bint Salem eased out of the speakers, and he couldn't help but sing along.

***

As the sports car passed her, she could hear the subject singing at the top of his lungs. The little Asian lady spoke out loud to her Bluetooth, "Okay he's away. Still eastbound in the curb. Playing Saudi karaoke with himself now; damn, he's awful too. Totally relaxed. I'm switching out at the next light. Tony, he's all yours."

She signaled her turn and slipped into the turn lane at the next street, and caught a glimpse of the subject looking back at her in his side mirror, as he drove on.

A male voice came over the radio, "Okay folks, I got him. Two for shade and still slipping away from the sun."

For the next forty-five minutes, this rolling surveillance continued. They knew roughly where he was headed but not the exact part of Scarborough. The last time they had tailed him he had expertly lost them within minutes of getting off the highway. Today he was taking a more direct route though the city. Now that they were deep in the east-end the traffic was much lighter. The surveillance vehicles eased back even further letting the helicopter maintain a visual. The eight spin cars rotated in and out of a spot about three back of the subject.

Raahil made his usual set of heat checks by turning into different gas stations in his neighbourhood. He would then come back out going the opposite direction. He also ran a couple of red lights to try and make any would-be followers bite. None did. Raahil did think at one point he had spotted that same Asian lady from the Danforth following him. He had quickly turned onto a dead-end street and waited for her to pass. When the car came into view, it looked the same, but he realized this driver was a younger looking Asian female. Her seat was reclined, and her hair was in pigtails. Raahil laughed to himself, *Sailor Moon*, he thought. He started the car and pulled back out onto the street turning the opposite direction from the Asian lady.

***

In her little compact car, the officer spoke again to the Bluetooth. "Ok, that was close. I almost turned right onto the street he was sitting on. His lights had just gone out, so I bypassed. He's sitting on the dead end watching the street."

The helicopter had lost him under some overhanging foliage and needed confirmation. "Air One. Okay we got him again coming off that cul-de-sac and headed away from you now." broadcast the chopper's spotter.

The surveillance team had gotten tense. Right now was the critical time. When a subject first leaves, and when they get close to, a location are the times when they are the most aware. So, all of these antics that were designed to help the subject detect surveillance were actually giving him away. It told the team, in particular the two lead Detectives, that their target was almost home.

***

Confident that he had not been compromised Raahil hit the dial button and spoke an Arabic name into the air. The Bluetooth immediately acknowledged the request and dialed the security detail he had with him earlier.

A deep Arabic voice came over the speakers. "Salam."

"Wa-alaikum." Raahil replied in Arabic. Then asked, "How is our house doing?"

"It's locked and clean." was the cryptic reply.

Raahil hit the end button and turned onto Orton Park Road from the north and headed south toward the building. He rounded sharply into the driveway and right for the underground garage. His associates were parked in the roundabout by the front door. Raahil dove the car down the ramp and all the way to the back of the lowest level to its parking space. He backed in and as he hit the button to kill the engine he smiled at the successes of the evening.

***

The spotter on board Air One coordinated the spin cars on the ground and had lined up two undercover officers to be in a position to get out on foot if the need should arise. When Raahil had pulled into the driveway to the projects, one of those cars was closing in on Orton Park Road along Lawrence. The officer immediately sped up and made the left onto the street just in time to see the taillights of the sports car plunging into the underground. The undercover officer wheeled his deeply tinted car into a visitor's spot near the front door. He climbed out and eyed the two men in the black sedan by the door. They were watching him with the same curiosity. The undercover pulled up his sagging jeans and adjusted the flat brim of his cap dragging it to an obscene angle his head. Rubbing his thick beard, the young black officer strolled past the sedan and into the lobby. He confidently walked to the panel and chose a random unit to buzz. The officer was watching through the vestibule glass at the elevator, as the numbers sank and B2 lit up above the door.

An older female voice answered the buzzer asking pleasantly, "Who is it?"

The undercover scrambled and played a gamble, "Its O'Neil from the 4th floor Mrs. …" He paused to look at the name next to the number he had pressed, "Walters. I forgot my keys. Can you let me in please?"

There was a long pause. The undercover wasn't sure if the lobby surveillance camera could be viewed in each apartment through a closed-circuit system or not. His head was down away from the camera. He still had one eye on the elevator lights, which were still in the basement. After what seemed like an eternity, there was a scornful sucking of teeth that came through the speaker box in the lobby. But the door clicked open nonetheless. The officer tried not to run to the elevator bank, as he entered the lobby. The lights showed that it was still on B2. Instead, he made a right turn and found a stairwell where he walked, half ran, up to the third floor hoping he didn't miss the moving elevator. Entering the third-floor hallway, he turned left back to the elevator bank and saw the lights changing from B1 to 1. He decided to wait for it to pass. He would watch and see where it stops. Then go up to the floor. The officer pulled out his department-issued smartphone and typed a text:

I'm in. Subject in elevator. Stand-by.

A minute later, the elevator he was watching stopped at 21, the top floor of the building. It stayed there as if it were being held for something or someone. The officer reached forward and pressed the call button to go up. He saw the second elevator start rising to meet him from the lobby. He texted again:

21st Floor. Going to go up and try to verify a door.

COPY , was the reply.

The elevator door opened, and the undercover officer stepped into the small box. He pressed 21 on the panel and leaned back against the wall for the ride. At 15, his ride was interrupted. The doors opened and a small Southeast Asian man stepped in.

"Going up." the officer told the man trying to shoo him out. The small man looked surprised. He glanced at the panel and saw what floor the man had selected. Unfortunately, the doors had closed and the elevator had started moving. The small thin arm of the resident extended and pressed 19 on the panel. The man turned and faced the undercover officer. They locked eyes, and the little man spoke with a British-Pakistani accent, "I know you are not from this building sir. You must have pressed the wrong button. If you please, you should not be going to that floor." The little man stood there smiling awkwardly. At the 19th floor, the doors opened again, and the little man stepped out into the hall and held the door waving the officer out.

The undercover officer followed, and the elevator closed, continuing on its way empty. The little man spoke again, "I see nothing. I say nothing. But they will be coming to see why elevator empty. You are going now. There." The man pointed to the south stairwell. The officer turned to look, when he turned back to speak the man was already quietly shuffling down the opposite corridor.

The officer extracted his phone again:

Had to bail at 19. Something is off here. Good to come out?

The response: All clear. Security GOA.

The officer made his way to the stairwell and walked back to the lobby. As he got closer to the main floor, he could hear men's voices below. They were speaking a foreign language he didn't recognize. He continued down, trying to walk as normally as he could so that nothing would seem out of the ordinary. When he reached the third floor, he could tell the men were standing at the entrance to the lobby. He thumbed his passcode back into his phone and typed a quick message to another number:

Call me in 1 min.

10-4 blinked the text bubble under his last message.

The undercover officer kept walking, timing his steps so the phone would ring just as he made the turn to the last set of stairs to the lobby. He gripped the railing and pulled himself around the corner and down the first step of the final eight stairs. The officer looked at the two Arabic men in suits standing by the door to the lobby. One man had it propped open with his foot, and the other was looking down toward the basement stairs. They both looked up when they heard his hand squeak on the plastic railing cover, as he made the turn. The man looking down the stairs, pulled a cell phone from his breast pocket and dialed a number. He immediately spoke in what the undercover assumed was Arabic. The man's eyes never turned from the officer, burrowing into him. At that exact moment the cell phone in the pouch of the officer's hoodie started singing. A custom ringer set to play a popular rap song and it was belting out of the pouch. As the officer drew the phone out the base line and last lyrics echoed in the concrete stairwell. He hit the green icon to answer the call just five stairs from the two men. Both of the Arabs watching him as continued toward them.

"Yes Auntie?" the officer tried his best Jamaican accent. "Okay okay Auntie. Meh so sorry fi dat. Meh come back again tomorruh and meh uh bring dat fi you." The officer lowered the phone from his ear so he could pass between the two Arab men. They were closely spaced at the door in a roadblock of sorts. The one man still had his phone to his ear.

The officer stopped on the ground floor and stood less than a foot from the man holding the door. They looked in each other's eyes. They officer kept up his charade, "Move pusseh." He sucked his teeth and held his head back, while he waved at the men angrily. The undercover was towering above both men and outweighed them by at least thirty pounds. Strangely that did not seem to bother either of these men. A large angry black man in a housing project stairwell didn't worry them, that was also interesting.

The man with the phone listened closely to it like he was waiting for some order. What the officer could not have heard was the Arabic voice on the man's phone stating, "Let him pass. It's nothing." All the officer knew was that the man with the phone hung up and taped his partner on the forearm. They stepped out of his way and allowed the officer into the lobby. Both men watched as he walked toward the vestibule doors. The officer sucked his teeth again and continued his conversation in that gibberish dialect he had been speaking.

***

Raahil had been listening to the Jamaican man speaking near his security detail and had given the order to let him pass. After he had spoken his last word, he thumbed the end icon and dropped the phone onto couch. Leaning back in the leather sofa in his living room, he returned to his thoughts. His jacket was off and draped over the chair by the door. His shirt was open, as was the balcony door. A cool gentle breeze blew the curtains into the apartment and bright moonlight shone intermittently into the living room. He looked down at the green-eyed Persian between his legs who was busily pleasuring him. The moonlight glistened off the caramel skin on her back. She reached up tossing her dark brown hair to one side and looked up at him with those hypnotizing eyes. Raahil felt his body tensing and pressed himself back further closing his eyes to relax. His thighs tensed, and he climaxed with the thought that he had just closed another perfect day. He started to doze off, as he listened to the rhythmic beating of a police helicopter nearby. It was no doubt chasing down some highly dangerous criminal…he laughed out loud. His companion just smiled at him from her perch on his shoulder.

Once the undercover officer safely reached his car in front of the building, an "All clear" message was broadcast over the radio system. Janine reached down and picked up the mic from between the seats keying the transmit button, "Security stay with him, and make sure he's clear of any counter. Then lets R/V at the rally point. Everybody else, freshen up – grab a coffee and meet there in 20." She put the mic down and took a deep drag on her cigarillo. Her partner stared out the window at the blackness of the parking lot they were in.

Janine turned to him. "Pepper. What the hell is going on over there?"

A long silence hung between them. The heat of the interior of the car kept it aloft for what seemed like hours.

Janine shrugged and gripped the steering wheel to straighten herself up. She took another long pull on the cigarillo, exhaling as she turned the key over. Janine was not surprised by the silence. It didn't bother her that her partner wasn't saying anything. That is how they worked together, she thought out loud, and he was more introspective. It was part of what made them such a great team – the yin to the other's yang, the salt to the pepper.

Janine eased the car out of the parking lot, as her partner turned and faced her. She checked for oncoming traffic and caught that look on his face, one that she had rarely seen, He looked surprised and overwhelmed by a thought hovering as yet unsaid.

The car jerked to a stop at the edge of the road. "Spit it out!" she barked at him.

His face relaxed, and in the most neutral of deliveries her partner turned to her and said, "I think we just hit on a terror cell."

The words hung in the air mixing with the tobacco smoke and the burnt sulfur of a fresh match as the big detective fired up another cigarillo as if it were a victory reward.

Janine put the car back in drive and while they drove she chattered non-stop. It was a twenty-minute drive to the rally point. Every so often she would pause and look at him to see if they were on the same track. He didn't even have to look at her. He just stared out the windshield periodically nodding his approval with the odd, "Uh-huh." As she pulled in behind the old Fairview Mall, Janine stopped talking. She did a quick mental review of the new working theory. Janine eased up to the pack of waiting cars, but before getting out, she reached across and grabbed hold of her partner's forearm.

He turned and looked at her curiously.

"No one." she said. "Not yet anyhow. We need to lay this out for Gaines first."

100

"Okay." He slid out of the passenger seat.

The pair walked over to the rest of the team and started the debrief of tonight's operation. Specific follow-on administrative and surveillance duties were given out, and thirty minutes later the cars all went their separate ways into the night.

Chapter Eleven

One day later, Paul Speed and Mike Carter where just finishing running an evening interior combat session in one of the college shoot houses. As the team started to clean up, Speed pushed the door open to the main hallway and flipped the status switch from HOT to IN USE. Poking at his press-to-talk he announced, "Off comms." into the mic. He peeled off his helmet, set it on the butt stock of the carbine hanging around his neck and fished into his dump pouch under a pile of empty magazines to find his lucky hat, the one he had been issued the day he arrived at The Group. He gave it a good beat across his thigh a few times to shake out any debris or casings then tugged it down snug on his sweaty head. The main door to the hallway of shoot houses opened behind him, and he turned to see a raggedy bunch of plainclothes officers walking his way. Each had a black nylon gun bag in hand. Some had their body armor hanging loosely around their necks. A couple of the guys sported standard goatees and the two women had their hair in loose ponytails. Leading the group was a man Speed knew very well. He had a long greying beard and had let his hair grow but there was no mistaking this face. He was the man who had taught Speed everything he knew about police sniping, not just the marksmanship piece but the fieldcraft as well. The pair had eventually had the opportunity to instruct on a number of sniper courses together. Carter was at the door as well.

The trio of snipers smiled at each other. The former Group sniper put his gun bag down and dropped a backpack from off his shoulder. He handed the keys to shoot house #3 off to one of his teammates as they passed. Head nods and the odd fist bump were exchanged with members of the team that recognized the pair of T.I.G. snipers. Once they were passed, the snipers took turns slapping hands. They exchanged that one-arm style hug while slapping each other on the back. That, "brothers from other mothers," type of hug. The old sniper spoke first, "Hey Speeder, I was on an op last night with Manny and The Gentleman. They had a rookie with them. They tell you about it?"

Speed shook his head and sipped from his Camelback, "Haven't seen 'em yet. They are starting a little later today, I guess because they were out with you?"

"Well. You guys need to get with them and maybe drop a line over to the Intel people. If you're not in the loop yet – they may have stumbled onto a new cell out in the east end." The old sniper said it unemotionally, as he bounced his gaze between the pair and stroked the end of his beard.

"Seriously?" Mike Carter asked. "We have a file we've been working on over the last few months. It's had traction and lost it more times than my old pickup in a snowstorm. You think it might be back on the road again?"

"Looks like it, brothers. We pinned the tail on a donkey last night, and he led us to a very suspicious setup. It's still very preliminary, but the dots are at least visible on the page now." They shook-hugged again, and as their old teacher grabbed his gear he smiled. "Be good fellas. See you out there."

As he turned to leave, the sniper team replied with a coordinated simultaneous shot, "Doubt it!" The former sniper knew the line was coming, and with a smile he trotted off to join his team.

Speed and Carter turned and headed back into the shoot house to help sweep up brass and replace the targets. Parker was sitting on a couch in what was the living room busily typing away on the shoot-house's assigned tablet, filling out their training log for the day. His rifle lay across his lap and his helmet was on the floor propping up his crossed legs. The rest of Team Four were in various states of dress. The load-bearing gear was lined up along the back wall and their rifles were leaned up in front of them with the open chamber facing out for inspection. Speed and Carter doffed their gear and rifles placing them in the same fashion then busied themselves with the task at hand, though both of their minds still raced over the insight they had just been given and how it might fit with what they already knew.

Old Fossil's boots peeled up off the sticky carbon-collecting mat outside the door. He announced himself and stepped in to inspect the range and clear the team to leave. Fossil smiled, as he looked around in admiration at the T.I.G. folks. He saw that everything was as it should be. Nate Syndon and Speed were just finishing a final sweep up and Carter was helping Karras empty the brass bins. The old-timer plopped down beside Parker on the couch and kicked the helmet out from under his feet. Only he could get away with something like that.

"Easy old man," Parker said, "or I'll tell the ladies at the home not to let you have your Jell-O at dinner time!" He smiled – which was rare – and the old range safety officer smiled back like a pair of childhood friends.

"Got a good team here, Glen. Best I've seen through these ranges in some time."

"Thanks Fossil. I appreciate that from you. You get to see 'em all. You're right, though. These are some real good men here."

Parker paused, as Bryan Robinson had decided to come scampering through the shoot house riding a broom like a horse. He had also decided to remove his shirt, which to many would be offensive enough. He was squealing "Yee haw!" as he galloped through the living room and out to a kitchen area and back again.

"Except that one." Parker broke out into full laughter.

The other Hogs pretended to reign in the wild hillbilly that was Robinson to no avail but to a good laugh by all the men. Once the shenanigans were over, Parker hit SEND on the tablet, which filed the training log on the T.I.G. Servers. It also sent a copy to the college Tactical Training Section – TTS for short. They weren't associated to the "tactical" teams or their training at all, but they facilitated all front-line uniform "tactical" training as it was. They were the clearing house for all training that occurred within the facility, whether they were the ones running it or not. The team collected their gear and old Fossil shook hands with the guys, he then took his leave to sign off another range outside. The hogs loaded back into the Sprinter assigned to them for the training today and organized their gear down the middle of the floor. All the operators found seats along the walls and propped their boots up on the bags in the middle. Bryan Robinson took the driver's seat, as it was the custom that the most junior team member did all the shuttling to and from training sites. Sergeant Sommers took the passenger seat and threw his ball hat up on the dash rubbing his head. In the back Speed was sitting next to Parker and taped him on the leg.

"Hey Glen, when we get back Mikey and I gotta follow up on some stuff. We might need to do a little OT off the books – okay?" the sniper asked his TL.

Parker looked over sideways at him from under the brim of his tilted hat. "Sure Speeder. You need anyone else?"

"No thanks, bud, we're good. Just going to take a run out to INTEL and sit with someone there about that file we have going. Depending on the conversation, we may be there for a while."

"No problem. I'll keep the big man in the loop. Just keep me posted on how long you are and we'll make the time up to ya'. Ok?" The T/L advised. He pulled his hat back over his eyes and rested his head back against the wall of the van. The rest of the guys were also dozing off or on their phones. Speed looked across at Carter. He had his head back and was actually snoring already, the van had barely pulled out of the parking lot. Speed kicked at his partner's feet and Carter raised an eyebrow from under the brim of his lucky hat.

"Change into civvies when we get back and then hit the Sniper Room. You good to go over to INTEL for a visit?" Speed asked.

Carter smiled, nodded then closed his eye and resumed snoring.

Speed pulled his cellphone out of a pouch on his vest and thumbed in the passcode. He selected messages and began typing to his wife:

Got a briefing at INTEL after work. Gonna be a little late, but I'll keep you posted.
Love you babe!

Hitting SEND, he watched the message switch status switch to READ. Then the reply bubble popped up indicating she was writing back. The little dots rolled over and over like they were boiling, much like he thought her temper might be.

***

Angie Speed sat in her cubicle on the other side of the city and felt her heart sink when she'd read the message. "Seriously?" she thought out loud.

Her best friend who sat across from her leaned back and popped an earbud out, "You say something Ange?"

"Yeah – but no. I didn't mean too…I don't know."

Her friend knew the look. "Hey how about after work I grab the twins and we slide by for dessert? You know they all love playing together."

This eased Angie's frustrations, and she remembered Paul was the type of guy that was called on for important work. It couldn't always be helped. She was just disappointed because this would be the last chance Camyrn and her would get to have dinner with him for a week while he went on afternoon shift. She had planned a nice roast beef dinner with potatoes and gravy and those little Yorkshire puddings she knew he loved. She had even picked up a bottle of his favorite merlot. Secretly she had hoped that maybe they'd make Camryn a little brother or sister tonight. But like any good police wife, she shifted gears. She adapted to the new situation and said to her friend, "You know what? That would be awesome! But you're coming for dinner too."

"Done." Her friend replied excitedly, and they went back to work.

Angie typed her reply to her husband:

K. Try not to be 2 late. Keep me posted PLS. Mary and the twins are coming 4 dinner. Luv U 2. B Good.

That last part, "Be Good," she had learned from Paul. Cops were always saying "Be Safe" to each other. Paul had told her he hated that saying. He said it was impossible for him to be safe, especially at The Group, because everything they did was inherently dangerous. There was no sense hiding from it, he had said. One night as they were sitting on the deck of the shed, stealing a few moments before he went to work, she had kissed him and said, "Be safe honey." Speed had put his bag back down and looking his beautiful wife in the eyes said to her, "Babe. There is no safe at work for me. So I figure I just gotta be good. Good at what I do. So, let's say that instead okay? BE GOOD."

Ever since that night that is all she ever said to him when he left besides, "I love you."

***

Speed smiled at the reply as it popped up on his screen, and typed back a simple: YOU BET!

He put the phone back in the pouch, leaned his head back returning his thoughts to what his old mentor had just told them. In his mind Speed was scanning all the information on his internal whiteboard.

Before long Speed felt the van slowing and banking for the off ramp, he knew they were close to the base. Everyone else started coming back to life as well. The van rolled up to the black gates, which opened automatically. Robinson wheeled the team up to the appropriate parking bay. The roll-up door was opened by the person working the front desk that day who monitoring the video screens, and the van was backed into the large garage. The team piled out even before it stopped moving. Sommers got out and went to hit the button to close the garage door. Speed immediately began handing out gear and lugging it back to their team room off the hallway in the back of the garage. Inside the classroom-sized team room, gear was laid out on the floor so each operator could move it over to their assigned stall and re-organize it the way they liked. The weapons bags were arranged on the cleaning table in the middle of the room and the cleaning supplies brought up from underneath. Speed and Carter quickly pulled their kit bags to their stalls and hurriedly un-packed. The stereo was thrown on and the hard classic rock that most of the guys liked blasted from the speakers. There were two desks in the team room. One each, for the Sarge and the team leader. Both Summers and Parker were already down to their T-shirts and up to their eyeballs in gun parts.

Speed hung his plate carrier in his stall and as he placed his weapons in his gun locker he called over to Parker, "Hey Glen. You good if we–"

Parker cut him off without looking up, "Get outta here Speed. You've got stuff to do. Take that old man with you." He waved the bolt from his C8 in their direction.

"Heeey!" whined Carter from his stall where he had just finished locking his guns away. The team laughed and Parker looked over at Speed, smiled and shot him a wink. Speed grabbed his uniform shirt off its hook. He retrieved a Steno pad and their project file from the makeshift cabinet they'd built in the room for each operator. He met Mike at the door, and the pair headed down the hall back to main part of the station and around a corner to the Sniper Room. Carter swiped his pass on the sensor and the door clicked open. Speed went straight to the first computer plugged in his secure token and logged on. Next he opened his email and waited while the program came to life dumping a dozen or so new emails into his inbox. As soon as he saw the reply from Detective Gaines, he clicked it open not waiting for the rest of the mail to import.

The email had no subject, and the body read simply, "Call me. ASAP." It was signed with an automatic signature with Gaines' direct line and cell phone number. Speed looked at Carter and asked, "Can you call and see if he's in while I grab the rest of our files? Tell him we are coming right over."

Carter picked up one of the internal phones and dialed the four-digit extension to Gaines' desk while Speed snapped pictures of the white boards and maps. There was no answer at Gaines' desk, so Carter hit '0' and got the Intelligence Section's reception desk.

A young civilian man answered the phone politely, "Intelligence, Mr. Jones. How can I help you?"

"Hey. This is officer Mike Carter from the T.I.G. Can you tell me if Detective Gaines is available?"

"I'm sorry, sir, but he is in a meeting with Inspector Nance right now. Do you want to leave a message?"

Carter replied that he needed the detective to know they were headed straight over to see him and asked that he not leave. The diligent young clerk advised that he would ensure that the detective got the message immediately. Carter hung up and looked at Speed, "All set. Let's change quick and fly out of here. It's rush hour man, this could take a while." Ten minutes later the snipers had signed out one of the unmarked pool cars and were humming up the highway to the Intelligence building.

Chapter Twelve

S trong hit END on his cellphone and walked back through the dirty garage bays. A couple of young kids from Orton Park were there sweeping out the bed of one of the trucks. Strong stopped next to them and told them to tidy up the garage when they were done. Gary Stewart popped up on the other side of the truck, he didn't like Strong's tone. Strong hadn't noticed him working on the far side of the big diesel pickup. Gary wiped his grease-covered hands and smirked at Strong.

"It'd sure go a lot faster if a big guy like you came and gave them a hand, James." He postured to the young muscle-bound gangster.

"Didn't see you there Gary. Funny man. Do I look like I'm dressed for that?" Strong said as he waved at his office attire for the day. His black suede shoes impeccably cleaned and neatly tucked under the cuff of a pair of black slacks. On top he wore a pale blue collared shirt compete with silver cuff links in the shape of maple leaves.

"Well I guess not." Gary quipped. "We'll take care of it. I just have to get the hydraulics working on this bed here first." Strong waved at them and walked away preoccupied by the pinging coming from his phone.

He strode through the reception area with his head down and didn't even look up when the green-eyed Persian girl behind the counter said, "Good afternoon Mr. Strong." He just grunted a hello and kept walking. When he reached the offices, he leaned on the door frame to O'Neil's space. Still texting, he said to his old friend, "Hey bro, I gotta bounce. I have some shit to look after. Cool wit' you?" O'Neil searched him for any clues but saw nothing. This wasn't like his old friend to not tell him what was going on. Just as he was about to ask the question the phone on his desk rang.

O'Neil looked at the display and saw that it was the receptionist. He keyed the speaker button saying, "Just one second baby." Hitting mute, he looked at his best friend staring blankly back at him. "You all right? Need some help?"

Strong tried his best not to betray his own lie, "Naw man. It's just my girl. The pregnancy is getting to her and I'm trying to set up that pad I bought outta town…anyway she's freakin' out man. I gotta go and help get some shit organized. That's all."

The pair of old friends studied each other for a minute. Finally O'Neil said reassuringly, "Ok bro. Let me know if you need anything?"

"Bet." Strong wheeled to his own office to grab the keys off his desk.

O'Neil un-muted the speaker and waved to James Strong as he flew past the door. "What's up baby girl?" he asked the girl on the other end.

"They would like you to join them at mosque tonight. And it didn't seem like he was asking. But I'll make it worth your while." she purred into the speaker.

Well how could he resist that offer, O'Neil thought to himself. "Okay. Tell them cool. We can jet straight from here." He hit END on the speaker and looked up at Gary who had taken Strong's place at his door. "Hey Gary. What's going on?"

"That truck is gonna need a new hydraulic motor for the bed. It can probably wait until later in the winter, just before the spring season. But she's basically shot now. Can't raise it anymore, so it's basically a normal pick-up now."

O'Neil didn't seem too bothered. "Place the order for the part but have them delay shipment until November." When Gary didn't turn and leave O'Neil asked, "Something else Gary?"

Gary Stewart was a smart old man who knew guys like the old O'Neil Facey well. He had learned about them from the days when he'd find himself curled up in a stairwell of some drug-infested inner-city building. Stewart would wake up unsure of where he was, but there always seemed to be that unmistakable stench of urine and puke in the air. Most times, a needle hung out of his arm and his belt, or a shoelace was in his hand. Gary had lain in one of those stairwells more than once staring up at a flickering florescent light tube wishing that God would just take him. Just let the heroin kill him once and for all. Let it seep into his blood, working its way up his arm and stop his heart so that he could finally get away from all this.

Then it actually happened. Fifteen years ago he had just fired up a twenty-dollar hit of black tar heroin and injected it into the only vein he could find between the big toe on his right foot. As he sat back in the corner of that stairwell getting the first waves of the high, something different happened and his heart raced in a way he wasn't used to. Gary's eyes went wide. Everything got very bright. The last thing he remembered was gasping for air and hearing the stairwell door open. An angel hovered over him. She was talking to him, but he couldn't make out her words. Her face was blurry, but he could smell her sweet scent. As she got closer, he could see that she had prettiness to her round face, it was just inches from him now. Her soft caramel skin was calming, and he wanted to go with her wherever she would take him. He closed his eyes and smiled...it was finally over.

Fortunately, or unfortunately, depending on your perspective, he woke up in the hospital to find the kindly round-faced woman at his side. As luck would have it, she was a part time nurse's aide who lived in the building. She was on her way to work when she stumbled upon Gary taking his last breaths of life. She had dialed 9-1-1 and expertly started CPR. This angel had saved his life.

Gary would never forget her, Lateesha Jackson. He seized that opportunity and found himself the help he needed to get clean. He did it the hard way, by choosing not to use methadone to wean off the drugs. Instead, he turned to cigarettes first and kept himself busy gardening. To stay occupied, he worked long hard hours and became very good at his new passion, so much so that he eventually landed two jobs – one for a small landscaping company and the other at the garden supplier where he eventually met O'Neil Facey. Gary felt so strongly about his life-saving event that he had an anvil tattooed on the top of his right foot. Right where he had taken his last hit of heroin and on the top of the anvil he had "Lateesha" written, symbolizing for him that was where it all stopped.

The former drug addict stood staring at the former drug dealer. Gary knew that he had to tread carefully with O'Neil, but the pair had built a sort of uncle-nephew relationship – not quite solid enough yet to offer "fatherly" advice but strong enough to be listened to. "Is everything ok with James?" He wiped his hands on his rag.

"Why?" the young boss had returned.

"Oh, I don't know. It's probably nothing, O'Neil. He's just been acting shady lately. Lots of whispered phone calls out back. But you know what? Let's just forget I said anything. Its none of my business anyway." Gary turned to leave.

"Hey Gary. He just has a lot going on. First kid. A new house in the 'burbs, and finally getting' out of the hood. It's a lot. But thanks. I'll keep an eye." O'Neil smiled at Gary and told him that he and the boys could have the afternoon off.

Gary returned the smile, "Thanks O'Neil. That'll mean a lot to those kids. They've been working hard all summer."

"I know."

Gary wheeled around and walked out to the garage. O'Neil watched through the window, as Gary delivered the good news to his crew. He watched the smiles grow, and the high fives slapped back and forth. They guys turned to face his window smiled and waved before putting their brooms away and heading out the back door.

O'Neil caught her reflection in the window. She had walked in and was leaning back against the wall just inside the door. Her long brown hair curled over her bare left shoulder. He loved the way she smelled. Am I falling in love, he asked himself. Swiveling his chair and trying his best not to look excited by her, O'Neil leaned back and asked her, "What do you want to do for the next two hours?"

She bit her lip and slinked over to his desk.

***

Carter wheeled the blacked out minivan into the Intelligence building's driveway about thirty minutes after they had left the T.I.G. office. They had made good time, and Speed secretly hoped he could make it home before his little girl's bedtime. At the gate Carter pressed the intercom and the male receptionist answered politely again, "How may I help you?"

"Carter and Speed to see Gaines, please." Carter replied. He heard the motor for the big gate start to pull, and as soon as there was enough room, he eased the van through, finding a parking space near the back door. The snipers grabbed their files and made their way to the entrance. As they walked, they each thumbed at their phones putting them on silent. At the door, they hit another buzzer. The receptionist this time didn't speak, just keyed open the door as he watched the pair on a monitor. Seconds later, the snipers stood at the edge of his desk.

The young receptionist looked up and smiled at Carter. "Detective Gaines knows you are coming but is still in a meeting. One of his civilian staff will be right out to take you in."

With that, the door to the back officer opened, and Naila leaned out looking around the lobby. "Speed and Carter?" she asked in their direction.

"Yup. That's us." Carter replied, as the pair made their way to the door. Carter leaned back and thanked the receptionist who simply smiled.

"He had eyes for you, pal."

Speed jabbed at Carter laughing as the door closed behind them.

"It's the gray hair Speeder. He can tell I'm experienced." Carter responded smiling sarcastically.

Naila giggled. As they neared the coffee room, she turned and introduced herself, "Sorry guys. I'm Naila Rashid. I'm one of Detective Gaines' analysts. He's tied up for a bit, but can I interest you guys in some coffee?"

The snipers smiled, as if to say, "Do you really have to ask?" They took her up on the offer and found seats at a small coffee table. Speed was trying to place her name, he'd seen it somewhere, then it came to him. He sat up and looked at her asking, half shouting, "You're the Rashid whose name is all over our Intel Reports for our file aren't you?"

She smiled humbly. "I suppose I am."

Speed stuck his hand across the table, and she took it sheepishly. Naila had a quizzical look on her face. "That's some real nice work there. I think we are actually here to see you. We need to connect some dots here a little more quickly so we can get back in the game. I think something is happening and we may be chasing it now."

Naila looked the snipers over and stood. "Come with me guys."

She led them out of the coffee room and into the back hall. At a double door, she swiped her card and continued to a vacant conference room. In the room she powered on the computer and plugged in her token to access the servers. As the computer ran it's authentication process she sent a text to Gaines and simply told him where she would be and that she would be starting the meeting.

She typed, ARE THEY CLEARED?

Gaines replied, YES. GO AHEAD.

Speed and Carter sat next to each other directly opposite the screen, excited to hear what the analyst was about to tell them. As the authentication process finished and Naila's desktop appeared, both snipers had to lean back at the sight of the blue-eyed Bostonian's smiling face. It took up most of the wall now. "He's cute." Speed joked.

Naila's cheeks reddened with embarrassment as she opened a secure file from the desktop to cover the face. *I'm such an idiot*, she thought to herself, as she hit the remote that turned the window next to the door from clear to opaque and simultaneously turned on the "OCCUPIED" indicator next to the door.

Naila double-clicked on the presentation that she had been working on today and the opening slide blinked up on the screen. She sat down at the head of the table and swiveled her chair to face her guests looking for their reaction. The snipers took a second to digest the title screen with an outward calmness and interest. Speed was leaned back sipping on his coffee and Carter was leaned forward on his elbows. The title screen read:

"ORTON PARK"

Crime Orientation: **TERRORISM**

Project Name: N/A

"Well. That confirms that." Carter said, as he sat back in his chair and played with his coffee cup. The title page made their theory concrete, but somehow it still took them by surprise.

Naila began her briefing. She expertly went through the intelligence in a clear timeline for the snipers. She started with the original intercept and the list of burner numbers they had discovered. She went on to share what the new about the recent conversion to Islam of O'Neil Grant his crew, and the company they had started. Naila continued outlining the relationship that the detectives at Source Management had been building with a middle eastern man who had led them to the Orton Park Projects. She connected how this tied back into the suspicious intercepts. The analyst detailed the surveillance that ended in the stairwell of the building increasing their suspicion. It was all very compelling.

The original intelligence the snipers already knew because that is all they had been given to plan with. The problem was they had been given two addresses nowhere near Orton Park for the original work-ups. That concerned Speed. "So why the original addresses in Rexdale?" he asked her.

"What you don't know is that we've been running a side project here. When intelligence started to dry up after the Train Bombers we began fishing for the next threat. We were given the task of widening our searches in an attempt to predict where that next threat would come from. We listened to everyone from the Freemen on the Land to Greenpeace. Not much in the way of results however." Naila shrugged. "It was getting pretty boring, I'll be honest." She sipped her tea and continued. "Then I hit that first conversation by accident. I'd been listening to some fringe radical extremist chatting up some lady and in that one conversation, well honestly I started daydreaming. I stayed on longer than I would have normally. Suddenly the tone of the conversation changes, and I get a feeling that something is up. The next thing I know is there is a different male voice and accent on the line being invited to prayers?"

Naila looked at the snipers expecting them to have the same level of excitement that she had. They didn't for some reason? She went on and explained, "In my experience, the pattern of speech coupled with the tone of the conversation and the fact that it had been routed by the receiver was enough to start increasing our focus. Well not at first – it took a little convincing. Initially we were focused on what we knew to be the highest demographic of radical conversations we were encountering. They weren't in the traditional Arab neighbourhoods. It was the Somali Muslims we focused on first since we didn't know where the call originated. That and the fact that the second male on the line sounded Canadian, Urban. I hate to say it like this, but he spoke like a young black kid."

Naila was honest and fallible, she was highly intelligent and above all else she was convincing as hell.

Naila continued with expert analysis of her working theory and what they had been able to put together. "We passed you that information a month or so ago about the Taxi Company right?" she asked.

"A little thin though." Mike Carter responded. "Seems like a dead end."

"Okay. Fair enough, but hold that thought." Naila requested.

Continuing, she outlined the connections to O'Neil Grant. Until very recently, they had only been able to say that he was a converted Muslim, that he attended a mosque that espouses some radical extremist views. Intelligence efforts made no connection between him and any of the radicals that were identified at the Mosque until just the other day.

"And then all the chips fall together pretty much by accident the other night." Naila went on outlining the co-incidences of several complex investigations coming together. She outlined the Source Management surveillance that was focusing on an informant giving up a drug dealer. They assumed this was engineered to open up drug markets. Then the strange set-up at the Orton Park building that screamed of something bigger. She connected how there was a takedown being planned to grab O'Neil Grant's lieutenant, James Strong. She shared the intelligence that a hard-nosed street cop had given them about O'Neil going legit and had converting to Islam. Naila told them more things they hadn't heard yet that until today were just pieces of a growing drug puzzle. She told the snipers that sections of the Major Crime Task Force were digging deep into the business dealings and associates at O'Neil's New Leaf Landscaping. They knew he was from Orton Park, and they knew most of his staff were young at-risk youth from the Park. They knew his new girlfriend was a young Muslim girl, also from the Park. They believed she was related to an influential member of the Mosque where O'Neil was attending. And they had discovered that O'Neil had recently been observed spending a great deal of time with the same man the Source Management team had followed home the other day.

"And the Taxi connection is?" Speed asked open-endedly.

"Oh right," the young analyst said, "that's still a little vague. But the one link we have is that the company's drivers are primarily Muslim, a mix of Somali and Arabs. The Arabs come from the same region as our target group. Strangely enough most of the work that company is doing is focusing in and around Orton Park of late."

"Circumstantial." argued Carter.

"Yes it is." Naila agreed. "But in the constellation of intelligence collected, it becomes suspicious. Weak right now, granted, but worthy of exploration."

A sensor beeped, and a magnetic lock released followed by the door opening. Detective Gaines walked in and took the seat at the opposite end of the table. "Sorry for being late gents. I'm Jim Gaines, nice to meet you both. I know you by reputation only, but it's a pleasure." Gaines smiled and nodded at the snipers then asked Naila, "So. Where are we?"

"Well sir, we are basically up to date here. They're read in on all the connections now."

Gaines had just come from a large meeting with all of the other heads in the Intelligence building, the purpose of which was review all of the major cases underway and look for links that the Major Case software had not found yet. The next step would be to begin coordination and consolidation of these investigations. Most were convinced it added up to terrorism. A few holdouts were not. What was the depth, that was the burning question? Was it simply financing? Were they recruiting for ISIS or AQ? Or was there a plan in the works to attack sites in Canada again? Gaines chose not to share the details of this meeting with the two snipers just yet. He wanted their raw impressions of what they had just been told. Gaines leaned back and twirled his glasses around in his hand. much like his mind was twirling all the competing information it had just received. Being the head of the Analysis & Assessment Section meant that Gaines was tasked with completing a full analysis of the information presented. He would set the course of action for the entire Police Service.

Gaines had two hours to prepare his report and he wanted some outside perspective. Let's see if these guys live up to their reputations, he thought to himself, waiting patiently for Paul Speed to log into a second computer in the room. The screen came to life and Speed's desktop took over the screen on the opposite wall from Naila's. Gaines chuckled to himself at the sight of Speeds desktop image – a ferocious looking razorback hog carrying a sword charging across a diamond shaped crest.

Speed let the chuckle go and pretended not to notice. He connected his phone to the computer and downloaded the whiteboard photos he had taken earlier. He organized them in the order he needed and selected the first image. Swallowing hard Speed dove into their theory,

"So we've been doing some predictive analysis on our own over at the T.I.G.. It started right after we were assigned those initial targets in Rexdale. Almost immediately, we noticed that there was a substantive link missing. We knew there were gaps in what you guys had but it was more than that."

Mike Carter jumped in to support his partner. "The picture was too incomplete for us. Between the Team Three guys and us, we started looking through a wider lens."

Speed continued, "I have some contacts over at the RCMP and ran some hypotheticals past them. More like…I dunno…cause and effect scenarios. What would cause this to be true? We tried to stay big picture you know. The trouble was keeping it close enough to the chest that we didn't set off any unnecessary alarm bells with the Feds.

"Anyway, we managed to do that. We set up a mini think-tank at our shop. What *you* may not know is that Mike and I have been working on degrees in world politics with studies on world conflict. Several of our professors are former CSIS analysts and case agents. So we've been able to bounce ideas off them as hypotheticals in our classes as well." Speed paused and waited for a second. For the first time in a long time, he was unsure of himself. He knew he was no intelligence analyst, but he was not a dumb guy either, and neither was his partner. Carter leaned back smiling and winked at Speed. That was all the reassurance he needed to get started, as if they were lying on the range plinking targets at a thousand meters, Paul on the trigger and Mike on the scope, both trying to read the wind and the temperatures to make the right call on the corrections so that bullet would drop right where they wanted it. He could hear Carter whispering the wind call, "Half value left to right at 5-10. Give me two left for wind." Speed would reach up slowly to the windage turret and without taking his eye off the target slowly turning the dial. Feeling and counting the eight clicks that made up the required two minutes of angle called for by Carter. That would aim the bullet slightly into the wind. He'd whisper back to Carter, "Sniper ready."

Carter would reply, "Spotter ready."

They would wait for the most opportune second to fire, spending those preceding seconds slowing their breathing and relaxing muscles. Mike would be lying to his right, side to side and slightly behind him with the spotting scope just barely above the height of his shoulder on the same line as the barrel of the rifle. Speed would slowly release the safety with his thumb and reacquire his grip, his trigger finger coming to rest lightly against the metal trigger right at the joint between the first and second sections.

When Carter felt the time was right, he would simply whisper, "Send it." They had shot so many rounds together that before one of them could actually get the word "it" out of their mouth the round would be leaping from the barrel. As the gun settled, Speed would calmly work the action bringing the bolt back, extracting the empty casing and loading a new round. He would scan the target looking for a follow up call from Mike. In this moment, Mike's wink was like a silent "Send it."

The sniper started again continuing to explain how their little think tank had built a plausible theory on this terrorism case. The snipers had been collecting bits and pieces of intelligence from other un-related operations they had been on in different parts of the city. They had noticed all the same things that the different intelligence sources had seen, primarily, that the Somali Muslims in the city did not have the organizational where-with-all to organize any sort of attack. In fact, what the snipers had witnessed over the summer was that many of the Somali factions were fighting amongst themselves. Several shootings had occurred between the power groups in the community. As such, their power base had been significantly weakened by a series or arrests. Secondly, the snipers had surmised that a power struggle of a different kind had taken place in the east end of the city specifically in the Arabic Muslim neighborhoods. Traditional drug dealing was being pushed aside as immigrants from the middle east rose in numbers in what were once traditional "Black" housing projects. The snipers had seen handouts in many of the old buildings looking for people to convert to Islam. Asking people to join one of the many new mosques being built. Then one of the Team Three snipers had a theory after noticing an interesting occurrence over several nights. What he had noticed was that there were always several of the well-known Orange and Green taxis parked at east end mosques.

Speed explained, "The unique thing about that is, those cabs are all from the Westend. Most of the drivers live in Rexdale and could go to Mosque in Rexdale. They are primarily Somali but have chosen to attend Mosque in the other end of the city with Arab Muslims. Why? After speaking with one of our old team guys who is on the undercover protection detail, our theory is that the real threat is being built and organized in Orton Park by whoever lives on those upper floors. They have built a relationship with the Somali community to use them, for what purpose we don't know. We also think that they have been converting local gang members to do all the heavy lifting in whatever they are planning." Speed paused for effect. "We think the big picture motivator is some connection between a regional issue that will be specific to wherever these people are from. That along with an ideological desire to see the West out of the region. Canada has been very active overseas lately in support of U.S. and U.N. operations."

As Speed clicked off the last image, he looked over at the analyst and her boss. Naila sat smiling and nodding in professional approval of their analysis. Gaines' expression was neutral. Speed sat back down next to Carter and swallowed the last of his coffee. The room was quiet – dead quiet. Gaines kept twirling his glasses. Then he sat forward in his chair folding the glasses and setting them aside. He looked back and forth between the two snipers, then Naila.

"Holy shit!" Gaines said, stunned, "They always say you Group guys are nothing but knuckle-draggin' thugs. Shit are they wrong on your two guys' accounts. I think Naila would agree that is some top tier analysis. I should tell you that the meeting I just came from basically came to the same conclusion. But you guys did this all on your own with no interest in the intelligence game. That is amazing."

Carter looked at him and rebutted his last statement though, "No interest in the Intelligence game…maybe…but we have an interest in protecting the people of this city."

Gaines shook his head humbly and reached out to shake their hands. "I know you do fellas. All I meant was it's not in your primary job description is all. But it is now. I'm going to ask for your help on building the intelligence picture here. I – *we* – can't take this to command just yet. Not until we dot a few more I's. Because when we do they will have to take it to the National Security folks on Ottawa. We want to make sure the package is complete."

"So where do we come in?" Speed asked, confused. "I don't think you want us to come do analysis for you."

"No no." Gaines laughed. "What I need from you guys is street level intelligence. We can't get close enough to these guys to know who they really are. I wonder if your skill sets might help us with photographing the players in that building. Can you do that?"

"Easy peasy." Carter said. "In fact, we've already been scouting out possible OP's along with ingress and egress routes."

Gaines was pleased at how well this was coming together. "I'll send the operational request to your bosses today. Can you start on it this week?"

"We'll start on it tomorrow." Speed confirmed confidently.

Chapter Thirteen

A team of hardened drug cops sat around their downtown office. They were going over the final details for this evening's takedown. The team was acting on informant information provided to them by the people over at The Source Management Unit. All they knew was that a large shipment of crystal meth was to be arriving tonight in Orton Park. It was likely headed for the Crip crew who ran those buildings even though they had been mostly quiet this past year. There was no information on who was making the drop or who was picking it up. So the plan was to tail the usual suspects. There were three potential targets for drug dealing in that area that the team knew of. James Strong was one of them. Earlier in the day a small surveillance team had picked him up at work and were spinning him back toward Orton Park now. The road boss for this team was a veteran of eight years in drugs and thirteen in total as a cop. The detective in charge had spent five years in the drug squad before being promoted a little over a year ago. She had recently returned to run the team for the east end of the city. Her guys gulped down the last of their coffee and polished off the Timbits as she finished the operational briefing from the corner of her desk, she sent them on their way with modest expectations for success.

"Ok gents, play safe but don't play fair." she joked with her standard line. "I'll start up the case here in the event we get someone and need warrants for cars or apartments." Looking to her road boss, she smiled and nodded.

The team filed out the door and she clicked on some old school rap that was live streaming off the internet. As she soaked in the melodic baseline of an Eric B and Rahkim classic, she reached for the phone and dialed the Tactical Intervention Group. The station operator answered and transferred her to the operational team Sergeant. Once she had the man on the line she let him know that the pre-arranged operation was underway. She passed along a cell number where her road boss could be reached and the team Sergeant reassured her that two of his guys were in subdued order of dress and already in the area. He gave her the cell number for one of the operators and a radio channel as well. The two heads of the different teams thanked each other and hung up.

The detective went back to work typing and hit #2 on her speed dial. As it rang, she paused the music stream. An older female voice answered the line. "Judge Bates."

"Afternoon, your honor. It's Detective Hammersmith calling from the drug squad."

"Hello Allison! Good to hear your voice again! How is it going being back?" The seasoned Judge asked. The pair caught up briefly and the detective cut to the chase, "Your honor I have my team out on a case looking to seize about six kilos or crystal meth. I was wondering if you'd be available to review warrants for us later should we run into some side issues we need to explore?"

"Of course Allison. Anything for you my dear. I'll be at the office for about another hour. After that you can call my cell phone. Do you still have the number?"

"I do your Honour. Thanks very much again!"

"Good luck." the judge said as she hung up. The detective clicked on the portable radio sitting at the edge of her desk in time to hear her advance spin team advising that James Strong was back at the building on Orton Park. She also got texts from two confidential informants that told her that her other two suspects were heading downtown. Strong was becoming a clear front- runner in the suspect category tonight.

***

Strong spun the big black sedan down into its parking space, ashing out the last of his joint. Blowing the smoke from his nose he climbed out of the car reaching behind his back to adjust the pistol. He pushed the door closed and made his way to the elevators. When he reached his apartment, Strong went to the spare room and slid a dresser away from the wall. Behind it a safe had been sunk into the drywall. He spun the lock by memory and pulled the door open. From inside he removed the $60,000 in cash that he agreed upon with the supplier earlier in the day. Strong tossed it into the black backpack with the other $75,000 he had *borrowed* from the business today. He eyed another item in the safe and decided to take it as well. But before picking up the item, he slid on a pair of latex gloves that were resting on top of it. Strong then lifted the firearm out and slid the chamber open to see if a round was ready to fire. It was. Strong carefully placed the gun in a paper bag and put that bag and the money in a backpack. Unlike the one on his waist already, this gun was a ghost. It had no traceable serial number and had not been fired in any criminal instances, making it untraceable to any other crimes. It was the perfect gun to use in a drug rip. The gun gave him an extra sense of confidence, especially if he needed use it tonight. With his bag packed Strong locked the safe and slid the dresser back into position. He peeled off his work clothes and headed for the shower, he turned on the water letting it run and heard his cellphone blip. He scooped it off the counter and read the message:

1 Hour

Strong didn't bother to reply. He just dropped the phone back on the counter and stepped into the shower.

Raahil's phone also chimed up on the 21st floor, his message said:

Trap set. 1 Hr.

Raahil typed back in Arabic smiling to himself then set the phone on the little coffee table next to him on the balcony:

Excellent.

He continued sipping at his coffee eyeing the parkette in the courtyard where tonight's drama would be unfolding.

Thirty minutes later, Strong was getting fidgety. He sat in the big leather chair in his living room flipping channels on the big screen TV that took up most of the small room's wall. He really should have someone with him for security. But he had promised O'Neil he was staying out of the game. In fact, he should not even have agreed to make the transaction at the building. O'Neil would find out for sure. The request to host the deal at the building had come from his supplier who wanted it to be on secure turf. So, stuck in the predicament of not wanting to let O'Neil know he was back in the drug game and not wanting the supplier to think he was ripping off O'Neil, which would surely have gotten back to him, here he was. Waiting to make a major drug deal on his own in the one place his boss was sure to find out. He was as nervous the first time he'd stood out on a cold corner to sling dime bags. Strong reached down and anxiously fixed the cuff of his baggy jeans one more time. The buzzing phone in his pocket made him jump when it went off in the pouch of his dark hoodie. He pulled it out and read the message. "Time to go to work." he whispered out loud to himself, he stood pulling the backpack over his shoulder. The drug dealer checked the pistol one more time, tugging the back of his sweater down to make sure it was covered. Out of his apartment he turned left to the stairs and out into the evening dusk. The sun was just about to set in the west, the nearby minaret's loudspeaker signaling the call to prayers. Strong looked over at the parkette he and O'Neil had paid for and built. He smiled to himself and made his way over to a bench in the back where he could see anyone approaching. He and his old friend had planned for this specific bench to be installed in this exact spot for this exact reason.

"Eyes on T1, the Strongman is at the circus." A surveillance member announced over the radio channel.

Strong checked his phone again,

5 MINUTES the silent message read. He scanned the surrounding area and saw nothing, no one. "Perfect." He thought.

***

O'Neil slid his shoes off setting them aside at the door. His large canvas court shoes stood in stark contrast to the cheap slip-ons that occupied most of the space. He looked around sheepishly for anyone he recognized and eventually made eye-contact with Mustafa Mahmood. The Mullah's brother waved him up to the front. O'Neil made his way through the congregation greeting several elders who smiled strangely at him as he went. When he reached the front row Mustafa shook his hand. Kissing his cheeks he said, "My brother would like you to take a place of honour in the front this evening as he leads us through prayers." Mustafa pointed to a prayer mat in the first row next to his own. O'Neil felt something in the air. He wasn't sure exactly what it was.

***

"He's on the bench. Checking the score on the big screen." was the cryptic reply. In her office the detective was listening, visualizing Strong sitting on the bench in the playground checking his phone.

"Taxi pulling up out front." another member of the team reported. This could be the drop they were waiting for.

***

The evening prayers were started with the customary greetings, as the Mullah took the podium. He looked down at O'Neil and smiled in an almost sinister way. It took O'Neil off guard and added to his growing suspicions. Then Mullah began, and the congregation followed along in the prayers. As O'Neil bowed and raised his hands to his face, he couldn't shake the feeling that something was going wrong.

***

Strong watched the thin man slide out of the back seat noticing both the taxi driver and his passenger were Somali. The driver was quite young as far as cab drivers went in this town and he was dressed in that ridiculous prayer moo-moo. The passenger approached him on a direct route without any regard for his surroundings. Money-hungry snake, Strong thought to himself.

***

"Target two is a male Somali about six feet. Got on a blue zip-up track jacket and jeans that look like they're two sizes too big." reported the officer over the radio.

Another member of the team chimed in, "He looks like that world champion sprinter from Jamaica. Let's call T2 The Runner."

The team scribe for the night got on the air, "Ok we have The Strongman and The Runner about to meet in the circus."

The Runner slouched on the bench beside The Strongman, as several sets of binoculars watched them from the shadows. At the same time, Raahil had gotten a text from the taxi driver saying:

Drop made. I'm waiting for him.

Raahil was sitting on his balcony watching the pair through the rungs of his balcony as he looked down on the bench in the courtyard. The sun sank deeper and deeper into the horizon, much like the fate of the men on the bench.

***

The Somali man looked at Strong. "Do you got the money, man?"

Strong rolled his eyes, "Of course fool! You wanna count it right here stupid?"

"Show me – show me!" the Somali man said getting excited.

Too much of that khat, Strong figured to himself. He reached between his legs and opened the top of the backpack so the money could be seen. The Somali man reached for it, and Strong caught his wrist. He squeezed tightly and locked eyes with the man. "Not so fucking fast asshole." Strong growled in a deep low voice. "Show me the product!"

Strong let go of the man's hand so he could open the duffle bag. Strong counted six identically sized Zip-lock bags each holding what looked like a kilogram of white crystalized substance. He smiled. Reaching behind his back he drew the firearm and swiftly drove the muzzle end right into the Somali's forehead. It knocked him clear off the bench and onto the ground. The man grabbed at his forehead wailing, Strong kicked him over onto his back. He stared straight down at the cowering Somali with his arm extended, the sights of the ghost gun lined up on the man's face.

***

"Gun gun gun!" came the excited announcement over the radio from the drug team member with the best vantage point. The Road Boss spoke calmly so everyone would hear and not question his order, "Takedown. Takedown. Takedown."

***

Raahil was surprised when he saw Strong drive the gun into the man's face. He typed to the waiting taxi driver:

The young taxi driver put the car in drive. He switched on his available light and slowly cruised out of the driveway. Two small black cars raced in past him with wild-eyed goatee wearing men behind the wheels.

***

The drug team converged on the gun-toting drug dealer and the soon to be dead Somali man with guns drawn, their blue raid jackets emblazoned with the Police Service's crest and the word "POLICE" across the chest and back. The silver badges swung from the chains around their necks and identified them as cops, even if the ballcaps, goatees, T-shirts and tattoos hadn't done it already.

"Police, don't move!" they were shouting, "Get on the ground! Drop the gun!"

Strong froze for a second, slowly releasing his grip on the pistol. It dropped making a loud slap and thud as it landed square on the Somali's face and bounded to the rubberized surface of the parkette. He grabbed the two bags and started running as fast as he could for the closest building. The cops chased after him, but he was getting away. As he pulled the stairwell door open, he looked back over his shoulder to see where they were. The cops had stopped running and were standing over the Somali man. One was handcuffing him while the other secured the gun. The rest just stood there smiling at him.

He never saw it coming. The 6'5" 235-pound operator from Team Two and his partner had been waiting in this ambush position as planned, just in case of this eventuality. When the drug team announced he was running their way, the operators had waited with guns up for him to come running through the door. But as the giant T.I.G. operator watched the door opening he saw that their target was looking the other way. The operator seized a rare opportunity for a dynamic finish. In one motion, the operator flicked the safety switch back to SAFE and slung his rifle behind his back. He then squatted and took two powerful strides forward. On the third stride, he drove his shoulder into Strong's stomach, simultaneously grabbing him behind the knees and riding him slightly upwards. The operator continued driving and scooped Strong's legs to one side. He then violently changed the angle of their momentum and drove Strong fast and hard down to the ground with an earth-quaking *thud*. The double leg takedown sent the two bags straight up in the air, and the whole courtyard went deathly silent. Birds were scattered into the nighttime sky. The bags landed, and a puff of cash blew out of the open zipper of one.

***

Raahil had to cringe and leaned away from the violence of the tackle. Initially, he thought for a second that Strong might actually get away. But when the police stopped chasing him, Raahil quickly realized there was an ambush coming. He could feel the air come out of the whole courtyard when Strong hit the ground. Luckily, it was rubberized or else his head would surely have been smashed open.

**

O'Neil's eyes shot open in the middle of prayers at the mosque, like the ground had just moved beneath his kneeling body.

**

The enormous operator pulled his shoulder out of Strong's diaphragm. He listened for a minute, as the man lay there motionless with his eyes rolled back. Unconscious. His partner was right on his heels during the tackle and slid around beside him in a cover position with his rifle up on threat. Seeing none, he relaxed and tucked the stock of his rifle into the crook of his arm, the muzzle pointing straight up, and with his left hand he keyed the press to talk on his shoulder. "One in custody, I'd say." Chuckling.

**

A white light took over Strong's vision, and initially that was all he could see. As he regained consciousness, he could see the monster standing over him. He had a rifle in hand pointing down at him, and the man was straddling his torso. Suddenly a sharp pain in his rib cage snapped James Strong back to the real world. He gasped in deeply, trying to catch his breath. His back arched, and hot pain shot through the ribs on his right side. His lungs felt like they were stuck together, and they refused to inflate. Strong rolled onto his side below the behemoth and looked to the sky. As he did, he saw Raahil on the twenty-first floor balcony. He was looking down on him like some sort of puppet master. Strong was sure he could see him smiling.

The officer looked down at Strong and patting him on the back asked politely, "Sir, would you kindly roll over and place your hands behind your back?"

Strong wheezed out an answer between gasps for air, as he clutched his rib cage, "I can't. Ribs broken."

The other operator keyed his mic again, and stated calmly, "Medics up." Within seconds, a pair of tactical paramedics rounded the corner dropping their bags next to Strong. The two T.I.G. operators stepped back into cover positions and began scanning the notorious buildings for additional threats.

The smaller of the two keyed his mic once again, "Gonna need your RB over here?" he said as a pair from the drug team made their way over to collect their prisoner and the evidence.

A phone rang in the larger operator's pocket. He retrieved the phone and looking at the screen answered the call."

As soon as the detective heard the call for medics on the air, she'd dialed the number that had been given to her for the operators. "How bad?" she asked.

"Looks like maybe some broken ribs." the giant operator on the other end replied sheepishly.

"Ok. Here's the drill. You and your partner return to your base. Notify your sarge on the way in of the potential for a Special Investigations Unit mandate here. I'll make the appropriate calls to the division and the Duty Inspector." She hated this. These guys would potentially be raked over the coals for protecting her people against an armed drug dealer. No one was dead. No shots fired. Just one asshole eating a big ol' piece of Karma cake.

The two T.I.G. men gave custody over to the drug squad team. They exchanged some handshakes and headed for their van in the rear lot. In the distance, they could hear the sirens from the marked cruisers responding to contain the scene for the potential investigation.

The smaller of the operators was on his phone again to their Sergeant. "Yeah. The guy basically ran right into us."

"Yeah Sarge, the detective is making those calls."

"Yup we're on the way back. Stood down – I know, I know." He threw his hands up.

When they reached the van, his partner looked over the roof of the vehicle at him and apologized, "I'm sorry man. I should have just grabbed him maybe."

"Are you kidding me? That was awesome!" his partner exclaimed jumping a little as he said it.

Chapter Fourteen

O'Neil physically shook his head, trying in vain to get rid of the strange feeling that had come over him during prayers. Something was wrong he could feel it in his soul. The Mullah Ameer had led the prayer session tonight, his reciting's stung like hot blades jabbed into O'Neil's subconscious. There was both a subtlety and a directness in the man's words, if that was even possible? He felt that the Mullah was both pensive and enraged as he addressed the congregation. That was also strange, the masjid seemed more full than usual. There were many new faces tonight, and with everything else was causing a burning in the deep spaces of his brain. As O'Neil followed a small group of elders to the basement, the lights grew dimmer as did the conversations, getting darker with each step below ground. There was more direct talk about ideologies and how to "strike back" than he had heard here before. As they rounded the final corner into the basement the dim hallway poured into a large banquet room. This room was well lit and stood in stark contrast to the hallway, and the mood inside the space was festive. O'Neil recognized some of Ameer's men standing guard at the entrance. As he went to enter Mustafa gripped him by the elbow and directed him to follow the Mullah into a second smaller room just to the left of the main door. O'Neil's heart stopped beating for a moment, and he felt his legs grow weak for the first time since he was a child. He walked into the room and saw the black flag with white Arabic writing hanging from the far wall. He recognized it, having seen it in too many YouTube videos showing the beheadings of "infidels" in the Syrian desert and other ISIS propaganda films. O'Neil looked at the black-clad men standing on either side of the flag holding AK47s. Bright LED recording lights came on, which caused the men to squint awkwardly. The camera operator turned and smiled a crooked tooth smile at him, and it was then O'Neil started to worry he was about to be beheaded. He stood in the doorway frozen. O'Neil had long ago lost sight of what those initial meetings had meant, when there had been talk of payback and retribution. He had forgotten about the fixed books where several kilos of fertilizer had been skimmed off his deliveries every month. But it was all making sense. He had been used. His men had converted, in good faith, to Islam. His drug trade and access to weapons were used to arm and fund this Mullah's plot. Maybe O'Neil had wanted to forget, subconsciously shoving the thought to the back of his mind, blinded by the new found ease of legitimacy.

Mustafa motioned him to a chair along the back wall. O'Neil sat with an obvious relief that at least he wasn't going to lose his head. A small group of women fussed over Ameer's clothing and applied a thin layer of makeup to the parts of his face not covered by his beard. O'Neil sat mesmerized in the corner of the room. He was trying to become one of the shadows. He desperately wanted out of this room that was becoming a metaphor for the contract he was trapped in. His heart was racing and it caused little beads of sweat to form along his brow, sitting at the edge of his prayer cap. The young criminal mastermind could not see a way out of this. He was fully trapped, physically boxed into the corner next to Mustafa and mentally checkmated by the Mullah.

As the scents from the hookahs hung in the room a strange energy set in. Ameer adjusted the black keffiyeh and his robe and leaned back in the chair set between the two guards. When he was comfortable, he nodded to the cameraman who raised a hand to silence the room and pointed at Ameer to begin.

"As- salamu alaykum. My name is Ameer Muhamed. I speak today for the millions of Muslims being oppressed by the powers of the West. I speak today for the Independent Islamic State. For the Caliphate. Too many of our requests for the West to remove their troops from the Middle East have gone unanswered. Too often our words and protests lack action. We need action to support these demands. The heads of too many Westerners have been lopped off to the blind eye of your governments. The time for action on your soil has come again, and this time – insha'llah – you *will* accept our demands. You will leave the deserts of the Middle East and let our people manage our own affairs, as we have for centuries before you and as we will continue for centuries after you."

"Now, I am not a stupid man. I am reasonable, and I know that it takes time to reverse the engines of a big machine like a Western Army of occupation. So, I offer this message as a warning to begin making preparations for your withdrawal. If in one week's time we have not seen evidence of this preparation and you have not released a statement to the same effect, we will release a second message outlining the consequences of your inaction. It is our hope that you will see this warning as a sign of faith and act accordingly.

Do not underestimate out resolve. We are prepared to kill Canadians and to die ourselves in sacrifice to our cause. Allahu Akbar!"

The red recording light blinked off and the cameraman stepped back. He looked around the room, which was eerily quiet. Out of the deepest shadow in the room came a softly spoken phrase. Almost like the man saying it wasn't sure of himself, "Allahu Akbar." Everyone in the room turned to see who it was. Others started to repeat the phrase, quietly at first, but the chant started to grow. As it grew, Ameer smiled. He didn't have to look. He knew it was O'Neil. As the chant reached a feverish pitch, everyone was looking in his direction. The man stood and moved from the shadows into the edge of the circle of light being cast for the taping. "Allahu Akbar, Allahu Akbar!" O'Neil shouted with the group. He glanced over at Ameer and caught him smiling. O'Neil bowed his head in reverence to the Mullah as the small crowd circled him and carried him out to the larger hall.

Trays of baklava were laid out, and fresh dark coffee sat in several large urns. The hookahs were carried into the hall and placed around the room. O'Neil found his green-eyed friend serving plates of pita and hummus and other Arab treats. She smiled, as he took his plate but kept her place and said nothing. O'Neil sat in a corner with Mustafa and two men he did not know sharing a hookah filled with some of the sweetest Persian hashish. Out of the corner of his eye, he saw Raahil enter and lean into the ear of one of the security men. The guard nodded and immediately left the room. Raahil and O'Neil caught each other's eye, Raahil waved to the younger man then turned and left. Mustafa distracted O'Neil by handing him the pipe and with that inhale O'Neil melted back into the celebratory atmosphere.

Back in the video room, several copies of the short film were loaded onto flash-drives after some quick editing. Ameer oversaw all of these final details. The drives were carefully prepared and then sealed into envelopes at a sterile table in the corner. The man there looked more like a surgeon or an infectious materials handler. Raahil watched from outside the door and shook his head, as he had thought this whole exercise was a little much. But he reminded himself that he wasn't running the mission. Once sealed in the envelopes, five couriers were summoned to the door. Each wore rubber gloves and was handed an envelope, then verbally given an address. They were told not to use any phones or computers to look up routes to their addresses until they were well away from here. They already understood that instruction, but it was repeated nonetheless.

The couriers immediately set off on the first stage of this mission. Courier #1 would be making his way to a little strip mall in north Scarborough, where he would hide the envelope behind the toilet tank in a local coffee shop. He then would find a seat and wait for a message on his phone. This text would direct him to contact the Orange and Green Taxi Company requesting they pick it up. The instructions to the taxi company would be to deliver the package to Channel 7 News, whose office was just around the corner.

Courier #2 was headed to a trendy downtown restaurant, where he would make a similar drop and phone call. This package was to be delivered to Channel 24 in the city's heart.

Courier #3 was also heading downtown. His package was for Channel 3 News. He would be going into a back alley gay bar off Jarvis Street where they knew there would be no cameras. This package would be left with the bartender, in exchange for $200, for pickup by an executive from Channel 3 that the Mullah's group knew to be a patron of this bar.

Couriers #4 and 5 had much different targets for their packages.

Courier #4 was delivering a package that would be sent directly to the Police Service. He would make his drop at a little café in the northwest part of the city. There this courier would expertly slide the envelope behind a seat cushion for pick up. It would be delivered to No. 23 Division in Rexdale. Ameer was sure that it would be quickly delivered to the Intelligence people.

Finally, Courier #5 was heading out to the airport. His was to be the trickiest of all the drops, and he knew there was a good chance he would be detained shortly after. So his detail came with an escape and evade plan to get him out of the country quickly. This courier would check in for his coach seat on a flight to Turkey, by way of London Heathrow. Once he was at the airport, he was to hide his envelope in a garbage can in the public washroom in the main portion of the airport. The courier then would immediately head for the airline's counter. Having gone through the check-in process on-line he should have only a short wait. He would get an express pass through security thanks to a false flight club member status. With any luck by the time the packages were delivered, opened, analyzed and the authorities contacted he would be halfway across the Atlantic. Once his first boarding call was made he would initialize all the pickups by sending a text to the couriers. Courier #5's package would be delivered to the RCMP office at the airport.

The terrorists had timed out the notifications and the drive times in several dry runs. They expected a small variance in the timings, but their instructions were for each to be dropped at 9 p.m. Five simultaneous deliveries. That marked the beginning of their plot to exact a measure of revenge on Canada for Its involvement in the Middle East conflicts.

***

In an off-puttingly bleak police interrogation room, in a police station not far from the celebrating Mosque, James Strong sat uncomfortably. He held his ribcage, like he held onto hope that some lawyer would burst through the door, slowly sipping a cold can of coke. The same two detectives who had followed Raahil home now sat across from him. The tall lean muscled detective with the easy way about him was taking the lead. His female partner was sitting back in the corner chewing on the little green spigot from her overpriced coffee. She sat cross legged waiting to take notes, she nervously spun a pen between her thumb and forefinger. They had been back at the station for about an hour since getting Strong cleared by the hospital. He still hadn't said a word. The tall detective stretched his legs out in front of Strong cramping the accused into a smaller corner of the room.

"How those ribs feeling James? The pain killers kick in yet?" The detective asked genuinely.

"I'm a be a'ight. Your pig got lucky is all." Strong was trying to be as confident as he could. Both detectives laughed out loud. The big man laughed the hardest.

"Oh okay. Should I bring him in here so you can have a second shot at him?" This time the detective's tone was mocking.

Strong winced at the words and he curled a little in his chair. "Man, fuck you." Strong retorted as strongly as he could. It was pretty weak really, and he knew it.

The detective sat forward and slapped Strong on the leg.

"Look man, we can play this tough guy game all night. Or we can just get to talking about where those drugs came from and what your connection is to the guys who brought them to you?" As he leaned back, he looked Strong in the eye. His experience told him there would be no confessions that night. The detective had read Strong's file and knew he hadn't risen to the number two seat in the Orton Park Crips by accident. So the moment Strong started to kiss his teeth in response and before the first syllable of the word lawyer could leave his lips the detective had snapped forward. With surprising speed, he had slapped the pop can out of Strong's hand. It sent brown pop splashing all over Strong, as it crashed into the wall. The female detective jumped in her seat, dropping her green stick and gasped. The big detective stood violently over the table. Towering over Strong. He kicked his chair backwards, it took a bite out of the wall beside his partner. The detective glowered down at the criminal who sat without motion or expression. Inside, however, Strong screamed in pain as the surprise of the violence had made him tense up. The pain in his ribs was overpowering the medicine. The big angry detective stormed out of the room and slammed the door behind him shaking the room again.

Outside the door, the detective took a deep breath and looked to his left at the Drug Squad road boss who had been watching through the two-way window. The detective uncurled a big toothy smile and calmly stated, "If she doesn't crack him after that, he ain't gonna crack at all."

Inside the room, the smell of the soda pop still hung in the air. The only sound was the fizzing of the remaining Coke in the aluminum can. The little detective didn't move from her chair. She was giving Strong lots of room to feel comfortable, like he had just won a small victory. She even sat in a sort of curled up position, as if she was also frightened by her partner's behaviour. After a few minutes, the detective uncurled herself a bit and looked Strong in the eyes. "Shit. Are you okay?" she asked warmly, opening a crack ever so gently.

The two detectives outside the room watched through the one-way glass as Janine went to work. This was her wheelhouse, she had debriefed dozens of gang members. Her trick was that she didn't rush into the "good cop" role. She built it up patiently. Compassion came first, to put him at ease, then she would build up the trust. "Go slow." she kept telling herself. She stayed in her corner on the other side of the room and continued to relax her posture, baiting Strong in as she did. Her shoulders eased down, and her hands rested on the arms of her chair, her feet on the floor. Janine's posture was slightly welcoming, but not overly so, otherwise the game would be given away. Janine let the tension slowly squeeze out of the room under the door. She waited another five minutes without a word between them, and then she started.

"Is it okay if I call you, James?" she asked in a soft inviting voice.

"Yeah sure. Whatever." was Strong's still irritated response.

"James, can we start over? I'd like to hear your side of this story."

"Screw you lady. You guys already broke my ribs, and that guy goes off on me! Tries to intimidate me! Oh hell no."

There was a sting in his voice, Strong was still angry and she thought this might take a while. "I'm not going to apologize for my partner James. You'd know I was lying anyway. He's had a long day, and well, he has a short temper to be honest. But he's not in here now. So why don't we just go over some background information. What's your home address, James?"

As Strong answered the routine questions, the hook was set. Janine started the slow jigging of the bait in the water, gently and rhythmically, getting him to answer questions she already knew the answers to. But it got his lips moving, and when that started to happen, she knew she had him. If she timed the crucial question just right, he wouldn't be able to help himself. So Janine jigged away, question by mundane question. After about an hour, she paused and set her pen down on the table. She had been inching her way closer to him with every other question or so. Strong sat leaning over the table paying attention. A rapport was building. When she had put the pen down, Strong wasn't sure what was next. But he was no longer fearful of the consequences, and strangely his ribs had stopped hurting. The detective looked across at him and rubbed her forehead.

"James, I have a pounding headache, so I'm going to step out for a second to get some water, do you need anything?" she asked. The little detective chose her words carefully. *Need* instead of *want*.

"I could use another Coke and something to eat maybe?" he asked. The hard look on his face tried to mask what was happening underneath. Strong didn't realize it, but he had just committed himself to telling her everything.

The small female detective stepped out into the corridor and smiled at the passing custodian then turned to her partner and the drug detective. Her smile said, *He's mine. Just a matter of time now.*

The custodian continued to the washrooms down the hall and stopped her cart to fold out a yellow caution sign at the door. She then grabbed a garbage bag and went inside. She did a quick scan of the washroom and saw that no one was inside. The small round woman retrieved a cellphone from the pocket of the modest purse around her neck, which hung over top of her burka. The cleaner keyed in a preprogrammed number followed by a brief text:

He is talking.

She pressed the SEND button and powered down the phone. The custodian removed the battery and SIM card, tossing the later into a toilet and flushing it. The battery she tossed in with the garbage bag she had removed from the receptacle. As she reached for the door, it swung open, and her heart jumped in her chest. A female uniformed officer pushed through the door and was also startled, her ponytail swinging as she apologized and headed for the closest stall. The stall door closed, and the custodian breathed a quiet sigh of relief. She continued her duties around the station, as if nothing had happened. At the front desk area, she went out to the public foyer and dusted the old trophy case. Next to the case was an electronics recycling drop box and she slid the phone from her pocket into the bin. She relaxed and finish her shift without another person even noticing she had been there.

Raahil was sitting with Ameer in a corner of the reception hall enjoying some of the dark coffee. The phone in his breast pocket buzzed signaling an incoming message. He excused himself and left the group moving to a quiet spot along the wall away from prying eyes. When he read the text he was instantly enraged but managed to keep his composure. They knew this might happen. In fact, they had planned a contingency to mitigate their exposure to risk when it did. He opened a new message and typed:

You're on.

***

The text caused a cellphone to chirp, and a banner popped onto the screen, the receiver picked the phone up from the desk and read the new message. Calmly the reader stood and gathered a black knapsack near their feet, checking a pistol over for a last time the receiver typed back a reply:

OTW

Chapter Fifteen

The two operators from Team Two had been left to sit in separate rooms. Departmental policy mandated that they were separated from one another and not allowed to talk to anyone except a Union representative or lawyer. Each of them waited patiently with their rep, to hear if the Province's Special Investigations Unit would be invoking its mandate. The larger of the two operators was just finishing off a medium sized pizza, his large boots resting on the corner of the conference table when the boss walked in. Vincent Wismer leaned in the door and looked at his man who seemed none too worried about the delay. Wismer nodded at the union rep, the man taking the cue gathered his things to leave.

"Big fella, I just got the call from the SIU Liaison. It appears they have decided not to invoke the mandate although it meets their threshold." Wismer told the inwardly relieved operator.

The union rep stopped and shook both their hands then he continued for the door as the giant stood and looked at his boss. "I'm really sorry sir. I should have pulled back on that one. I'll be more careful…"

Wismer cut him off sharply, "Hey! Don't you ever apologize for protecting yourself or your brothers and sisters out there. That's what I pay and trained you for. When justified, you employ every tool to the fullest of your abilities. Do you understand me? I'm proud of you kid, damn fine job!" He said it loud enough for the rest of the building to hear. As the big operator moved through the door thanking his boss, Wismer stopped him again, "Besides, I just watched the takedown video…that was highlight reel quality. Terry Tate type stuff."

The big operator smiled and headed down the stairs to the team rooms looking for his partner. As he wheeled into the Team Two room he saw Speed and Carter sitting there. His partner was telling the story of the takedown and stopped as soon as the big man entered, "Sorry big fella, I had to tell 'em!"

Speed and Carter jumped up and shook the big man's giant hand, "Nice job brother!"

"Wanna watch it, pal?" called his partner from under the TV the team had hanging on the back wall.

Without hesitation, the big man grabbed an energy drink from the fridge and stepped over the back of the couch onto a vacant seat. Carter sat beside him, his partner in a recliner to the right working the controls and Speed standing behind the couch.

The Team Two operator selected the proper input and queued the proper file. The screen blinked and a frozen image appeared. Carter and Speed studied the screen trying to figure out what neighbourhood it was in. As the video started to play, they could see that it was shot with a camera from a park behind a playground, an area between two buildings. A lone male came from the building on the right. He made his way diagonally across the screen to a bench on the near left. As the camera pans in and out to give perspective Speed recognizes the two white buildings, "Is that Orton Park?"

"You bet." the big man says over his shoulder.

"The target is James Strong from the OP Crips. We are set in an ambush position in this stairwell." The big operator reached forward and points at the stairwell door just visible in the shadows to the left of the screen. They all watch the meeting followed by Strong's muzzle punch. Then the takedown team comes rushing in. The camera pans to follow Strong as he ran to the door. Then everything seems to go into slow motion. The anticipation of what is about to happen building with every one of Strong's steps. They watch him stop and open the door while looking back over his shoulder. When the door starts to open, you can just make out the two operators moving in the background. Then in a flash, like the video was suddenly thrown into fast forward, Strong is crashed to the ground. All four of the men sitting there jump back from the TV at the hit. "OH DAMN!" someone shouted. They replay it several times in slow motion and increase the perspective in order to see all the intimate details. At one point, they can see Strong's head whip around violently then slam onto the rubberized ground. The bag of money flying through the air hitting the ground and burping up a dozen or so bills. They can see the second operator moving to cover his partner with a look of surprise on his face. As they rewind it a fourth time to watch Strong drive the Somali man in the face with his muzzle, the perspective zoom is still on its highest setting and Carter sees something deep in the image.

"Pause it!" he yelled. "Go back to when we first see this guy coming from the round-a-bout at the front." He directed the controller.

"What did you see Mike?" the operator asked obviously confused.

"There. See what I see Speeder?" Carter points at the image on the screen and looked at Speed with wild excitement in his eyes.

Speed stares at the image of the Orange and Green taxi sitting there. What looks like a young Somali man is behind the wheel. Goosebumps pop up on Speed's arms. He knows what this means, they were right. "Guys can we roll it forward slowly and keep this taxi in the frame?"

The controller zoomed the perspective back out and played it forward in slow motion. Just as Strong stands over the Somali after knocking him off the bench the cabbie slowly drives away. He freezes the image one last time as the door number for the cab comes into view – 1023.

"This mean something to you guys?" the two men asked Speed and Carter.

"It sure might." Carter replied guardedly.

"Can we get a copy of this?" Speed asked the big man. The big operator wasted no time and popped the flash drive out of the TV, he plugged it into the computer on the Team Leader's desk, downloaded a copy, and emailed it directly to both Speed and Carter.

"If you're asking Speeder, then it has to be important. There you go." They shook hands and parted ways. The Team Four snipers swiped their way into their own team room just down the hall and Speed jumped into a seat at Parker's desk. After logging into the computer he opened the email containing the video and immediately clicked the FORWARD button, Speed puts Gaines' name into the recipient list and Cc'd Naila. In the subject line he wrote simply: Connection?

In the body of the email, Speed outlined the origin of the video and its connective issues. As soon as the message was gone, Speed opened another new message and addressed it to both Sergeant Sommers and Glen Parker:

Subject: Surveillance Operation Request

Sarge, Glen,

Mikey and I have been requested to assist Intel with an urban surveillance operation. The timeline is open-ended, but it is in relation to the previous file we've been working. We would like to get started tomorrow afternoon if that works for you guys and our team manpower? It is important that we launch on this as soon as possible.

We will both be available tonight on our cell phones for questions.

Thanks in advance,

Paul Speed

SWT#4

Regular guy

Speed hit send and signed off the computer. He looked over at Carter's stall and watched him checking gear. "All good?" he asked.

Carter didn't look up from the MAWLS laser as he slid new batteries into the device and function tested it against the floor in front of his stall. "All good bud. Batteries swapped on all the Giz'. Just need the okay to launch I guess?"

Almost on cue, both of their phones chirped at the same time. Speed and Carter looked at their phones and read the same text messages, from Parker:

Green light. Keep me in the loop for a security detail. Be good.

That message was followed quickly by a message from Sergeant Sommers:

You're GTG. Stay connected with Glen. Be good lads.

The snipers smiled at each other and headed for the door. They would be back in early tomorrow to write up the Operational Plan and submit it to the staff sergeants for approval. Once the OP was approved, they would be off and running. For now though, time to get some sleep; the next few days may not hold much of that for the pair of police snipers.

Chapter Sixteen

In the lunchroom, Strong's interrogators searched for something for him to eat. The vending machines were empty of anything worthwhile. One of the rookie members of the drug team happened to walk by head down, headphones on.

His boss reached out and grabbed him by the shoulder strap of his black backpack. "Hey Jamal. Where you headed?" the detective asked.

"Oh hey boss. I was just lookin' for you. Gonna make a coffee run for the guys, you all want anything?" the surprised rookie offered.

His boss fished into his pocket and pulled out his corporate credit card, issued to the detective for times just like this. "Put the coffees on the card and grab a cold cut sub from the deli next door for our friend here." the detective said waving his thumb in the direction of the interview rooms.

The young drug officer waved the card over his shoulder replying, "You got it, boss."

The detective turned and looked at the partners from Source Management. "Good kid. I like him, he's gonna go places."

The young officer got in his car and headed for the coffee shop up the street. He placed the order for a traveler box of coffee telling the employee he would be back to pick it up. He then strolled into the deli next door. Inside, he smiled at the old European woman behind the counter and ordered the best smoked-meat sub she can put together. He asked for simple toppings, but as an extra he requests sundried tomatoes. He happily paid with the boss's card, thanked the woman, and ducked back into the coffee shop where he picked up the box of coffee. The young officer slid back into his car, the smell of the smoked meat mixing with the aroma of fresh coffee in an awkward stew. Before he headed back to the station, the officer opens the submarine wrapping. He moved the tomatoes, hiding them under the meat hoping Strong won't look there. The officer knew something that the other's did not, information that had been shared with him many months ago by a member of Raahil's security team. They told him that Strong had a severe allergy to dried fruits and vegetables. The officer remembered it had something to do with the sulphates that were used to preserve them. If eaten, it would likely send him into anaphylaxis and stop his heart within minutes. The information had been passed to him as part of a contingency plan should the need arise to eliminate Strong. The terrorists had always believed Strong was the weak link from the local street gang. The officer rewrapped the sandwich and fired up the engine.

Back in the station, the rookie dropped the coffee off to his team first, and then brought the sub to the detectives waiting near the interrogation room. "Best I could get," he told them, "smoked meat on a fresh white bread stick." He handed the sandwich off to the female Detective.

"That's great, thanks." replied the female detective with a wink, as she took it. She grabbed another can of Coke from a table and turned toward the interrogation room. The young officer returned the credit card to his boss and went to rejoin his team; there was still a mountain of paperwork to finish. He purposely chose a desk where he would be able to watch the door to the room Strong was in, anticipating the chaos. He sat stroking his substantial beard, while he quietly prayed to Allah that the food would be enough to do the job.

***

The female detective came back into the room and placed a submarine sandwich bag on the table in front of Strong, along with the Coke can and a bag of chips. Maybe it was because he was so hungry after the adrenaline dump of this evening, but that sandwich smelled like nothing he had ever smelled before. He was salivating at the aroma and the scent of that smoked meat circled him like the perfume of a gorgeous woman. He smiled and thanked the detective as he pried open the can of pop with one hand and took a long sip. The detective sat back down on her side of the table. She blew gently across the top of a fresh coffee, which also smelled amazing. He would make her get him one of those next. Strong unwrapped the sub and pulled open the top bun. The aroma of the warm smoked meat wafted into the room again, just like lifting the lid on a pot of his granny's oxtail stew. He scanned the toppings trying not to look like an ingrate.

The detective started talking again distracting him. "So, when did you come over from Jamaica again James?" she asked sounding sincere enough.

James placed the top back on the sandwich and raised it to his mouth. He was about to bite but stopped to answer, "About twelve years ago, when I was eight. I came with my grandparents. My mum was a drug addict and died over there, and my daddy…well I never even really knew him, so." The sub hovered inches from his mouth while he spoke. His body was curled over the top edge of the sandwich in anticipation of the meal. The moment the last word left his mouth, Strong took a hefty bite. He didn't even notice the large piece of sundried tomato he was chewing on, he was so hungry. Strong swallowed

140

without hardly chewing at all. He kept eating one large bite after another. He was ravenous. About to take his fourth bite, Strong felt the tingling and swelling in his throat. He knew what was happening but was powerless to stop it. His eyes went wide with panic, and he dropped the sandwich on the table. His throat was closing rapidly, and his heart was racing. Strong was gasping for air, clawing at his throat. He slapped at the table and begged the detective with his eyes for help. No words would come out of his mouth though.

***

The female detective watched in amazement as Strong devoured the sandwich. She knew she had him right where she wanted him. Suddenly he dropped the thing and grabbed at his throat – wild eyed. She put her coffee down and asked if he was all right? Strong was no longer able to form words due to the swelling. It was all he could do to gasp for air. His right hand was holding his throat and his left frantically pawing at the sandwich, ripping it apart.

"What's wrong James?" There was panic in her voice now.

The door flew open. Her partner immediately grabbed Strong from behind thinking he was choking. The big detective tried in vain to perform the Heimlich maneuver while Strong still scratched at the sandwich. Strong managed to pull the meat off revealing the hidden culprit. His heart racing and eyes bulging, he pointed frantically at the sundried tomatoes.

The female detective shoved the table out of the way and yelled, "He's having some sort of allergic reaction. He can't breathe, and is going to die if we don't get him an EpiPen and to a hospital fast!" She watched his neck and face swelling and his skin turning a dark shade of mahogany.

The drug detective grabbed the phone of the wall outside and hit the page button, yelling into the receiver, "Anyone with an EpiPen to the interrogation rooms, NOW! And someone call an ambulance!" He hung up, his team crowded around the doorway to and see what was going on. The two Source detectives kept trying to help Strong find some oxygen. But Strong's heart was already being over worked by the stress of struggling to breathe. At 8:45 p.m. his heart could not take anymore and it stopped beating all together. He took two final gasps of breath and with his eyes fixed on the female Detective he passed. Strong's final thoughts were panic and anger – the fucking police had just killed him.

The two detectives slumped against opposite walls. They sat staring at each other, stunned. The big detective kicked the table in frustration sending the submarine scattering all over the floor. He looked down at Strong's bloated face and neck and yelled, "What the fuck!"

A chubby middle-aged policewoman elbowed her way through the crowd, out of breath. She was waving an EpiPen in her hand. She froze at the door.

The female detective looked up from the floor and saw the tell-tale blue and orange tips. She smiled at the woman, "Thanks. But it's a little late." A moment later, a pair of medics pushed through the crowd into the room. They attempted in vain to revive Strong. Their supervisor stood at the door noting their actions, as he dialed a base hospital. The detectives pulled themselves off the floor moving to the hall outside the little interview room's door, waiting for the inevitable. Janine typed a text to her boss letting her know about the death in custody and what would become an SIU investigation. The drug team detective gathered his people in a corner and kept them there quietly waiting for the Officer in Charge to arrive.

The on-duty Staff Sergeant arrived at the commotion and leaned in looking at the two detectives from Source. "Dead?" the OIC asked.

The medic supervisor hung up his phone, "Just pronounced by the doc' at Sunnybrook."

The old Staff Sergeant looked around and with a nod of his head motioned the three detectives to the coffee room.

Inside he asked, "Okay. Who is wearing this?"

The detectives looked at one another. Then the large detective from Source Management spoke up, "Staff, Janine and I were the only ones in the room. The drug guys were all in the other office working on their reports."

"Who brought the food in to him?" the Staff Sergeant inquired?

Janine looked up at the drug detective. She gave him that look that said she didn't want to put his guy under this kind of pressure. The drug detective spoke next, "Unfortunately boss, my junior guy bought the food and delivered it to these guys. He never went in the room, though." He hoped the last part would be enough to keep his man in the clear.

"Jesus Murphy." the Staff half shouted. "You and you, subjects," he said pointing to the two Source detectives, "and all your people are witnesses. I'll find separate rooms for you two." He again pointed at the Source Management Detectives. To the drug detective he shouted, "And you get your people writing their notes."

With that done, the Staff Sergeant set about organizing the scene until one of his sergeants could come in and take over. The body was covered up, the area sealed off and uniformed officers put on crime scene duty inside their own station. The staff sergeant notified the Operations Center, who in turn would notify the liaison officer. They in turn would notify the Special Investigations Unit itself.

The young rookie drug officer managed to send one more text before having to destroy this phone. He typed:

Gone.

He kept his head down and his hoodie pulled up, hands under the edge of the desk. He worked smoothly to remove the SIM card and battery, easily snapping the SIM card in half. Then he dropped the battery catching it between the toes of his shoes so that it didn't clatter onto the floor. He let it slide off his toe under the desk, pushing it as deep under the desk as he could reach. The young officer got up and slinked off to the only washrooms available; they were in the foyer. Teammates patted him on the back in consolation, as he passed. He sure seemed to be taking this pretty hard, they were thinking. When he entered the foyer, he passed a used electronics receptacle. He casually dropped the phone in just as the front doors swung open. The SIU Liaison Inspector burst through and blew right past the drug officer, straight through the access doors looking for the staff sergeant. The young officer went to the bathroom and washed his face and hands, as he whispered to himself anxiously, "Allahu Akbar" over and over.

Chapter Seventeen

A decorative fountain splashed water against the sides of a large slab of black granite in the middle of the newly renovated terminal. Off to one side sat a slender Arabic man. He was professionally dressed in a well-tailored dark blue suit and crisp white shirt. He wore no tie, and his collar was open. The man's beard was closely shaven, and his hair was cut neatly. He sat alone in a row of seats next to the fountain that occupied the dead space between the various gates. The man watched with interest as a toddler tried reaching into the fountain's pool, the little girl's mother slowly losing patience with each splash of the water. The man reflected inwardly at what he knew was going to happen in the next few days and smiled. The mother caught him smiling and mistook it for amusement at the toddler's antics.

"God, I wish she'd just settle down for a nap. Sorry if she's bothering you."

"No bother at all, love." He used the British accent he had been practicing for months. The mother scooped up the child and returned to her gate across the way. The child wailed loudly over her mother's shoulder reaching for the fountain as they left. Sitting there he stared at the bubbling fountain, the terrorist courier listening for the chimes of the intercom. He craned his ear toward the ceiling to listen.

"Attention all passengers on flight 1098, Turkish Air, bound for Turkey via London Heathrow. This is your first boarding call. All passengers needing assistance or those travelling with small children please make your way to the gate now. Thank you."

People stood and gathered their carry-on bags. The courier punched a passcode into the lock screen on his yet un-used phone. He opened the text application and thumbed open one of five draft messages. He selected each in sequence hitting send. Each message contained a different set of instructions, one for each of the Orange and Green drivers. These were the details of where and how to pick up their packages. The man waited for confirmation that all were delivered, and then he sent one last pre-loaded message, to Raahil:

My Taxi is ordered. I will see you later.

Once the text was delivered, he powered down the phone. The man calmly removed the SIM card and placed it in his pocket. He went over to the fountain and sat on the edge staring down into the pool like he was making a wish. The man placed the small black smartphone on the edge next to him and sat fiddling with a Loonie in his right hand. When the second call for his flight came he stood purposely knocking the phone into the darkness at the bottom of the fountain and tossed the Loonie in after it. No one even batted an eye. The man turned and made his way to his carry-on bag. As he stooped to pick it up, he snapped the SIM card between his fingers and slid it into a garbage bin next to the bag. Grabbing the handle he lifted the bag over his shoulder and headed for the gate. At the counter the man reached into his breast pocket and removed his boarding pass, the pleasant attendant tore the end off and handed it back to him with a smile saying, "First class, Mr. Almadi. Row 6, pod two." The man smiled and nodded, taking back the pass and boarding the plane.

He found his first-class pod and slid into the luxurious leather seat kicking off his shoes. A steward came by and offered him a glass of wine. He took it graciously and put his nose to the rim of the glass. As he leaned back in his seat, he inhaled the deep notes of mahogany and black cherries from the merlot. The warm dark aroma helped to ease his nerves. The man reclined and continued scanning the passengers boarding behind him in hopes he could pick out any air marshals. At the same time, he eyed the air crew for any sign that the authorities were about to hold the plane back. But all the passengers looked the same. They were all tired people settling in for a long flight. The boarding was as routine as any other, and eventually the cabin door was closed and secured. The man felt the plane switch to its own power and the pressure build in the cabin. The plane eased away from the gate, and as it started to move the co-pilot came over the intercom. She introduced herself and the pilot and hoped the passengers would enjoy the almost seven-hour flight.

At the same time the plane was making its way out to the end of the runway for takeoff, five Orange and Green taxis were arriving at their pick-ups. Two drivers fished in behind toilet tanks, one inside a seat cushion, another in a garbage can, and one from the hands of a bartender. The taxis then scattered across town to their destinations. A short time later and at roughly the same time all five of the deliverymen walked into the lobbies of three news stations and two police stations. The airplane rocketed down the runway and the big jet lumbered into the night sky at 9:05 p.m. and this courier was gone forever.

***

O'Neil was still in shock, as he drove back to the buildings. He had given them the appearance that he was committed to the cause, however, internally he was scrambling to find a way out. His green-eyed girlfriend sat silently staring out her window beside him.

The rain that beat down on the car as they drove made it hard to tell where the red and blue flashing lights were coming from. As they neared the buildings the lights were reflected off the tall white buildings, but two hundred meters up the road O'Neil took his foot off the gas. He let the car coast past the news outlet trucks and police cars. At the driveway a policeman was posted along a line of crime scene tape. The officer's hat was pulled low, and the collar of his raincoat was pulled up in a losing battle to shield his neck from the driving rain. O'Neil pulled close to the tape and the officer leaned down at the window.

"Residents only." the uniformed officer said very officially, apparently not recognizing O'Neil.

"I live in fifteen. There." O'Neil said in a passive reply and nodded toward the building. The officer pulled out a memo book noted the time and took down O'Neil's name and apartment number. He lifted the tape and announced into his radio that a resident for building fifteen was coming through. As he drove O'Neil wondered what the hell could have happened. Had one of his former crew been murdered? He couldn't see the telltale orange blanket covering a body anywhere. The police seemed focused on the courtyard. But there was nothing there except for some of those little yellow numbered evidence cones.

O'Neil turned right into the driveway for the underground access that was actually under the southern building off Lawrence Avenue. He drove slowly through the crowd of cops looking at their faces. Their features blurred by the rain streaming down the car's windows. He did see one face he knew. Standing by the front door to his building O'Neil saw officer Immes under the awning. Immes nodded solemnly at the car and touched the brim of his hat in a salute. The gesture seemed odd to O'Neil and yet somehow it was not entirely out of place. O'Neil accessed the garage and made his way inside. He drove down and then back toward his own building and his numbered space. As the car rounded the last concrete column he saw Raahil and two of his security men standing next to the parking spot. O'Neil coasted in between the concrete pillars and killed the engine. His girlfriend was out of the car before the engine had even stopped running. She made her way to the elevator door without looking back for him. O'Neil didn't bother to call after her. He was still trying to figure out the bigger problem that seemed to be in front of him now.

"What's up Raa'?" O'Neil asked.

"We need to go upstairs to speak with Ameer. But we cannot be seen together, so you will go with Jameel first, and I will follow shortly." Raahil wasn't asking – he was ordering now. O'Neil nodded and stepped off with the security man conspicuously in tow. In the elevator the security man inserted a control key and switched the elevator to *Service*. He held the button for the twenty-first floor closing the doors. O'Neil could feel the beads of sweat building on his back. When they reached the floor it was as quiet as a library. The men stepped off the elevator and turned toward the Mullah's apartment their footsteps echoing in the silent hall. Another security man stood in the Mullah's doorway apparently waiting for them. The trio entered and O'Neil was ushered into a back bedroom that served as an office, there he found the Mullah seated at a large mahogany desk.

The room smelled of old paper books and shisha. A laptop sat open in front of Ameer next to an antique desk lamp. The walls were one continuous bookshelf holding texts in both Arabic and English. O'Neil saw books on economics and religion as well as works of poetry and novels. He recognized some of the authors, Clancy, Patterson and Child; he was a fan of the action thriller genre as well. O'Neil also noticed two ornate copies of the Koran and one paperback copy of the Bible. The Bible was on the edge of the desk and had many colourful tabs sticking out of its pages. O'Neil found himself at the edge of an expensive looking Persian rug taking in the room when the Mullah, without looking up from the laptop, asked him to sit.

"Have a seat O'Neil. Would you like anything? Coffee, tea, soda, water? Anything?" he asked in a warm gentle tone.

"I'm good." O'Neil replied. "But what's goin' on?" He probed cautiously. He was trying to process everything that had gone on tonight, and it was about to get more confusing.

"O'Neil. I had to be the one to tell you this…" The mullah paused for effect. "I could not let the police try and spin this to you. It HAD to come from me."

"What did? What the *hell* is going on man?" O'Neil was panicking, and he didn't like this feeling.

The mullah got up from behind the desk coming around to the front. He sat back against the heavy frame and placed a hand on O'Neil's shoulder.

"The police killed James tonight O'Neil. They murdered him in a police station while they interrogated him." The mullah watched the words as they ran around O'Neil's head taunting him. O'Neil's expression changed from scared to utter disbelief. He sat frozen in the chair.

"What? How? What do you mean, what are you talking about? He was going to his new place to set some shit straight with his girl?" O'Neil protested, speaking quickly, the panic obvious in his voice. But somewhere inside himself he knew it was true. He knew this was the strange feeling he gotten during prayers.

The Mullah slid the laptop around to face O'Neil. On the screen was a picture of the badly swollen James Strong lying on the floor of a small room with a table and two chairs. Several other people's legs were in the image, but O'Neil could not discern anything from that. He reached out and grabbed the laptop in disbelief. If he hadn't seen James' signature diamond earrings and the tattoo on the top of his right hand, O'Neil wouldn't have recognized him at all. O'Neil dropped the laptop onto the desk and fell back in his chair this time slumping in defeat.

The Mullah offered him some words of comfort, a passage from the Quran,

No soul perceives what it will earn tomorrow, and no soul perceives in what land it will die. Indeed, Allah is knowing and acquainted.

But he didn't let the phrase linger for long before he dove right into the heart of the meeting.

"You see why we need you, O'Neil. It's not just Muslims they are after. They have wronged you and must pay. We will ensure you have your pound of flesh, my young brother." the Mullah went on for another half hour, preaching and consoling. All the while O'Neil kept nodding and agreeing, but he was not really listening. His mind was trying to figure out a way to verify this story and turn this situation around. When the Mullah was finished, O'Neil stood abruptly and thanked him for his support. Leaving he gave the standard "salam" over his shoulder as he steamed for the door. He passed through the hallway, and the security man at the door turned his back to him to open it. O'Neil saw the bowl of burner phones on the hall table and he quickly reached out, plucked an old flip-phone off the top and pocketed it inside his prayer gown as he walked. O'Neil left the apartment telling the security man in the elevator to take him to the 4th floor. After the short ride, he walked off the elevator and keyed his way into the apartment.

The apartment felt cold. It was empty and dark. O'Neil pulled his prayer cap off and threw it at the kitchen counter, as he walked to the living room. He fell down onto the leather couch and sat in the darkness. The hardened criminal doubled over covering his

148

face and cried like a child. All the years of being a hard-ass and suppressing his feelings had caught up with him. Every locked away tear burst out, he could not catch his breath and he sobbed violently in the darkness for thirty minutes. Alone. There was no one to comfort him at the loss of his longest and best friend. O'Neil clutched at his ribs that were starting to ache with the sobbing and felt the phone inside his gown. He pulled it out and sat staring at it for a long time.

Finally, he decided what he had to do. He reached out and flicked on a lamp, wiped the tears from his face, and sobbed one last time then abruptly stopped. He put that weakness away, that was it, the gangster's grieving process complete. The old O'Neil was going to have to come back now. The gangster opened the phone and powered it on as he retrieved a tattered business card from the drawer of the coffee table. There was a handwritten phone number on the back. O'Neil hesitated momentarily, his thumb hovering over the buttons, he ran the scenario through his mind one last time. Then he punched in the ten digits and held the phone to his ear.

***

In front of the building, police officers and SIU investigators scampered about under black umbrellas and rain-soaked hats, and a cell phone rang in someone's coat pocket. Tim Immes pulled the phone from his raincoat and looked at the screen not recognizing the number. He was about to hang up and thought better of it. Maybe it's one of the homicide detectives, he thought to himself. Immes thumbed the accept call icon and put the phone to his ear. "'Ello?"

***

The small-framed cab driver approached the counter at the City's largest television news outlet and eyed at the young receptionist busily typing away while babbling into a headset connected to her impressive desk phone. The dismissive stout woman looked up and him and mouthed the words "One Second" with a raised index finger and inflated lips. He smiled back with a ghoulish, misaligned smile that made her look twice. The receptionist noticed the manila envelope in his hand and stuck out hers with her palm up as is if to say *Give it here*. The cabbie placed the package in her well-manicured hand, and she paused her phone conversation, "Sandra, hang on for one second will you?" And looking ever so interrupted, she asked the cabbie, "Do you need me to sign for it?"

"No miss." The cabbie turned and made his exit, still smiling that hideous smile as he left. The receptionist turned the envelope over and saw that it was marked simply NEWSROOM.

"Sandra, I gotta run. See you at dinner hun'." She hung up and pressed the speed dial for the News Director's office. A woman answered and was told that a package had arrived for her. She said she would be right out and hung up. The receptionist placed the envelope on the edge of the tall counter and went back to surfing the web for the latest gossip on her favourite Hollywood celebrities. A minute later, the thirty-something news director came through the doors and picked up the envelope. She turned on her heel and went straight back through the doors into the busy newsroom looking the envelope over as she did. The woman could feel what seemed like a small USB device inside and tore the edge off the envelope. A field reporter interrupted her looking for some advice, "Am I okay to quote this guy?" he said pointing at the screen?

The news director pulled her glasses onto her nose and leaned into the reporter's computer screen. She read the reference notes the reporter had taken in the field and thought about the repercussions. When done, she stood up removing the glasses, "I think we'd better leave him as an unnamed source for now. Better for him; we don't want those guys going after him. Ask editing to digitize his face and voice okay."

"Thanks." the reporter said turning back to the screen and picking up the desk phone. The news director pushed through her office door with her shoulder. She plopped down in her antique leather chair and swiveled back in front of her screen. The device was plugged into the slot on the side of the large display, and she waited for the icon to appear on her desktop. When it did, she double clicked it, and a window appeared listing the one file on the device – a video file with no label information. She was about to click it open when her phone rang. She hit the speaker button, "Hello?"

"Jamie. Did you just get a package delivered? A small USB with a video file on it?" came the excited male voice on the phone. It was her counterpart at the city's second largest television news outlet.

"Actually, yeah I did. I was just about to open it. Why? What's up?" she asked more intrigued now.

"Okay. You have to watch it. You're not going to believe what's on there, though! You can open it, we had our IT guys scan ours first and there's no malware. I'll stay on the line."

The news director double clicked the file and watched her screen turn black. Then the video started. First with a shot of the black and white flag associated to the Islamic extremist groups from the Middle East. Next the image transitioned to some very well put together footage from what appeared to be terrorist training camps. There were

150

exploding cars, flashes of 9/11 images, and beheadings. Then the screen faded back to blackness. The music died off. Slowly the screen brightened and a man is seen sitting on a throne-like chair with two large men beside him holding assault rifles. Her mind raced and she scribbled notes on a pad as fast as she could without even looking down. The experienced news investigator wasn't even processing what she heard – she was just trying to capture the words in case the thing self-erased or corrupted. Her ears were perked at what this man outlined, who he was and what his group wanted. She wrote the timeline down and circled it thinking to herself, "That's impossible." When the man made his first reference to Canada, she immediately hit the call button for the on duty producer.

"My office. Right now." she barked. The producer knocked and entered headset dangling from his belt. The woman simply pointed at her screen. As the producer came behind the desk and they all listened as the man started to list the consequences of inaction.

"This is real time? Here?" asked the Producer incredulously.

"Looks like." said the voice from the phone's speaker.

"It's Paul over at Channel 24." the news director informed her producer.

"Can anyone verify if this as legit? Who are these guys?" The Channel 24 News director asked.

"I tell you what, Paul," the woman offered, "let's agree to work together on this. I'll make that call for now and get approval from the station manager shortly. It shouldn't be an issue. You get your people tracking down everything they can about this group. My people will start working on regional analysis."

Her counterpart and friend was in instant agreement.

"Sounds good. I'll do the same here. Can we agree to split the field work and interviews?" he knew she would go for it. They would cut Channel 11 out since they had been playing dirty at news scenes lately. They hung up the phone, and both news directors immediately pulled their people into planning rooms. The teams began reviewing the footage again and set the framework for the night's leading story.

***

Similar reactions were had at both the 23 Division Major Crimes office and the RCMP Airport Detachment. At 23 Division, the MCU detective immediately called over to Combined Forces Operations – Intelligence Section. He spoke with the detective on duty.

"I'll be right over." the detective said immediately. The Intelligence Detective grabbed a secure laptop and headed for the Tech Crime Section down the hall. Sticking her head in she queried the group, "Anyone available for a job right now? It's urgent." A senior officer in the back stood up and grabbed their coat and laptop bag, "I'm free." They headed to the parking lot. The Tech officer noticing that the lady from Intel seemed to be in a big hurry.

At the RCMP detachment, the duty NCO took receipt of the package and analyzed the USB device. Being much more suspicious, he contacted their Internal Security Section first. The member on the other end suggested the NCO insert the USB into a stand-alone laptop. The NCO ran a malware program on the laptop, which found nothing after it scanned the file. The member hung up as the NCO double clicked the file. As it opened his head fell into his hands. He couldn't believe what he was seeing. The seasoned NCO scanned the quick list of numbers under the blotter on his desk. He picked up the receiver on the desk phone and dialed the number for the Integrated National Security Enforcement Team (INSET). The duty NCO advised the member on the line of what he had received and was told that an INSET investigator would be there within the next two-hours. The NCO was asked not to play the file any further for fear it may self-erase and to not remove the USB device from the laptop. In addition, the NCO was advised that this was officially a National Security "Protected C" investigation. As such, he was under orders to say nothing to anyone in the office about the video's existence.

Chapter Eighteen

Immes stood on the edge of the rain. "'Ello." he said again, this time more forcefully.

"Immes?"

Immes recognized the voice immediately. He couldn't believe what he was hearing. Why now, after all these years, after all their run-ins? Immes suddenly realized he was holding the phone out in front of his face, staring at the screen in disbelief.

One of the other cops nearby asked, "Everything all right there Timmy?"

Immes waved him off and stepped into the rain, away from the growing cluster of cops who were looking to stay dry. "Yeah." He replied to the caller. "O'Neil?" he asked just to be sure.

"Yeah man. We need to talk."

"You name the time and place, I'll be there." Immes knew this had to be a big deal if O'Neil Facey had finally decided to call him.

"Okay. Listen, you know that old burger joint out in the west-end on Dundas?"

"Yeah I know the one. I thought you liked Johnny's out here better?"

"Too close to home, man. Can you be out there in an hour?"

"I will make it happen. I'm on this scene here now, but I'll find a way."

"Okay. Cool. Hey Immes."

"Yeah?"

"I appreciate this." He wanted the cop to know this was a legitimate meet.

"No problem."

Big Tim Immes pressed END and immediately stepped out back out of the rain looking for his sergeant. As he wiped the rain drops off his face, he found the woman standing in the lobby of the building. She was in a conversation with one of the suits. Immes was fiddling with his hat as he walked over and tried to get the sergeant's attention. When she finally looked his way, she could tell it was important. "Whaddya need Immes?" the veteran sergeant asked.

"Sarge, I just got a call from a source who may have information about all of this." Immes made a big wave of his hat at the complex and looked up at the ceiling as he said it. The experienced Sergeant got the meaning immediately and nodded.

"Okay. Be safe."

Immes thanked her and donned his hat heading back into the rain to find his scout car. Jumping in he raced back to the station. He would need to change into his street clothes, he couldn't meet O'Neil in uniform.

O'Neil hung up the phone and sat for a minute staring at the black display. Then he forced himself to stand. He made his way to the kitchen and in the back of the pantry he fished out a bottle of Jamaican rum hidden away after he had "converted." Five separate times, Raahil and his security team had come and searched the apartment for items of sin. They caught him once but never again. The bottle was disguised as malt vinegar, and they had never once looked at it. O'Neil spun the top off and took a long hard pull straight from the bottle. He swallowed hard, squinting as he fought to keep the strong alcohol down. He went to his room and removed his prayer gown hanging it in the closet. He stood in front of the dresser scanning the open drawer, eventually settling on a pair of conservative looking jeans. He pulled on an old plain white T-shirt and grabbed one of his flat-brim hats from the shelf along with a black Gore-Tex jacket. Everything smelled brand new. He had almost forgotten what that smell was like. He put on one of his modest watches, nothing to showy and decided to pass on any other jewelry. O'Neil was going to be a long way out of his territory, with no back up, and he had enemies where he was going. Before he left, O'Neil removed the bottom left drawer and reached into the void where he felt the familiar cold grip of his pistol. He preferred the old Colt 1911 for several reasons. Yeah, it was heavier than many modern handguns, but it was battle proven. The single stack magazine meant the grip was narrower, which leant to a better control of the weapon. It also leant to a smaller profile for concealing, and the fact that it was a .45 caliber meant it had stopping power. In his previous life, O'Neil had a lust for the lavish, so he had the grips customized in old ebony with his initials engraved. He checked the magazine by hitting the release and letting it fall into his opposite hand. Finding the mag was full, he slapped it back into place and heard the click as the mechanism grabbed the mag. O'Neil slid the gun into the leather holster that was sitting inside his waistband at the small of his back. He slipped into a pair of black cross trainers by the door and took one last look at himself in the mirror. He smiled – he was back to his truest self. The gangster grabbed the rum and took another long pull on the bottle then headed out. O'Neil made his way to his car and prayed he would not be stopped by either the cops or the Arab security team. Fortunately for O'Neil, the Arabs were lying low and staying clear of the police presence. As for the cops, they were still focused on the courtyard. So O'Neil eased himself into the seat of his two-door coupe and fired up the engine setting off for his meeting.

***

Immes was waiting when he arrived. The downpour this evening had kept business at the burger joint slow. The officer was in street clothes and had selected a quiet booth in a back corner. The unlikely pair made eye contact when O'Neil came in. He took his time and ordered a banquet burger and chocolate shake before sliding into the booth across from Immes. It gave him a couple extra minutes to collect himself. They both scanned the other patrons, as they sat there. Neither saw anything to scare them from this meeting.

The odd couple sat across from each other in an awkward silence for what seemed like an eternity. Immes picked at his fries, nervously twirling them around in the pile of ketchup on the edge of the burger wrapper. O'Neil took a sip of his shake then set it down on the tray. He pushed his tray away and sat back in the bench. The gangster adjusted the brim of his hat so he could better judge Immes' reaction when he asked his questions. But he also wanted Immes to see him and know he was being sincere. Immes returned the posture letting O'Neil know he was ready to hear whatever it was.

O'Neil started slowly and deliberately. "Immes, I need to know something. I need you to tell me the truth, and if you can do that, I will open your eyes to something you never even knew existed. Can you do it? Can you be completely honest with me, dawg?"

Immes knew the only answer was, "Yes." And he delivered it with all the sincerity he had in his soul. He delivered it with his heart, his tone and his eyes. He *was* being honest anyway, he had never had any real hate for O'Neil. So his sincerity was easily visible to the gangster.

O'Neil had been studying Immes' face for any hint of a lie. He found nothing but the honesty. Taking a deep breath, O'Neil asked his question, "Did they kill my boy, Immes? Did they kill Strong?"

The question actually startled Immes. He wasn't even sure if O'Neil had known that Strong was dead yet. He had only nodded to him earlier because he figured O'Neil knew about the takedown.

"Kill him? Jesus. No way man!" Returned Immes shocked. "Why would you think that?"

"I was told you guys killed him. Maybe to get to me, I dunno."

Immes could see that O'Neil was barely keeping it together. "O'Neil," started Immes compassionately, "I'm sorry about what happened, but why would the police ever do that? What do we gain by that? And no offence, you're really not that big of a deal, man."

"So what the fuck happened then?" O'Neil probed further, shouting, causing the old man behind the counter to whip around and look at them.

Immes smiled and nodded as he took a sip of his drink. "Here is what I know." The officer started with the details of the takedown.

"Wait wait wait." O'Neil stopped him, pointing his straw at the big cop. "You're telling me that Strong was there to make a dope pickup? That you guys had a fink who told you it was on?"

"Yeah, that's exactly what happened. Ok yeah, sure he got smashed by one of the TIG guys but—"

O'Neil cut him off again. "I don't care about that part. That's just the game. Tell me somethin', how did the other half get there?"

"Not sure? Taxi I think I heard." Immes replied a little confused?

"You know what kind?" O'Neil was on the edge, leaning across the table on both elbows now, his tone rising again.

"No. But why does it matter, O'Neil? What is this all about?"

"Somethin' bigger than a dope deal. That's what." O'Neil shot back in a whisper across the table.

"Look man, all I know is he had some sort of medical emergency at the station. An allergic reaction or something?"

"That's interesting, Immes. I needed to know if it was true or not that you guys killed him. I believe you, and I think I know who did. And why." O'Neil let the statement hang in the air for a minute.

The big officer sat back again, a dissatisfied look spreading across his face. Just as Immes was about to answer with the standard, *It was just an accident*, but O'Neil cut him off one last time.

"Terrorists Immes." he whispered while leaning over his half-eaten burger and looking the big cop dead in the eyes. "And I can tell you everything. But not here."

Suddenly, in this one brief conversation, it was very clear to O'Neil that he was being setup as Ameer's patsy. O'Neil Facey was no one's patsy.

O'Neil's words sat heavily in the both with the pair. The statement had sucked all emotion and sound out of the room. Everything was frozen. There were no smells. No nothing. Just this big, huge thing sitting there, pressing down on them both. Immes slowly twisted in his seat his eyes fixed on O'Neil. He pushed his hat back on his head and mouthed the words, "Holy shit." He sat there for another minute almost unable to breath. The gravity of it all was sitting on his chest. Immes leaned back into the table and quietly said, "There's a procedure for this sort of thing. You have to meet with some detectives and lay it all out."

O'Neil didn't hesitate. "I'm in. Can we set it up right now?" That one question took O'Neil through his fourth metamorphosis. He had gone from drug dealing to professional landscaper to terrorist and snitch in the space of a year.

Immes nodded feverishly as he scrolled through the contacts on his phone. He found the one he was looking for. He hit the text message icon then typed his message:

I have a very important source I need you to meet. His information has ties to what happened last night. This has national security implications. I'm with the source now – reply ASAP.

Immes looked at O'Neil and placed the phone on the table. He tapped the screen once more to make sure it was on silent. Seeing the icon in place he lay it flat again in front of himself.

"This shouldn't take very long." A soon as the word "long" left his lips, the phone buzzed on the table. Both men looked down at the screen:

Bring him to our office. Are you covert? Do you have cover?

Immes looked up at O'Neil, "Well. You still wanna do this?"

The reply was immediate from O'Neil, "Yeah, I have to. For my boy Strong."

Immes typed back:

Covert. No cover. Public place.

The person on the other end of the conversation wrote back quickly:

Stay put. Send the location, will send a cover team to move you here.

Great job Tim!

***

The big detective from Source Management had been isolated in the division's community room, which felt more like a boardroom than a place to foster police-community relations.

"Oh, there'll be some meetings coming up in this room in the next few weeks." He rolled his eyes, as he talked out loud to himself. When his phone had buzzed in his pocket, he wasn't sure if they would let him look at it. The union rep and the SIU investigator had just arrived to interview him. They both looked a little surprised when he thumbed in the access code and held the phone away from them.

"What?" he said. "The sources don't know I'm with you guys. This message is privileged." He continued to read. He kept his poker face on but inside was dancing like a lottery winner. He copied the message to his partner who was sequestered in another office. Then he typed his response to Officer Immes.

Janine was sitting alone eating a slice of the customary pizza bought by the union. She picked up her phone and dropped the slice of pizza on the table as she read it. She quickly typed back to her partner:

I'll make the arrangements.

Her first call was to The Group. Janine got the operational sergeant and laid out her request. Immediately his team leader and one of his snipers were on the detail. The sergeant gave her the TL's cell number and said they could be on the move in ten minutes. Janine thanked him and hung up. Next, she dialed the extension for her office and got one of the other detectives on the line. They exchanged pleasantries, and Janine cut it short. "Bill, I need you to prep the office and conference room one for a level five debrief. Should be there within the hour. Tim Immes is the handler and will be coming in with the source and a TIG cover team. Got it?"

"Roger J, on it now." The detective hung up and set to work right away.

Janine got the location for the pick-up and sent it to the Group TL and got a COPY as a reply text. She let her partner know everything was in place, all she had to do was wait for the SIU to let her leave. She took another bite of the cold pizza and tried not to let her mind run wild. Janine stood and paced in the small room, her mind playing over dozens of scenarios. She was trying to guess who the source might be and what they might know? Either way, she knew this could be the break they needed.

Chapter Nineteen

Immes saw the black SUV pull into the lot, parked facing the window and flashed its lights twice, just like they had agreed.

"Your ride or mine, O'Neil?" Immes asked, as he finished the last of his diet pop.

O'Neil smirked, "Won't be the first time I been in your car, Immes. Plus, I can't be seen driving into wherever we're going."

Immes smiled. "Ok man, let's go." The unlikely duo headed out to the lot. Immes nodded to the two operators in the black SUV, as he keyed the remote to the unmarked car.

O'Neil swung himself into the passenger seat and when the doors were closed he looked over at Immes. "Where we headed?"

Immes faced him. "Going up to the Intelligence building."

"You trust me enough to take me there?" O'Neil asked clearly surprised.

"The fact that you called me was the first step in that O'Neil. The second was the Intel people seem very interested."

Immes gave the cover guys from The Group a thumbs-up and put the car in drive. The thirty-minute ride to the Combined Forces Building was pretty quiet. There was a nervous anticipation in the car. Not hostile, not standoffish. It was more like being on a first date and you were driving the girl home. Both of you were wondering if there would be a first kiss. Would it be a home run or a first-baser? When Immes finally pulled up to the big gates, he had leaned out to press the intercom button. As he was about to request entrance, the gates opened automatically.

"I guess they're expecting us." He laughed and looked over at O'Neil who was staring at the floor and fidgeting with his phone. Immes pulled around the lot in a wide loop coming back toward the employee entrance, he could see a detective waiting patiently just inside. The Group truck had followed the whole way and was also angling for a parking spot, which were plentiful given the time of night. Immes found a spot just a few spaces from the door and pulled in. He killed the engine and turned to O'Neil, "Now you're going to have to leave that gun here, O'Neil." He pointed to the small of his back.

O'Neil was shocked, partly because in the anticipation of what was about to go down he had forgotten it was there. "How'd you—"

The cop stopped him, "Know?" Immes finished the sentence. "Shit, I've been watching you fidget with your guns for years, man. I knew you were carrying. Take it out in the footwell there and empty it. Then put in the glovebox. Be slow about it, or those guys in that black truck are gonna light us both up."

O'Neil looked out the windshield at the intimidating man in jeans, a plaid shirt and some trucker style ball hat. He stood strongly at the front of the black truck across front of them. The man had a short-barreled assault rifle across his chest as he watched O'Neil intently. The gangster moved slowly and didn't see Immes motioning to say *It's okay* to the operator who was inching closer to the car. With the gun stowed away the pair exited the car and were escorted to the door by the TIG operators, where they were all greeted by the detective.

"Gents, welcome to Intelligence. If you'd please follow me."

The detective led them down a short hallway and into a large conference room. One of the TIG operators took a post outside the door. The other asked O'Neil to put his hands on the wall to be searched. O'Neil actually thanked Allah for reminding him to leave his holster in the car too. The search was negative, and the operator nodded to the detective and Immes then left the room. The two TIG operators would take turns for the rest of their shift rotating between stationing themselves at this door and in their vehicle in the parking lot until the next shift came to relieve them.

O'Neil slumped into one of the comfortable leather swivel chairs. The escorting detective spoke first, "The detective that will be handling your information will be with you shortly. Unfortunately, I have to ask that you both remain in this room until you're done here. My next request is that you both place your cellphones in this tray please."

Both O'Neil and Immes dumped their phones into the deposit box, which they watched the detective lock. Holding it under his arm he asked, "For now, is there anything I can get you?"

O'Neil smiled "Good thing we ate, huh Immes?" he joked. "Seriously though, can I get a coffee and maybe a cookie or something?"

"Coffee thanks." Immes added.

The detective smiled politely. "I will have a carafe brought over shortly, and I'll scrape up what I can find for snacks. Give me a few minutes." He left. As the door was opened, O'Neil saw that the Group operator outside the door had some sort of load bearing vest on and his rifle slung over top of that. The operator gave no facial indication of what he thought was going on, he was just doing a job. The man sipped his coffee and scanned the hallway then nodded at some unknown person out of O'Neil's view. The door closed, and O'Neil looked over at Immes, who was rubbing both his eyes with the heels of his hands.

"Taking this pretty serious huh?" O'Neil asked, looking for confirmation.

"Uh yeah." Immes replied tiredly and maybe a little sarcastically from under the brim of his hat.

The door opened again, and the detective returned placing a tall carafe and two mugs on the conference table. There was also a bowl full of milk cups and sugar packets. "Sorry but we are out of cream. I'll be back shortly with some snacks."

O'Neil picked the bigger of the two mugs and spun the handle toward himself. Immes poured the coffee. O'Neil stared at the dark liquid as it poured into his cup and started laughing out loud at the crest on the mug when he realized which unit it was for.

"Well this is ironic." he said turning the logo to face Immes. Even Immes had to laugh, the wording on the cup read: SOURCE MANAGEMENT & WITNESS PROTECTION UNIT

In the middle was the Unit's crest. The two of them sat laughing for several seconds, which helped vent the tension out of the room. When the detective returned a few minutes later the pair were wiping the tears from their eyes while still giggling. The detective smirked and slid a large bowl with several varieties of bagged chips and assorted vending machine goodies across the table, he nodded to Immes and headed back out the door.

The time passed slowly, and the temperature in the room felt like it had dropped a few degrees. An hour had passed since they had arrived, and O'Neil was getting fidgety. The Source Management Unit Detective watched him on the screen in his office. The time was right, O'Neil was ready to talk. The detective sent a quick text to Janine and her partner:

He's ready. Heading into poly him now.

Her reply was quick:

Great Bill. Thanks, we are OTW.

The detective grabbed his laptop and a backpack from the floor and headed to conference room #1. At the door, he showed his credentials to the operator posted on the outside and swiped his way in. He immediately scanned over O'Neil making a quick first impression. Calm, confident, poised, he thought to himself. "Gentlemen, my name is Detective Bill Neely. I am the polygraph examiner for the Service."

161

The man set up his equipment. Gone were the days of a big bulky polygraph machines with a continuous running sheet of paper like an ECG at a hospital. Nowadays, all he brought was his powerful, yet thin, silver laptop and a heart rate strap with a finger pulse monitor. In fact, he probably could run the software off his smartphone or a tablet. O'Neil removed his jacket and set it on the chair next to him. He stood up so the detective could strap him in and then settled back into the chair. O'Neil's left hand rested palm down on the table. The detective got comfortable in the seat next O'Neil and opened the program he used to run the test.

Looking over the frame of his glasses at Immes, the examiner said, "Officer, you'll have to wait outside for this portion." He motioned toward the door with his head.

Immes got up with his coffee and smiled at O'Neil. Exiting the room, he leaned on the wall beside the operator guarding the door.

The door closed, and O'Neil swore he felt the temperature rising now. He wasn't nervous, at least he didn't feel like he was, but he could feel his armpits getting moist.

The detective arranged a legal-size pad next his laptop and removed his glasses. He looked at O'Neil and in a very calm and inviting voice said, "Mr. Facey, just try and relax. Don't try to beat the machine, just answer truthfully. Are you ready to begin?"

O'Neil replied without reservation or fear of what he was about to do. "Yes sir, I am."

With that, the examination began. The examiner had been fed some basic information by Janine and her partner and he used that information to examine O'Neil's level of truthfulness on those facts and set the baseline. The exam was to be a test of O'Neil's suitability as a level five source. The process would last about forty-five minutes.

***

Outside the door, the two Source Management lead Detectives had arrived. They were making acquaintances with the TIG operator and Immes. Janine and her partner each shook Immes' hand in amazement; the timing of this was almost too good to be true. As such, they would tread carefully. How had he been able to pull in such a high priority source?

"How the hell did you land him?" the big source detective asked skeptically.

"I didn't. That's the thing, he called me." Immes told them as surprised as anyone. "He wanted to know if we, the police, had killed James Strong."

The Source detective's eyes went wide.

"Like someone had told him we killed him on purpose, and he wanted me to verify or deny it." Immes continued.

162

The two partners from the Source Unit were frozen at the statement and shot each other looks of amazement.

"What?" Immes asked.

"They fucked up, man." the big detective told him. "They tried to use Strong's death to lock O'Neil into their plan. It looks like that just backfired."

The door opened, and the polygraph examiner emerged from the room, expressionless like the good poker player he was. The four cops outside the room all scanned his face for some hint at how it had gone. Nothing.

"Well?" Janine asked finally.

Detective Neely cracked a partial smile, "Preliminarily of course, he looks like the real deal, Janine. I'll have a full report ready for you tomorrow."

The polygraph expert nodded to the small huddle of investigators and headed back to his office. The two Source detectives smiled at each other then at Immes. Heading to the door to the conference room, the tall detective motioned for Immes to join them, "Come on Immes, he's your source. Time for the intros and a formal video statement."

O'Neil watched the group enter and saw that they looked pleased. That was a good start.

The tall salt and pepper haired detective who looked like he was mixed race of some kind came around the table first with his hand extended. He wasn't rushing over, just respectfully approaching. "Hey man. I'm Detective Felix DeLeon from the Source Unit." They shook as he said it. O'Neil smiled and nodded.

The female detective was around the table next. "Detective Janine Byers. Pleasure to meet you. Do you need anything before we get started?"

O'Neil just shook his head.

"Ok then O'Neil, why don't we just start at the beginning, okay?" Janine said. "Tell us what you know about a terrorist cell operating out of the Orton Park Projects."

"I need to know that you'll look after Strong's girl and their kid." O'Neil responded, "And me too obviously."

"O'Neil, I assure you that if the information I think you are about to give us is what I think it is, you will be well cared for. I mean look how seriously we're taking this, and you haven't said a word yet." The tone of her reply and her soft voice immediately put him at ease.

O'Neil Facey started talking. The words didn't come easily at first; he struggled against his old habit of lying to the police and an archaic code of not snitching. But gradually those things faded away, the room felt like it had gotten warmer as if on purpose. The gangster walked them through everything he had seen over the last couple years. With the clarity of hindsight, he was able to recognize the slow infiltration that took place. Every one of his words made him a little more comfortable in his new role as an informant, a "source" for the police. O'Neil talked about the transition from low-income, primarily black residents to multi-generational Arabic families. He was able to describe it in economic terms for them. The once steady line-ups of drug addicts coming to his buildings that dwindled to a slow trickle, how he had been forced to branch out for territory, which had been costly in terms of both his business's exposure and loss of manpower due to arrest or death. Still, he had managed to continue making enough money to stay comfortable. Then he told them about the night that he and Strong had been confronted by the Arabs in the stairwell and brought to the twenty-first floor where they had first met the Mullah.

O'Neil slowed the story, as he sipped on another coffee. The detectives were on the edges of their seats. That soundproof room was so quiet that you could hear the whir of the small cameras as they zoomed in on him. He pictured a technician in another room sitting at a computer making sure they captured the most minute movements on O'Neil's face. He figured some computer program had been analyzing his facial patterns and tone of speech throughout the entire interview. O'Neil readjusted himself in the big leather chair and started again. He sat up tall to show them that this was the part they all wanted to hear about, and for Strong's sake it was the part he needed to tell them.

"It started simply enough. They wanted to pay me to for my drug business and have me lay low. They would organize and run my crew mixing in some of their people and product. Heroin and opium is their thing. I agreed. Why not get paid to not work? Shit, it's a no brainer. I was banking social assistance cheques, their payoff, and I kept a small crack business running on the side downtown in Vanauley Walk. Everything was going smooth. Then in the spring they call and want to meet to discuss some new idea, that landscaping business I run now. They were going to pay for setting up the company. In the beginning, the only request was that I convert to Islam, which I had already told them I was interested in. I also had to process whatever orders they sent to me. I didn't want to lose the money flow. I looked at it as a way out of the game you know?"

"Okay. So, they have you open a front business. What's the goal?" the big detective from Source, Felix, probed.

O'Neil eased slowly into the next part, "I didn't see it at first either. Then I'm sitting with Strong in a club, and it hits me. They want fertilizer to make bombs. The initial startup purchase for my company alone was huge. But my company had also been set-up as the buyer for three other companies who were all starting up at the same time. One is out east in Whitby, one is west in Georgetown, and one is way up north in Sudbury. My company processes the orders and has the supplier ship direct to the other companies. I've never been out to any of them."

The detectives exchanged stunned looks around the room until Janine broke the silence and asked O'Neil to continue.

"Look, I'm no snitch. And I really didn't care that much that they were possibly planning to blow shit up around here. They were treating me like a king. We were partying, buying expensive cars and things on the company dime. I had hooked up with a girl from their floor – you know they own the whole top floor right? It's like its own world up there. Security teams, servants, whole apartments for meetings. Wild! I was going blind to what was happening. Then tonight happens, and it's like they're trying to shut the door behind me and lock me in." O'Neil pauses again, this time embarrassment showing on his face.

Felix DeLeon jumps in, "O'Neil, don't beat yourself up for not seeing their play. Guys like this are professionals. People we will have to take very seriously."

O'Neil looked up and smirked. "I know I know. I'm just pissed I let them get over on me. Anyway. The other night they asked me to Mosque with them. It all felt kinda weird. I was being paraded around the Mosque like a prize. After prayers, we go downstairs and they make me watch one of those terrorist videos being made. You know, like from the Internet? I was frozen, man. I knew what I had become…I was going to be their fall guy. They had set me up. I decided right there that I was not going down for this. But I had no way out yet, so I played along."

"After some celebrations in the Mosque basement, I went home and came across the crime scene. I was trying to reach Strong, so we could figure a way out, but he wasn't answering his phone. He was supposed to be sorting some shit out with his girl. She's having a baby in a couple of months. I had this bad feeling something had happened to him. I pulled into my spot, and I see two of the Arab security guys. My girl and I get out of the car, and she just bounces. Doesn't even look back. The head security guy, Raahil, tells me to head up to the twenty-first to see their boss. When I get there, this guy Ameer tells me that the cops have killed my best friend. He wants me to use that as anger to help them."

DeLeon interjects, "But that was a fluke accident. It was likely a drug overdose, or some sort of allergic reaction. We won't know until tomorrow. How could this Raahil have known anyway?"

O'Neil sat back. "I wondered the same thing. No one would know this, but Strong has a rare allergy to dried fruits and vegetables or some shit. Did he eat anything while he was in custody? If he did, check what was in it. And then I figured they must have someone working on the inside as well. That fact on top of how he knew about Strong's allergy scared the shit out of me! This guy can reach out anywhere and find out anything. Shit, he probably knows I'm here already."

O'Neil was relieved that the whole story was out, but he was also scared of the beast he had just pieced together. O'Neil would spend the next two hours with the detectives filling in the blanks and organizing a strategy that would see him playing double agent for a little longer before they could pull him out. When it was over they all shook hands and headed for the parking lot door. Stopping short the group waited for Immes and the TIG operators to bring the vehicles around. Cell phones were turned on and immediately started buzzing, they were slipped into pockets to be answered later.

"O'Neil, I can't thank you enough for this." Janine said. "We will be in touch on how to proceed. Okay? For now, stay safe and just go along with whatever they ask you. If it's really serious, text one of us and we will guide you through it."

The door opened and the TIG operator nodded at O'Neil signaling it was time to go.

"Holy shit Janine." Felix said as they closed the door and walked back to their desks.

Janine was glued to the notification banners on her lock screen, "Oh my God Pepper! They've already sent the first message out. We are going to be running to play catch-up on this now!"

Felix had his phone out, too, and the pair were in a full sprint to their office to start making calls and planning their next moves.

Chapter Twenty

Early the next day, Mike Carter and Paul Speed strolled through the back door of The Group's building to prep for a sniper training evolution. As they passed the staff sergeant's office, he waved them in. Staff Sergeant Farmer asked them to shut the door and sighed deeply as he dropped his glasses onto the desk.

"Boys, it's on. We are going to have to speed up the timeline on your planning for that Archangel operation. Take a look at this." Farmer turned his monitor so they could see and hit play on the video file. The snipers watched in amazement as the terror cell's video played. They were both searching for clues as to the origin or location but found nothing. When it was done the pair of snipers took a seat across from the old staff sergeant.

"Okay Staff. What now?" Carter asked.

"Luckily for us, they screwed up already. It would seem they've pissed off one of their own, significantly enough that the person has come forward as an informant. The information is pointing at Orton Park as the base for these guys—"

Speed interrupted. "That might explain the weirdness over there the last few months. Mike and I have been working on a theory with some people from Intel."

"Quite possibly. I received an email from the boss there that outlined what you two have been up to. Great work. The formal request from Intelligence came in this morning. They want you guys to set up over there and get some eyes on that twenty-first floor. They would like pictures of as many people as possible. Go put your plan together and launch on this ASAP." Farmer directed his men. He had a serious look of concern on his face that was not lost on the snipers. They excused themselves and headed straight for the team room.

Team Four's room was empty, and as the snipers swiped their way in, the fluorescent lights clicked on taking a second or two to heat up. Carter started to wheel black cases out to the garage and load them into a van. Speed sat at Glen Parker's desk and powered up the computer. While he waited for the authentication process, he called Parker at home, filling him in on the details of their new tasking.

"Glen, you think we can get the team in on a call-back to help Mike and I get inserted into those buildings? I have an idea how to make it happen – but it'll take some time to setup, and we will need some bodies." Parker assured his sniper that he would make the phone calls and get as many guys in as he could.

Carter returned and sat across from Speed chewing on a stir stick, "What else needs doing, Speeder?"

"Mikey, I have an idea on how to get us into that building. Can you find out who has the contract to service the HVAC there? Then give them a call and see if they are agreeable to this?" Speed went on to outline the details of the insertion plan for his partner. When he was done, Carter smiled a mischievous smile at him.

"That sounds great, but what about avoiding the roof all together? Maybe we can get lucky and find an apartment on the twenty-first and be inside? Less exposure than the roof."

Carter had a good point, Speed thought. The trouble was going to be finding someone police-friendly enough to let two snipers take over their apartment.

The snipers set to work on their separate tasks. It would take them through several coffees and phone calls, but about midday they were stretched out on camping chairs in front of their stalls reviewing the plan and equipment lists. Speed pulled his lucky hat down over his eyes. "I think we got it covered, Mikey. I'm going to grab some shut-eye while we wait for the guys."

Carter was already snoring in the chair beside him.

***

In a dusty old warehouse north of the city, four mini vans were parked with their noses into the back wall. Their back doors were open, and a group of mechanics were busily pouring over the interiors. All interiors had been gutted, except for the driver and passenger seats, and the men were in the process of installing fabric sheeting behind those seats. In the opposite corner sat twenty-four large blue plastic shipping barrels with their lids off; beside that sat an ominous pile of commercial fertilizer bags. There was also an empty parking space for a larger vehicle that had not yet arrived. An older Arab man watched the work from a modest office mounted high in the opposite corner of this warehouse. He was reviewing a checklist while he chain-smoked unfiltered cigarettes, a blue haze hanging in the air above him. He wiped a palm full of grime off the window and recounted the barrels he could see on the floor below.

One of the mechanics came to the door. "The vehicles will be ready later today. Shall we start loading the fertilizer into the barrels?" he asked in a thick Arabic accent.

The man behind the desk just nodded and waved his cigarette at the worker. As soon as the worker left, the foreman retrieved a cellphone from the desk drawer. It had never been powered on before today. The man punched in the memorized numbers and reclined in the rickety old chair to watch another news report on the released video: "This is Siobhan Murphy reporting from outside Police Headquarters. Once again we anticipate some sort of statement later this afternoon from the Chief of Police on the investigation into the video released by an apparent home-grown group of terrorists. The group has made a series of demands of the Canadian Government that are to be met within the week. I turn it over to our partners at Channel 3 for more on that aspect of the story."

"Thanks Siobhan. That's right, I am live in Ottawa outside the residence of the Prime Minister where we are also standing by for a press conference…"

Denise Dobson droned on for another few minutes before the foreman remembered to hit send on the phone.

When the line picked up a female answered politely, "Hello, may I help you?"

The foreman replied in code, "Please tell my friend that the flowerpots are ready. Ask if I should begin filling them now."

"I will pass along your message sir. He will get back to you shortly. Have a nice day." And she hung up.

The foreman lit another cigarette and got up from his chair. He refilled his mug with the burnt and biter black coffee from the pot on the old coffee maker and went to stand at the window again. He scanned the floor of the warehouse, and through the dusty haze the foreman smiled to himself as he watched the first bags of fertilizer being emptied into the barrels. He jumped and spilled coffee on his dirty shirt and tie when the little phone on the desk started buzzing. The foreman looked at the display and read the reply he had already anticipated:

Please begin filling the pots. Thank you, the water truck is on the way.

At a separate warehouse on a completely different side of the city, a refueling truck full of diesel started up. Two young Arabs climbed into the cab, and as they pulled the truck out of the garage, they waved to another worker who hurriedly closed the doors. The landscaping company yard was in their rear-view as they made their way out of the industrial complex toward the highway for the drive to the bigger yard of their sister company to the north.

***

By mid-afternoon, the rest of the Hogs were rolling into the team room. Big Greg Karras kicked the chairs of the two snipers startling them awake.

"Snipers huh? Brothers, I had you both."

The big man laughed, as he dropped into his own chair. Parker was at his desk, and Damon Fernandes came through the door with a large box labeled for Speed.

"Speeder, there's a box here for you."

Speed pulled a knife from his pocket and slit the packing tape open. He pulled back the box tabs to reveal several sets of blue coveralls with the logo of a local heating and cooling contractor on them. The company had even included a couple of magnetic labels for the vehicles. Speed handed out the uniforms to the team and with a nod from Parker he started the briefing, where he outlined the mission and its objectives. Once everyone was clear on time appreciation the guys quietly split off to their stalls to get ready. Someone fired up a portable speaker and the music of the latest pop sensation filled the room.

The operations order had been left on briefing screen behind the Sergeant's desk, and the guys took turns standing under it to note the specifics of their tasks:

<u>OPERATOR – CALLSIGN– TASKING– VEHICLE- WEAPONS</u>

Parker D01 / T/L / Vehicle #1 / Passenger / Pistol / MP7

Robinson D09 / Security / Driver V#1 / Pistol / MP7

Leo D04 / Sec / breach / V#1 / Pistol / C8

Speed S4 / Sniper / V#1 / Pistol / Sniper Gear

Fernandes D10 / Security / Driver / V#2 / Pistol / C8

Horowitz D02 / 2i/c / V#2 / Pistol / MP5

Syndon D07 / Sec / Breach / V#2 / Pistol / MP5

Carter S4A / Sniper / V#2 / Pistol / Obs Gear

Several hours later, as the terrorists maneuvered their pieces into place, two very crafty snipers snuck into position as well. The team arrived earlier in the evening just after sunset when most of the building's residents were at prayers. A group of eight men in total had come in two vans labeled with the name of a local heating and cooling repair company. The men had come, presumably, to work on the A/C units in the easternmost building that seemed to be acting up today for some reason. Although it had been a cool fall day,

170

the air conditioning units kept powering on and dropping the internal temperatures in the buildings below twenty degrees Celsius. Raahil's security detail had watched them enter and had even called the company to confirm the job was legitimate. The receptionist had said it was. They would be there for some time, the receptionist had told her inquirer. They watched as the men had lugged several cases of tools in through the shipping doors. The repairmen, once inside, had gotten into the service elevator and headed for the roof top A/C units. The security men watched and counted as eight men appeared on the roof coming from the elevator room. The repairmen set to work on the units and the security men grew bored of watching. They quickly returned their attention back to their regular routines.

Two of the repairmen went back to the elevator room unnoticed and took the elevator one floor down to the twenty-first floor. On the floor, they cautiously exited the elevator and headed to an apartment at the far end of the hall. The men had with them two black cases and two black backpacks. At the door one of the men pulled a knife from his pocket quietly slicing through two police crime scene seals along the frame. He inserted a key and the men entered quickly closing the door behind them. The pair of men stood in the darkness for several minutes and let their eyes adjust, their noses had to adjust as well to the stench of death coating the walls.

A police cruiser pulled into the roundabout and stopped in front of the east most building. It was exactly the same time it had come every night this week. A young officer got out and made her way inside the building. She went to the elevator and pressed the call button. When the elevator arrived she entered and pressed 21 then leaned back in the corner for the ride. The doors opened, and she exited the elevator turning in the same direction the two repairmen had. She stopped in front of the same door the men had entered, and with no surprise or shock she quietly withdrew two new seals from her vest pocket and placed them over the ones that had been cut by the repairmen. She drew out her flashlight and held it quietly against the peephole giving two quick flashes. She then calmly walked back to the elevators trying not to smile.

Inside the apartment, the two repairmen had been watching the peephole waiting for the signal. When they heard movement outside the door, they froze and waited. Two pinhole-sized flashes blinked in the peephole, and the men knew they were secure. The first man peeled open his dark jumpsuit and withdrew his cellphone. He then pulled a dark green shemagh from around his neck draping it over his head. The glow from the phone's screen being trapped inside and thus not a compromise to their position. He typed a message to their team on the roof:

In position. All Secure.

On the roof, one of the workers stopped what he was doing in front of one of the large A/C units. One of Raahil's security team watched from the opposite building. The worker took out a phone and looked intently at the screen. He appeared to tap at the screen typing back a message to someone.

The worker read his screen and typed his reply:

Solid Copy. Dusting off, be good boys.

Speed read the message inside the crime scene apartment and flashed a silent thumbs-up to Carter. On the roof, the men took their time replacing the covers on the A/C units and packing up their gear. Roughly an hour had passed since they had arrived and suddenly the A/C units settled back into their regular program. The men loaded into the elevator and headed for their vans without another look from the security men at Raahil's building. The repairmen quietly pulled away and the buildings went quiet again.

Inside their apartment, Speed and Carter set to work building their OP. The snipers crawled on their bellies along the parquet floor to the hallway between the bedrooms. Once there they slowly pulled the bedroom doors closed. Getting the cases there was going to be problematic but they had developed a solution. They couldn't have the cases rumbling across the floor, it would signal the residents below that someone was in the apartment. Their solution was a felt pad applied to the backside of each case so that it would slide across the parquet without a sound. The snipers had strung out para-cord as they initially crawled, and Speed now slowly pulled the first of the cases toward their position his backpack riding on top. Speed passed the case and pack to Carter and started on retrieving the second. Carter slid into the bathroom with the equipment and sat on the edge of the tub with a red headlamp pulled onto his forehead. He set to work setting up their communications gear, laptop and down room. He retrieved a black wooden board from the case and laid it across the width at the end of the tub, there he set up the laptop and radio. Next he dug out a thick black cloth cut to the width of the door opening. He stuck Velcro strips around the frame then pressed the cloth to it. Now that the room was isolated he powered on the laptop and radio. Carter plugged an earpiece into the radio and keyed the mic twice signaling they were up and running, and waited for the return double click. Once it came he immediately shut the set off. No one could be sure

172

that their targets didn't have scanner capabilities. Even an encrypted broadcast could compromise them.

Speed had slithered into the first bedroom while Carter was working. The room at the beginning of the hallway would become their observation point. He crawled in front of the closet and began pulling the pile of dirty clothes, discarded shoes and assorted junk out into the open space on the floor around the bed. Speed was careful to leave space for them to move in and out. Once the closet was empty, he slid himself in and as quietly as possible popped the bottom runner for the sliding door out of its track. Standing up he eased the upper portion of the slider out of the top track ever so slowly. One of the top runners stuck and he tried in vain to ease it out of the jam. He took a calculated risk and forced the door free. The pop seemed to echo through the whole courtyard and Speed was sure he had blown the mission before it was even started. Speed stood still and let the noise settle. After five agonizing minutes of holding the door in place, he eased it forward three feet. Carter was on his belly below Speed and placed two homemade kickstands in the bottom of the door that would hold it in place. They hung two sheets of the black fabric on either side of the extended door. The one on the side closest to the door was cut about three feet up from the floor. Which allowed a place for the snipers to crawl under and into the closet. Inside the closet Speed removed the shelf and clothes bar setting them in the corner and opened up a tall folding stool and a camera tripod. After clicking the camera into position Carter slid back out to the hall where he waited between the second room and the bathroom. Speed stepped up to the repositioned door and took a deep breath. He pulled his combat knife from his belt and ever so slowly he slid it through the door material at the lens's level. He cut three sides of a rectangle and pulled it inwards. Speed next placed black screening in the opening to obscure the lens as it sat there.

Satisfied with the setup Speed slid out into the hall and joined Carter. They shared a smile in the darkness and traded places. Carter reached back into the second case and removed another digital SLR camera sliding a black nylon over the long lens. He crawled back into the room made his way along the floor into to a corner blanketed in deep shadows. Carter draped an old bedsheet that they had painted to match the interior walls, based on crime scene photos they'd reviewed, he then slowly stood and let his eyes adjust to the lighting in the courtyard through an opening made for the camera. He stared at the twenty-first floor across the way. The buildings were the same exact height but the lay of the land pushed this building slightly higher than its sister. This gave the snipers the advantage of being able to look slightly down into the opposite floor. As Carter brought the camera up he snapped the first pictures of the inner sanctuary of their targets. Speed was sitting in the bathroom/down room and thanking a higher power for how lucky they had gotten. They had been more than surprised when they had heard about this sealed apartment. A man had been found dead in the kitchen under some suspicious circumstances here earlier this week. The body had been removed but the apartment had not yet been cleaned and was being held as the local detectives continued their investigation. Everyone involved had decided the compromise to that investigation was worth the interest of National Security. Sealed warrants had been written to allow the snipers back in the apartment without compromising the potential homicide investigation. It was risky, but it was a risk all involved were willing to take in this instance.

Not much was happening across the way, as Carter snapped pictures of the exterior of the building. When he was finished he low crawled back to their little hide and sat up behind the large telephoto lens. Looking across, he could see details of the apartments on the twenty-first floor. Carter reached down to the backpack at his feet and pulled out an old aluminum clipboard that had long since been spray-painted into a generic camouflage pattern. Before going any further he pulled a bag of loose-leaf tobacco from a pocket and packed a substantial ball into his cheek. He then quietly opened the folding storage tray taking out two sheets of white grid paper and a pencil, and started scribbling notes under the dull red glow of the headlamp. Carter noted the number of balconies, doors windows and anything else that seemed unique. Periodically, Carter would peer up into the lens to check for any activity. The sniper then draped a black towel over the camera lens and slowly pulled down the screening. Carter was confident that he was deep enough in the shadows that he could not be seen, but he was still cautious not to let any light shine off a camera or range finder lens. He slowly brought the range finder to his eye in his right hand while covering the lens with his left then slid his fingers away from the device's lens and laser. He marked the distances from their position to the doors and windows at Ameer and Raahil's apartments. The sniper periodically stopping to note each on the diagram he was building on the grid paper as he went. With that task complete Carter replaced the screening and made a quiet whistle to Speed.

Speed reached under the screen and tapped his partner on the foot to let him know he had arrived. The pair switched places, and Speed went to work behind the lens now. He had with him a pair of binoculars, all the lenses on their equipment had been covered in pieces of black nylons cut from old pairs of their wives hosiery. Speed slowly scanned back and forth across the opposite floor for any sign of activity. Most of the rooms he found were in darkness.

Carter was back in the bathroom and had just lit a camping stove for coffee. He returned to the hallway and opened the second black case retrieving a small gray dish antennae. It would boost the signals from their communications gear. Carter carefully slid the small dish inside the door of the second bedroom next to the bathroom and pulled the wire under the door, leaving it partially ajar. He ran the cable up along the doorframe and hung it in place using some sturdy peel and stick hooks. The cable continued into the bathroom around the vanity mirror and plugged into the laptop over the tub. Next Carter ran a Trojan horse program from inside the Wi-Fi application. This allowed them to piggyback on any wireless signal they could find. Carter waited for the program to run and selected a strong signal from the top of the list. He watched as the Wi-Fi icon at the top of the screen lit up with four dark bars. Next he opened the web browser and searched for satellite images of the opposite building. Click, cut, paste, and he dropped the image into their planning file. Working steadily, Carter plugged the camera into the USB port and started the download of his initial images. He used an editing program to overlay the details onto the satellite imagery. The small pot on the camping stove came to a boil, and Carter reached out of the tub and made two small cups of instant coffee. He took one to Speed and returned to his computer, where the file had just finished saving and sending. Speed sipped at the hot coffee while he continued scanning the building. True to his training, he was memorizing the terrain. He made mental notes on the angles of fire and the layouts of each of the apartments, the time passing slowly as it always did on an observation job.

The sun started to poke at the horizon and the weary sniper team, who had traded positions several times through the night, welcomed the change. The warm orange glow of the pending sunrise teased at the day waiting to begin. Already the two buildings buzzed with activity. Men were filing out of the lobbies and walking down toward the Mosque, all dressed in the standard prayer garb worn by devout men. The minaret speakers sounded the call to morning prayers from the nearby Mosque. Carter rubbed his tired eyes knowing the sun would be up in the next ten to fifteen minutes. From his position deep in the closet, the angle made it impossible for him to see the men leaving the buildings on the ground level. But there was a bustle of activity on the floor directly across from him. Several men in suits and dark sunglasses were posted at internal doorways now. Women were scurried about the insides of the adjacent apartments. Carter eased the camera over to a bedroom window to his right. This one was at the far end of the building and as the drapes were pulled open he saw a woman there in a loose-fitting hijab. A pair of hands wrapped around her waist from behind. They grabbed onto her breasts and a man's face appeared over her shoulder. Carter clicked rapidly on the camera's trigger, capturing their faces. The man appeared to be in his fifties with short dark hair; the woman seemed considerably younger, maybe in her twenties, he thought, as he clicked another picture. Carter looked at the display on the camera and zoomed the image in closer. The girl had the most piercing green eyes. She seemed to be looking back directly at the camera as the older man groped her, she seemed indifferent to the man's advances. The images ran through a USB line into the laptop and popped up on the screen as Speed was resting his head against the back of the tub. They were automatically uploaded to the Department's servers by way of the highjacked Wi-Fi signal where the analysts back at intelligence would study them.

***

Ameer pulled away from her and cursed her for not returning his gestures.

"Are you not enjoying your time in Canada? Or should I send you back to the little village your father came from?"

"No I am sorry. You exhausted me last night is all. Let me go and help with the preparations for today." She lied, hoping he would not force her to perform again.

Ameer turned from the closet where he was pulling on his prayer gown and barked, "Get out of here." He thought to himself that she was becoming a liability. He may have to deal with that problem sooner than later. Raahil passed the young girl in the hallway on the way to the Mullah's room. He thought about stopping her, but she looked distracted. He watched, as she walked with a distinct purpose into the kitchen and asked an older woman what she could do to help.

Ameer was adjusting his dishdasha when Raahil appeared at his doorway. The Mullah nodded him into the room and Raahil closed the door quietly as he began with a whispered voice.

"I have given the order to begin readying the explosive mixture in case we need to speed up our timeline."

Ameer placed a hand on his shoulder. "Excellent idea." he praised then added coldly, "I think our young lady friend will need to be removed from the equation today as well." he motioned with a nod toward the kitchen.

"I will see to it personally." Raahil said, holding back his disappointment. He had also enjoyed his private time with her; apparently the Mullah had grown tired however. The pair of men and two security escorts went to the elevators where they met the Mullah's brother Mustafa. The disheveled misfit was already stuffing his face with some sort of pastry he had swiped off a tray in front of one of the apartments.

"salam." he mumbled through a full mouth.

Raahil turned his eyes away, rolling them as he did, and returned the greeting.

Ameer smiled painfully, "Salam brother. Could you please pull yourself together before we get to prayers this morning." he said while brushing the crumbs off the protruding belly of his younger brother. Mustafa shrugged and lumbered into the elevator ahead of the group. The entourage melted in with the other men heading to prayers and made the short walk to the mosque taking in the brisk October morning.

Just inside the doors, Ameer saw O'Neil removing his shoes and smiled at him. O'Neil smiled back camouflaging his anger. He didn't noticed Raahil approach from behind and was startled when the man took hold of his elbow.

"When prayers are over make your way to the Mullah's floor so we can talk some more, understood?"

They were ordering him around more and more frequently now. O'Neil angrily pulled his elbow away muttering, "Yeah sure." He shuffled away with the crowd to perform his ablution ritual before entering the inner sanctuary of the mosque.

When prayers ended, O'Neil walked back to the buildings with the congregation chatting casually about life and Islam with his brothers. O'Neil was still a touch apprehensive about his debriefing with the Intelligence cops last night. What he had done went against everything he grew up believing. He had seen men killed for being mistaken as a snitch. O'Neil put extra emphasis into his prayers this morning pleading with Allah to keep him on the right path. Intrigued by the Islamic religion, he was embracing it more every day. Over this past year, O'Neil had spent more time in a place of worship than in all the years of his young life combined. He was still lost in thought when he reached the Mullah's building. A stern looking security man standing just inside the vestibule waved him in. O'Neil rolled his eyes and sucked his teeth as he followed the man to the elevators.

Reaching the floor, O'Neil again found himself amidst a celebration of sorts. All the apartment doors were open except for Ameer's at the end of the hall. Tables of food were being set up, as the women scurried in and out of the apartments. There were a number of security men lining the hallway and the usual compliment outside of the Mullah's door.

O'Neil was looking for his green-eyed girlfriend. He had been spending so much time with her lately, but he had not seen, or heard from her since she left him in the garage last night. He wanted desperately to find her and ask why she had just left him there, but she was nowhere to be found. O'Neil poked his head into several of the apartments, as he made his way to the Mullah's door. In each case, the women would turn away from him; to him it felt like they were embarrassed for him or maybe hiding something. When O'Neil reached for the doorknob to Ameer's door, one of the security men put a hand on O'Neil's chest stopping him.

"Just wait." the man had said in that dark murky accent common to the Arab security team. The man patted O'Neil down before opening the door for him. O'Neil looked at the man puzzled. "New policy." was the only explanation the man would give.

***

The older Middle-Eastern man, who they had nicknamed Godfather, rose from the living room couch and moved toward the door. Initially Speed couldn't make out who was there, but he could see Godfather shaking hands with someone. By the way he leaned forward he figured they were exchanging greetings. Then Godfather gestured toward the living room, and a second man became visible.

CLICK CLICK CLICK.

***

O'Neil followed the Mullah to the couch and sat across from him. A handsome middle-aged woman appeared and delivered a tray of coffee and sweets. She said nothing and slid through the room with her eyes cast at the floor. Ameer sipped his coffee, then looking at O'Neil said, "We are going to prepare our second message today. I want you to ride with me to the taping, and I want you to stand beside me, as I address the infidels. Will you do that for me?"

The question could only be answered one way, and O'Neil knew it. "Inshallah. Of course, I would be honored." O'Neil lied to the Mullah. It was his only play.

***

Speed clicked off several more pictures of the young black man and Godfather talking and shaking hands. Carter was on the computer again watching the pictures upload and get send to the servers. An email message popped up in the corner of the screen marked urgent. It was from Detective Gaines at Intelligence. Carter immediately clicked it open and read:

SUBJECT: Photo catch download!!HIGH IMPORTANCE!!

178

Guys,

Are these pictures coming across in real time? The black guy in that living room is O'Neil Facey. He is our source, and I have just been given permission from the Chief and the Crown attorney's office to use him as an agent. He is now under your protection whenever possible.

Please reply to this message that you understand the information above, ASAP!

Gaines

Carter quickly typed back in the subject line:

Solid Copy.

He hit SEND and slid off his stool. Carter went and sat on the floor outside the bedroom where he could hear Speed busily clicking away. He whispered a hiss to get his partner's attention. Speed replied in a soft whisper, "Yeah."

"The black kid in your last haul. Sitting with Godfather. He is the source. Well actually, status change, he is the agent. Added mission, protect the agent whenever possible. Suggest codename Judas." whispered Carter over his shoulder as he sat with his back to the doorframe.

"Solid copy on Judas." was all Speed needed to say. Carter went back to the computer and relayed the new code name for the agent in an email to Gaines. He then tore open another pack of rations and prepared the morning meal. Carter ate his half and left the other for Speed. When he was done, he stood and urinated in a bucket they had found and replaced the towel they were using to suppress the stench. Carter stretched to loosen up for his shift behind the lens and three minutes later he was sliding on his belly back into their little sniper hide. As he stood to allow Speed room to slide out he noticed the new furniture. Speed had setup the shooting tripod and Hog Saddle and unboxed their rifles. Both were leaning in the corner with the suppressors screwed on. Carter hoisted his onto the tripod and tightened the sides of the saddle. He adjusted the tripod to his height and made sure his line of bore and line of sight would clear the cutout. When he had finished settling the weapon in place he did a quick scan of the target. He snapped a few pictures of some of the women and security detail that he could see now that the sun had shifted. Many interior doors remained open giving him a view to the hallway. Then he leaned back on the closet wall, his eyes slowly adjusting to the shadowy cocoon. Carter scanned the maps and images taped against the back of the closet door in front of him. There was a completed range card which had distances to key features marked prominently in red along with headshots of the people they had identified. If the person had been given a codename, it was also written in red ink under their face. So far they had the older Arab man (Godfather), a slightly younger chubby Arab man (Sonny) along with a total of eight security men that were simply numbered one through eight. A number of women were pegged to specific apartments and named after famous female TV sitcom characters – Peggy, Marge, Laverne, Shirley and Debra. Carter re-read the range card and reached over to his .308 dialing the elevation turret to compensate for the furthest distance in their arc of fire, an even two hundred and twenty yards. He gave the rifle two full minutes of elevation or eight clicks, and settled into his routine of observing the building.

***

O'Neil and Ameer made their way to the garage with the security entourage in tow. As they entered the sub-floors Mustafa went to his own SUV. He called to his older brother, "Ameer. I am stopping by to see Raahil before I meet you at the taping. I will only be fifteen to twenty minutes late."

Ameer smiled and waved his brother off. The big hemi engine roared to life, and Mustafa squealed out of the underground. O'Neil and Ameer climbed into the backseat of the large sedan, and two of the security men sat up front, the other two following in a second sedan. The cars were started and the little convoy slipped out of the underground, carefully spacing themselves out by two minutes, so as not to appear conspicuous.

Chapter Twenty-One

Mustafa's big SUV pulled into the gravel lot at the back of New Leaf Landscaping and parked next to one of the work trucks. The considerable man rolled out of the truck's cab, adjusting his designer sunglasses as he headed for the back door. He used his master key to open it and made his way inside. The garage was empty except for a small plain looking minivan parked in the middle. The chemical smell hit him, and he scrunched his face; he hated the smell of the topsoil and fertilizer, added to that today there was also a fresh smell of salt. A new pile of the stuff had been delivered and sat in the corner waiting for the snow to come.

Mustafa could hear voices coming from the office area. He bent over, looking through the window into O'Neil's office and could see Raahil and two of his security men standing there. Mustafa jogged excitedly, albeit slowly, through the garage and into the offices. Stopping at the door to O'Neil's office, he stared at the young green-eyed girl. She was seated in the middle of the room crying. Her limbs were secured to the chair with plastic flex ties, and she was bleeding from the mouth. Her hair was a mess and her clothes torn. Mustafa made a low disgusting growl, as he licked his lips and started to undo his belt. The young girl was reeling away from him, as he moved toward her. Raahil turned and saw Mustafa entering the room. Before Raahil could get between them, Mustafa was on her, grossly kissing at her neck and trying to shake his pants from his plump hips. The other security men were frozen, but Raahil stepped forward and powerfully thrust-kicked Mustafa, hitting him hard on the lump of fat and excess skin hanging sloppily over his hipbone. The kick sent him spinning off the girl and tumbling awkwardly onto the floor, his belt-buckle jingling mockingly as he rolled around. The security men stepped forward, but Raahil held his hand up. He continued to move on the stunned Mustafa. Raahil stepped around Mustafa's feet and drove a hard kick into his liver, the man's hairy belly jiggling with the wave of the blow.

Mustafa groaned in pain as he rolled on the floor. Between gasps, he looked up at Raahil and sputtered angrily, "You will die for this."

Raahil was terrifyingly angry at this point. Although Mustafa was several inches taller than the head of security and outweighed him by at least fifty pounds, Mustafa was paralyzed with fear. Raahil bent over the cowering Mustafa yelling directly into the man's face. "You are a complete idiot! Did you drive here in your own car Mustafa? Did you?

Did you not consider the security cameras on the other buildings that will place you at what is about to become a crime scene?" Raahil drove another kick into the spoiled fat man's side as he continued his tirade. "And just what did you think we were going to do here? Rape her like an uncivilized animal? Leave our DNA all over her so that we could be connected to her murder later? I should have let you." Raahil paused, he was panting with anger, the veins in his neck bulging with each beat of his heart. "And who do you think you are to barge in here like this anyway? This is not part of your job."

Mustafa had managed to sit up against a wall and was huffing as he held his aching side, "My brother will order you be killed for treating me this way." He tried to counter weakly. Raahil pulled a cellphone from his pocket and dialed the ten-digit number to the Mullah's personal cell phone. He held it out with his thumb hovering over the SEND icon.

"Do you really want to take the chance that he won't order me to kill *you* for nearly compromising everything we have done?" Raahil was waving the phone around the room. Mustafa dropped his head.

He feared he knew the answer would not be in his favour and muttered, "No."

Raahil ordered the fool from the room and sent one of his security men to keep an eye on him. As Mustafa dragged himself out the door, Raahil pulled on a pair of latex gloves and picked up a five-pound mallet he had brought in from the garage. He stood over the green-eyed beauty. He was saddened at what he had to do next, he had come to enjoy her. He brushed her hair back with his free hand, the tears streaming down her cheeks had matted strands of her hair sticking them to her cheek, but she didn't make a sound. The room was eerily quiet. Raahil could feel the adrenaline rushing through his veins down to his hand clenching the mallet. He shook a little. He raised the heavy instrument over his head and looked the girl in the eyes one last time.

In the waiting room, both Mustafa and the security man jerked around to look at the office when they'd heard the sickening *thud*. They could hear the chair topple over followed by a second *thud* and loud cracking sound. Raahil and the security man exited the room. Mustafa could see little blood droplets sprayed across Raahil's neck and face and the sleeve of his right arm. Raahil removed the shirt and wiped his face with it. He stuffed it into a paper bag one of his men had produced along with his pants and shoes. He then opened a duffle bag Mustafa had not noticed on the reception desk. From the bag, Raahil changed into a new pair of jeans and fresh button-down shirt. The entire time, Raahil held an unwavering angry stare on Mustafa.

As he combed his dark hair he finally spoke. "I will not speak of this to the Mullah. But step out of line again, brother, and I will not hesitate to tell him everything, and he *will* order me to kill you. Do you understand?"

Mustafa stood gingerly and huffed, "I will meet you at the meat shop." He shuffled out through the back of the garage to his car, the big engine roaring as he sped away.

"You can send an email from the computer in the office to all the employees telling them that the business will be closed for the next three weeks." Raahil instructed one of the men. "Tell them it is so that he can take a vacation and grieve the loss of his friend." He turned to the other. "Make sure the blinds are all closed so she isn't found too early by accident, and when we leave be sure to use his security code to set the alarm." The two security men made quick work of their tasks and returned to the mini van where Raahil was just getting off his phone.

***

Ameer ended the brief phone call with "...that's fine. Thank you. I will see you shortly." He turned and faced O'Neil. "Young brother O'Neil. This is a very big step today. Are you ready for this?"

O'Neil paused to think about his answer then proceeded cautiously. "I feel like I get closer to Allah every day. If this is what he wants from me, then I am ready."

Ameer smiled confidently, knowing he had made the right choice in selecting this young man. O'Neil smiled back at him. Ameer thought it was a smile of admiration. In reality O'Neil's bright white smile was concealing a plot to kill him. The car turned in behind a long commercial building and stopped at a small loading dock. The driver exited the vehicle and knocked at the door. A small, faded sign read, "Green Tree, Halal Meats." An older Arabic man opened the door with a smile and waved them inside. O'Neil went first nodding to the man as he passed. He overheard the man asking Ameer about his daughter.

"Is my daughter working for you again today my friend? I have not seen her in many days now." the man asked. O'Neil didn't hear the response, but Ameer had an arm around the man's shoulder and both were smiling and nodding.

The group made their way to the basement. There they found the same set as at the mosque, the camera crew standing by patiently. O'Neil was guided to a washroom where he was given a black robe and keffiyeh to don. On the counter sat an AK47 with that ominous curved magazine hanging out from under the receiver. O'Neil quickly dressed in the clothing he had been given. He grabbed the weapon off the counter, and thought to himself, "I can't be this lucky. They'd never give me a loaded gun to hold near him." O'Neil wasn't familiar with this particular gun, but he had held enough other ones to know there had to be a release button for the magazine. He found it just as the door opened, and Raahil stuck his head in. The magazine fell to the floor and rattled noisily. O'Neil bent down sheepishly and picked up the magazine. As he turned it over, he could see that it was as empty as it had sounded.

Raahil stared at him for a long time. He was analyzing his actions and demeanor. "Are you almost ready?" he asked skeptically.

"I'll be right out." O'Neil replied trying to hide the nervousness in his voice. Raahil closed the door and O'Neil signed heavily. Collecting himself, he hastily wrapped the scarf around his face. As he walked toward the set, he saw Ameer sitting in the big chair reviewing his script. A woman came over and fussed with the keffiyeh around O'Neil's face. She then pushed him onto the set to a place to the left of the Mullah. O'Neil looked around for direction and decided to mimic the pose Mustafa had adopted on the other side of the Mullah. Ameer handed the script back to someone, O'Neil couldn't see who through the bright lights shining in his face, he barely made out the camera operator's countdown and the little red light turn on atop the camera. The Mullah's voice was barely audible to O'Neil, now in a daze. He was tunnel visioned by everything happening around him, and the lights were having a dizzying effect on him. O'Neil's whole life seemed to be spinning out of control. He heard Ameer repeating much of the same things from the last taping.

And then the mood changed.

Ameer's tone switched to something low and angry. O'Neil listened. He could not help turning his head at this point to look at Ameer as he heard him saying, "Since you do not take our demands seriously and have refused to show us that you wish to negotiate our terms, I am left with no choice but to carry out my threat. I warned you that we were not to be taken lightly. There are twenty-four hours remaining in our stated timeline. You have those remaining hours to show us your commitment, or we will begin killing the people of this country."

The lights blinked off, and the camera shut down. The same man sat at a computer and started the editing process. The other people in the room were busy chatting or packing equipment. O'Neil saw the Mullah and Raahil huddled in a corner and eased his way over. He overheard only three words, "Union Station" and "Buses".

184

Ameer noticed him first. "Well done O'Neil. You are truly one with us now." The Mullah hugged him tightly and kissed his cheeks. O'Neil tried his best to act normal, but he was afraid his reservations were starting to show. The production wrapped up, and everyone made their way back upstairs.

The little shop owner was there again looking like a lost puppy. The man tugged at Raahil's sleeve. "Sir, if you haven't seen my daughter, should I call the police to look for her?"

Raahil stopped abruptly and guided the little man back into the shop. "No no effendi. Leave that to me. I will have my people look for her. She is probably just sick. It's been going around the building."

As the convoy pulled away, the old man stood in the doorway to his modest shop nodding and waving goodbye. O'Neil desperately needed to get to his cell phone.

***

At the training center, Team Three was on the ranges. The training cadre put the assaulters through a series of outdoor move and shoot drills while dismounting vehicles. The snipers were on the long range with the Cadre's lead sniper trying to get through a qualification shoot. This wasn't going well. Josh Bender and his partner Handsome Jack were fighting it today. Josh had qualified on the first pass with a perfect score, but they were onto Jack's third and final attempt. The trio had gone over the rifle from tip to tail after the second failure to make sure it wasn't something mechanical. They had even had the armourer bring out the bore scope to see if the barrel had reached its replacement time. It had not. The gun had been cleaned for a third time and left to cool. The trainer looked at his watch and told them to ready their gear. The snipers headed out to the firing line and the trainer looked at Jack, "C'mon Jack. Just slow yourself down and let's get this, okay buddy?"

Jack settled in behind his rifle on the 300-yard firing line and began the process of slowing his breathing. The shooter went through his pre-shot checklist just as the Special Forces instructors had taught him. Bender lay along his right side and just slightly behind him. Everything looked perfect, Bender was on the spotting scope and reading the wind. It had died right off, these were near perfect shooting conditions. Slightly overcast, no wind, no mirage boiling off the ground. No other distractions like cars or radio transmissions, just the shooter and his weapon.

Bender whispered to his partner, "Zero value winds – three hundred yards." Out of the corner of his eye, he watched Jack reaching up slowly and adjusting the elevation turret to the appropriate setting. His hand slipped slowly and quietly back to the trigger and rested there gently, waiting for the call.

A raven cawed in the distance but otherwise the world was still. The trainer stood over them and straddled their legs, watching all of Jack's movements. He leaned down to read the elevation turret and saw that it was dialed appropriately to four- and three-quarter minutes of angle, then nudged Bender's foot letting him know he could begin.

Bender took a slow breath and whispered, "Spotter ready."

Jack replied, "Shooter ready." Jack breathed out slowly and began taking the slack out of the trigger, ever so slowly. Steadily.

"Send it." Jack heard the words and finished his trigger squeeze, as the punctuation to the order. The gun leapt and settled as Jack worked the bolt chambering a new round. The shooter scanned down range, he wouldn't be able to see the impact point, but his partner would with the big spotting scope. Both men stayed on their glass, one scanning and one waiting. The target for this portion of the qualification was a three-inch black circle. The cold shot had to land in that circle.

"I can't see it. Have them mark it," was the nervous response from Bender. The trainer radioed down range to the man working the bunker and asked him to mark the target. The trio watched as the target was lowered and raised again with an orange marker in the center of the black circle.

"Hit!" the trainer announced with measured excitement. The snipers breathed a sigh of relief and picked up their gear. In this next phase, they would run with all their operational gear to the 400-yard line and back. Jack would have ten seconds from the time they hit the dirt to fire three rounds into a black rectangle painted in the chest of a target down range. The rectangle was three inches wide by six inches long. Bender shouldered his backpack and Jack his drag bag. They bumped fists and took off running. They panted heavily as they returned to the 300-yard line. Both were already pulling their bags off and getting gear out. The pair hastily dropped into the dirt and Jack dropped the rifle over the top of the drag bag not bothering with the tripod.

The trainer was calling out, "Ten…nine…"

Jack forced his breath out and held it. He squeezed off the first round and worked the action.

"Seven…six…five…"

Jack fired his second shot and tried to steady himself.

"Four…three…two…" He squeezed off the third and final round and let the gun settle. Both sniper and spotter rose to their knees to catch their breath. The target went down and reappeared with two orange markers in the rectangle. It meant one of two things. Either one round had missed the target entirely or two rounds were so close that one marker covered both. Which was it? The radio crackled, "Three hits."

The snipers smiled and readied themselves for the final five rounds of the course of fire. In this phase, Jack would have to hit a moving man-sized target three times in the chest cavity for them to count. He accomplished that without much trouble, although the trainer noted Jack seemed to be struggling with getting his eye relief just right behind the scope. The final two rounds would be fired with no time limit. These were two of the most difficult shots to make. The sniper would have to put both rounds inside a rectangle that went across the eye area of the target. The scoring area was only 2 inches tall, but it was 6 inches wide. Essentially the scoring area went from the eyebrows to the bridge of the nose, and from the outside of one eye to the other.

The pair of snipers settled in, and Jack sent the two rounds. He worked very deliberately at setting up and squeezing the rounds off. When the gun settled after the last round the trainer called the range cold and the lights around the range and on the control tower switched from red to green.

Gear was stowed back in bags and loaded on shoulders for the walk back to the target to verify the scores. All the targets that Jack had shot in this attempt were pushed back up for viewing. He walked straight to the last target. One round had landed right between the eyes but the second was straddling the line of the rectangle off to the right side.

They stood looking at the target for a few seconds. Then the trainer spoke, "Well it's a pass finally, Jack. But you'll have to shoot it again next week and qual on your first pass or be stood down."

Jack obviously was not happy with his performance. "Yeah yeah. I know. Shit."

"Is something else going on, Jack? Are your eyes bugging you? You seemed to really struggle with your eye relief today." the trainer asked, just doing his job. It was not the kind of question any shooter wants to have to be asked or worse yet have to ask themselves. Jack was furious, not at the trainer for asking but at the thought of it happening.

"I sure as hell hope not." he said.

Chapter Twenty-Two

Team Three was the operational on the evening shift that overlapped with the night shift to accommodate for the volume of work during the overnight hours. Word was already spreading around the unit like wildfire about Handsome Jack's struggles on the range. The team was out on patrol, but Jack was squirreled away in the planning room, huddled over a computer at one of the desks. As per The Group's protocol, the sniper team coming on shift was required to check the sniper room for any pending operational plans that need additional work. As Speed and Carter came in from their detail, they took a second to duck their heads into the planning room. Speed didn't see what Jack was looking at, but he could tell that he was engrossed in it. The Team Four snipers took a quick glance at the status board and saw there was nothing for them to cover and headed off to their own team room. Jack didn't even look up when Speed left the room.

Team Four readied itself for another night shift, and the weather people were all calling for a cold early November night. Speed and Carter found their Team in the room, all still in their sweaty gym clothes, busily prepping their personal gear for the shift. The TV in the corner of the room was tuned into a hockey game, an original six rivalry. Speed and Carter had been extracted from their observation post just a few hours ago, where they had spent nearly a full twenty-four hours compiling intelligence on the twenty-first floor of the terrorist's building. The pair still had hours of administrative work to do, but Speed's favorite team, the Boston Bruins, were back in town to battle the hometown Leafs, and he found himself procrastinating, as he reclined in front of his equipment stall. So far, the teams were both off to good seasons, and Speed, as always, was torn as to which to cheer for.

Some of the guys had pulled their chairs under the screen and were tinkering with their kit as they willed the Leafs to a victory. Speed's phone chimed; it was a video chat request. He smiled at the phone's screen, as Angie and little Camryn's faces came into view. It was their bedtime ritual when he wasn't home. Speed hated not seeing them for extended periods like this. He loved them so much for being supportive of his job and its negative side. He and Angie had watched too many of their friend's marriages end in divorce and swore to each other that would not be them. He winked at his beautiful wife as she held the camera in front of little Camryn squirming her lap.

The Bruins scored again and went ahead 5-2 in the second period. The guys up close to the screen booed relentlessly, as Speed roared along with his wife and daughter on the phone. John Burke turned and tossed an empty box of ammunition in Speed's direction laughing.

Angie asked Speed, "So, anything on the go for you guys tonight?"

Speed shrugged, "Not yet. The Team Three guys are still out, and there isn't anything in the hopper that we know of. Hey – you remember Handsome Jack right?"

"Sure, the sniper with the scar. That's the guy right?"

"That's him."

"Okay sure. Is he okay?"

"He's fine. Well, mostly I guess. He has been really struggling on his sniper qual's lately. Word is they may take his rifle from him. That would really suck for the guy."

Angie smiled. "Paul. Are you worried about your eyes, honey? You're too young."

"I know. But God, this must be killing him." Paul replied concerned.

"Maybe you should go talk to him and be a good friend. See if you can help someway?" Angie Speed was always the voice of reason. Her outside perspective was what had kept Speed grounded through the early part of his career. She smiled at him as Camryn made fishy faces to the camera.

Speed burst out laughing. "Camo, you're a riot!" he exclaimed making the same face back to her. "Okay girls, I gotta run. Love you." They blew each other kisses and ended the call with their traditional, "Be good."

As Speed pushed himself out of his stall his beloved Bruins scored again to close out the second period.

"I think Chinese for dinner tonight there, Burkie. Looks like I'm gonna win that bet." Speed rubbed big John Burke's head, as he passed and got an angry grumble in response. He headed down the hall toward the sniper room to look for Jack and to set to work compiling the intelligence haul from the past 24 hours.

***

O'Neil had finally managed to get free of the celebrations taking place up on the twenty-first floor. Rather than head straight back to his own apartment where he knew they might come and look for him, O'Neil went to an old girlfriend's unit on another floor. The young woman let him in without questioning why he was there. A toddler sat playing in the living room while the TV flashed images of some popular kids program she had recorded. The show periodically grabbed the kid's attention with some bright colors or funny sound.

"Taesha, I just need somewhere private to make a couple calls. You okay if I do that here?" he asked her politely.

"For sure boo. Only if you stay, have dinner and kick back after." She was obviously lonely. O'Neil was too, and he needed somewhere to hide out for a bit to get away from what was going on upstairs.

"Okay sure. I'll stay for a while." he said, only half sure. O'Neil patted the little one on the head and went into the bedroom to make his call. He watched, as the young mother stopped by a mirror in the hall to fix her hair smiling to herself. She went into the kitchen and started pulling open cupboards looking for some dinner. O'Neil closed the bedroom door and pulled a phone from his pocket. He dialed the number given to him by Immes for these contacts and sat on the edge of the large bed.

"Go ahead." It was Immes' voice.

"They are going to put bombs on buses man." O'Neil whispered.

"Which buses? When?"

"I'm not sure, but I don't think it's the city ones. I think it's the other ones that run out of Union Station. I think the plan is to make this their warning for not meeting the demands. That's all I know, man." O'Neil felt a little helpless but knew he could only do his part. He just hoped the cops would do theirs.

"Okay. I'm on it, stay safe man." Immes hung up.

O'Neil went back out to the living room and fell into the couch beside the young woman. She had freshened up her make up, he noticed. There was a knock at the front door, and an older woman entered smiling at O'Neil. He smiled back recognizing the woman as Taesha's grandmother. The older woman gathered up the toddler telling him to kiss his mommy. The young woman kissed the little one, as they left and locked the door behind them.

She turned and faced O'Neil with a seductive bite of her lip. "No pressure Face. No strings."

***

Immes was on the phone with the Felix DeLeon from the Source Handling Unit and he relaying to the detective what O'Neil had told him. "Jesus!" the big detective replied. "That doesn't leave us a whole lot of time!"

Chapter Twenty-Three

10:00 a.m.

The following morning, newsrooms across the country were all switching to the feeds from Channel 3 and 24. Anchors Denise Dobson and Siobhan Murphy had become the recognized authorities on the latest domestic terrorism story, and the two stations were still sharing roles in disseminating the information to the viewing public. The television screen switched to a live feed of Siobhan Murphy standing in a police conference room. The police crest hanging in the background behind a large dark wood podium, the bright TV lights soaking it in fluorescent white light. Siobhan had a look of deep concern on her face as the camera stared at her. She was obviously unaware they were live. Realizing that she was in fact ON, the professional reporter quickly switched to her news delivery face. Siobhan began matter-of-factly addressing her audience and went through a brief restating of the facts. Just in case anyone had missed part of the story that was being covered nightly on every station in the country. The young reporter turned abruptly as a number of police officers flooded into the crowded room. A uniformed spokesperson addressed the room and introduced the tall gray haired officer with the blue eyes to her left. He wore an expensive suit and seemed important, although Siobhan had never seen him before.

"Inspector Nance is here to give a brief statement as to the status of this investigation and answer a few questions." The young spokesperson went on to outline the rules for the question-and-answer period following the statement. Then she stepped back from the podium, Inspector Nance taking her place. He deliberately opened a tablet in front of himself, scanned the room, and took a sip of water. The suspense in the room was palpable as the camera zoomed in on his face. His blue eyes piercing millions of screens across the country. Nance purposely held the silence for a moment and then spoke directly to the camera,

"Last evening a second demand video was received from the terrorists. This demand video…"

***

Angie was in the kitchen at the sink cleaning up from breakfast. She had the little screen on the counter tuned to the news. She stared at the screen. As Nance started to speak, she looked up through the window, and saw her husband at the Shed looking in at the TV hanging in there. He was stoic, arms folded but he didn't seem surprised or shocked. Her husband was leaning on the rake like that famous picture of Ken Dryden leaning on his goalie stick. She heard his phone ring and watched as he dug into his pocket to retrieve it. It was like Nance's voice on the television was talking directly to Speed.

Nance continued, "We will not stop working on this investigation until every last co-conspirator is in custody and the people of this city and this country are safe. We will throw every single resource without prejudice at this investigation."

As he finished that sentence, she watched Speed nod and his demeanor changed. He didn't look nervous or rushed. He just calmly put things away and shut the shed. The look on his face told the story, an intense focus was written there. She knew he was already *on the job* as they say. He turned to close the shed door as he answered another call on his phone. She knew this would go on until he left for work

Angie placed the dishes back in the sink and started filling Tupperware containers with food for her husband, she knew to pack things he could eat without warming. He wasn't likely to be sitting anywhere near a microwave for the next several hours.

Speed came in the back door staring down at his phone, still texting and called out to his wife, "Babe. I'm getting…"

Angie cut him off. "Called into work. I know; I saw Barry on the news too. I packed you some lunch." She handed him his lunch box and a large stainless steel water bottle that he had covered in stickers from various tactical supply companies.

Speed smiled at her and pushed the ball cap back on his head. "I love you Angie." He gave her a tight hug and a gentle kiss. His mind was somewhere else already though.

Angie stopped near the counter and kissed him again. "Don't be good today honey – please be great."

Speed smiled over his shoulder and finished writing something on the notepad on the counter. He turned and kissed his wife again and thanked her. He grabbed his go-bag and lunch box then headed out the door. Angie locked the door behind him and returned to the kitchen. She slumped onto a stool, tears running down her cheeks as she read the note he had taken time to leave her and Camryn:

Mommy and Camo,

I love you guys very much! Camryn, be good for mommy and I will see you soon. You are the greatest ladies in the world! - Love, Dad

In the warehouse north of the city, the workers had finished mixing and packing all the components into the trucks. The trucks were lined up along the back wall and no one was permitted to go near them. In a small makeshift workshop, the bomb maker was putting the final touches on three additional explosive devices, which were then carefully packed into identical bags ready for delivery to the commuter bus terminal this afternoon. Upstairs in the offices of the same building, the suicide bombers were going through their pre-attack rituals. They shaved, washed and prayed together. Mullah Ameer Mahmood was there, overseeing the process. Mustafa was also there, but he was hulking around a table of food and wine. Raahil was busy seeing to the security arrangements, his entire team of security men was also present; most had AK47's slung over their shoulders. Three taxis and their drivers were waiting just outside the building to deliver the bombers and their packages to the terminal. Alone in the middle of the hustle and bustle, O'Neil Facey sat nervously in the main garage area trying desperately to figure out how to get a message to Immes. Raahil had taken his cell phone when they had left early this morning.

***

As the press conference finished, Siobhan Murphy managed to get an interview with Nance. "With me is Inspector Barry Nance who is the officer in charge of the Intelligence Division. Inspector can you elaborate on what you know and where the police are in this investigation? Are we any closer to making arrests?"

Nance smiled politely. "Siobhan, we are making great progress in this investigation. We still have work to do, but it's all coming together very quickly, and I am confident we will see a successful conclusion to this investigation. Thank you, but that is all I can say at this time." Nance excused himself by answering his phone as he stepped away from the camera.

***

10:45 a.m.

Speed was at the TIG building along with every other operator in The Group. Three of the sniper teams were remaining in street clothes and being assigned to plain-clothes surveillance of possible targets. The three other teams were being sent out to overwatch the three major bussing centers in the city. The gun teams themselves were being spread around the city to cover those terminals as well, but the focus would be on the Union Station terminal.

Speed and Carter were detailed to cover a bus terminal in the east-end. It was a link between the longer route buses coming from out of town and the local buses coming into the city. They were dressed in unassuming jeans and button-down shirts, the pair had been so busy lately that they each had a few days of growth on their faces. They quickly loaded extra pistol magazines and rechecked their weapons, the aggressive rock music playing in the background was in stark contrast to the guys as they got ready. No one was angry or aggressive. No one was getting pumped. It was business, they were focusing on the job at hand. Calmly going through the rituals of checking and re-checking equipment.

Carter looked at Speed. "I have a feeling we should take our operational gear and long guns with us Speeder. I don't think we will be getting back here."

"Good call pal." Speed slapped his partner on the back, and they packed their sniper gear and long guns, along with their assault gear and weapons into several soft bags. Speed grabbed his Colt carbine with suppressor and red dot sights. Carter opted for the trusty MP5; he had his modified with a red dot sight, suppressor, and vertical fore grip. Magazines were loaded and all of their kit was put in the back of an old Suburban. The snipers checked back in with Parker and got the OK to head out.

The guys loading trucks in the bays waved, and the snipers got an enthusiastic, "Save some ass-kickin' for us." That was Bryan Robinson leaning out the back seat of another truck as the pair of Team Four snipers headed out the door. At 11:45 a.m., the exit gate swung open and three separate vehicles slid out onto the road and rolled in different directions hoping to head off the bombs.

***

12:30 p.m.

O'Neil wandered around the old building looking for a phone that may have inadvertently been left lying around. He was becoming increasingly worried that he wouldn't be able to contact Immes in time, as the terrorists looked to be getting ready to leave. The bomb bags had been moved near the door and were waiting for their assigned bomber to pick them up and get into a taxi. O'Neil stood at the makeshift buffet table near the bottom of the stairs that lead up to the office area. He heard the door open, and the Arabic music spilled out to the garage. Ameer exited and made his way down to the bombs stopping to stand over them saying some sort of blessing. There was a lot of chanting of Allah Hua Akbar coming from upstairs, and O'Neil watched as each bomber came out clean-shaven and dressed like any other ordinary Canadian. One even had on a hat with the Maple Leafs blue and white logo on it. Each was handed a pill to swallow;

194

O'Neil figured it must be some sort of drug to keep them motivated, ecstasy maybe? The chants grew as the trio came down the stairs. Each one stopped to get their bag, Ameer grabbed each by the shoulders and kissed their cheeks, then sent them out the door one at a time. The door closed behind the last one and the men still inside the garage erupted in cheers and shouts. O'Neil looked down at the table and saw a cell phone sitting there like a gift. Just as he was about to grab it a big hand slid under his and swiped it away. Mustafa glared at O'Neil and turned away walking up the stairs.

***

1:15 p.m.

An operator sat in front of a screen in a quiet restricted corner of a Canadian Air Force base in Ontario. The operator and a second airman's eyes were fixed on large screens that could be mistaken for a flight simulator. The images on the screen showed a large warehouse with several cars in the lot. The operator announced to his superior that the three green and orange taxis he had reported on earlier were taking on passengers, each was carrying a gym bag. The taxis were in motion and leaving the location.

This information was passed on by secure transmission directly to Nance's phone. It was then bumped to Gaines, who relayed it to his surveillance teams. The drone operator kept widening his orbit so he could watch all three vehicles as long as possible until the spin teams were in place. As good as the security had been by the terrorists, when they took O'Neil's phone this morning they couldn't have known he would miss a check-in with his handler. This would necessitate the Source Management people pinging that phone. When they found that the phone had been off a request was made, through various federal channels, to have it powered back on and tracked.

National security served as a very powerful motivator, and the request was approved immediately. The phone was eventually triangulated to this garage north of the city. At that point the police had then gotten a surprise offer of assistance from the Department of National Defence. The Canadian Military's Special Operations Units were being kept in the loop all along with this National Security investigation, and the Government felt it was in the Country's, and their SOF unit's, best interest to assist in any way they could just in the event a request should come through Parliament to allow those units to act domestically. The drone had been launched almost immediately from a secret facility in northern Ontario, and the very delicate sharing of information and resources began. The vetting of the shared information was going through the RCMP's tactical team in the province, ironically two Group operators were currently seconded to this team and naturally keeping their buddies informed. So the gray drone continued to silently circle high above the city outside the visual range of any prying eyes.

***

1:30 p.m.

Two of the spin teams were on their targets and tracking them into the city. A team from the TIG had joined each surveillance team and was trailing at a distance to intervene if necessary. But a delay was being caused by the third team's inability to find the last taxi.

In the Combined Operations building, some technological wizardry was taking place. The drone operator had relayed the information on the taxis and their fleet numbers, and a computer tech was using those fleet numbers to mine for information. She had been able to backdoor her way into the company's dispatch system to see who was driving the three taxis. The taxis were not showing as active on the company system. So the technician tried a different approach. She attempted to get access to their phones and see if there was an outside chance they were being used as a GPS. By adding these pieces, she hoped to find the third taxi, but that would take time.

The deeper the taxis went into the city, the harder it would become to track them with the drone and for the surveillance team to remain undetected. The spin guys were acting with the assumption there would surely be counter surveillance following these cabs and were staying a little looser than normal.

In a strange twist, Raahil had suggested not to send a countersurveillance team, as he felt the larger footprint would be too easy to spot.

"And besides," he had said, "I am supremely confident that no one knows who or where we are. The cab drivers will ensure they are delivered."

***

The teams from The Group had orders to takedown the taxis as soon as one of the taxis committed to the bus terminal. The spin teams would initiate the car stop and the Group team would deal with the driver and any occupants.

The computer technician struck pay dirt and was able to access two of the phones. They were in fact being used as GPS to guide those taxis onto their targets. Both were heading to the downtown bus terminal next to the train station. A message was sent to Gaines. He again forwarded it to the spin teams and the TIG team sergeants. The technician was having little success locating the third taxi, however. She had the driver's name and found he did own a cell phone, four in his name actually. Two were showing as sitting still at the University of Toronto Reference library. One was stationary at an

196

apartment building near Don Mills Road and Lawrence Avenue, and the last one was showing at a high school in the same area. So it was up to the drone operator and the available spin team to find the taxi without her help.

***

2:50 p.m.

Unsuspecting citizens started their exodus from work and there was a steady stream of bodies heading into both the bus and train terminals.

There was still no sign of the third taxi.

The two they were following had not committed to the terminal yet, so the police held back. The surveillance guys were gripping their steering wheels tightly, as they resisted the urge to pull up closer to the cab. The Group operators were also getting restless in their vans as they checked and re-check their lights and sights.

***

In the taxis, the air conditioning was on even though the temperature outside was cool enough for the heat, the mix of nerves and drugs was making the bombers sweat and they didn't want to draw any extra attention to themselves. The cabs were in their final stages of approach. As planned, each was doing a random circuit around downtown before committing to the terminal.

***

Speed and Carter paced on the platform at the east end bus terminal looking for anyone acting suspicious. The place was empty, and they knew they were about to miss the takedowns in the city. They were helpless, Carter radioed to the snipers from Team One who were at a platform just like this one north of the city.

"Sierra four to Sierra one, you guys having any luck there?"

"Negative Four. It's basically a ghost town here."

***

3:05 p.m.

A message blinked onto separate cellphone screens in the two taxis.

Make your deliveries now.

At the same time the company dispatcher sent a text message to the third driver over his computer dispatch system telling him the same thing. All three cabs made their moves toward the terminal. Three suicide bombers started their prayers silently to themselves.

The surveillance and tactical teams immediately arced to intercept the taxis. The third taxi could still not be located, but the computer tech had been able to get the fleet number

197

– 7708 – from the dispatch message. The last spin team would be scanning the area for that cab.

Fleet number 7708 had been parked right around the corner from the terminal. It had arrived within a minute of receiving that dispatch message. The bomber had left the taxi and taken a spot in line for an outbound bus to Oakville. He was calm and had successfully blended in with the crowd. The oblivious businessmen and women stood or sat with their newspapers and cellphones and waited for their bus home. As the buses started pulling up to the various loading points the other two taxis arrived at the opposite end of the terminal from [7708]. Cab [7708] pulled away quickly and began heading north. The driver was trying to distance himself from the scene. The rushing cab caught the eye of a passing surveillance car and the officer quickly put the information over his radio. He U-turned and sped after it, his surveillance team and their attached set of Group operators racing to catch up.

***

3:15 p.m.

The first bus in the terminal pulled out onto the road and headed south toward Lakeshore Boulevard. At the same time eight unmarked surveillance cars screeched and skidded around the two taxis on either side of the street at the opposite end of the terminal. The bombers were just getting out. Two large black vans also screamed up the road. The surveillance operators were bailing out of their cars and running away from them, clearing the lines of fire for the Group operators coming in to effect the arrests. As the surveillance people passed the tactical men, four small black metal cans were floating through the air toward the taxis, two each per cab. The scene sent the people on the platform scrambling for cover. A second later, four loud concussions echoed through the downtown as black and gray-uniformed tactical operators rushed forward. Several people on the platform screamed. The men moved rapidly toward the two would-be bombers, who were frozen with shock. The bomber closest to the terminal tried to run and climbed over the hood of the closest surveillance car with his bag in hand.

He ran toward the buses yelling, "Allah Hua Akbar." After only about ten yards, the back of his head exploded, and he fell forward landing flat on his chest. The pursuing operators dove for cover behind cars trapped on the street. The bomber's gym bag tumbled rudely to the ground with him, coming to rest a foot or two beyond his body.

198

"Hit." Josh Bender whispered to his partner, as they lay on the roof of Union Station looking east. Handsome Jack smiled, as he worked the bolt loading a new round and scanned the area for more targets.

"Sierra three – shot out, shot out, shot out – one cold badger." Bender announced into the radio.

The second bomber was stuck in the cab, the doors had all been pinned by the surveillance cars. The Group operators had backed off and tried to call the bomber out through a window. He refused to move. The bomber was praying frantically and he pounded on the window in a futile attempt to get out. On the sidewalk nearby, an unnoticed Arab man was trying in vain to make a phone call, but he was unable to get a signal. He tried desperately over and over even yelling in Arabic at his phone. Handsome Jack heard the man and looked down over the ledge from his sniper hide and thought the man might be trying to initiate the bomb remotely.

"Possible accomplice. He's trying to remote initiate the package. Just north of the takedown, east side. Male middle-aged Arab yelling at his cell phone." Jack put the information over as fast as he could. The operators at the rear of the takedown that were holding security positions started racing up the street at the man.

The man with the phone didn't notice them right away because he was staring at a black SUV that had slipped in unnoticed and parked at the curb during the initial takedown. This truck had an assortment of thick antennae and a large bubble on its roof. Two large men had slipped out of its interior pointing guns at him with serious anger in their eyes. The man stood there locked on them while he repeatedly thumbed send on his phone. Out of nowhere, he was kicked off his feet and onto the ground, and two other men in gray were on him wrestling his hands behind his back. One of the men from the electronic disruption vehicle picked up the phone and calmly powered it off.

***

3:20 p.m.

The surveillance team caught up with taxi 7708 and executed another dramatic high-risk stop on a busy downtown street. When the smoke cleared from the distraction devices, the tactical operators had smashed out all the windows of the taxi and pulled the driver through his opening. He was on the street in handcuffs, as they radioed the all clear. The cab was empty.

Back at the terminal, officers were busy evacuating the platform and remaining buses of civilians in case one of the bombs should go off. Dozens of uniform police swarmed the scene. Roads were blocked and yellow police tape hung. A bomb squad truck parked at the top of the road on a hill looking down on the unfolding scene below.

**

3:24 p.m.

The final bomber held his bag on his lap and looked nervously around the interior of the bus. There was only himself, the driver and four other passengers. He was confused. Why hadn't the bombs gone off? They had been assured that there would be remote detonation. What was going wrong? As the bus pulled further away from the terminal and turned under the Gardiner Expressway, the man opened the bag to look at his bomb. Maybe he had knocked a connection loose? The screen on the phone attached to the bomb flashed NO SIGNAL. As he sat staring in disbelief, the screen turned green and stopped flashing. He saw the display change to INCOMING. The bomber looked at the ceiling and yelled, "Allahu Akbar!"

**

Raahil watched a video feed being supplied by an associate positioned near the scene in a nearby office tower. He had been using a hardline video feed. When Raahil realized the bombs weren't going off, he started to dial them himself and finally made a connection to the third bomb. As he saw his phone connecting, Raahil also yelled, "Allahu Akbar!" He could see the horrendous explosion and smoke rising from under the expressway, as the camera panned to the west.

**

O'Neil dropped his head and tried to hide his sense of failure.

The explosion rocked the downtown area from underneath the elevated expressway a few short blocks from the terminal. When the first officers arrived on the scene, they found one of the green and white buses torn open like a tin can. It stunk with the smell of burning rubber and plastic. A cloud of black smoke and gray dust hung over the scene and the overhead expressway had buckled, a section had fallen dropping a vehicle some one hundred and twenty feet to the roadway below. Three young college students were left dead inside. A second car that must have been beside the bus when the bomb went off had careened into a concrete pillar and trapped the driver. Anyone inside the bus was gone.

Chapter Twenty-Four

While there was chaos downtown, every other corner of the city had gone deathly quiet. Word of the explosion spread quickly, and people were frozen in front of any TV screen they could find. In the big box electronics stores, they huddled around the walls of TVs on display. On sidewalks, people hugged perfect strangers with tears rolling down their faces while they stared through the display windows of the department store. In a Tim Horton's, twenty or so customers stood scattered though the coffee shop all facing the screens above the fireplace where the news channel was broadcasting the story.

Shocked and awed.

Barry Nance sat in a conference room with Jim Gaines and three other analysts, Naila being one of them. They watched a large screen with a live feed from the drone. The drone operator reported robotically on the damage as he circled the scene.

Nance rubbed his forehead and looked at Gaines.

All Gaines could manage to say was, "Fuck!"

Nance shook his head, "This isn't over. Let's pull ourselves together and grab up the rest of these guys before another bomb goes off. We start working right now." By the end of his statement Nance was yelling which was not his normal style.

"I want the Major Incident Command Center fired up immediately and the required unit commanders notified. Gaines, get your analysts tearing these guys lives apart strand by strand. I want something workable within the hour."

Gaines, along with Naila and the other analysts, were already up and moving to their part of the building. Intelligence analysts and detectives began scurrying throughout the building. As they did, a buzz started across the entire Intelligence community. Phones rang repeatedly, and computers hummed through data base searches. You could feel the vibration of the Intelligence engine now running at full tilt, people from the various sections were doing their part. The collective power of their intellect was being brought to bear on finding the rest of this group. Nance was on his phone, before the door had closed behind Gaines and his people, giving orders to the Tech Support Section.

Speed and Carter sank in their truck staring out the window.

"Holy shit Mikey! Holy shit!" was all a stunned Speed could string together for a sentence.

Their radio cackled again. All teams not active at the bombing scene were ordered to rally back at the TIG base for retaskings. Carter threw the truck in drive and pulled out of the lot heading for the highway.

"Gonna be a long night, Speeder."

"Yeah it is." replied Speed with some sadness in his voice, as he hit the switch, firing up the lights and siren.

In the warehouse, some of the terrorists were celebrating a victory. Mustafa was dancing and chirping away like a fat old hen. Ameer leaned on the railing looking down at Mustafa smiling with a satisfied look on his face.

Raahil came to his side and spoke calmly next to his ear. "At the risk of ruining this little party, I do not believe we have reason to celebrate. We were lucky to get just one of those bombs to explode. We should send the trucks now. We have been compromised, there is a leak somewhere."

Ameer turned to face his old friend and closest advisor. He smiled genuinely. "Raahil you have always been the voice of great caution. But is not the time to panic. We were interrupted, yes. But Allah wants to see us succeed. If we rush those trucks out, they will surely be intercepted by the authorities. They do not know about this place. We will send the trucks as planned in three days' time."

Raahil could not believe what he was hearing. He searched himself to see if he was overreacting. He knew he was not. The Head of Security knew his job, and he knew that this mission was fully compromised. If only one thing next to Allah was true, he was sure that this was it. "Make me this one compromise then. Let's get as far away from here as we can for now. If the authorities come, we do not want to be here."

"Fine." Ameer agreed. "We will go to the house in the east end and wait for our final act."

Raahil left his side to make the arrangements for the move. Vehicles were loaded, and the building was left in the hands of a small security detail. As the group was loading into the vehicles in the parking lot another drone settled into an orbit over the location. This new drone happily captured video of more license plate numbers and hovered above the small motorcade as it made its way out to the highway. Eventually the convoy turned off the highway, and the drone settled into a new orbit over an upscale residential neighbourhood in the northeast part of the city. It was just eighteen kilometers from the Group's base. The drone operator was not able to get a look at the faces of the people getting out of the vehicles due to some passing cloud cover, but she marked the house, and as ordered, held her orbit over the house.

***

Hasty plans were being drawn up for tactical assaults on the twenty-first floor of the Orton Park building. Speed and Carter were still in that general area and were retasked over the radio. They would reinfiltrate their old OP setting up overwatch for Team Six and cover them as they arrived. The trick would be how to get into the building with their gear this time? The snipers didn't have the luxury of the air conditioning repair company ruse they had used previously. Carter wheeled the old truck into a lot across the street. The sun was just setting, and they could hear the call to prayers echoing through the neighbourhood. The snipers watched, as the men streamed from the building and headed to mosque. Looking at each other, they decided that was as good a time as any. They accepted the risk of being seen going into the building. The snipers mitigated some of that risk by using the front lobby of the opposite building. This way they would be entering on the side that faced away from the terrorist's balconies.

Sitting in the visitor's parking, they eyed the lobby. They were waiting for the right time to move. Speed was in the passenger seat and closest to the door. The pair watched the elevator open, and an elderly resident make her way slowly out into the lobby. Speed grabbed his pack and a black gun bag from the rear seat. He strolled across the walkway to the lobby like he owned the place and entered the vestibule just as the little lady opened the door. He held it open smiling as she passed. Carter followed Speed's lead. The pair of snipers jumped in the elevator and headed for the top floor.

***

In the Joint Operations Command Center, the TIG Staff Sergeants Ray Farmer and Frank Goodhall liaised with Nance's Intelligence head. They were trying to nail down locations for immediate entry. A Federal Crown attorney was on hand, and a judge had been driven over as well to authorize the warrants. Information was still very scattered at that point. Sorting through the list of possible of targets was becoming a monuments task. Tactical teams from jurisdictions around the city were also put on standby. The teams at the Group were given a two-minute notice to move order, and the men geared-up sitting in, on or near their assigned vehicles waiting to be assigned a target to hit.

Two addresses were immediately at the top of Naila's list. The entire 21st floor at Orton Park was obvious, but she wanted to send the Group to New Leaf Landscaping.

"It's a great place for them to have staged an operation like this." She had argued. Gaines rolled it over and decided everything was going to be hit anyway.

"Let's do it. Send the boys in gray the address."

Naila typed a quick email to Farmer and Goodhall, which they immediately added to the list and assigned it to a team. The Sergeant for Team Two heard his phone rattling in the cup holder in the console next to him. He sat forward and checked the screen, then called for his team to saddle up. The men quickly donned the rest of their gear and checked their weapons as they jumped on board. The other teams stood and watched as Team Two pulled out into the evening. As the van rolled out of the garage, the men it passed slapped its sides, comforting their brothers inside.

***

Ameer went straight to the bedroom and lay down falling immediately to sleep. Mustafa went straight to the refrigerator and hunted for food. Raahil was standing in front of the TV watching the news his arms folded and a concerned look on his face. O'Neil entered the living room and fell into the couch.

"How did they know we would be there?" Raahil asked the TV, hoping it would actually give him an answer.

Mustafa shouted from the kitchen with a mouthful of dates, "I bet this little asshole told them!" the fat man shouted, waving a finger in O'Neil's direction. "We should kill him Raahil!" Raahil hushed Mustafa with a finger to his pursed lips. He looked at O'Neil and wondered.

***

Speed and Carter wasted no time getting into the apartment. They weren't worried about being discreet, as they popped the door open with a mini pry-bar. Once inside, they wedged it shut behind themselves. Speed went straight to the end of the hall and opened his drag bag. He slid the black and tan rifle out of the bag and quickly spun the suppressor onto the end. Carter camped out near the first bedroom with his MP5 around his neck watching the apartment door. Speed was already in the room glassing the opposing building. Carter was up on comms advising Team Six that the sniper team was in position.

Speed saw no one on security so he edged into the second bedroom and up within a foot of the window. He looked down and saw the roundabout was empty.

Speed reached up to his left shoulder and keyed his mic. "Sierra Four to Team Six – Number one side is green, target floor is green, light activity."

"Copy. Long Final." came the reply from the T/L. The snipers know knew the team was about a minute away. They listened for the call of "short final," followed by the T/L's call of "out out out."

A minute later, those calls were heard, and the team slipped out of the van like a family of church mice. They staged at a side door that led to the stairwell. An operator stepped out of the line and pulled a tool off the back of his plate carrier, he slid it into the crack of the door and peeled it open, the team stealthily disappeared into the stairwell.

Three of the operators split off from the team on the second floor and made their way to the opposite stairwell to act as a blocking force. This group would hold on the landing to the twentieth floor out of the way of any crossfire. It seemed to take forever for the team to reach the target. The snipers listened while the two elements reported their floor positions to each other as they slowly climbed the stairs. Eventually both sides halted on twenty.

The T/L called the snipers for a SITREP and got a short reply from Speed.

"Green."

Seconds later, the team hit the floor. Speed could see women scrambling from apartment to apartment. He focused his rifle on the last unit. He knew it had been the busiest with male activity the last time. Speed panned his rifle back across to the opposite end of the floor and watched as Team Six worked their way along. They were in the second apartment now. He swung his rifle back the other way and saw a man in the living room of the last apartment holding an AK 47. It was leveled at the door.

"Gun Gun Gun. Last unit. Male in the living room, AK pointed at the door." Speed reported calmly, waiting for a response from the T/L, his safety off and his finger gently caressing the trigger.

"Copy Sierra Four. We are still about four apartments away from there. Keep me posted. I'll advise when we are on the door."

"Copy."

Speed waited, watching the man with the AK, who kept changing his position. Eventually the man dropped the gun on the kitchen counter. He lay down out of sight in the living room waiting for the police to come and get him.

"We're on the last door Sierra Four." the T/L announced over Speed's headset.

"Gun should be on the kitchen counter, inside the door to your left. Target was last seen going down to the floor straight off the door in the living room area." Speed reported back.

A second later, the door flew open, two distraction devices exploding in the room. Speed watched the team spill in, converging on the terrorist in the living room. He heard an operator in the kitchen report the gun back to his T/L and Sergeant. Then the team called the all clear followed by checking in one by one.

"Twelve warm badgers at this site. Roll in the uniforms for support." the Sergeant called over the radio. Speed and Carter quickly packed their gear and headed for their truck.

***

Team Two had finished clearing the New Leaf Landscaping building, but they were frozen in the office, shocked at the site of the young girl lying there with her skull caved in. The report of the body sped its way through the various chains of command.

Everyone had the same two questions on their minds. Where had the leadership of this cell gone to hide? And what were they planning next?

***

The drone operator had relayed her intelligence on the east end house to her leadership. They however, were sitting on it. Paralysis by over analysis was setting in. The SOF teams were currently on standby and evaluating the situation. The RCMP were stalling any request to set them loose domestically and a heated debate was taking place behind parliamentary doors hours away from the scene in Ottawa, so the cozy little house remained an unknown. Night had set in, and a cool fall wind was picking up. On the quiet little street in Scarborough, families settled down in front of their televisions. Like the rest of the country, they waited for the latest news on the unfolding terrorism event in their backyard. The people of this neighbourhood were none the wiser to the new residents down the block. The blinds were drawn, and maple leaves blew across the lawn like at every other house here. A little gray dot in the night sky continued to silently circle the unsuspecting street.

***

Not knowing about the terrorist's safe house, Naila was left to whittle away at their known addresses. She and two other analysts scoured through records found at the Orton

Park building. A false wall had been uncovered, and a treasure trove of information had been found that was being connected to items gathered at the landscaping offices.

One of the junior analysts noticed it first. She studied it for a time trying to place its usefulness. Naila saw the perplexed look on the woman's face. They had just found an interesting piece but couldn't see where it fit into the puzzle. Her eyebrows raised with excitement, and she showed it to Naila.

"I think I found them!" she exclaimed.

The analyst was holding an electronic shipping receipt. It showed fertilizer shipments on a regular basis from another company to New Leaf. The analyst had dug a little deeper and discovered that several numbered companies were owned by one larger company. This company was based just north of the city. Naila played a hunch. She sent the address to the Group without even asking Gaines' opinion on the intelligence or his permission to launch the team.

Chapter Twenty-Five

The address popped onto the screen on Staff Sergeant Farmer's phone. He asked one of the assistants in the operations center to run a background on the address.

The officer immediately replied, "No need, Staff. That's the building we had the drone covering earlier today. Same company – same address."

"Is DND giving us anything from that location now?" Farmer asked.

"Yes sir. I can put the live feed up on the main screen." The officer made some quick mouse clicks, and the images appeared on the main screen. The perspective was high over a commercial neighborhood. It looked rural to a degree, as there were no other buildings close by like in the city.

"Audio?" Farmer asked.

The officer made another mouse click and the drone operator's voice came over the loudspeakers in the MICC.

"Can we talk to the pilot?" It was Staff Sergeant Goodhall this time.

"Yes Staff, we can. What would you like to say?"

"Ask him to zoom his camera in on the main door and then the truck parked in the dark behind the main building."

All eyes in the command center watched as the image zoomed in closer and clarified itself. There was nothing to see at the main door except for a faint slice of light squeezing under the threshold. The drone's camera panned over to a dark shadow. The grill of an old SUV was barely visible. As the drone pilot focused the night vision camera, the image cleared up, and the silhouette of a man became visible. There was a bright glow of a cigarette, which overpowered the screen forcing the operator to pan the camera back out. Clearly visible across the man's chest was an AK47. Behind him as the drone circled, they could just make out a stream of light escaping through the cracks of another access door.

Inspector Wismer placed his hands on the shoulders of his two Staff Sergeants. "Meeting right now in the conference room."

He nodded in the direction of a glassed-in conference room that overlooked the MICC.

In the conference room Wismer was direct and brief. "We are not waiting around anymore. The government and the military can't decide if this is terrorism, but the Chief has. We're sending the boys in on this. I want it contained tonight, and we will green light them early in the morning. All of our friends want to play. But that is going to be your call as to who we let in on this. Get it planned up and the teams moving within the hour. That's it."

"Sir." the two staff sergeants responded in unison. The pair headed back into the main area and grabbed two tactical planners, brought them into a second conference room, and placed a conference call to the administrative sergeant back at the TIG office. The framework was already in place; they only needed to close up the walls. All the teams were called back to the TIG to reorganize and stand ready to move.

***

Word reached the anonymous little house that the police had moved on their apartment and the New Leaf offices. They were informed that the green-eyed girl's body had been found.

Mustafa was furious and screamed at O'Neil. "I knew we never should have brought this animal so close to us! He is the weak point! For sure he put them on to us!"

His spit flew everywhere, and he foamed at the mouth. His hair was a mess and his eyes bloodshot and wild, he looked like a rabid animal.

"Maybe you should lay off the ecstasy tabs you keep asking me for, Mustafa!" O'Neil yelled back at him. He hoped that the aggressive counterattack would be enough to protect his cover. "You're paranoid! Think about it. I haven't had my phone all day, Raahil has it."

"He's right Mustafa. I do have his phone." Raahil interjected calmly, holding the curtains open slightly and scanning the street without looking back at them.

Ameer joined them, still looking optimistic and turned to Raahil. "I fear it has been our lust for that young girl that may have undone this plan. I think that the anger of a father who has just found out his daughter is lost forever has cost us. I would like to go speak with this man. Perhaps we can still use him."

Raahil made one final security request. He did not want them to use the cars they had come in. This old neighbourhood had a lot of big old maple trees whose branches provided privacy in a backyard, or a covered escape route for those trying to avoid being seen. They left the lights and TV on, and the little group made its way out the back door. They pushed through a hedgerow and a broken fence into the yard behind. Going around the side of the house, they stopped at the side door. Raahil gambled. In such an affluent and established neighbourhood, crime rates would be low, which meant doors would be unlocked. Inside the mudroom, he found a set of keys for the large boxy SUV in the driveway. His gamble paid off, and they climbed into the luxury vehicle slipping quietly out of the driveway for the short drive to the old man's apartment.

***

Around the warehouse north of the city, three tactical teams floated through the darkness in the surrounding fields like a predawn mist, each settled into a predetermined position. The team's snipers had crept in first and already had eyes on the building. The difficult part was coordinating the communications between Group Team Five, York Region Team Two and part of the Team from the RCMP. A common encrypted channel had been setup that all their radio sets could receive. It meant each sergeant carried two radios, and there would be delay in the sharing of information. The drone continued its lazy orbit above them. The operator noted the blinking of thirty green IR strobes that sat motionless in the grass and brush just on the edges of the property.

A lengthy and heated discussion took place between Staff Inspector Wismer, the Chief of Police and the General Liaison Officer from CANSOFCOM about what information was being withheld. Eventually, the liaison relented and released the information on the terrorist's safe house and immediately a team was detailed to hit the address.

***

Team One stopped at the end of the road and approached the target on foot. They expertly hugged the shadows along the fronts of the other houses. Sierra One and One Alpha watched through their night scopes, as the team eased up on the neighbouring house. The point man had his rifle up at threat ready. The rest of the team with their muzzles up looked like the hair on the back of an angry dog's neck.

"Green." reported the sniper team, which started the entry team moving to the door.

An explosive tech approached the front door covered by the point man and placed a strip of explosives along the edge of the door. The pair retreated a few steps followed by the flash and loud bang, the door splintering and falling to the inside The team made its entry behind the explosive breach. Two minutes later they reported, "All clear. No one inside."

***

Goodhall slammed his hands on the table and startled the quiet room.

"Jesus! We had them!" he shouted in disappointment.

210

Naila dug furiously through the piles of intelligence, trying to connect who this dead girl was. Then she remembered a picture Speed and Cater had sent her from their night of observations. She pulled it up on the screen placing it next to the image of the dead girl. It wasn't a perfect match due to the horrific injuries, but close enough. Naila called Gaines and outlined what she had. She theorized that the girl's family might be able to help. He agreed and sent a plainclothes team to bring them in for questioning.

***

Raahil and Mustafa had made their way up to the old man's apartment. At the door, they forced their way in. Mustafa slammed the door shut, as an old woman came running at him screaming. He slapped her across the face with the back of his hand, dropping her to her knees. The woman immediately stopped crying and sat holding her jaw. Raahil went to the kitchen table where the old man was frozen with fear.

"You have betrayed us, my friend. The Mullah would like to see what use you can be to us now."

Raahil grabbed him by the collar and dragged him to the door. One of the man's other daughters came from her room. She had a bat in her hand raised over her shoulder. The young girl ran face first into the muzzle of Raahil's pistol. He pushed the gun hard into the fleshy part of her cheek just under her right eye causing a small circular cut that began to seep blood. The anger boiled in him, not at her per se, more at his lack of control over the unfolding situation.

"Put the bat down and go sit on the couch Habibi." The order was soft but direct. The pair of terrorists withdrew from the apartment and headed back to the car with the old man. He was shoved into the back seat beside O'Neil. Raahil climbed in next and sandwiched him in the middle.

"Now where do we go?" Ameer asked Raahil looking back in the mirror. He had no plan for this. He was showing that he was completely out of his element and was handing control over to Raahil. Ameer had stopped fighting, given up. Raahil could see it in his eyes.

"We go to his shop. We film one last video message and we send the trucks. We kill him and then we split up and try to get back home. It is our only move at this point, my friend." Raahil was trying to be reassuring. He held only a sliver of hope that they would survive this, but someone had to steer the ship. One of these brothers wasn't capable, and the other had suddenly stopped trying

Gaines stood over Naila's shoulder looking at the screen. Documents cluttered the desktop, as she opened and scanned them quickly. Coffee cups and half eaten containers of Chinese takeout were scattered across her work area.

"Where would they go Naila? Where else—" Gaines was interrupted by the beeping of his phone.

He read the screen. "Shit! They took the girl's dad."

Naila didn't even look up. "That's it! I've been trying to find a connection to this family and the old man. Why use him? Different neighbourhoods. He comes from a different country…why him? Then I see it. His daughter went to an art school in the Orton Park area, and her best friend lives in those buildings. She had been spending a lot of time over there. She's been carded in the courtyard like fifteen to twenty times, right up until about the time when the terrorists take over the twenty-first floor. Look at the picture the snipers grabbed." Naila pulled it up on the screen. "Now she wears hijab and is right in the main target's apartment?"

"So they were using her for something." another analyst theorized.

"Yeah they were. This girl had been hanging out with all of Facey's soldiers. Soldiers this cell would need for their heavy lifting. But that's not all. This might have been a total coincidence but her dad owns a meat shop in the east end as well. I looked at the floor plans; it has an unused basement that in the original design was meant to be a little reception hall of sorts."

"Perfect for filming clandestine videos." Gaines started to close the loop. "So they pull her in to lock down the soldiers and likely as bait for Facey, but also as a way to own her family. Look we saved your daughter you owe us. Okay Naila, send the shop address to the Group guys. I'll see about getting that drone re-tasked. Let's give them all the other associated addresses we have so they can wrap this up all at once."

Gaines turned and started texting furiously on his phone. Naila sent her message to Farmer and Goodhall, listing the shop and several other addresses.

Goodhall handed his phone to the planning Sergeant and sat back looking up at the big screen. A rookie clerk came by and replaced their coffee carafe, Goodhall taking the opportunity to refill his cup. It was just turning one in the morning. This would be ending one way or another in the next few hours, he knew.

At the TIG, operators loaded magazines, replaced their radio batteries and fussed with equipment. Snipers went in and out of the sniper room printing off photos of their assigned targets, then trotted back to their team rooms to prep ghillie suits and urban hide kits. The team rooms were buzzing. Different music rolled out of each room mixing with the sounds of close-knit men preparing to do dangerous work. No one spoke of the danger, they just kept busy. Eventually all the teams filtered into the garage for a large-scale briefing, minus the snipers who had been deployed already. The overall mission was stated via video link from the MICC by Staff Inspector Wismer. He wished all the teams good luck and closed by saying he would see them back at the base for lunch. When he signed off, the teams broke off into smaller groups and went through their pre-operation briefings. One by one, they slipped out of the garage and into the night, heading for pre-arranged staging areas. Parker looked down at his watch and pressed the light. The pale blue screen on his Garmin told him it was 02:00 hrs. He let go of the button and leaned his head back against the wall for the short drive. He let his mind drift over his immediate action drills and a list of what ifs.

Chapter Twenty-Six

The snipers from Teams Three and Four had spent the better part of an hour sliding across two gravel rooftops, one on either-side of the Green Tree Halal meat shop.

"Why couldn't this have been one of those green roofs with the grass?" Carter was complaining.

Speed and Carter would be responsible for the front of the shop while Bender and Handsome Jack covered the rear. The shop was situated in a commercial strip mall. It sat right on the far west end of the structure. There was a main shop area in the front and the back had a kitchen/butchering area. There was also a third exit from the west side, just one door.

Speed eased his rifle forward in behind the makeshift air conditioner cover they had built as their sniper hide. He and Carter were laying side by side in the shadows now. Carter got on the radio over the sniper channel and relayed what they could see. It wasn't much but there were lights on in the back part of the shop and they could see shadows moving about. He went through a final confirmation on who each of the players were and how they were coded, "Badger One is going to be the calm slim fit one. We've been calling him Corleone".

"Badger Two will be the fat ugly one. He is tagged Sonny."

"Badger Three is an older male. We think he is the boss. Tag him Godfather."

"Dove One is our hostage."

"Dove Two is our agent that we believe is still with them. He's the black kid. Tag him Judas."

"Sierra Three and Three Alpha copy. Be advised. We have a black SUV out back. We sent the plate in, and it was reported stolen tonight."

Carter replied quietly. "Copy."

Other sniper teams were going through the same procedures around the city. The teams themselves had all arrived at their staging locations and were settled in waiting for the order to move.

***

Raahil and Mustafa dragged the old man down the stairs to the basement and turned on all the lights. They had not brought a camera and would have to film this message on a cell phone, which would be downloaded to the laptop Raahil had in his bag and onto the one remaining flash drive. Then they would call for one of their preferred taxis to pick it up.

The old man pleaded from his knees. "Where is my daughter, sir? Why are you doing this to me? I've been very helpful and grateful for what you have done for my daughter and my family."

Raahil was organizing the computer and the camera while Mustafa was guarding the old man. Mustafa reared up his foot and smashed it into the man's face crumpling him into a heap on the floor. He stood over him and began raining punches down onto him with all of his weight. Raahil watched at first and then became sickened at the sound. He shouted for Mustafa to stop.

But when he moved to intervene, the Mullah appeared at the bottom of the stairs and held his hand up at *Raahil* to stop. "You will let him finish."

The beating continued for another twenty seconds until the obese man ran out of energy and punctuated his tirade by spitting on the old man. "We killed your bitch daughter. She was troublesome, and you are better off without her! But you will get your chance to see her again when we are done punishing you for your betrayal!"

O'Neil had joined them and stood watching the unfolding drama. Mustafa was wild and crazed. Raahil was rattled, but a sense of calm seemed to have come over the Mullah.

"Is everything ready Raahil?" the Mullah asked.

"Yes. Whenever you are ready." was the unusually sheepish reply from Raahil.

There was no banner this time, and there would be no hidden faces or AK47's. This video was a going to be a last-ditch effort at salvaging their plan. Mustafa dragged the old man to his feet and held him up next to Ameer. They had bound his wrists with some cords. His face was swelling badly, and he could hardly stand on his own. But the old man didn't even whimper. O'Neil watched him closely; a single tear ran down the man's cheek. He watched it slowly drop to the floor splattering in the blood that pooled by the man's feet. O'Neil didn't listen to Ameer speaking, as Raahil held out his phone recording the message. When it was done, Mustafa dropped the old man to the floor and stomped on his ribs and face again.

O'Neil thought of the green-eyed girl. He couldn't take this anymore. Where were the cops? He was done standing on the sidelines. The young, athletically muscled O'Neil ran over and dropped his shoulder, burying all his weight into Mustafa. It didn't knock the man over, but it did knock him back a step. Most importantly, it got him to stop.

Raahil was there as swift as the fall breeze, his pistol pressing against O'Neil's temple. "Ameer?" He was asking for permission to shoot O'Neil.

"Not yet Raahil. He hasn't played his part yet."

Mustafa forced O'Neil to help drag the old man back up the stairs and drop him in the kitchen where Raahil set the laptop down and copied the recording to the flash drive.

"Make the call for the taxi, Raahil." the Mullah ordered.

Raahil dialed the number and made his request. Then they waited, wrapped in the tension of their unraveling plan.

***

03:45am

The taxi cruised onto the side street a block from the meat shop and was immediately stopped by a surveillance team. The driver told them that he was making a pickup at Green Tree Halal Meats. The team detained the man and seized his cell phone. The road boss for the team called the MICC and advised them of the situation.

***

3:50 a.m.

Mustafa was growing increasingly impatient. Between bouts of shouting at the old man for betraying them and beating him, he would scour the shop for food.

"Where is that fucking taxi?" he kept yelling.

***

Sierra Three Alpha – Handsome Jack – had moved his position slightly away from his partner so he could cover that side door as well. After settling in, Speed made an announcement on the sniper channel.

"All Sierra units switch to the common channel and check in at 0425."

***

4:15 a.m.

Carter pulled his dark green keffiyeh over his head, covering his phone, and sent a text to his unit commander:

All Sierras in position Sir. Will come up on comms at 0425.

The lights came on in the front of the shop, and Speed was able to make out Badger Two/Sonny. The grotesque man was going through the display cases, his shirt looked like it was covered in blood. Badger One/Corleone and Three/Godfather also appeared in the background. Corleone was pushing Dove One toward the open area in the shop and sat him at a table. Speed swiveled his scope back to the doorway leading to the rear

216

kitchen area. He had seen a flicker of movement, Speed recognized the person immediately. It was Dove Two/Judas, the agent, O'Neil Facey.

"Sierra Four – INFO INFO INFO."

Speed paused to make sure the air was clear. "I confirm, all guests have checked in at the party. Currently all are in the front of the location."

***

The person quietly monitoring the sniper channel sent a text to Wismer. He smiled at the screen as he looked down at it on the oak table and thought to himself, "I know."

***

4:27 a.m.

The sniper teams around the city were all checked in and on the common assault channel. They listened as their teams moved into their final positions. Speed watched as Bryan Robinson and Damon Fernandes slid along the front of the stores toward the meat shop. They took cover in an alcove two doors down in front of a fabric store.

Speed acknowledged to the command center that he had been given the authority to engage the terrorists without having to request permission.

"Sierra Four, we confirm Lightening Order at this time."

***

4:29 a.m.

Raahil new something was wrong. The cab should have been here. He grabbed the old man by the collar pulling him out of his chair. He drove him at the door with his gun pointed to the back of the man's head.

"Go check the back door. Something is not right!" he yelled at Mustafa and the others. Mustafa and Ameer ran for the back door, more out of a chance to flee than anything. Mustafa threw the door open and stepped out holding it open for Ameer who stopped in the threshold just in the shadows. Mustafa eyed the black van to his right whose doors were flinging open. Raahil was also peeking out the front door at the same time looking for the infidel assaulters that he knew must be coming for them.

***

Speed's voice broke the sterile silence of the MICC, as it leapt from the radio channel being broadcast in the room.

"Sierra Four…Corleone at level one door one holding a gun to the dove's head. Looking around nervously. We have a solution."

There was no panic in the man's voice that anyone could tell across the common radio channel. Yet lying on the roof of small business kitty-corner to Green Tree Halal Meat Store, or target one, one hundred and thirty yards away, were two men whose hearts just jumped.

"Sierra Three…solution on Sonny at the door on the black side. He's with Godfather, Sierra Three Alpha. Do you have a solution for Godfather?"

Men pressed their headsets tightly against their heads as they listened to the current exchange. Three other men were sliding their trigger fingers onto their triggers and pushing their weapons off safe.

"Sierra Three Alpha…No. Negative at this time."

"Sierra Three, I've lost Godfather. We still have solution on Sonny. Options Sierra Four?"

Speed's direction was clear and immediate. "Simultaneous. Then scan for Godfather for a rapid follow-up. Ready? Alpha Team standby. On my count, five…"

The air around the snipers went still. Sound disappeared from their environment, and the faces in their crosshairs seemed to be moving in slow motion. Speed felt the hair on his arms stand up and bead of sweat trickled past the corner of his left eye.

"…four…"

His right index finger caressed the trigger on the modified Remington 700 until it found it's sweet spot, about halfway from the tip of the finger to the first knuckle.

"…three…"

Handsome Jack and Speed smoothly started to pull their triggers backwards, taking out the slack. Jack slowly inhaled and held his breath. Speed adjusted his sight picture slightly as his target, Corleone, leaned forward.

"…two…"

The two shots were fired at exactly the same time from suppressed rifles on opposite sides of the building and were barely whispers in the night as the snipers reported over their radios, "Shot out, shot out – lightning, lightning, lightning!"

The worlds in and around several locations came alive with the sounds of doors crashing and the concussions of distraction devices echoing through quiet streets.

***

Mustafa hit the ground with a *thud*, as Handsome Jack worked his bolt backwards and then forward again chambering a fresh round. He came back on target looking for Godfather. Bender smiled quietly, his way of saying, *I knew you still had it in you, pal.*

218

Team Four flooded along the back wall of the business and halted at the door long enough to toss in two distraction devices. One operator stepped out to confirm Mustafa was dead with two more rounds to the man's face and then rejoined the entry.

***

At the front of the store, Speed worked his bolt, as fast as he could. He had barely heard Carter calling, "Hit, target down." on the radio next to him. As Speed's scope settled back on the front door, there was nothing but a pink mist of brain matter floating where Raahil's head had been. Speed struggled to catch his breath, as he pushed the adrenaline back down in his system, he instinctively scanned the inside of the store for the third Badger – Godfather.

Speed saw O'Neil crawling on his knees to the door and watched, as he pulled the old man back in through the opening to a corner just as the kitchen door flew open. There were flashes from the distraction devices going off. Ameer was running toward the front door.

There were TIG operators in the kitchen, and two of them slid through the door into the shop. Their guns were leveled at Ameer, green lasers danced across the room and painted the man's face, as he stopped at Raahil's body lying half in and half out the open front door. Speed was on his trigger again but didn't have a shot due to the position of one of the TIG men in the room.

The two operators spread out away from each other in an attempt to maximize their arcs of fire should Ameer refuse to comply. Outside the shop, Robinson and Fernandes had crept closer and were only one store front away. They were no longer hugging the building but were instead out in the open. One was on a knee with the other standing over him both of their guns up and ready, their lasers painting the back of the man's head.

Ameer froze weighing his options. He was analyzing the scene, and he slowly looked out the door up in the direction of Speed and Carter's hide, he couldn't see them, but he knew they had to be there. O'Neil was pushing the old man into the ground and trying to calm him.

"Shhh. Be still I'm not going to hurt you. Just lay still."

The TIG operators in the room with Ameer were Parker and Karras. Parker calmly give Ameer commands to lie down on the floor, but the man wasn't listening or maybe he couldn't hear. Speed watched, as the look on Ameer's face changed from analyzing to committed. Suddenly Ameer turned and squatted, as quickly as his aging body would let him, and he tried to grab Raahil's pistol out of his hand. He barely even made the turn.

Both Parker and Karras fired several times. The rounds slamming into Ameer's torso and as he fell to his knees Parker firing one more fatal shot to the middle to Ameer's face striking him just above the bridge of his nose, the body crumpling awkwardly to the floor. Speed dropped his head away from his scope, closing his eyes for a moment and taking a deep breath.

The team continued through the building securing both the old man and O'Neil. A security perimeter was established, and the snipers watched as an ambulance rolled up to the front door. The snipers stood on the edge of the roof for a short time and digested what had just happened, but only for a moment. The sniper pair quickly repositioned themselves with a view out into the neighbourhood and announced to Parker and the command at the MICC, "Target One secure, Sierra's Four, Four Alpha on security overwatch."

Bender and Handsome Jack followed suit.

***

In the command center, there were cheers shouted and hugs shared, as the bleak concrete room took on a relieved tone. Wismer, Farmer and Goodhall sat motionless and quiet at the head table. The three tactical commanders had not moved since Speed's first call over the radio. Wismer leaned back with his hands folded behind his head and a look of satisfaction on his face. Goodhall looked like he had seen a ghost and sweat profusely; he slowly rose from the big table and made his way to the back of the room away from all the celebrating.

Farmer was frozen in his chair, his hands were on the table in front of him and he was sitting straight up still looking up at the screen with the plotted positions on it. "Holy crap Vince! They pulled it off." he said to his boss.

Wismer was looking down at his phone, which was pinging like a slot machine now. Looking over the edge of his glasses he asked the old staff sergeant, "You didn't think they would?"

"It's not that I didn't trust the men boss, but this…well it was different."

There was a silence for a minute, as Wismer scrolled through the incoming congratulatory texts.

Farmer looked over at his boss and spoke again. "I can't do this anymore, boss. I'm done. I'm going to take some time off, and I'll file my papers in a few weeks, but I'm done."

Wismer looked back at him blankly.

Farmer continued as the celebrating buzzed on around them, "I realize that this job has passed me by. I've been holding on because I love this place, this job, these men, but I just can't do it anymore."

Wismer smiled, "I know Ray. I've seen it in you for a while now. You've been a huge asset to this outfit. It'll be a shame to see you go."

Farmer stood and shook hands with the Tactical Intervention Group's officer in charge and made his way to the door. As Wismer sat back down, his phone chirped again. He looked at the display and read the email from General Brown (probably not his real name). The Commanding Officer; Canadian Forces – Special Operations Forces Command. It read:

Inspector Wismer,

It is with the most sincere admiration and professional respect that as the C/O of the Canadian Special Operations Forces Command I extend congratulations on behalf of all the men and women in the command and myself. Job well done sir. Just as our motto, Viam Inveniemus – *We will find a way*, says, today your men truly found a way. Please share this with all involved.

Additionally – once you've completed your internal debriefs and after action reports I would like to invite your commanders and select team members to come and present a case study of the operation at our training center. It is my hope that this may in future lead to increased interoperability between our units and an opportunity to share lessons learned. I hope you will consider this offer.

Congratulations again on an excellent operation and a job well done!

Regards,

Brig. Gen. R. Brown

CANSOFCOM

Wismer took the time to write a quick reply and slid his phone back into his pocket. He waved across the room to the Chief of Police, who was being prepped for the press conference; the Chief smiled and offered a thumbs-up. Wismer returned the gesture as he rose to join his remaining Staff Sergeant at the snack table. Patting Goodhall on the back, Wismer quietly led him out from the room and out to the parking lot for the ride back to the TIG building. Wismer had a promise to keep and wanted to get back his men.

Epilogue

The teams from the Group eventually made their way back to their base. Prisoners had been turned over and were being looked after by their brother teams from Peel Region. Equipment was being hung in its place, vehicles were gassed and parked, and radio batteries placed back in the charging slots. Some of the men were just sitting around staring off into nowhere, while others were hugging their brothers. A much smaller group was quietly huddled on the station's rappel tower braving the cold morning air.

These men sat on the highest level of the tower staring out toward the morning sun. Most had dark sunglasses covering their eyes. Some still had camouflage paint streaked across their faces. The lead sniper from the training section sat on a railing in front of the group waiting for them all to arrive. Once all twelve snipers were assembled, coffee mugs in hand, the S/L placed a bottle of 20-year-old Macallan on the ledge. He reached in his pocket and removed something, he slammed his hand down next to the bottle revealing, as he pulled it away, his sniper section challenge coin. One after the other, the snipers dug into their wallets or pockets and copied the gesture. Each man held out their mug and was given a share of the scotch. Most had cigars hanging out of the corner of their mouths as well and a box of matches was passed around to light them. The SL next raised his glass and saluted each of them separately and gave a small dissertation of each man's contribution to the craft. The scene was like that of a group of samurai taking part in a sacred sake ceremony, each bowed their head to the SL in response to his words. The SL saved Handsome Jack, Bender and Speed for last. This was a first for police snipers in this country, three police snipers from the same agency had been forced to make kill shots during the same operation.

"To you three. For the courage to protect our brothers, for a steady heartbeat and smooth trigger pull, and, for your dead-eye accuracy. We salute you." He raised his mug.

The other nine snipers copied the gesture in unison, saluting their friends and shot back the warm scotch.

The lead sniper poured a second round and raised his mug again.

"To *all* of you men who laid in the shadows. Like Angels watching over your brothers. *Ex Umbris Venimus* (From the shadows we came)."

"Ex Umbris Venimus." they replied together as they clanged mugs. The warm aroma of good cigars surrounded the snipers, the cloud of smoke encircling them and hugging them together. The snipers stole this time not as a way of celebrating the death or the killing of human beings, but as a way to celebrate surviving the test of men. This was a validation of their skills, their training and their mettle as warriors.

In a groundbreaking arrangement, a new protocol had been put in place with the SIU. The new procedure was there to facilitate police shooting investigations during large-scale operations like this one, born out of these special circumstances. The cooperative effort had led to a seamless and rapid investigation of the shootings as they occurred during the takedown phase of the operation. Almost immediately, a crown attorney, a defense attorney and two high-ranking investigators from the Special Investigations Unit had made determinations on each shooting. This oversight group had been given access to sensitive information and was allowed to observe in the command center. That meant they were able to access information in real time and thus make a quicker determination as to the legal consequences for any officer involved shooting incidents. As such, Jack, Speed, Parker and Karras were cleared of any wrongdoing before their gear had even been put awa

***

Down in the team rooms, there was a quiet sense of accomplishment. There were high fives and head rubs, as men went about the business of reorganizing their equipment for the next day's assignments.

The adrenaline would need hours to ease out of the building. Goodhall and Wismer made the rounds, stopping at every team room. They shook every single member's hand then respectfully disappeared letting the boys have their time – not, however, before pulling each sergeant into the hall separate from their teams where the boss handed over a bottle of his favorite whiskey as a token of his appreciation. Through the afternoon, The Group enjoyed a hearty meal supplied by the thankful staff from a nearby hotel, after which the men slowly trickled out of the building. Unfortunately, Team Six drew the short straw and had to stay on duty for the rest of the day, but the city remained placid in the aftermath of the pre-dawn takedowns and the guys were able to spend the remainder of the shift going through the process of cleaning their weapons and gear. Eventually the Hogs said goodbye to each other and headed for home as well.

In the cool midafternoon Speed walked through the mudroom door, kicking his boots into the corner. As he came through the door into the main hallway Angie and Camryn ambushed him with hugs. The family stood there squeezing each other for what seemed like an eternity, Angie with tears rolling down her cheeks. She stepped back and pushed them away laughing.

"They're happy tears." she told him.

Camryn had ahold of Speed's hand and wouldn't let go. She could not possibly understand what had just happened. His little girl led him to the couch in the family room.

"Wanna watch cartoons daddy?" she asked innocently. Speed smiled and pushed her bangs back.

"You know I do."

The three of them curled up on the couch next to a fire and just held each other as they laughed at the ridiculous antics of some bird and a cat.

***

In the days and weeks following the operation, connecting leads would be chased down and co-conspirators would be arrested during more raids. Naila would be promoted to senior analyst in charge of all Intelligence operations, and she and Gaines would receive an award for their work. Gaines knew it didn't really belong to him, and he transferred back to divisional police operations taking a job as Divisional Detective where he stored his award in the bottom drawer of his desk.

Inspector Nance was promoted to Superintendent and given charge of all investigative operations, his span of control included drugs, vice, robbery, sex crimes, computer crimes and homicide.

There were award ceremonies, memorials, town halls, debriefs, case studies, testimony, interviews and Monday morning quarterbacking still to be done. That was the custom in the wake of such a precedent setting event. Most observers would be applauding the outcome, but the true professionals would be highly critical of themselves. That was the case at the Group.

The individual team debriefs were heated and thorough, and most of the teams would hit the shoot houses within the next few days to go over, in minute detail, each footstep of their part of the operation. Speed and Carter were on the long ranges in those days confirming zeroes and just shooting to relax. Handsome Jack left The Group almost immediately to replace old Fossil at the ranges and was a perfect fit. He stood out there on the range with the other snipers as they talked their way through the operation.

At the CANSOFCOM compound analysts obsessed over every line and page in that little leather journal. It had been recovered from the breast pocket of Ameer's jacket after he was shot. Since then Special Operations soldiers from around the world had been slipping quietly into non-permissive countries to eliminate various connected terrorist targets.

The one thing that went right back to normal was the volume of work the unit had to tackle. The day after the takedowns teams were back out talking a suicidal woman off a balcony. One team worked with the K9 unit to track a pair of meth addicts that had robbed a veterinary clinic at gunpoint taking its Ketamine supply. And others took in doors on drug warrants as the pace of operations fell back into its regular patterns. New members joined the unit as older members like Pinky and Jack moved on. A huge retirement bash was held to honour longtime member of the Group Staff Sergeant Ray Farmer. His replacement was not a former team member, and he would struggle to get up to speed on the what's and how's of the Group.

Speed and Robinson had become fast friends and routinely spent time on days off with the families. Robinson became a welcome third wheel to the evening fire pit scotch nosing outside the shed at Speed's place with Carter.

Angie and Speed would announce that she was pregnant again and that they would be having a June baby. They agreed that they did not care to know if it would be a boy or a girl.

In the early spring on a cool Sunday night, Speed sat with his feet up on the edge of the stone fire pit, Camryn wrapped in a blanket on his lap. Uncle Mike and Uncle Bryan were also there sharing stories and a drink with Paul. Angie stood at that big window again and subconsciously rubbed the little being in her belly. Her cheeks warmed, and she smiled as she stared out at them. Their life wasn't perfect, but it was certainly worth it, a tear trickled down her cheek and she laughed to herself, *Pregnancy hormones.*

She wiped it away with the back of her hand. Speed caught the glint of her wedding ring in the shadows and knew she was at the window. He sent a smile in her direction and hugged little Cammie, who snuggled into his arms. He winked to where he knew Angie was trying to hide as he mouthed the words, "I love you."

Damn snipers. she thought, as she stepped back from the window crying again.

AUTHOR's BIO

This is Peter's *first* novel, and he has more books in the works. This book started out as a hobby and an outlet for work stress, and has spent many years growing. Eventually Peter found the professional witting help he needed, and the book moved forward to what you have just read.

Peter grew up in the east end of Toronto, Ontario Canada, the son of two teachers. His interest in writing developed while at university where he took some courses in the literature field out of sheer curiosity.

He left university early to start his career in law enforcement, which eventually led to him spending twenty-one years as a police tactical operator. During that time he was fortunate have been trained in several specialized skills, eventually becoming a team leader and following that a team Sergeant.

Throughout this time Peter developed a deep love for coffee and writing short stories, which were often based on his experiences. He has appeared on podcasts in the police genre and been published in a major police training magazine.

Manufactured by Amazon.ca
Bolton, ON